GENA SHOWALTER

Beauty Awakened

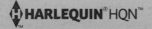

Recycling programs
for this product may
not exist in your area.

ISBN-13: 978-0-373-77743-3

BEAUTY AWAKENED

Copyright © 2013 by Gena Showalter

Printed in U.S.A.

First, to my amazing new editor, Emily Ohanjanians,
for taking me on and not vomiting
when I explained my "process."

To Marie, who takes care of me in so many ways!

To my mom and dad, for answering every single one
of my book-related calls and never saying,
"This again? But we went over it yesterday—for an hour."

To my agent Deidre Knight, for always having my back.
Even when I say things like
"So…here's what I want to do next."

To Jia Gayles, for always being willing to help with promos.

And to Jill Monroe, for too many reasons to list.

God is good. All the time, God is good.

Beauty Awakened

PROLOGUE

SEVEN-YEAR-OLD KOLDO sat as quietly as possible in the corner of the bedroom. His mother was brushing her hair, lovely dark ringlets spun with threads of the purest gold. She perched in front of the vanity, humming softly but excitedly, her smiling, freckled image reflected in an oval mirror. He couldn't help but watch her, fascinated.

Cornelia was one of the most beautiful creatures ever created. Everyone always said so. Her eyes were the palest violet, edged by lashes the same brown-and-gold mix as her hair. Her lips were heart-shaped, and her pale skin glowed as brightly as the sun.

With Koldo's inky hair, dark eyes and deeply bronzed skin, he looked nothing like her. The only thing they had in common was their wings, and perhaps that was why he was so proud of the glittering white feathers cushioned by plush, amber down. They were his one redeeming feature.

Her humming suddenly ceased.

Koldo gulped.

"You're staring at me," she snapped, all hint of her smile gone.

He cast his gaze to the floor, as she preferred. "Sorry, Momma."

"I told you not to call me that." She slammed the

brush onto the marble counter. "Are you so foolish that you've already forgotten?"

"No," he replied softly. Everyone lauded her sweetness and gentleness as much as her beauty, and they were right to do so. She was generous with her praise and kind to everyone who approached her—everyone but Koldo. He'd always experienced a very different side of her. No matter what he did or said, she found fault. And yet, still he loved her with all of his heart. He'd only ever wanted to please her.

"Hideous little creature," she mumbled as she stood, the scent of jasmine and honeysuckle drifting from her. The purple fabric of her robe danced at her ankles, the jewels sewn into the hem sparkling in the light. "Just like your father."

Koldo had never met his father, had only ever heard about the man.

Evil.

Disgusting.

Repulsive.

"I'm having friends over," she said, flicking her hair over one shoulder. "You're to stay up here. Do you understand?"

"Yes." Oh, yes. He understood. If anyone caught sight of him, she would be embarrassed by his ugliness. She would rage. He would suffer.

She peered at him for a long while. Finally she growled, "I should have drowned you in the bathtub when you were too young to fight back," and stomped from the room, the door slamming shut behind her.

The rejection cut bone deep, and he wasn't sure why. She'd said far worse countless times before.

Just love me, Momma. Please.

Maybe…maybe she couldn't. Not yet. Hope unfurled in his chest, and he raised his chin. Maybe he hadn't done enough to prove himself. Maybe if he did something special for her, she would finally realize he was nothing like his father. Maybe if he cleaned her room… and had a bouquet of fresh flowers waiting for her…and sang a song as she drifted to sleep… Yes! She would hug and kiss him in thanks, the way she often hugged and kissed the servants' children.

Excited, Koldo folded the blankets he used for his pallet on the floor and jumped to his feet. He darted through the room, picking up the discarded robes and sandals, then fluffed the pillows strewn around the center rug, where Cornelia liked to relax and read.

He ignored the wall of weapons—the whip, the daggers and the swords—and straightened the items on the vanity: the brush, the bottles of perfume, the creams for his mother's skin and the pungent-smelling liquid she liked to drink. He polished every necklace, bracelet and ring in her jewelry box.

By the time he finished, the room and everything in it glistened as though brand-new. He grinned, pleased with his efforts. She would appreciate all that he'd done—he just knew it.

Now for the flowers.

Cornelia wanted him to stay here, and had he promised to obey her, he would have. But he hadn't promised. He'd told her only that he understood her desires. Besides, this was for her, all for her, and no one would see him. He would make sure of it.

He strode to the balcony, pushed open the double doors. Cool night air wafted over him. The palace was situated in a far realm of the lower heavens, neighbored by thousands of stars twinkling from an infinite expanse of black velvet. The moon was bright and high, a mere sliver curved into two upward points.

The moon was smiling at him.

Encouraged, Koldo stepped to the balcony's ledge. There was no railing, allowing his toes to curl over the side. He flared his wings to their full length, the action bringing a cascade of joy. He loved flying through the sky, soaring up and zipping down, rolling through the clouds, chasing birds.

His mother knew nothing of this. "You are never to use your wings," she'd announced the day they'd begun to sprout from his back. He'd planned to heed the command, he had, but then, one day, she'd been screaming about how much she despised him, and he'd climbed to the roof so that she wouldn't have to gaze upon his ugly face. His misery had distracted him and he'd fallen down, down, dooown.

Just before landing, he'd flared the previously·unused appendages and managed to slow his momentum. He'd crawled away with a shattered arm and leg, broken ribs, a punctured lung and a fractured ankle. Eventually, he'd healed—and he'd next jumped on purpose. He'd been addicted to the feel of the breeze on his skin, in his hair, and had craved more.

Now, in the present, he dived headfirst. The air slapped at him, and he had to swallow his whoop of satisfaction. The freedom…the slight edge of danger… the rush of warmth and strength… He would never get enough. Just before impact, he straightened and leveled out, his wings catching the current. He landed softly, his feet already in motion.

One step, two, three, *annnd* he was a mile into the

forest. Not because he was fast—though he was—but because he could do something his mother and the other Sent Ones he'd seen could not. He could move from one place to another with only a thought.

He'd discovered the ability a few months ago. At first, he'd only been able to whisk a yard, then two, but every day he managed to go a little farther than before. All he had to do was calm his emotions and concentrate.

At last he reached the stretch of wildflowers he'd found the last time he'd broken the rules and left the palace. He plucked the prettiest from the ground, the petals the perfect shade of lavender, reminding him of his mother's eyes. He brought them to his nose, sniffed. The mouthwatering aroma of coconut clung to him, and his grin returned.

If Cornelia asked where he'd gotten the bouquet, well, he would tell her the truth. He refused to lie, even to save himself from a punishment. Not only because other Sent Ones could taste when another being lied—unlike him—but also because lies were the language of the demons, and demons were almost as evil as his father.

His mother would appreciate Koldo's honesty. Surely.

Hands full of moist green stalks, he sprinted out of the forest and leaped into the atmosphere, going higher and higher, his feathers ruffling in the wind, the muscles in his back straining in the most delightful way. Up and down his wings glided. His heart thundered in his chest as he landed on the balcony and peeked through the doorway. There was no sign of his mother.

Breathing a sigh of relief, he entered the room. He emptied Cornelia's favorite vase of old, dried flowers, then added the new and watered the stems. He returned to his place in the corner, folded his legs and waited.

Hours passed.

More hours passed.

By the time the hinges squeaked to signal the door was being opened, his eyelids were heavy, his eyes as dry and scratchy as sandpaper, but he'd managed to stay awake and now jolted to eager attention.

A soft fall of footsteps. A pause.

"What did you do?" his mother gasped. She spun, taking in every inch of the bedroom.

"I made it better for you." *Love me. Please.*

A sharp inhalation of breath before she stomped over, stopping just in front of him and glaring down with fiery hatred. "How dare you! I liked my things the way they were."

Disappointment nearly crushed him, so heavily did it settle in his chest. Once again he'd failed her. "I'm sorry."

"Where did you get the ambrosia?" Even as she spoke, her gaze jerked to the double doors leading to the balcony. "You flew, didn't you?"

Only a beat of hesitation before he admitted, "Yes."

At first, she gave no reaction. Then she squared her shoulders, an action of determination. "You think you can disobey me and never suffer any consequences. Is that it?"

"No. I just—"

"Liar!" she shouted. Her palm smacked against his cheek, the force of the impact propelling him into the wall. "You're just like your father, doing what you want, when you want, no matter how anyone else feels about the matter, and I'm not going to tolerate this behavior anymore."

"I'm sorry," he repeated, trembling.

"Believe me, you will be." She grabbed his arm and hauled him to his feet. He didn't struggle, allowing her to toss him onto the bed, on his stomach, and tie his wrists and ankles to the posts.

Another whipping, he thought, not allowing himself to beg for mercy she wouldn't show. He would hurt, but he would heal. He knew that for a fact. He'd earned a thousand other punishments just like this one, but he'd always recovered. Physically, at least. Inside, his heart would bleed for years to come.

His mother selected a blade from the wall, ignoring the whip she normally wielded.

She was going to…kill him?

Finally Koldo tugged and twisted, but he wasn't strong enough to fight his way free. "I'm sorry. I'm really sorry. I'll never again clean your room, I promise. I'll never again leave it."

"You think that's the problem? Oh, you foolish boy. The truth is, I can't let you loose. You're tainted by your father's vile blood." The fire in her eyes had spread to the rest of her features, creating a wild, crazed expression. "I'll be doing the world a favor by limiting your ability to travel."

No. *No!* "Don't, Momma. Please, don't." He couldn't lose his wings. He just couldn't. He would rather die. "Please."

"I told you not to call me by that wretched name!" she screeched.

Panic caused little crystals of ice to form in his

blood. "I'll never do it again, I promise. Just…please, don't do this. Please."

"I must."

"You can take my legs. Just take my legs!"

"And make you dependent on me the rest of your life? No." A slow grin lifted the corners of her lips. "I should have done this a long time ago."

A second later, she struck.

Koldo screamed and screamed and screamed… until his voice broke and his strength drained. Until he saw his beautiful wings on the floor, the feathers now soaked in his blood.

Until he could only close his eyes and pray for death.

"There, now. Hush. It's done," she said almost gently. "You lost what you did not deserve."

This was a dream, surely. His mother was not so cruel. No one could be so cruel.

Soft, warm lips pressed into his tearstained cheek, and the jasmine and honeysuckle of her scent overshadowed what remained of the coconut. "I'll hate you forever, Koldo," she whispered into his ear. "There's nothing you can do to change that."

No, not a dream. Reality.

His new reality.

His mother was far worse than cruel.

"I don't want to change it," he said, his chin quivering. Not anymore.

A tinkling laugh escaped her. "Is that anger I hear? Well, well. You're already more like your father than I knew. Perhaps it's time you met him." After a moment's pause, she added, "Yes, in the morning, I'll take you to your father's people. You'll realize just how good I've been to you—if you survive."

CHAPTER ONE

In a world of darkness, the smallest light is a beacon.

Present Day

KOLDO STALKED DOWN the ICU ward of the hospital. He and the warrior with him were hidden from human eyes and protected from human touch. The doctors, nurses, visitors and patients misted through them, completely unaware of the invisible world playing out alongside theirs. A spirit world that had given birth to this natural world, the human world.

A spirit world that was the true reality for all creation.

One day, these humans would discover just how exact that statement really was. Their bodies would die, their spirits would rise—or descend—and they would begin to understand the natural world was fleeting, the spiritual eternal.

Eternal. Just like Koldo's irritation seemed to be. He didn't want to be here among the humans, on yet another silly mission, and he really didn't like his companion, Axel. But his new leader, Zacharel, wanted him busy, distracted, for he suspected Koldo teetered on the verge of breaking a heavenly law.

Zacharel wasn't wrong.

After everything Koldo had endured in his father's

camp…after escaping and spending centuries searching for his mother, Koldo had finally found her—and
locked her inside a cage in one of his many homes.

So, yes. Koldo teetered. But he wouldn't ever cause
the woman irrevocable harm. He wouldn't even lower
himself to break one of her nails. For now, he simply
hoped to teach her the horror of being trapped by circumstance, as she had taught him. As she was still
teaching him.

Later, he would… He wasn't sure. He no longer liked
to consider the future.

Because of his abhorrence of Cornelia, Koldo had
landed in the Army of Disgrace. It was a terrible name
for such a choice defensive force, but it was one that fit
nonetheless. The members were the worst of the worst,
the baddest of the bad…male and female Sent Ones who
were in danger of damnation.

For various reasons, all twenty soldiers had ignored
prized heavenly laws. They were meant to love, but
they hated. They were to help others, but they really
only hurt. They were to build up, but they only ever
tore down.

Three months ago, the members had been given
one year to mend their wicked ways, or they would be
stripped of their abilities and kicked into hell.

Koldo would do whatever was necessary to keep that
from happening—even deny himself true vengeance.
He refused to lose the only home he'd ever known.

Axel grabbed him by the arm, stopping him. "Dude!
Did you see the meat bags on that girl?"

And there was reason number one why Koldo had a
problem working with Axel. "Could you be any more

disgusting?" He jerked from the warrior's hold, contact with another not something he enjoyed.

"Yeah," Axel said with an irreverent grin. "I could. But someone, and I won't say your name, K, my man, needs to get his mind out of the gutter. I wasn't talking about her chesticles."

Koldo ran his tongue over his teeth. "What, then?"

"Hello. Her demons. Look."

His gaze slid to the room at his right. The door had been in the process of closing and now clicked shut, blocking the occupant from view. "Too late."

"It's only too late when you're dead. Come on. You gotta see this." Axel strode forward and ghosted through the entrance.

Koldo's hands curled into fists, and he battled the urge to punch a wall. They had a mission, and distractions only extended their time in a place crawling with demons laughing at the pain the humans suffered and whispering into the ears of anyone who would listen.

Can't survive, they said. *There's no hope.* And these humans…so many were puppets, with clawed hands tugging at their strings. If they failed to fight back, they would become casualties in a war between good and evil, either in this life or after death. One way or another.

That's just the way things worked.

The Most High ruled the heavens. "He" was actually a sacred trinity consisting of the Merciful One, the Anointed One and the Mighty One, and He was the King of kings, His word law. He had appointed several underlings throughout the skies. Germanus—or Deity, as some of Koldo's kind called him, referring to a title, nothing more—was one of those underlings. A king answerable to the King.

Germanus led the Elite Seven—Zacharel, Lysander, Andrian, Gabek, Shalilah, Luanne, Svana—and each of those seven led an army of Sent Ones. Zacharel, for instance, led the Army of Disgrace.

Sent Ones looked just like angels, but they weren't actually angels. Not in the sense the world knew, at least. Yes, Sent Ones were winged. Yes, they waged war against evil and helped humans, but in actuality, they were the adopted children of the Most High, their lives tethered to His. He was the source of their power, the essence of their very existence.

Like humans, Sent Ones battled the desires of the flesh. They experienced lust, greed, envy, rage, pride, hate, despair. Angels, in actuality, were servants and messengers of the Most High. They experienced none of those things.

Mind on the mission.

Koldo straightened his spine. Zacharel had tasked him and Axel with killing a specific demon here at the hospital. The demon had made the mistake of tormenting a patient who knew about the spiritual world around him, a male who had called upon the aid of the Most High.

The Most High was love personified, willing to help anyone who asked. Sometimes angels were dispatched, sometimes Sent Ones. Sometimes both, depending on the situation and the skills needed. This time, Koldo and Axel had been chosen. They had been nearby, headed to a training session, when Zacharel's voice had whispered through their minds, imparting instructions.

Axel peeked his head through the center of the door and said, "Dude! You're missing it!"

"The person in that room is not our—"

Grinning, the warrior once again disappeared.

"Assignment," Koldo finished to no one but himself. His anger intensified.

Control yourself.

He could move on and fight the demon he was supposed to fight, no problem, but according to Zacharel's orders, he wasn't to proceed without his partner.

Grinding his teeth, he marched forward. He slipped through the iron obstruction without any difficulty, stopped and glanced around. The room was small, with multiple machines attached to the motionless blonde female on the bed. A redheaded female sat next to her, chatting easily.

The redhead had no idea there were two demons standing behind her, pretending not to see the Sent Ones in the room.

"Two of the guys in my office got to arguing about who could run faster," she said, "and soon bets were flying."

Her voice had a whispery quality, as if filled with smoke and dreams, and it settled over Koldo like warm honey. And yet, with the soothing came a tensing. Every muscle in his body knotted up, as if preparing for war. He...wanted to fight such a delicate human? But why? Who was she?

"I felt as if I was standing in the middle of a stock exchange or something."

Laughter bubbled from her, such beautiful laughter, pure, with nothing held back. The kind he'd never experienced himself.

"They decided to race in the parking lot instead of have lunch, and the loser had to eat whatever's in the plastic bowl in the break room fridge. The one that's been in there for over a month and is now black. I heard the cheers as I was pulling out of the lot, but I didn't get to see who won."

Wistful now. Why?

"You would have voted for Blaine, I'm sure. He's only five-nine, so he wouldn't tower over you *too* badly, and he has the cutest blue eyes. Not that his looks have anything to do with his speed, but I know you, and I know you would have wanted him to win regardless. You've always been a sucker for baby blues."

He could only see the top half of her, but judging by the fragility of her bone structure, she was a tiny thing. Her features were plain, her skin as pale as porcelain, and her eyes as gray as a winter storm. Her mass of strawberry hair was pulled into a high ponytail, the ends curling all the way to her elbow.

There was an air of fatigue surrounding her, and yet, there was a sparkle in those winter eyes.

A sparkle the demons behind her would soon snuff out.

He forced his attention on the pair. One was posted at her left and one was posted at her right, and both had a proprietary hand on her shoulder. They were Koldo's size, with dark, pupilless eyes that reminded him of bottomless pits. Lefty had a single horn protruding from the center of his forehead, and crimson scales rather than flesh. Righty had two thick horns rising from his scalp, and dark, matted fur.

There were many different types of demons, and they came in all different shapes and sizes. From the first of their kind, the fallen archangel Lucifer, to the viha, the paura, the násilí, the slecht, the grzech, the pică and the envexa. And sadly, many more. Each sought the destruction of mankind—one man at a time, if necessary.

Amid the types of demons, there were ranks. Righty was a top-of-the-line paura, and all about fear. Lefty was a top-of-the-line grzech, and all about sickness.

Demons liked to attach themselves to humans and, through whispers and deceit, infect them with a toxin that caused their anxiety levels to spike, in the case of the paura, and the immune system to weaken, in the case of the grzech. Then, the demons fed off the ensuing panic and upset, weakening the humans further and making them easy targets for destruction.

The girl must have been a veritable buffet.

Just how sick was she?

Lefty gave up trying to ignore Axel and glared at him as he danced around, slapping his face and saying, "I'm hittin' you, I'm hittin' you, what're you gonna do about it, huh, huh?" in the good-ole-country-boy accent he sometimes liked to use.

Koldo despised demons with every ounce of his being. No matter their type or rank, they were thieves, killers and slayers, just like his father's people. They left chaos and confusion in their wake. They ruined. And this pair wouldn't leave the girl unless forced— but even then she could welcome others.

His chest burned as he switched his focus to the girl on the bed. But…his gaze lasered through the wrinkled cover, the thin hospital gown, and even skin and muscle. What he saw astonished him.

To him, the blonde was now as transparent as glass, granting him a glance at the demon that had wormed its way inside her body. A grzech, different from the one plaguing the redhead. This one had tentacles that stretched through the blonde's mind and into her heart, draining the life from her.

The Most High often blessed Sent Ones with specific supernatural abilities during difficult situations, things like this X-ray vision, as he'd heard others call it. Until now, Koldo had never experienced anything like it. Why here? Why now? Why this girl and not the other?

The questions were overshadowed a second later, when, in the blink of an eye, Koldo learned exactly how this had happened to her, the information seeming to download straight into his brain.

Born at twenty-six weeks, the blonde and her red-headed twin had struggled to survive the heart defects they'd been born with. Multiple surgeries were needed, and both almost died countless times—each time nullifying any progress made. Throughout the years, their parents had become fond of saying, "You have to keep yourself calm or you'll have another heart attack."

Innocent words meant to aid the pair—or so it seemed.

Words were one of the most powerful forces known—or unknown—to man. The Most High had created this world with His words. And humans, who had been fashioned in His image, could direct the entire course of their lives with their words, their mouths as the rudder on a ship, as the bridle on a horse. They produced with their words. They destroyed with their words.

Eventually the blonde had come to believe the slightest rise in her emotions would indeed cause another painful heart attack, and with her belief, fear had sparked to life.

Fear—the beginning of doom, for heavenly law stated that what a person feared would come upon them. In the blonde's case, the fear had come upon her in the form of the grzech. She'd caught his notice, and she'd been such an easy target.

First, the demon breathed his toxin into her ear, whispering destructive suggestions.

Your heart could stop at any moment.

Oh, the pain...it's unbearable. You can't live through that again.

This time, the doctors may not be able to revive you.

Demons knew human eyes and ears were a doorway to the mind, and the mind was a doorway to the spirit. So, when the blonde had entertained the terrible suggestions, constantly rolling them through her mind, the fear had multiplied and become a poisoned truth, causing her defenses to crumble, allowing the demon to slink inside her, create a stronghold and destroy her from the inside out.

She had indeed had another heart attack, and the necessary organ had weakened beyond what human medicine could repair.

Did the Most High want Koldo to help her, even though she wasn't his current mission? Was that what this unveiling was about?

Sighing, the redhead leaned back in her chair, returning Koldo's attention to her. Once again, he saw flesh and blood rather than spirit. The Most High's gift hadn't extended to her.

He didn't have time to wonder why. A waft of cinnamon and vanilla hit him, quickly followed by the sickening scent of sulfur. A scent the girl would not be able to shed, as long as the demons stayed with her.

"It's about time for me to go," she said, rubbing at the back of her neck as if the muscles were knotted. "I'll let you know who won that race, La La."

Did she have any idea that evil weighed her down and stalked her every move?

Did she know she was full of demon toxin, just like her sister? That, if she didn't fight, she would end up in the same circumstance, the demons worming their way inside her body?

Koldo could kill Lefty and Righty, but again, other demons would sense what easy prey she was and attack her. As unknowledgeable as she clearly was, she would surrender again.

For any kind of long-term success, he would have to teach her to wage war against the toxin. But to do so, he would need her cooperation and time. Cooperation she may not give. Time she may not have. But…maybe *she* was the one the Most High wanted him to help. Maybe Koldo was to save the redhead from the blonde's fate.

Either way, the choice to aid her—or not—was Koldo's. Germanus and Zacharel might issue orders, but not the Most High. Not even when He revealed a truth. He never overrode free will.

"You want in on this, buddy?" Axel asked him, continuing to slap at the now-snarling demons behind the redhead. "'Cause I'm about to take things up a notch."

"A notch above annoying is merely irritating," he said, inwardly fuming because he already knew he was going to pick the mission. Survival always came first.

Why was he fuming, anyway? He liked the sound of the girl's voice—so what? Who was she to him? No one. Why should he care about her and her future?

"We have a duty," he added. "Let's see to it."

Immediately guilt attempted to rise. No matter who she was—or wasn't—he was cold and callous to leave her to such an evil end, wasn't he? His father would have made the same choice. His mother would have— He wasn't sure what she would have done. She still seemed to love everyone but Koldo.

"Ah, come on, hoss," Axel said. "Stop and play, that's my motto."

"*You* come on," he called to Axel. "Now!" Before he changed his mind.

"Sure, sure." Axel worked his way behind the demons and kicked one in the back of the knees. The other twisted swiftly to bat the side of Axel's head with a meaty fist, sending the warrior propelling through the far wall.

Koldo stepped in front of his brethren when he returned to the room, preventing him from springing into a full-on attack. "Touch him again and you'll discover my talent with the sword of fire," he told the demons.

Loyalty mattered to Koldo. Deserved or not.

"Yeah." Axel didn't sound upset or even winded. He sounded happy. "What he said."

Koldo threw him a glance, saw that he'd raised his fists and was hopping from one foot to the other. He could not be thousands of years old. He just couldn't be.

"You're the intruders here," said the demon that had pretended Axel's head was a baseball. His voice was as jagged as broken glass. "The girl is ours."

He struggled against the urge to hurt and maim the demons as he reached back, grabbed Axel by the collar of his robe and tossed him through the only door into the hall. "I pray we'll see each other again," he told the fiends.

They hissed as Koldo stalked from the room.

Axel stood in the middle of the walkway, black hair shagging around a face he loved to claim women saw in their fantasies—because he saw it in his own. His electric blues glared holes in Koldo. "Dude! You wrinkled my clothes."

They were back to "dude," rather than "hoss." Clearly the warrior had no idea just how volatile Koldo's emotions were. Every step farther away from the girl darkened his mood. "What do you care? We're to engage in battle, not model the current fashions from the skies."

"Duh. But a guy's gotta look his best, no matter the occasion." An orderly walked by, wheeling a cart piled high with trays of food, snagging Axel's attention. He followed, tossing back a delighted smile. "I smell pudding!"

How sublime. *I got stuck with the only winged warrior with ADD.*

THE FUN AND GAMES ENDED the moment Koldo and Axel closed in on the targeted demon. The human the creature tormented was restrained to his bed, and drugged, too, if the drool leaking from the side of his mouth was any indication.

A slecht hovered in the air at his right, whispering vile curse after vile curse.

"G-go away," the male managed to gurgle. He could see the demon, but not Axel and Koldo. "Leave me alone!" The more he spoke, the stronger he became… but not yet strong enough.

You couldn't slay a dragon if you had not yet learned to slay a bear.

Axel shocked Koldo by surging forward without a

word, his wings shooting from his back. The demon only had time to look toward him and gasp before the warrior unsheathed two double-edged short swords from an air pocket and struck.

The swords were a gift from the Most High and something every Sent One was given. Axel's wrists crisscrossed to form a very effective scissor, chopping the demon's head from its body in a single heartbeat of time. The pieces thudded to the floor before evaporating into ash.

Deep down, Koldo had expected to carry the weight of the battle. This was... This was...

Not fair.

The human sagged against the bed, his head lolling to the side. "Gone," he sighed with relief. "It's gone." He closed his eyes and sank into what was probably his first peaceful sleep in months.

Axel tossed the black-stained weapons back into the air pocket. "Dang, I didn't mean to do that again."

Again? "You've killed so quickly before?"

"Well, yeah. *Every* time before. But once, just once, I'd like to only injure my opponent and get a little thrusting and parrying in before I deliver the death-blow. Well, see ya." Axel flew through the ceiling, disappearing from view.

The man was as much a mess as Koldo. No wonder Axel had been given to Zacharel.

Just how wildly did he teeter at the edge of falling? As close as Koldo?

Go home.

Good advice, and miracle of miracles, it sprang from his own mind. He meant to heed it. He did. But a single thought changed his mind. The redhead. He wanted to see her. Muscles tensing all over again, Koldo whisked back to the blonde's hospital room.

Only, the redhead was already gone.

Disappointment hit him first, followed by a new tide of frustration and anger.

He whisked to his home hidden in the cliffs along the South African coast. A flash, the action was called. He'd learned a lot about himself and his abilities since being dropped in the middle of his father's camp all those centuries ago.

A man will do just about anything to survive, boy. And I'll prove it to you.

His father's words—and yes, Nox had indeed proven them.

Just like that, the frustration and anger spilled over, and he roared. He beat his fists against the walls, over and over again, soaking his knuckles in crimson, cracking his bones as well as the stone. Every punch was a testament to a centuries-long rage, a soul-deep pain that had never gone away, and a festering wound he knew would never heal.

He was what he was.

He was what his parents had made him.

He'd tried to be more. He'd tried to be better. Each time, he'd failed miserably. Darkness constantly flooded him, banging against an already unstable dam made of tainted memories and corrosive emotions. A dam he was only able to rebuild after outbursts like this one.

The punching continued until he was panting and dripping in sweat. Until skin and muscles were shredded, and the broken bones exposed. Even still, he could have taken another thousand swings, but he didn't. He forced himself to exhale with measured precision and imagine a cascade of darkness leaving him.

The dam refortified.

Aches and pains made themselves known, but that was okay. The banging had stopped. For now, that was all that mattered.

He padded across the living room. Along the way he fisted the collar of the dirty robe and yanked the material over his head. He dropped the garment on the floor, wind and dew whipping around him without any hindrance. He had no doors to block the gales, no windows to silence the song of nature; the entire house was open to the elements. Even better, the ceiling, walls and floor had been *formed* by the elements, presenting a showcase of glittering dark rock.

He stopped at the ledge overlooking a magnificent rushing waterfall pounding into the jagged stone below. Heavy sheets of mist rose from a turbulent sea, enveloping his naked body.

He came here when he desired privacy and peace. The turbulence around him had a way of making his mind seem calmer than it was. The wind kicked up, rattling the beads he'd woven into the length of his beard.

Once upon a time he'd possessed a head of hair to match. Long, thick and black, intricate beadwork woven throughout the prized strands. Now... He scrubbed a hand over the smoothness of his scalp. Now he was bald, his precious hair sacrificed in favor of vengeance.

Now he looked like his father.

Before he could stop it, his mind took him back to one of the many times he'd stood at the bottom of a deep, dark pit, thousands of hissing serp demons slithering over feet that had been flayed like fish…around a neck that had been sliced like Christmas ham.

Serps were very much like snakes, and they had continually sunk their fangs into him, all over him, dripping venom straight into his veins. But through it all he'd stood utterly still, remaining strong, refusing to so much as groan. His father had promised to remove a finger for every sign of weakness he exhibited. And when he ran out of fingers, he had been told he would lose his hands, his feet…his arms and his legs.

Back then, he hadn't yet reached full maturity—hence the reason his wings had not grown back—and he would have been unable to regenerate the limbs. He would have suffered all of his life, and he—

Beat the ugly memory to the back of his mind, where it belonged. So his father had tortured him for eleven years. So what? He'd been rescued by Sent Ones, and had later become part of an army himself. Not the one he was currently in, but a different one, commanded by the now-deceased Ivar. Back then, Ivar had been the best of the Elite, and being under his command had been an honor.

Yet, in a fit of temper very much like the one he'd just displayed, Koldo had thrown that opportunity away, besting Ivar in front of his men.

Regret still haunted him. Such a lack of respect for such an admirable man…

Koldo had been kicked out of the army and left on his own—for a while. He'd used the time to return to his father's camp and obliterate everyone and everything.

The single greatest day of his life.

He reached up and gripped the rock above him. *Now I'm part of this new army, led by a man once known only as Ice.* Tomorrow, Zacharel would have another mission for him, one far below his skill level. Koldo knew this, because his leader had sent him out every day for the past three weeks, allowing him no time to break a heavenly law and bring judgment upon his head. At least, supposedly.

Koldo could lie.

Koldo could steal.

Koldo could kill.

He could do any number of other things their kind was not to do. But he wouldn't.

Thankfully, he wouldn't have to worry about being paired with Axel. Zacharel liked to assign him a new partner for every new mission, probably to keep him off-kilter.

Sadly, it was working.

And yet, there was one bright light, he realized. The girl from the hospital in Wichita, Kansas. The redhead. He still wanted to see her.

Surely she wasn't as tiny as he seemed to remember. For all he knew, she possessed the long, lithe legs of a dancer. Surely her hair wasn't the sweet color of strawberries. It had to be fire-engine red or an ordinary dark blond. Surely he'd imagined the purity of her tone. Surely.

He straightened, anticipation overshadowing all else. He *had* to know, the desire a living entity inside him.

First, though, he would have to hunt her down.

CHAPTER TWO

KOLDO SPENT THE REST of the night digging through the heavenly archives kept on every human ever to live and learned several interesting tidbits about the blonde and the redhead. The comatose girl was Laila Lane, and the other one, the one he wished to observe, was Nicola Lane. They were twenty-three-year-old twins, with Nicola being older by two minutes, and unmarried.

So young. *Too* young.

The two were identical. The only reason Laila had blond hair was because she'd bleached it, hoping to be "unique." The girls had no other family, and relied only on each other. Their parents had died in a car accident five years before.

Koldo left the library and flashed to Laila's hospital room. Once again Nicola was nowhere to be seen. But he wasn't worried. According to the gossiping nurses, she came every day. He had only to wait.

He strode to the edge of the bed. This time, the Most High's gift was not in operation, so, when he looked, he saw the blonde rather than the demon hiding under her skin.

The sight was almost as bad.

Her hair was dry, thin and matted. There were bruises under her eyes, and her lips were chapped. Her skin was severely yellowed, her liver obviously shutting down.

She wouldn't last much longer.

The Water of Life was a powerful liquid capable of repairing the most damaged human flesh, and the only thing capable of saving her. It would also rid her of the demon. But her thoughts, words and actions would influence its continued success.

The grzech could return to her and try again to poison her. So, even if Koldo fed her the Water, she would have to learn to fight the forces of evil—and then actually fight. Was she willing to engage in any kind of battle?

Maybe. Maybe not. Either way, Koldo wasn't willing to suffer and sacrifice, and he would have to do so to even approach the shoreline of the River of Life. First, he would be whipped. Second, he would be forced to give up something precious to him. Last time he'd relinquished his hair. And there was no telling what he would be asked to give up next. His ability to flash? His captive mother?

Never!

The practice had not been created by the Most High, and wasn't even supported by Him. But Germanus refused to end "a tradition that had been with their kind since the beginning," as a means of proving the depth of their determination. So, once again free will prevailed and the practice continued year by year. Koldo saw no way around it.

The room's only door opened suddenly, and Nicola stepped inside. Koldo straightened, and even tensed at the sight of her. He frowned. His body had only ever reacted this way before battle. Why was this happening with her?

At least she had no idea he was there. He was in the spiritual realm, and she in the natural, so he was blocked from her gaze.

He looked her over from bottom to top, then back down—far more slowly. That fall of strawberry curls was once again in a ponytail, the thick length tumbling over one shoulder. There were dark circles under her eyes, and the color in her cheeks was high. Her lips were swollen from being chewed. Despite the heat outside, a worn pink sweater draped her shoulders, the lapels pulled tightly together.

She was a tiny fluff of nothing, just as he recalled, her frame heart-wrenchingly delicate. He towered over her, and could easily break her in half with a single twist of his wrist.

Can't ever touch her, he told himself.

For some reason, the tension inside him only increased.

The same demons stood sentry behind her, following close at her heels. They spotted Koldo and spewed a mouthful of dark curses.

"Why are you here?"

"What do you hope to gain?"

He ignored them, and they decided to do the same to him, perhaps hoping he would go away this second time, too.

"Hey, La La," she said softly. "It's Co Co. I'm told you've taken a turn for the worse."

The words were encased by a thick, grim shell, yet still her voice stroked over him. A feather tickling. A brush of velvet caressing. He savored the odd sensations, even...liked them?

Nicola pushed the smallest chair next to the bed, struggling under its weight. The demons snickered at her. Angered, Koldo stepped toward her, intending to help her, but immediately forced himself to still. Now wasn't the time to reveal himself. He would frighten her.

The demons caught his aborted action and scowled at him. So much for ignoring him.

"You're not welcome here, Koldo," Lefty said.

Responding to a demon invited conversation. Conversation invited lies. Koldo wasn't so foolish as that. But he wasn't surprised the creature knew his name. With as many demonic kills as Koldo had made throughout the centuries, the entire underworld knew of him.

"We can *make* you leave," Righty proclaimed.

Fine. He was foolish. He said, "You can try." No matter what, they would fail.

Nicola reached out and gently patted her sister's hand. "Oh, did I tell you? Blaine won the race."

The monitors beeped steadily, the comatose girl never moving, never twitching.

Sighing, Nicola sat back in the chair and began to relay the trials of her workday.

This time, he would help her, Koldo decided. To start, he would have to do something to ensure she listened to him, and actually acted on what he said.

That was the only way she would come out of this.

And perhaps it was his only way out, too. In saving her, he might finally find some sort of atonement.

Atonement. The word echoed in his mind. It was something he sometimes craved, but not something he deserved. Sometimes, when he closed his eyes, he could still hear the agonized screams he'd caused…could still feel the barb of his victims' fear.

Clenching his fists, he resolved himself. He could do this. And so could she.

"You're going to get better, La La," she suddenly announced, as though drawing hope from his thoughts. "You have to recover. I won't allow anything else. I'm the big sister, and you have to do whatever I tell you to do. Nothing else is acceptable."

Gaze locked on Koldo, Righty bent down and whispered into her ear. Spreading poison.

The color drained from her cheeks.

Lefty squeezed her shoulder, and she slumped forward, as though some of her energy had evaporated in a puff of smoke.

She stopped talking victory, and went back to discussing her day.

Koldo rubbed the back of his neck. What had just happened was a prime example of the life she had probably always led, pulling herself up only to be knocked down again.

Well, no more.

His body tensed all over again, preparing for war. But this was different than what he'd felt when Nicola had first entered the room. There was no sense of anticipation, no hint of excitement. He just wanted to flat-out raze his enemy into the ground.

He held out his hand and summoned a sword of fire—another gift every Sent One received from the Most High. One he always had a right to use.

Righty and Lefty jolted to attention, gnarled wings popping from their backs.

"You sure you want to do this?" Righty asked with a gleeful smile. The horns on the creature's head grew... grew...becoming monstrous ivory towers. Fangs stretched between his lips, extending past his jaw. "You'll walk away, but you'll be in pieces."

The same grotesque transformation overtook Lefty, little sparks of fire flashing underneath his scales.

Koldo didn't bother with a response. He simply launched forward, blade arcing through the air. The two demons flew apart, moving out of harm's way. He expected the action and went low as he landed, twisting to the right. Flames slicked over Righty's thigh.

The demon grunted from the pain, the scent of burned hair filling the room.

Koldo jumped up, kicking a leg forward and a leg backward, nailing both of his opponents at the same time. He landed, and they recovered enough to leap at him, punching. He blocked one, but purposely took the other's abuse, grabbing on to Lefty's arm and holding tight as he used the appendage as leverage to swing up both of his legs into Righty's throat with a brutal *slam slam* of his booted feet. Then he flipped Lefty over and tossed him to his back to stomp on the creature's face. Bone crunched, suddenly a jigsaw puzzle that needed to be put back together.

Before the second stomp, Lefty rolled to his feet and bounded on the bed—the females utterly unaware— and, without pausing to consider a wiser way, slammed into Koldo's back. A long, thick tail wound around his middle, squeezing. The hook on the end sliced all the way to Koldo's intestines.

Lefty raised sharpened claws, intending to slash through his windpipe, but Koldo flashed to the other side of the bed. The moment he landed, he leaned forward and grabbed the end of the creature's tail, jerking and spinning Lefty's entire body.

As the fiend careened forward, Koldo flashed behind him and swung his sword. The demon tried to dodge, but wasn't fast enough. Fire met scales and bone, and scales and bone immediately lost. The demon's arm detached, spraying black blood over the floor.

Blood the humans would never see.

A howl of agony erupted as Lefty grabbed the appendage and flew out the window, into the afternoon sunlight. Unlike Sent Ones, demons couldn't regenerate limbs. The creature would have to have the arm reattached.

Deep down, Koldo knew this would not be their last battle.

Cursing, Righty turned in a half circle, his gnarled wings sweeping in Koldo's direction. He could have dodged, but he chose to allow the end of one wing to clip his ankles, knocking them together, sending him flying to the floor. The beads in his beard rattled as he hit, air bursting from his lungs. He pretended to lose his hold on the sword, and the weapon vanished.

Righty dived on top of him, just as he'd wanted, fangs bared. Koldo punched with all of his might, and broke the demon's nose, sending fragments of cartilage into his rotting brain. Then, Koldo flashed behind him, summoning the sword of fire, swinging. The demon shot forward, staying low. But not low enough. The scent of smoke and sulfur filled the air. A loud *thump* sounded. One of the creature's horns was now missing.

Features contorted with rage, the demon hopped to hoofed feet, black blood leaking down his face, from his busted nose. Roaring, he lunged. Twisting left, twisting right, Koldo stepped into the battle dance. Righty knew when and where to move, sometimes managing to avoid injury. They tangoed from one side of the room to the other, up the walls, down the walls, on the floor, across the ceiling, rolling over the bed, falling through Nicola as she continued to chat with her sister, not so much as a hitch in her breath.

Koldo released the sword and grabbed a fistful of fur on the demon's chest. He launched the creature through the far wall. A second later, the fiend raced back into the room.

"The girl is mine," Righty snarled, stalking a circle around him. "Mine! I'll never let her go."

"You were foolish when you decided to follow Lucifer rather than the Most High, and you're foolish now, to think you can best me. You fight from a place of defeat, and you always will." Long ago, the Most High had crushed all the forces of hell. But still the creatures struck at humans, determined to hurt those the Most High loved.

And the Most High loved all humans. He wanted to adopt them, as He'd done the Sent Ones.

A hiss of rage sounded. "I'll show you defeat!" Rather than initiating a full-scale attack, the demon backed one step away, two…three. A slow grin lifted the corners of his lips. "Yes, I'll show you defeat. Very, very soon." With that, he disappeared through the wall.

Koldo waited, at the ready, but the demon never returned. No doubt, he'd gone to recruit a few of his friends.

I'll be ready.

Only problem was, "very, very soon" told Koldo

nothing. In their realm, one day could be as long as a thousand years and a thousand years as short as one day.

"What the heck is going on?" Nicola exclaimed. "It's like two boulders have been lifted from my shoulders." As she spoke, a smile lit her entire face, transforming her from plain to exquisite. Her pale skin took on a radiant sheen, her eyes becoming the color of summer rather than winter.

The moisture in his mouth dried.

"Oh, La La. It's wonderful!"

Wonderful, yes, but still the toxin flowed through her veins. That would have to be dealt with.

He would have to find a way to gently reveal himself to her, something he'd never done with a human. He would have to garner her trust, something he'd never before cared to try. But when? How? And how would she react?

Be as shrewd as a serpent yet as harmless as a dove, Germanus used to tell him.

Funny, but Koldo was far less assured of his success with the girl than he'd been with the demons.

CHAPTER THREE

The next day

THE ELEVATOR DINGED, and the double doors slid open. Nicola Lane stepped inside the small enclosure, relieved to find she was alone. She was—

Not alone, she realized with a jolt of surprise. Oh, wow. Okay. In the far corner, a very tall, very muscled man shifted from the shadows. How could she have missed him, even for a second?

The doors closed, sealing her inside with him. *I don't judge by outward appearance. I really do not judge by outward appearance.* But oh, wow, wow, wow, he had to be a time-traveling Viking sent here to abduct modern women to give to his men back home—because they'd killed all the women in their village.

I watch too much TV.

He certainly gave off an all-dangerous-all-the-time vibe. And now, it was too late to avoid a possible pillaging.

Her heart fluttered, the warped beat making her light-headed.

"Floor?" he asked, his deep voice filled with more jagged edges than a shattered mirror.

"Lobby," she managed to reply, and he pressed the appropriate button.

It was a miracle the entire elevator didn't split apart from the force he used.

There was an exaggerated shake, and the cart began to descend. The scent of morning sky and—this could have been mere fantasy on her part—rainbows filled the small enclosure, and every waft came from the man. It was, quite possibly, the best cologne she'd ever smelled, and like the ladies in the AXE commercials, she had to battle the urge to lean into him and sniff his neck.

And wouldn't he just love that? He would demand to know what the heck she was doing, she would panic and her heart would give out, just as Laila's had, and… and…she wasn't going to think about her beautiful, precious Laila right now. She wasn't going to think about losing another loved one. First her mother, father and br— No, she wasn't going to think about that, either. She would break down.

And was that delicious heat coming from the Viking, too? For the first time in years, Nicola felt enveloped by warmth, the cold from her medications and poor circulation finally chased away.

The man turned and leaned against the wall, facing her fully. In that moment, she decided "very tall, very muscled" wasn't an adequate description for him. The tallest, most muscled man she'd ever seen in person or on TV worked better, but again, the description failed to capture the essence of his absolute gigantorness. He. Was. Huge.

And okay, yeah, he was also quite beautiful despite his murdering-and-pillaging aura. He had bronze skin, a gleaming bald head and a black beard tied by three crystal beads. His eyes were a surprising shade of gold, and capped by two thick brows with a prominent arch in the center. He wore a white linen shirt and white linen pants, each garment flowing as fluidly as water. On his feet was a pair of combat boots.

And she was studying him as if he were a bug under a microscope, she realized, horrified by her behavior. Nicola had often gone to school with electrodes taped to her chest and tubes sticking out of her clothing, so she knew the pain of a single wide-eyed stare. Her attention darted to the glittery pink tennies her twin had given her for their birthday last year.

"I'm quite large, I know," he said in an accent she couldn't place. At least he hadn't sounded offended.

Still, her stomach bottomed out. He'd noticed her examination of him, and now sought to…comfort her for her rudeness? How unexpected and sweet. Well, then, she would be brave.

She raised her chin and forced herself to meet his gaze. "Maybe I'm just amazingly tiny," she said, trying for humor.

His eyelids narrowed menacingly, hiding all that gold, leaving only the black of his pupils. "Do not lie, even through implication. Not for any reason, not even to be nice."

Her fingers went numb, and her heart once again fluttered. He was okay with staring, but joking was a killing offense. Good to know.

"Lies are the language of evil," he added in a gentler tone.

A gentler tone, but still intense.

The elevator stopped, the doors opened and a short, heavyset man took a step inside.

"You'll take the next elevator," the big guy announced.

The smaller man instantly froze. He licked his lips, backed up. "You know what? You're right. I will." He spun and raced away.

For a moment, Nicola considered following his lead. There was being polite, and there was being wise, and the two didn't always intersect. The fact that the Viking wanted to be alone with her couldn't bode well.

The doors began to draw together. Now was her chance to run.

But… she couldn't do it. "You didn't yell at him," she pointed out, unsure why she was having trouble keeping quiet—and why she'd stayed. "You seem like such an equal-opportunity yeller."

"I didn't yell at you, either," he said with a frown. A moment passed. He nodded as if he'd just realized something important. "You're sensitive. I'll be more careful."

What, he dreaded her wrath?

He studied her as intently as she'd studied him, causing her to squirm. "You are five-two, aren't you?"

"Five two and a half, thank you." She never forgot that very important half!

"That's a somewhat decent height for a woman, I suppose."

"For an eight-year-old boy, too," she grumbled.

"Not any that I know," he replied, deadpan.

Was he teasing her? Or was he just that blunt?

Finally the box stopped for good, and the doors opened to the lobby. Her companion politely waved her forward. She offered a bemused smile, said "Thanks" and hurried out—alive.

Almost alone, she thought wistfully. She would be able to sort through her thoughts and figure out what she was going to do when her sister… When Laila…

She couldn't think the word, even though she knew it would happen sooner rather than later. A mercy for Laila. Another sorrow for Nicola. She wasn't sure how many more she could bear and still survive.

Most people with their condition and underdeveloped heart died in their late teens. But she and Laila had lasted into their early twenties, a true miracle in itself, and she should be thrilled with the time they'd had together. And yet, she wanted more. For both of them. Laila wasn't satisfied with her life, and a person should be satisfied before they died. Right?

Nicola just…well, she needed to decide on a plan of action *today*. For once, her mind wasn't shrouded by a thick veil of fear and anxiety. And why were people looking at her as if she were a hideous beast monster determined to—

Not her, she realized, but the man beside her. The giant from the elevator. Nicola stopped, and so did he. He failed to maneuver around her, as if her slight presence was somehow blocking his path. She faced him fully, anchoring her hands on her hips. He stepped three feet away from her, and she found herself shivering all over again.

The heat *did* come from him.

He peered down at her, his golden eyes framed by the blackest, most luscious lashes of all time, so unexpected in that rough-and-tumble time-traveling-warrior face.

"Can I help you?" she asked.

"No, but you can have coffee with me."

No, he'd said. Meaning, she couldn't help him. He *really* took the honesty thing seriously. And had he just…asked her out? "Why would you want to do that?" she wondered aloud. And why hadn't she just said no?

She had to return to work, like, soon. Her lunch hour was almost over.

"I'm not ready to go home."

Ah. Not a date, then. He simply craved a distraction from whatever had brought him to the Palace of Tears and Death, and oh, could she sympathize. And she wasn't disappointed that he wanted nothing romantic from her. Really. Her mother had been right. Boys equaled excitement and excitement equaled another heart attack. And really, she hadn't ever missed boys and excitement all that much because she'd always had Laila. But Laila was…was…

"Coffee sounds great," she croaked as her chin quivered. Clearly she needed a distraction, too. The planning could wait. So could work. Pulling herself out of this pity pit was more important. "There's a little shop down the far corridor."

He stepped up beside her, and all that delicious heat returned. They kicked into gear, earning several more stares and even a little whispering. People had to be shocked by the difference in their sizes, and she couldn't really blame them. The top of Nicola's head failed to reach the man's massive shoulders.

"So, what's your name?" she asked.

"Koldo."

Cold-oh. Had to be foreign. "I'm Nicola."

"*Nicola.* Latin, meaning 'a victorious people.'"

They turned the first corner, though the scenery didn't change. All of the hallways were the same: white and silver with signs posted along the walls. "Uh, did you just secretly look that up on a cell phone I can't see or did you already know?"

"I knew."

"Why?"

"The words we speak are important, powerful, and since names are spoken every day, directed at specific individuals, people often become what they are called. I like to know who I'm dealing with."

Well, she wouldn't tell him she was the most defeated person ever and shatter his illusions. "What does *Laila* mean?"

"Dark beauty."

Interesting. Laila was fair, but she *was* lovely. "What does *Koldo* mean?"

"Famous warrior."

A warrior, as she'd first assumed? She wondered if he was in the army. "Are you truly famous?"

"Yes."

No hesitation. No pride. In his mind, he must have simply stated a fact. She admired his confidence. "So, what do you do, Koldo?"

"I'm in the army."

Nailed it!

Two more corners, and they reached the shop. He directed her to an empty table. "What would you like, Nicola?"

Her name on his lips…an embrace and a curse, all rolled into one. It was a little disconcerting. "Oh, I can—"

"You won't offer to give me money, and insult me," he said, and for once he sounded genuinely offended. "Now, then. Let's try this again. What would you like? I'm buying."

She smiled. No one had ever insisted on buying her something to drink. Most offers came from the coworkers who knew about her situation, and were mere tokens. The moment she mentioned taking care of her own bill, the other person immediately acquiesced. "An herbal tea, please. Something without caffeine. And thank you very much."

A nod, and he was off, leaving her chilled. She watched as he approached the counter. Watched as the punked-out cashier stared at him with utter fascination. He didn't seem to notice as he placed the order and waited for the drinks...and muffins, scones and croissants from the looks of it.

What kind of woman would capture his attention? she wondered.

Another warrior-type probably. Strong, capable, with big-enough bones to withstand any kind of abuse—uh, contact.

He returned a few minutes later and spread out a feast before her, the scent of berries, yeast and sugar wafting up and making her mouth water. She hadn't eaten in forever, it seemed, because she'd been too consumed with worry for Laila, dread over paying bills she hadn't begun to make a dent in and, well, trying not to drown in a sea of despair.

Today was different, though. Even as upset as she was, she felt better than she had in a long, long time, and her stomach rumbled.

Cheeks flushing, she claimed her tea and sipped at the burning liquid, savoring the sweetness. "Seriously, Koldo. This means a lot to me. A thousand times thank you wouldn't be enough."

"It's very much my pleasure, Nicola."

So polite. She liked that.

And the likes were certainly outweighing the dislikes now, weren't they?

"The food is for you, as well," he said, pushing a muffin in her direction.

Her eyes widened with astonishment. "All of it?"

"Of course."

Of course, he'd said. As if she was used to eating for an entire legion.

"You will keep up your strength," he added. "Right now, you're too pale, too frail."

She wasn't insulted. She *was* pale and frail. Nicola selected one of the croissants, pinched off a warm, buttery corner. "So…were you here visiting someone?"

"Yes."

Though she waited, attentive, he offered no more than that. "I'm sorry."

"Don't be. I'm not."

Annnd…again he offered nothing more. "Do you come here often?"

"That could be the plan, yes."

Silence.

Talkative much? But okay, no problem. They weren't really here to get to know each other, were they? They were here to forget their lives, if only for a little while. "I'm here a lot." Every day, in fact.

"Perhaps we'll see each other again." He lifted a steaming cup of coffee to lips as plush and red as candy apples and gulped. His expression never changed, the fiery temperature somehow *not* melting and welding his tongue to the roof of his mouth.

"Perhaps," she offered.

Again, silence.

What were girls supposed to talk about with boys they weren't interested in romantically? Because, if she were being honest—something he would definitely approve of—this was kind of painful. It wasn't what she'd expected or hoped for.

"What do you do when you're not here, Nicola?" he asked, at last taking up the reins of conversation.

Relieved by his efforts, she relaxed in her seat. "I work. I'm an accountant every weekday morning and afternoon." A job guaranteed to keep her blood pressure steady. She could crunch numbers, sort receipts and design a financial plan to get anyone out of debt. Anyone but herself, that is. She was still working through her parents' bills, and her and Laila's medical costs were still stacking up. "I'm a checkout girl at an organic food market every evening and on weekends."

"Neither of those jobs sprang from a childhood dream."

No, but dreams died…and if you weren't careful, the ghosts would haunt your present. "Why do you think that?" She wasn't fond of her jobs, but she'd always done whatever was needed to survive.

"I'm highly observant."

And quite modest.

"So, what did you *want* to do?" he asked.

Why not tell him the truth? "I wanted to live," she said. Really live. "I wanted to travel the world, jump from airplanes, dance on top of a skyscraper, deep sea dive for treasure and pet an elephant."

He tilted his head to the side and steadily met her gaze. "Interesting."

Because she'd mentioned activities rather than a career? Well, there was a reason for that. She'd never known how long she would live, so a career had seemed pointless. "What about you?" she asked. "What did you want to do?"

"I'm doing it." He refused to look away. "You could still do all of the things you mentioned."

"Actually, I can't. My heart couldn't take it." Let him assume she meant her nerves would get the better of her rather than the truth.

"You're right."

Wait. "What?"

"If words are the power of life and death, you just pointed a loaded gun at your head."

"What are you talking about? That's absurd."

"You speak what you believe, and you believe you're doomed. If there's one thing I've learned throughout the years, it's that what you believe is the impetus for your entire life."

A spark of anger caused her heart to skip a beat. "I believe in reality."

He waved a dismissive hand through the air. "Your perception of reality is skewed."

Oh, really? "How so?"

"You believe what you see and feel."

"Uh, doesn't everyone?"

"Everything in this natural world is changeable. Temporary. But the things you cannot see or feel are eternal."

She slammed her tea on the tabletop. Liquid splashed from the hole in the lid, burning her hand. "Lookit. Maybe you're not getting enough oxygen up there where your head lives, but you sound like a crazy person."

"I'm not crazy. I know you can be healed."

Healed? As if she hadn't tried everything already. "Some things can't be changed. Besides, you don't have any clue about the things I've done or the future I have."

"I know more than you think. You're so afraid to live, you're actually killing yourself."

Heavy silence descended. *He'd...nailed it,* she thought. She'd watched as fear slowly ate away at her sister's happiness, tainting every aspect of her existence. And in the days before she'd landed in the hospital, that's all Laila had had. An existence.

Her stomach had always hurt, ruining her appetite. Nicola was already striding down that road.

Laila had lost weight, and even her bones had seemed to wither. Give Nicola another few months.

Laila's hair had lost its glossy sheen. Blue and black smudges had become a permanent fixture under her eyes. Yeah, another few months should take care of that for Nicola, too.

"Somewhere along the way you lost hope," Koldo said, and there was a grim quality to his voice, as if he had suffered a loss of his own. "But if you'll listen to me, if you'll do what I say, your heart and body will mend and you'll at last do all the things you've always wanted to do."

"Are you a doctor?" she demanded. "How do you know that? And what do you think you can do for or to me that hasn't already been tried?"

Ignoring her questions, he said, "Selah, Nicola."

And with that, he disappeared, there one moment, gone the next.

CHAPTER FOUR

DETERMINED TO PROVE A POINT to Nicola, Koldo flashed out of the hospital to his underground home in West India Quay. The place of his greatest shame.

The place he kept his mother.

The small, hidden cave was illuminated by a soft green glow emanating from a lake of water uncontaminated by human life. Air so fresh it literally crackled with vitality enveloped him.

Just like the home in South Africa, he kept no furniture here, no wall hangings, no decorations and no amenities of any kind. Unlike the other home, there was a cage, a bucket for food, a bucket for water and a blanket. He would have provided his mother with a bed, but then, she'd never given him one.

"Well, well," she said. "Look who's returned."

And there she was. Cornelia. A name that meant *horn*. And she was certainly that. Sharp and deadly, able to puncture a man's heart and coldly walk away as his very life drained from him.

She sat in the corner of the cage, wearing a robe made by human hands and natural fabric. One Koldo had tossed her after ripping off the one made in the skies, for the robes their people wore could clean themselves and their wearers. But he hadn't wanted Cornelia cleansed in any way. He'd wanted her to know the feel of dirt that could never be scrubbed away.

Her skin was pallid, her freckles a stark contrast. Her long hair had been shorn and now fell to her ears, the locks tangled and sticking out in spikes. He hadn't been the one to do this deed. A few weeks ago, she had been captured by a horde of pică and dragged into hell in an attempt to force Koldo to betray Zacharel. He hadn't. He had rescued her instead.

He had no idea what else had been done to her, only that torture had, indeed, taken place. When he'd found her, she had hovered at the edge of death, and that was the only reason she hadn't fought him as he doctored her back to health. Now, here they were.

Her, as hate-filled as ever.

Him, shockingly dissatisfied with the situation.

As a child trapped under his father's reign, he had dreamed of punishing her in the worst of ways. And he still wanted to. Oh, did he want to. The desire was always there, burning in his chest. But he hadn't. He wouldn't. He'd allowed himself to do little things, like denying her the bed and proper robe, but nothing else. He was nothing like her, and every day he proved it. He would come here, pit himself against the pull to act and then leave.

Wise men knew not to even approach the door of their temptation, but Koldo hadn't yet convinced himself to stop.

"Hello, *Mother*."

She sucked in a breath. "I should have cut your tongue out of your mouth when I had the chance." She tossed a pebble at him. The stone bounced off his shoulder and tumbled to the floor.

"Just like you should have drowned me. I know."

Her eyes narrowed, long lashes fusing together and hiding the violet depths he so often saw in his nightmares. "I hadn't the stomach for violence back then. But your father... I expected better of him. He should have done what I could not."

"Oh, never doubt that he tried." Many times.

Koldo thought back to the day Cornelia had flown him over his father's camp and dropped him. As weak and agonized as he'd been, landing had hurt more than the brutal removal of his wings.

A huge, bald man with more muscles and scars than Koldo had ever seen stomped toward him. Cornelia called, "Meet your son, Nox—may you destroy each other," before flying away.

Nox. A name that meant *night.*

Koldo had blacked out seconds after that, only to awaken on the floor of a spacious tent, the bald man looming over him, grinning widely, his eyes as black as his name implied.

"You're my son, are you? Raised by a do-gooder angel."

His mother? A do-gooder?

"I'm betting you're filled with silly notions about right and wrong," Nox had continued. "Aren't you, boy?"

Concentrating on the words had proven difficult— everything inside Koldo had been screaming at him to run and never look back. But he'd been trapped inside a body too weak to move or flash. All he could do was watch as thin curls of smoke wafted from the male's pores, scenting the air with sulfur.

That's when realization had slammed into Koldo

with collision force. A bald head, bottomless eyes and black smoke could mean only one thing. Nefas. His father hailed from the most dangerous, vile race in existence. A race that sneaked up on humans, poisoned slowly, painfully…destroying utterly. A race without a conscience.

A race just like the demons.

The Nefas were death dealers. Soul suckers.

The age of their victims never mattered. The gender of their victims never mattered. They lived to inflict pain. They killed. And they laughed while doing it.

"No worries," the man had said. "You can unlearn."

Nox had wanted Koldo to embrace the Nefas way of life, and Koldo had resisted…at first. But every time he'd tried to escape, flashing away, his father had been right on his heels, easily finding him and dragging him back—punishing him. Once, Nox had tied him down and poured acid down his throat. The time after that, Nox had plucked out one of his eyes and nailed it to the bar of his cage, so that he could watch himself watching himself. Koldo had had to win the eye back—and stuff it back in. By then he'd been a little older and had been able to partially heal it. Still, his sight had never been the same.

Bitterness and hatred had taken root inside him. Why him? Why had no one saved him? How much more would he be forced to endure?

Finally, he'd lost his will to fight. He'd given in. He'd raided villages. He'd helped his father and the other soldiers fit their mouths over their victims' mouths and suck out innocent souls, leaving only lifeless shells.

A man will do just about anything to survive, boy.

It was the only one of his father's lessons that he'd taken to heart.

Now, Koldo was certain he'd passed the point of redemption. He could have fought harder. *Should* have fought harder. That he hadn't... Guilt would always ride him, and shame would always fill him.

He had too many memories. The dark kind that never went away. Each one made him long to pluck out his eyes, just to blank his line of sight, or cut off his ears, just to quiet the screams.

Over the years he'd earned a big-enough name to draw Germanus's attention. An army of Sent Ones had swooped into his father's camp to destroy Koldo, had seen the scars on his back and mistakenly assumed he wasn't Nefas, for Nefas could not grow wings, and Koldo had obviously had them at one time. So, the soldiers had captured him instead.

That had been the beginning of his new life.

Germanus—a name meaning "brother"—could have and probably should have slain him despite his origins. Koldo had been feral. He had snarled and cursed and attacked anyone who neared him. After all the things he had done, after all of the people he had killed, he was supposed to forgive himself and adopt the "do-gooder" approach? Impossible!

But Germanus had looked deeper than the surface, had seen the shame and guilt in Koldo's eyes. Emotions raw and intense, even back then.

The king of the Sent Ones had spent the next several years coaxing Koldo from his rages, doing his best to comfort a young male with such a damaged past, ensuring Koldo was trained to fight the right way, that he had a safe, comfortable place to sleep, that he always had a proper meal to eat.

It had been Koldo's first taste of actual caring and concern, and he'd soon grown to love Germanus—would still die to protect him.

"Why did you mate with Nox?" he asked his mother as he stalked around the cage.

"Why not? He was a very beautiful man."

Some women would find such a dangerous male attractive, Koldo supposed. Despite the bald head and dead eyes, he'd had a face far lovelier than any Koldo had ever seen. A purity of features, a radiance most beings could only ever dream about.

"Did you hope to tame him? Did you think you would be the one to change him?"

Cornelia pushed to her feet, always keeping her gaze on him, never permitting him to have her back, where her beautiful white-and-gold wings lay. She expected him to remove them. She was right to do so. It was one of his biggest temptations.

"Evil cannot be changed," she said.

"Did he betray you for another? One of his own kind, perhaps? A female better suited to his particular tastes? Or, perhaps he turned to *many* other females."

"Shut up."

But he couldn't. He was closing in on the truth. Even as sickness churned in his stomach, he said, "He used to laugh about you, you know. Said you loved him, begged him to be with you, to stay with you. Said you sobbed when he left. Said you—"

"Shut up, shut up, shut up!" she shrieked, racing to the bars where Koldo stood. She shook with so much force he was surprised the reinforced metal held steady.

The ferocity of her reaction should have pleased him. This was what he'd always wanted from her, after all. Rage, frustration. Helplessness. Mirroring what he'd felt for so many years. But the sickness intensified. How could he do this to a female? Any female?

How could he hurt another of his kind?

She spit on his boots. "I hate you. I hate you so much I can barely breathe past it. I hate you so much I'd rather rot in this cage than pretend I love you or say I'm sorry for the way I treated you. I'm not! I never will be. You were an abomination then and you're an abomination now. The day you die is the day I rejoice."

Hurt and fury joined the collage of other emotions, the darkness in his mind thickening, once again banging at the dam. He stepped back, away from her, lest he lash out and end her—becoming just like his father. The scent of jasmine and honeysuckle followed him.

Even here, she carried the despised fragrance with her.

What had an innocent little boy done to elicit this kind of rejection? How could she blame Koldo for his father's treatment of her?

How could Koldo still hurt, after all this time?

"If ever I die," he said, "you won't be the cause. You're too weak. You've always been weak, and that's why Nox let you go."

Again she spit on his boots.

Hands fisted, he flashed to his home in South Africa. He had sixteen residences throughout the world, each tucked securely away from prying human eyes, but more and more this was the one he preferred, the one where he spent most of his free time.

Before he even manifested, he was beating at the

walls, tearing the newly healed skin on his knuckles. Blood splattered. Bone snapped.

This time, the rage failed to drain as quickly.

Hours seemed to pass before he was shucking his clothing, ripping the material in his haste. The shirt and pants hit the floor and drew together of their own accord, the tears and halves forming a perfect robe. Cool water droplets splashed against his bare skin as he peered out at the turbulent waterfall.

That woman...

He punched the side of the wall, dust and debris ghosting through the air. Always she reduced him to *this,* to a man who felt as if his heart had been cleaved from his chest, stomped on, sliced, kicked around and burned to ash. He *had* to gain the upper hand with her.

Otherwise, he would kill her.

When Cornelia breathed her last, her spirit would leave her body. But she would not go up, would not spend the rest of eternity with the Most High in the Heavens of heavens. She couldn't. To die with hatred blazing in her heart was to go down, down, down. It was a spiritual law no one—not even a Sent One— could supersede.

Devilish things could not coexist with divine things.

Reason number one Koldo was in such danger himself.

Cornelia deserved such a fate, yes. She deserved to suffer for all eternity. But he wasn't going to be the one to send her to an early grave. He wasn't like her— if he had to remind himself every day, he would. More than that, he wanted...what he could never have. Answers. Her love.

Absolution.

He gritted his teeth. No, he wasn't like her—and he no longer wanted those things. A taste of vengeance was all he craved.

The thought hit him, and he paused. There was no way someone like him could help a female as fragile as Nicola, was there?

He should have stayed away from her, he realized. But he hadn't, and now it was too late. He'd flashed away from her to prove the existence of supernatural activity, hoping to force her to accept it and take the first step toward fighting the demons. Now she knew.

Now she would ask questions.

If she asked the wrong people, they would give her the wrong answers.

He scrubbed a hand over the smoothness of his scalp. He had to stick to his plan.

And that wasn't such a bad thing, he told himself. Nicola intrigued him. Her voice, so soft, so sweet…so addictive, a caress his ears already craved again. Her wit. Her resilience. Her bravery. He'd snipped at her, yet she hadn't sobbed and begged for mercy.

Throughout her very short span on earth, one disaster after another had befallen her. Perhaps the demons were responsible, or perhaps the imperfect world. Perhaps both. Whatever the reason, he wanted better for her. The better he himself had found with Germanus.

Koldo just had to teach her how to fight the toxins. And he had to do it while keeping her calm. Fear would strengthen what the paura had left behind, and tension would weaken her immune system, strengthening what the grzech had left behind. Without fear and tension, the toxins would fade. With hope and joy, the toxins would fade faster.

Bottom line, what you fed grew and what you starved died.

Would she be able to look past her negative emotions and see the light?

A spark of anticipation beaded, somehow overshadowing the nearly overwhelming cascade of acid his mother had caused. Despite everything, he couldn't wait to see Nicola again, to learn what she'd decided about his disappearance. If she'd convinced herself she'd imagined him, or if she'd accepted he was something other than human.

"So not the view I was hoping for," a male voice said from behind him.

Still naked, Koldo spun and faced Thane, the second-in-command of Zacharel's army. Thane, meaning *freeman.* And the warrior certainly seemed to be everything the word implied. The male's carnal appetite was well-known. He hunted a new lover every day, discarding those he finished with as if they were dirty tissue.

And yet, even knowing that, women still flocked to him, as though he was the only male in creation with curling blond hair and big blue eyes.

"What does Zacharel want me to do this time?" Koldo demanded, reaching into the air pocket at his side to withdraw another robe. He yanked the material over his head, trying not to stare at Thane's wings. They arched over the warrior's wide shoulders, sweeping all the way to the floor. Pure white was broken up by dazzling gold. Trying—and failing.

"It'll be better to show rather than explain," Thane said, an odd note in his voice.

That didn't bode well. "Very well. Lead the way."

CHAPTER FIVE

THE NEXT WEEK PASSED in a blur for Nicola. Every day she woke up at the butt crack of dawn, went to work, went to see her sister on her lunch hour, went back to work, went to her second job and toiled until the wee hours of the night before at last heading home, watching TV to unwind, then falling asleep for four measly hours—and the cycle started all over again.

Now, she sat at her desk at Estellä Industries, watching the clock. *Come on, noon. Get here already.* The only aspect of her life that had changed was her thinking. She couldn't get Koldo out of her mind. Who was he? *What* was he?

After his disappearance, she'd asked the girl at the coffee shop whether or not she'd actually spoken to a giant of a man with a bald head and beaded beard. The answer hadn't surprised her.

"Are you kidding me? I'm not blind. But, uh, are you guys dating or, like, is he available? Because I already wrote my number on a napkin if you want to, like, give it to him."

Unless they'd shared the same hallucination, Koldo was real and Nicola wasn't crazy. Or maybe she was, despite that. She'd actually taken the napkin, curious to know what Koldo's reaction would be.

But…what was he? she wondered again. What did

say-la mean, the last word he'd spoken to her? She had no idea how to spell it, so she hadn't been able to look it up online. And how had he vanished in the blink of an eye? Was he some kind of ghost that more than one person could see?

With as many near-death and death-death-for-a-minute-or-two experiences as she'd had, she knew there was an afterlife. Several times she'd floated into it. Once, she'd even talked to some kind of being.

Isn't this nice? he'd said. He'd had pale hair, eyes as clear as the ocean and a pair of beautiful white wings. He'd been handsome in a classic movie-star kind of way, and had worn a long robe as he'd tried to urge her down a long tunnel. *Isn't this peaceful? Just let go of your old life and you can have this forever.*

He'd reminded her of the angels she'd seen in picture books, but there'd been something about his tone… something in those eyes…she had fought him, wanting to return to Laila, and for a second, only a second, his affable mask had fallen away and she'd gotten a glimpse of bright red eyes, gnarled bones and fangs.

A monster. A monster just like she used to see as a child, before therapy and drugs had convinced her otherwise. Now she wasn't sure what to think about Koldo and the monsters and had no idea how to figure it out. There was an overload of information out there, but nothing had jelled with her.

The right answer would elicit peace; she knew that much. Peace always accompanied truth.

Koldo would just have to tell her. *If* he ever showed up again.

And he had to show up! Did he really know how to heal her heart? If so, could Laila's be healed, as well?

The more she wondered, the more hope filled her. To be able to fall asleep and not wonder if she would wake up, or if Laila would still be alive…to never fear losing another sibling. To be able to walk up a hill, holding Laila's hand, without either of them passing out…to be able to skip and jog and jump…to be able to dance! Oh, to dance. To fall in love, get married and have children. To live, *really* live, as they'd used to dream, before tragedy convinced them to deal in "reality" rather than "fantasy."

Koldo had said he would be visiting the hospital again, but hadn't mentioned when. If he waited much longer, she might strangle him when he appeared, just to release a little steam. Every day she looked for him so diligently the nurses asked her if she'd like a Xanax or ten to help her relax.

When has anything good ever happened to you?

The question wafted through her mind, and she frowned.

Being optimistic will only lead to crushing disappointment.

No. No, that wasn't true.

You don't need one more thing to worry about right now.

Her hands curled into fists. Before meeting Koldo, she might have caved under the weight of those thoughts. She definitely would have battled an upset stomach, paced a thousand miles without ever leaving her chair and frayed the edges of her nerves until her limbs began to shake uncontrollably. Now…

"I'm not listening to you." Or herself. Whatever! She had hope for the first time in years, and she wasn't letting go. She leaned back in the chair at her desk. "He'll keep his word. He'll turn up, and he'll answer all of my questions."

The depressing thoughts stopped, and she breathed a sigh of relief.

A knock sounded at the door.

"Are you Nicola Lane?" a hard, biting voice asked.

Nicola blinked rapidly and focused on the beautiful woman in the open doorway. She was tall, slender and black, with a fall of jet-black curls. Shadows consumed eyes the color of chocolate. Koldo's were lighter, like caramel, and— Wow, Nicola must be hungry.

The woman wore a black-and-white tailored jacket, a pencil skirt and mile-high stilettos that perfectly complemented toenails painted black-and-white. Everything about her screamed style, sophistication and cold-blooded calm. So, what was she doing here, at the middle-class stress capital of the world?

"I'm Nicola, yes."

"Well, congratulations. I'm now part of your department."

Sarcasm on the first day. Wonderful. "Are you Jamila Engill or Sirena Kegan?"

Frowning, the girl said, "Jamila Engill."

"Pretty name." She wondered what *Jamila* meant. No doubt Koldo would have known.

"You have two new hires?"

"Yes." Nicola tugged the lapels of her sweater closer together to ward off the chill blasting from Jamila's attitude. Okay, fine. It was from the overhead vent. "Please, have a seat and we'll get to know each other."

Jamila marched into the office and slammed onto the far chair. Chin high in the air, she twined her hands in her lap and kept her gaze narrowed on Nicola, her back ramrod straight.

They were gonna have fun together, she could tell.

Five days ago, her very jittery, very irritable boss told her that he'd decided to hire two more accountants. Shock had nearly drilled Nicola to her knees. She'd been begging for a new hire for months, and every time she had been told to "make do."

Currently, she was doing the work of five people. At first, she had managed. After Laila's hospitalization, she'd begun to fall behind.

"So...what will be expected of me?" Jamila asked tightly.

Nicola explained a little about the operating system, and even though she hated sharing personal information with a stranger, she added, "I'll be as much a help as possible as you learn, but the truth is, my sister is... dying—" even voicing the word was difficult "—and she... Well, I'm being pulled away from the office more and more." Sooner or later, Jamila would have found out anyway. Phone calls would have come in, paperwork would have blasted through, or coworkers would have mentioned it.

This way, it was out in the open from the start.

Jamila leaned back in a pose that should have relaxed her. Instead, she appeared more rigid. "I'm sorry."

People always said that. Nicola wondered what Koldo the Honest would have said.

Just the thought of him caused her heart to flutter. She cleared her throat. "Sometimes we have to confront employees who haven't turned in their books. They'll make excuses, but you'll have to stay on them."

"That won't be a problem."

No flinching, and no paling.

"Good, then you should do fine." *Unless you keep glaring at me like that.*

"Hey, y'all. I'm Sirena, and I'm reporting for duty."

Nicola's attention shifted to the girl now standing in the doorway. She was taller than Nicola by an inch, maybe two, and wore an ill-fitting black jacket and matching pair of slacks, with a pink button-up top breaking up the darkness. Her hair was long and blond and as straight as a board. Her eyes were as wide as a doll's, a mix of brown and blue; a pair of horn-rimmed glasses perched on her nose.

"Oh, my," she said, shutting the door behind her. She glided to the other chair and eased down, then extended a small gift basket. "This is for you. I was just so excited to work with you, I couldn't help but show it."

How sweet. "Thank you." Nicola accepted the offering with a smile. A jasmine body wash and a lotion scented with honeysuckle.

"Look at this place." Sirena gazed around. "It's not big, but it's homey and wonderful, isn't it?"

Homey? Wonderful? Not even close. The room boasted plain white walls and a concrete floor painted gray. The only furniture was the desk, Nicola's chair and the two chairs in front. Not one of the three had a cushion.

Her first few months in the office, Nicola had hung pictures of her family on the walls, but every time she'd looked at them, memories had flooded her.

She'd heard her mother shout, "What are you doing, laughing like that? Excitement of any kind isn't good for you. Do you *want* to die and send me spiraling into another depression?"

She'd remembered her father patting her on the head and saying, "Every night I go to sleep afraid I'll never again see my beloved girls."

Well, his fear had come true, but not for the reason he'd thought. His life had been cut short by a drunk driver, and he *hadn't* seen them again.

Pictures of Laila only served to remind her of all she would soon lose. Her best friend, her confidante, her cheerleader. Her very heart.

"You'll be able to decorate your cubby however you like," she said, fighting a quiver in her chin.

"I can't wait!" Sirena's happy tone chimed.

Jamila stiffened, as though offended.

A knock boomed from the door. The entrance swung open before she could bid the person on the other side to enter. Dexter Turner peeked his head inside. He had a full head of dark hair and brown eyes that were puppy-dog sweet.

"Hey, Nicola, I was wondering—" His gaze landed on Jamila, widened, slid to Sirena, widened still more, before finally settling on Nicola. He gulped. "I, uh, didn't know you had company."

"I can leave if you want," Sirena said, eager to please.

"You're fine," Nicola told her, not wanting the women to vacate just yet. Dex had asked Nicola out several times, and she'd always told him no. In high school, she and Laila had been forbidden to date for their own good. Then, after their parents had died and they'd been on their own, they'd both gone a little crazy, going out with anyone who asked.

Granted, only five guys had asked Nicola. But then, she was glad there hadn't been more. She had hated every minute of every date. The nervousness had been too much for her, especially since each of the boys had expected her to be more experienced than she was, considering her age. She had stuttered, and she had squirmed in the uncomfortable silences that followed.

After vomiting before the last one, and nearly passing out during dinner, she had decided not to date until her doctors discovered a way to regulate her heartbeat once and for all.

Not Laila, though. Laila had flourished under the attention. A few months ago, she'd even made a go of a serious relationship. But the two had fought and fought and fought, and all that strife had put a strain on her body. She'd ended up in the hospital. Of course, when the doctors told her that she would never leave, the guy had walked away and never come back.

"I'll just catch you later," Dex said, and shut the door.

Several beats of silence passed.

"Is he yours?" Jamila asked.

"Nope," Nicola said. "I'm single."

"Well, I think you two would make an adorable couple," Sirena said, her hand fluttering over her cheek as if she were flushing. "Just adorable."

The phone rang, and Nicola picked up the receiver, grateful for the distraction. "Nicola Lane's office."

"Miss Lane?" A strong male voice. Familiar.

"Yes," she said, her heart suddenly pounding erratically.

"This is Dr. Carter at County General."

Dread spiked, and she experienced a rush of dizziness. "What's happened?"

"Nothing good, I'm afraid. Your sister has taken another turn for the worse. How soon can you get here?"

WHAT DID I DO to deserve this? Koldo had spent the past six days with Thane. An eternity, surely. A punishment, definitely. They had traveled to the Downfall, Thane's place of business. A palace of iniquity, to be sure. One that would have been visible to the human eye if not for the cloud surrounding it. But it had to be this way. Only the Most High, Sent Ones, angels and demons operated in the spiritual realm. Other supernatural creatures, like the ones Thane entertained, would have been unable to visit otherwise.

The entire place was in the process of a very slooow descent toward the earth, moving a mere inch a day.

Falling.

As the members of the Army of Disgrace might at any sign of misconduct. *Symbolism at its best,* he thought. But then, wickedness of any kind caused a separation with the Most High.

The club would eventually end up in hell.

Won't think about that.

Other than successfully completing the three demon-killing missions Zacharel had assigned the entire army, Koldo and his companions hadn't left the club.

Thane and fellow angels Xerxes and Bjorn lived there, and Koldo wasn't certain how they were allowed to maintain their status as Sent Ones. But he now knew why they had been given to Zacharel. More than using a new woman every night, they fought whoever angered them with brutal intensity—and nearly everyone they encountered angered them.

Now the four of them were in the bar, sitting in a shadowed corner. Different immortal races wandered about, drinking and dancing, their hands wandering. From the trouble-happy Harpies to the scream-happy

Phoenix, and everything in between. Vampires, shape-shifters, the Fae and countless others.

The snake-shifters were considered the most dangerous, with the Phoenix a close second. But the race that topped them all? The race no one ever considered, because everyone liked to pretend they were nothing more than a nightmare? The Nefas.

Koldo was very glad no one knew about his father. Gladder still no one ever would. Even the Sent Ones who had rescued him from the camp all those centuries ago had no clue about his origins.

"Having fun?" Thane asked him.

"Why am I here?" he demanded.

The warrior tossed back a shot of vodka. "Haven't we gone over this? Because Zacharel commanded us to stick together, and I refuse to live in one of your hovels."

Koldo's frustration level spiked. He was to have a permanent babysitter now? No. Absolutely not. He refused. Something would have to be done. "What about our mission? The one you couldn't tell me about? The one you had to show me?"

"I never said there was a mission."

Must not kill a Sent One.

"But if I had told you I wanted you to come to my place and enjoy yourself," Thane continued, "you would have said…"

"No." Never.

"And there's the reason I *implied* there was a mission."

Koldo banged his fist into the table, earning several what's-up-with-the-angry-beast glances from nearby patrons.

His gaze swung to Bjorn, who sat on Thane's right. "Is he always this tricky?"

"Are you always this curious?" was the irritating reply.

Bjorn had dark hair and tanned skin veined with the same gold that wove through his wings. His eyes were a rainbow of colors, from the lightest of blues to the darkest of greens, with shades of pink and purple thrown into the mix.

His name was Scandinavian for *bear*. Again, another perfect fit.

Jaw locked, Koldo looked to Xerxes.

Xerxes, Persian for *monarch*. The male had long white hair pulled back in a jeweled torque. His skin was the color of milk and lined with scar after crisscrossing scar, each in jagged patterns of three. Arresting, yes, but it was his eyes that truly held a person's attention. They were a bright ruby-red, and glowed with an endless rage matched by few.

I'm one of the few.

"Are they always this cryptic?" Koldo asked him.

"Are you always this annoying?"

All three males chuckled at their own ridiculous wit.

Koldo refused to envy their friendship, or their complete ease with each other. He'd heard they'd met inside a demon fortress, each a prisoner—each tortured. He'd had no one during his own years of anguish, and perhaps that was why he preferred his solitary life. The fewer people privy to his secrets, the less likely he was to face betrayal.

"I've introduced you to many beautiful females, hoping one of them would entertain you—and free me of the burden of you," Thane said, tossing back another vodka. "You've refused them all. Why?"

"I have no interest."

"Have you *ever* been with a woman?" Bjorn asked.

"No." He'd had no desire. He still didn't. Except… every day since he'd come here, Zacharel had granted Koldo an hour-long break from Thane. He'd spent the first half of that hour with his mother, resisting the urge to hurt her, and the second half with Nicola, watching, hidden from view.

He would ensure no demons were following her. He would wonder what she'd look like if she laughed with all of her heart, carefree, and his blood would heat in the strangest way. A tingling heat. Almost…electrifying. He would begin to step into the natural realm, catch himself and back off. What if his presence caused her heart undue stimulation? What if he hurt her? He had the hands of a killer, after all.

So, he would remain in the spirit realm. But the tension within him had gotten worse. The hum of anticipation had gotten stronger.

He had no idea what to do, what to think.

Even still, he was eager to speak with her, to at last discover what conclusion she'd drawn about him. How was he to kick things off, though?

Your sister is going to die, but I can help you save yourself.

I'm a Sent One. Heed my words.

I'm a cold, hard man. I've done terrible things. But have no fear, I won't harm you.

"A virgin," Xerxes said with a tinge of…envy? Surely not. He motioned to a female. "We must change that."

Smacking bubble gum, a blonde Harpy approached

the table. She wore a sequined bra and spandex shorts, her hair braided at the sides in two perfect ropes. "What's up, guys?"

"We want you to give our friend a lap dance," the scarred warrior said. Then, to Koldo, "I bet you can't resist *that*."

Her gaze slid to Koldo. She was a pretty little thing, with wide green eyes and freckles scattered across her nose. He wasn't into freckles. "You want me to cozy up to *this* guy?" she asked, hitching her thumb in his direction.

"Yes," Xerxes replied, deadpan.

"He looks like a cold-blooded killer."

In Koldo's case, looks were not deceiving. "You don't have to—"

"So *of course* I'll give him a lap dance!"

Wait. What? "No, thank you. I don't want—"

"Whoohoo, this is gonna be fun." She fist-pumped the air. "Are you prepared to soar?"

"We're already in the skies, sweet," Thane said, clearly fighting a wave of amusement.

She rolled her eyes. "Whatevs. He knew what I meant. Didn't you, Killer?"

"I would rather you not—" Koldo began, only to be cut off again.

"Move the table," the girl said, rubbing her hands together. "I want to get this party train out of the station *the right way*. And that's my way, in case anyone missed my meaning."

Koldo pinched the bridge of his nose as Bjorn and Xerxes stood to obey the Harpy. Before the warriors could get started, he stiffened.

Not because of their intentions, and not because

of the Harpy. Deep inside, where instinct sizzled and crackled, he experienced a sudden knowing.

Nicola was in trouble.

"I have to go." He jumped to his feet, accidentally sending the table toppling the floor.

"Well, that's one way to do it," the girl muttered.

Zacharel's orders stated that Koldo was to remain with Thane twenty-three hours a day. If he disobeyed, he risked punishment. He'd already used up his hour away today. "And you get to come with me," he told the warrior, pointing at him to show there would be consequences if he was ignored.

"Wait. You're leaving right now?" The Harpy's pink, glittery lips fell into a seductive pout. "But I haven't even started yet, and I've got some wicked-cool moves. Did I mention I'm very bendy?"

Thane's gaze narrowed on Koldo. "We're not leaving. We do, and I'll never get you back here."

The warrior had just as much to lose as he did, Koldo realized—and that gave Koldo all the bargaining power he needed. "We'll return. You have my word. Until then, you had better follow." He informed Thane of where to go and flashed to the hospital, but…Nicola wasn't there. He flashed to her office. She wasn't there, either. He did, however, spot a Sent One, as well as a girl he didn't recognize but thought he should.

There was no time to question either female. He flashed to Nicola's house, but his redhead wasn't there, either. Her second job…nope. Back to the hospital, where he materialized at an empty nurse's station and used the computer. A good decision. Laila had been moved to a new room.

Thane landed just in front of him. He tucked his

wings at his sides as he looked around. "What are we doing here?"

"You're waiting for me to conclude my business, and I'm in the process of concluding my business."

Without another word, he flashed to Laila's new room. And that's when he found Nicola, sobbing over her sister's body.

CHAPTER SIX

KOLDO ASSESSED THE SITUATION quickly. Laila's heart monitor was racing. There was a sharp odor in the air—the scent of impending death. There was a wheeze to her breathing, even with the machines doing all of the work—the *sound* of impending death. Though she wasn't dead, her spirit was already halfway out of her body, about to ascend or descend whatever path she'd chosen for herself.

She wouldn't last much longer. Once the spirit was all the way out, the body couldn't survive.

Nicola's forehead rested on the bed, her delicate shoulders shaking as she cried with the intense force of her despair. Despair…a mix of both fear and tension, strengthening both of the toxins. Soon, every demon in the hospital would be hungry to feed off her.

"Nicola," he said, stepping into the natural realm and becoming visible. His first word to her in all these many days. He shouldn't have waited until tragedy struck, he realized.

Her attention whipped up to him, and red, swollen eyes landed on his face. She gasped, "Koldo," with a big dose of surprise. Her nose was stuffed, her voice no longer smoke and dreams but scratchy. Strands of hair clung to splotchy cheeks. "What are you doing here? How did you find me?"

How could he explain that he'd felt her pain, when he wasn't sure how or why he'd done so? Ignoring the question, he forced his gaze to move to Laila. "She's dying."

A pause. A trembling, "Yes. I shouldn't be crying. I knew this was coming." Nicola covered her face with her hands, wiping away the tears, perhaps even trying to rub away the tension. "She needs me to be calm. *I* need me to be calm."

So do I.

"But…"

"You hurt," he said.

"Yes." Sighing, she fell against the back of the chair. She released a breath, drew in another, and her nose wrinkled adorably. "Last time you smelled wonderful. This time you smell like a brothel."

He wasn't embarrassed by the insult. Nothing had ever or would ever embarrass him. He was…overheated. Yes. That's why his cheeks suddenly felt as though they were on fire. "And how do you know what a brothel smells like?"

"Fine. You smell like what I assume a brothel smells like. Cigarettes and alcohol and conflicting perfumes."

"My apologies." The first part of what she'd said at last penetrated. Before, she'd thought he'd smelled wonderful.

His body tensed, just as before. But there was no urge to inflict pain…he wanted only to touch her, to offer comfort and—he wasn't sure.

The beeping from the monitor sped up.

Nicola traced her fingers over her sister's hand, then stopped, just stopped, as if the action were too much for her.

How much strength had she lost since his last visit?

No matter the amount, the answer was the same. Too much.

"What are you, anyway?" she asked almost absently.

"You haven't figured it out on your own?"

"No. How could I?"

"There are many ways."

"Name one."

"Easy. A sensitive spirit."

She expelled a weary breath. "All I know is you aren't human."

"Correct."

"So why don't you just tell me?"

"Would you believe me?" If he admitted he was a Sent One, she would, perhaps, have no idea what that was. If he used the word *angel,* she might have certain expectations he would be unable to meet. "We can discuss it later. Right now, why don't I help your sister?"

Immediately he wished he could snatch the words back, but did he? No. He'd said them. He would deal with the fallout.

Eyes as wild and turbulent as a winter storm widened. "How?"

"I…can buy her a little time. She'll strengthen and she'll awaken, but I don't think she'll live more than a few weeks," he rushed to add. She had to be swimming with toxins. Not only that, she would still have no internal or external barriers against the demons. Barriers she would have to learn how to erect. Barriers she might not have time to learn how to erect.

"A few weeks," Nicola parroted.

"Not long, I know, but—"

"I'll take it!" she shouted, as though she feared he would change his mind.

So eager for so little. "But you haven't yet heard my terms."

Her beautiful mouth edged into a frown. "You want something from me?"

Many things. "I'll buy your sister a few weeks, and in exchange you'll do what I tell you, when I tell you, until the day I release you from my charge." He had no idea how long it would take him to rid her of the toxins and teach her enough to survive on her own.

"That sounds like something I've heard on the late-night news. Are you expecting me to become your sex slave?" Her tone wasn't scandalized, but curious.

"No," he replied with a frown of his own. "I don't want you in that way." He didn't, did he? He hadn't lied to Thane and the others. He was a virgin. Desire wasn't something he was familiar with, and he wasn't sure he would recognize it.

He knew he admired Nicola's loyalty to her sister. He knew he wished he had someone who loved him half as much. But seeing her naked was…intriguing, he realized, the blood heating in his veins, becoming molten, scorching him. A heat that had nothing to do with rage. It bubbled up, washing away the cold man he knew himself to be.

Perhaps he *did* want her in that way.

The very idea nearly sent him stumbling backward. His mind reeled. But…but…but she was so dainty, so fragile. He dwarfed her. Could crush her. Why her? Why now? Desire for her was implausible. Impractical.

"No," he croaked. He couldn't.

"Oh," she said, her shoulders slumping. "So, you want me to obey you when you tell me to…what?"

"Stay calm. Embrace peace. Sow joy."

"Sow?"

"There is an irrefutable spiritual law that states a person reaps what they sow. Therefore, if you sow joy into others, you will reap joy for yourself. Right now, you need joy."

"Calm, peace, joy," she echoed hollowly. As if he were insane.

Maybe he was. "Yes."

"Why do you want me to feel those things?"

If you don't, the toxins will build up, and eventually you'll die, just like your sister. They weren't exactly calming, peaceful, joyous words, so he remained quiet.

"Wouldn't you rather have me, I don't know, grow a beard, get taller and play the part of Koldo in a little production called *What You're Asking Is Impossible?* Because that I think I can do."

Silly human. For the first time in his life, he wanted to smile. "No."

Desperate, she said, "How about the number of the coffee shop girl? I could give you that, and we could call it even."

Coffee shop girl? "Remember when I told you I could help you heal?"

"As if I could ever forget."

"This is the way."

A moment passed. A moment she spent blinking at him. "Calm, peace, joy," she repeated. "Tell me my sister will live longer than a few weeks, and it's done."

As if he was in control of how long her sister survived. But she didn't know that, and she was trying to buy more time. "I'm sorry I wasn't clear. I gave you my top offer. There's nothing more *I* can do on your sister's behalf. Therefore, there will be no negotiating of my terms."

"I figured, but I had to try." She offered the same bright smile she'd given him in the elevator, and he had the foresight to capture a mental picture this time. One he would remember on the worst of nights, when the past threatened to rise up and swallow him. She was proof there was more in the world than darkness and pain.

"Do we have a deal?" he asked.

"We do."

He nodded. "Very well. Don't allow the doctors to take her off life support. I'll return shortly."

"But—"

He left before she could finish her sentence. Right now, every moment counted.

He flashed to Thane, who paced in the hospital hallway, and told him where he was going. Then he flashed to Zacharel's cloud in the lower level of the skies. He had no wings and couldn't hover outside the entrance to await permission, which was why Zacharel had given him an open invitation to enter—as long as he remained in the foyer.

"Zacharel," he called. Walls of swirling mist surrounded him, obscuring his vision of the rest of the home. But that's the way clouds worked. They opened only as you moved through them.

His commander stepped through the haze, his black hair askew, his robe dirty, torn and speckled with blood. Solid gold wings arched from his back, patches of the feathers missing.

Protective instincts rose. "What happened to you?" Koldo demanded. "Do you require aid?"

Zacharel's dark head tilted to the side, his emerald eyes glassy, as if he'd…cried. "No aid is currently needed. You'll find out what happened with the rest of the Sent Ones. A meeting will be called very soon, and every army will be there. Until then…what are you doing here, Koldo?" The last was said on a weary sigh.

Koldo liked and respected Zacharel. The warrior had taken responsibility of the most unruly army in the skies, and wasn't afraid to get his hands dirty to help each and every one of his men out of trouble.

"I gave Annabelle a vial of the Water of Life and I need what remains."

Zacharel stared at him for a long while before saying, "Why do you want it?"

"Is there any left?" he asked, refusing to state his reason when he wasn't yet sure there was a prize to be had.

Ignoring *his* question, Zacharel turned and motioned for Koldo to follow.

After only a few steps, the cloud opened up, revealing a living room suited for the richest of humans, with a velvet-lined couch, one half of it backed and the other half open. It was ideal for any Sent One and human pairing. There was a matching recliner, an intricately carved coffee table made of crystals from all over the world. A tapestry hung on the far wall, the words *Perfect Love Casts Out Fear* scripted in Greek in the center.

Clearly Annabelle had decorated—Annabelle, who sat in front of the coffee table, poring through books, furiously writing passages down in a notebook.

"Hey, Koldo," she said when she glanced up. She had a fall of straight, blue-black hair and rich amber eyes. Her Japanese mother and American father had certainly shared the perfect blend of DNA to create her, he thought, for there wasn't a single flaw to her exquisite features. And yet, she couldn't compare with Nicola. A fact that delighted him. Why?

He inclined his head in greeting.

Zacharel eased onto the couch behind her, enfolding her between his legs. Refusing to give precedence to the urgency inside him, Koldo claimed the recliner across from them. He had no wings, so the back of the chair offered no restriction to his movements.

A white-hot pang blistered through his chest.

"You asked if there was any left. There is," Zacharel said.

"Oh, what are we talking about?" Annabelle asked, dropping her pen.

"How much?" Koldo insisted, ignoring her.

"A single drop."

Annabelle grinned with delight. "The Water of Life, then."

A drop. That was enough for what Koldo planned. "I wish to purchase it from you." The words seemed to be pushed through a tunnel of broken glass. He'd shed blood for this liquid. Had lost his hair for it. And now he had to give something else?

Annabelle had kept her end of the bargain, he reminded himself. She had kept Zacharel out of the heavens while Koldo searched for his mother. The Water was hers. Not his. So yes, he had to give something else.

"Again, why?" Zacharel asked.

"I hope to save a female." At least for a little while.

Annabelle tapped a finger against her chin. "Human?"

He offered no more. That information wasn't necessary.

"The female you have locked away?" Zacharel asked tightly.

He knew Koldo had a Sent One trapped somewhere because Koldo had rescued *two* females from hell, all those weeks ago. His mother, and one of Zacharel's soldiers. That soldier had been lost to the pain of her injuries and should not have been aware of Koldo's actions. But aware she had been. And she'd told Zacharel everything she'd witnessed.

Zacharel had no idea Cornelia was Koldo's mother, and he had yet to demand Koldo free her. Maybe because he knew Koldo would simply hunt her down again. Instead, he'd kept him busy with all those missions and now the babysitter, hoping to restrain him from any further wrongdoing.

One day Zacharel might realize nothing could restrain Koldo.

"No," he said. "Not the one I have locked away." Again, he offered nothing more.

"She is—"

"Not up for discussion."

Zacharel popped his jaw, the very picture of a commander who'd had too much lip from his subordinate. "You're supposed to be with Thane, watching him. What are you doing with a human female?"

So Koldo was to keep Thane from committing a crime, not the other way around? "I'll return to Thane. You have my word. Now, will you sell the Water to me or not?"

Emerald eyes crackled with angry flames. "Not."

Koldo looked to Annabelle.

Seemingly delicate shoulders lifted in a shrug.

"Sorry, but I know better than to tango with Zachy when he's gone stubborn."

No, she didn't. She tangoed with "Zachy" no matter his moods. Koldo had seen her—and he'd seen her win.

Teeth grinding, Koldo popped to his feet. "Very well." He would try and purchase a drop of the Water from someone else. If he failed, if he had to approach the Heavenly High Council, he…would not, he thought. He could endure a whipping, no problem, but he still wasn't sure what sacrifice they would next require.

Therefore, he *had* to find someone willing to sell him the Water. If he failed to return and keep his part of the bargain, Nicola would never trust him. And if she never trusted him, she would never listen to him. Never find comfort with him.

Never reap the joy that she needed so badly.

He marched out of the living room.

"Koldo," Zacharel called.

He stilled, his muscles knotting from strain. *He's your leader. Show him respect—even though you would enjoy ripping his head from his body.* Slowly he turned and faced the warrior. "Yes?"

"I won't sell it to you. I will, however, give it to you." Zacharel reached into an air pocket and withdrew a clear vial. A single bead of Water rolled and glistened at the bottom. "The very day you gave Annabelle the vial, I poured a drop into a separate container and saved it for you, waiting for the day you would need it. I only pray you use it wisely. It's a second chance…and I won't be offering you a third."

CHAPTER SEVEN

NICOLA WAS LIGHT-HEADED and close to fainting. Her nerves were frayed, her heart alternating between fluttering painfully and stopping as though squeezed by an iron-hard fist. Koldo had been gone sixteen minutes and thirty-two seconds. During that time the doctor had come back expecting to turn off Laila's machines. Ending her. Forever.

How was Nicola to remain calm, embrace peace and sow joy like this?

She had asked for more time, and the doctor had tried to talk her into hurrying along.

Laila's in pain.

She's ready to go. Her body can't endure on its own, and her mind is already gone.

She'll never recover from this.

Nicola had refused him.

Finally, he had left the room. But he would be back. She knew he would be back.

If Koldo failed to return in time…

Laila will die today, she thought, and nearly vomited.

Her light-headedness increased, and she wasn't sure she had the strength to remain lucid much longer. If she passed out cold…

Again, Laila would die.

If. If. If. How she hated the word! She—

Koldo stepped into view, as though he'd opened a doorway she couldn't see.

Relief speared her, and she leaped to her feet. He was as big and strong as she remembered—maybe bigger, maybe stronger—and he was a warrior. In some kind of army, he'd said. As long as he was here, Laila would be safe.

Except, his eyes held a grim taint.

Why grim?

She looked him over, searching for a clue. He wore the same flowing white shirt and pants as before, the same combat boots, looking comfortable, stylish and ready for action. There were no specks of blood to suggest he'd had to fight his way here.

All that grim was for Laila, then.

"Koldo," she croaked.

He nodded in acknowledgment. "Stop worrying, Nicola."

"First tell me the bargain stands." The words rushed out. And wow, had she really put her trust and hope in a stranger like this? A stranger of such dubious origins?

Yes, actually. She had. Laila's survival was too important.

"It does," he assured her.

Good. That was good. "Where have you been?" *Ugh. Watch the accusation. You don't want to send him fleeing.*

"Here and there."

A lovely nonanswer. "Well, are you sure this will work?" Whatever "this" was.

"I'm sure she'll hurt," Koldo said, once again ignoring her question, "and she'll scream, but her body will heal. What happens after that will be up to her. Do you still wish me to proceed?"

Nicola had a little talent for dissecting tones and unveiling a supposition only hinted at. What had she just gotten from Koldo? He didn't think the results would be worth the effort. Well, too bad. She did. Laila was worth anything. Her sister deserved a second chance. No matter how short.

"I do," she finally replied.

"Very well." Koldo stepped up to the bed and gently pried Laila's lips apart. He opened his hand to reveal an empty vial…no, not empty. A single droplet of water rolled at the bottom, glistening in the light.

He placed the vial over Laila's open mouth, paused. He inhaled sharply, as if trying to force himself to act. His hesitation caused Nicola's worry to magnify. Maybe this wasn't the best decision. Maybe she had made the deal with Koldo for her own selfish needs.

"Is there another—"

But she was too late. Koldo had just tipped the droplet onto Laila's tongue.

Nicola waited, expecting something to happen right away. The screaming he'd promised, perhaps. Or maybe, miraculously, a smile.

A minute passed, then two, and nothing changed.

Koldo released a heavy sigh. "It's done," he said, and met her hopeful stare. "I must return to my duties or face—never mind. I shall come to you tomorrow, and your time in my care will begin."

For the third instance in their acquaintance, he vanished.

"But—"

There was no time to lament or rage over his newest defection. Laila unleashed the promised scream. A scream that nearly busted Nicola's eardrums. Worried all over again, she rushed to her sister's side. "Laila, darling, what's wrong? What do you need?"

Her sister responded with another scream.

Two nurses burst into the room, both unwinding stethoscopes from around their necks.

"What's going on?" one demanded.

"I don't know," Nicola replied hoarsely. Koldo had fed her sister a drop of…what? Not water, that much she now knew. But she couldn't mention the warrior without sounding utterly insane.

And if they doubted her sanity, they would refuse to allow her to see Laila. Laila's fate would fall into someone else's hands, and someone else would get to decide to turn the machines off.

"Step back," the other said, even giving her a little push.

They checked the monitors and wheeled a machine closer to the bed. Laila's entire body began to violently shake.

"Is she going to be okay?" If Koldo had actually done something to harm her sister, Nicola would… She would… There were no actions vicious enough.

Another nurse came rushing in. "What's the problem?"

"Get her out of here," the others commanded, motioning to Nicola.

Nicola was too weak to fight as she was dragged from the room. The nurse raced back inside, shutting the door, leaving Nicola standing in the hallway. Tears leaked from her eyes, cascading down her cheeks. She flattened her hand over her heart. The flutter was gone, but the beat was too hard, too fast. Black spots began to wink through her vision. Breath singed her lungs even as her blood chilled.

Her sister was in there, screaming and screaming and screaming, and obviously in more pain than ever. Her sister could be dying right this second, but Nicola wasn't with her. Only strangers.

How could she have done this? How could she have risked so much, without knowing more?

The black spots thickened. Her breath heated another degree, and the chill in her blood turned to ice-thickened sludge. Knowing she would pass out at any moment, Nicola tried to sit down. But her knees gave out a second later, no longer able to hold her weight, and she toppled forward.

Her face slammed into the tiled floor, and she knew nothing more.

SOMETHING PRIED NICOLA'S eyelids apart, and a bright light suddenly chased away the darkness. Little details claimed her attention. There was a throb in her temples, a steady beep, beep, beep in her ears and a stream of cold in her arm.

A voice beckoned to her, but she couldn't make out the words. A brighter light was flashed over one eye, then the other. She tried to turn away, but her head was too heavy to move. She tried to reach up and push the stupid thing away, whatever it was, but her arm was even heavier.

She felt as though she'd fallen asleep at the wheel of a car and woken up inside a mangled heap, her weakened body pinned in place. Help had yet to arrive.

"Nicola?"

Scratch that. Help had arrived.

She blinked rapidly, and finally managed to focus. A man loomed over her. He had dark hair, dark eyes, and his skin was beautifully black. He wore a lab coat and had a stethoscope draped around his neck. Dr. Carter from County General, she realized. Laila's doctor.

"You fainted," he said, his tone gentle.

"No, I—" Had fainted, yes. The memory played through her mind, and she saw herself in Laila's room. Koldo had fed her sister a droplet of something, then vanished, and her sister had begun to scream. A nurse had shoved Nicola out of the room and fear had overtaken her.

Now she was lying in a hospital bed, hooked to an IV and wearing a paper-thin gown.

"Your heartbeat has been regulated," he informed her.

Don't care. "Laila," she said, trying to sit up.

Dr. Carter kindly pushed her back down. "You knocked your skull pretty hard when you landed. In fact, you have a concussion, and we're going to keep you for the rest of the day and night."

"Laila," she repeated, her voice a mere croak.

His lips curved into a slow smile. "It's the most amazing thing. Once we got her calmed down, we noticed her vitals were actually stronger than they'd been in weeks. We drew some blood, and the results astonished us. Her liver and kidneys are finally working properly, and her heartbeat is steady."

"She...she..."

"Just might live," he confirmed.

Just like that, undiluted joy burst through Nicola, as

potent as any drug. Joy Koldo had sown into *her*. Laila was on the mend! Koldo had told the truth. He had—

Saved her twin for a little while, Nicola recalled. Only a little while. Ribbons of disappointment threaded through the joy. He'd said he could buy her sister time, nothing more.

Before, that had seemed so promising. Now? She wanted more.

Time. Time. The word echoed through her mind in tune with the ticking of a clock. How much time did her sister have? Koldo had said she wouldn't live more than a few weeks, and when Nicola peeled back the top layer of those words and peeked inside, she realized Laila could drift away much sooner. In a matter of days.

Tomorrow, even.

An hour from now.

"I want to see her," she rushed out.

Dr. Carter's smile widened as he turned to the side and waved his arm toward the patient in the bed beside hers. "You can."

Her gaze landed on the beautiful blonde buried under a mound of covers, and her joy returned full force. Tears flooded her eyes. Her beloved Laila was stretched out on her side, facing her, the color in her cheeks healthy for the first time in months. Her eyes were closed, her breathing even. Her chest rose and fell on its own, with no help from a machine. Her lips were curved in a grin. A soft, happy grin.

Nicola had worried for nothing, she realized. In fact, she had actually harmed herself. Had she remained calm and trusted Koldo, she could have enjoyed hearing the news of her sister's recovery while on her feet.

She could have whooped and laughed and watched as Laila strengthened. *I'll never make that mistake again.*

"It's a miracle," Dr. Carter said. "If she continues to recover at this rate, she should be able to go home in a few days."

"Really?"

"Really. Right now she's resting, and I suggest you do the same. We'll be checking on you every few hours." He reached out, squeezed her hand. "If you need anything, let us know."

"I will. And thank you."

He nodded and strode from the room.

Nicola stared over at her sister, marveling. How many nights had she and Laila lain awake in the same bed, snuggled up to each other, whispering and sharing secrets? Countless. And they would have that again.

Laila released a soft sigh and—

Oh, wow, wow, wow.

Nicola rubbed at her eyes, but…she could still see an ugly little monkey with tentacles instead of arms perched on the side of Laila's bed. The creature was glaring at Nicola with hatred in his eyes as he stroked Laila's arm, as though trying to capture her attention.

A hallucination? Surely. She was concussed, after all. But…but…it looked so real. Just like the monsters she'd seen as a child.

Koldo materialized at the side of Nicola's bed, consuming her attention and overwhelming her thoughts. Any other time, surprise would have jacked up her heartbeat. Because really, she didn't think she would ever get used to watching a man appear from thin air. But there were currently very strong drugs in her system, preventing any kind of adverse reaction.

"Do you see that?" she demanded.

"What?" he replied, looking around.

The monkey was gone, she realized. "Never mind."

He peered down at her and frowned. "I was granted permission to return, to leave the thorn in my side for another hour, and check on you. Apparently, I'm a beast to be around. And I find you injured?" There was a thread of anger in his tone. "Why are you injured?"

"I hit my head when I passed out," she admitted.

"And why did you pass out?" He leaned over and traced calloused fingertips across her forehead, exactly where she'd hit it during her fainting spell. A sharp lance of pain caused her to wince, and he drew back, a gleam of shame in his eyes.

A part of her mourned the loss of him, pain or not. He'd just given her a nonmedical-related touch, and it was the first she had received since Laila's admission here. She'd liked it. A lot.

He was so warm. So vibrant.

So…necessary.

"Well, it's kind of a funny story." Suddenly nervous, she twisted the sheet on her bed—and maybe the drugs weren't so strong, after all, because her heart skipped a beat. "You see, you had just given my sister that drop of liquid and disappeared, and she had just started screaming—"

"As I told you she would do."

"Yes, but I wasn't exactly prepared and…"

Understanding dawned, lightening those golden eyes to a bright, otherworldly amber. "You worried."

"Well, yeah. Did I mention Laila was screaming?"

His lips pursed. With irritation? she wondered. Yeah. Definitely with irritation. He looked ready to murder her. It probably wouldn't help his mood if she told him that he suddenly reminded her of a male model flashing Blue Steel. Or Magnum. And that he was really, really, really good-looking. Like, superbeautiful.

I have to watch less TV on the nights I can't sleep.

"We're not off to a good start," he said.

"I'm sorry."

The apology earned her a short, curt "Do better."

"I will."

"See that you do."

So bighearted of him. "So, what did you give her?"

A pause, then, "I'm not ready to share that information."

Judging from the hardness of his tone, he might never be ready. "Well, are you ready to tell me what you are? Besides a soldier, I mean."

"You still have no guess?" he asked, his features darkening with disappointment.

She bit her lip. "I've been busy."

"Lesson number one," he said. "People give priority to what's important to them."

"That's true, but I have to work two jobs. I've had to care for my sister. I've had to sleep whenever possible."

"And you couldn't spare a minute here, and a minute there? Of course you could have! Instead, you give me excuses."

And excuses weren't allowed in Mr. Koldo's classroom, obviously. He was going to be fun to hang with, wasn't he? "Oh, yeah, well, how am I supposed to do the peace-and-joy thing if you continue to be mean to me?"

He jolted a step backward, as though shocked. "I'm not mean."

She peered at him, doing her best to radiate mock

sincerity. "Koldo, do you know the definition of the word *mean?*"

"'Nasty. Unkind. Cruel.'"

"Maybe for some. But the Nicola Lane definition is 'pain in my rear.'"

He rubbed the back of his neck. "I will endeavor to be nicer, then."

She suddenly felt a little guilty for teasing him. He'd taken her seriously. "Will you at least give me a hint? Maybe tell me where you go when you vanish?"

"I go to the spirit realm," he said, watching her intensely.

"So...you're a ghost?" As she'd first suspected?

He flashed his teeth in a fearsome scowl. "Ghosts do not exist."

Wow. "O-kay." There was a glimpse of the Viking pillager from the elevator. The one who had a major beef with lies. "So you're not a ghost. Got it."

"There are no ghosts," he reiterated sharply. "Human spirits go up or down, but they never linger or come back. What people consider ghosts are actually familiar spirits and familiar spirits are dem—" Sighing, he scrubbed a hand down his face. "Never mind. I have more to teach you than I realized."

A bead of worry she'd told herself she wouldn't feel joined the guilt. "You won't change your mind, will you?"

Annnd he flashed his teeth in yet another fearsome scowl. "How could I? A bargain was struck."

And he was always a man of his word. She'd already known that about him, and had to stop inadvertently insulting his sense of honor. He might stick around no matter what, but she wanted him as happy as she was supposed to be while he was doing it. "Why do you want to teach someone like me, anyway?" Nicola had nothing to offer in return. "And what do you want to teach me? I thought you only wanted me to do the calm, peace, joy thing."

He looked away, saying, "Perhaps I know what it's like to suffer one travesty after another, desperate for hope but discovering none." He studied her sister for a long while. "I just pray Laila proves to be as accepting as you."

"Would that help her? Save her for more than a few weeks?" A whisper. A desperate rasp.

"Honestly? Only she knows the answer to that. I can teach her what I teach you—and no, I won't share the details yet. You're drugged, and will forget the most important parts. I'll do everything I possibly can to make her feel calm, at peace and joyful." A flicker of doubt in his eyes, followed by…anger? He shook his head and added, "But will she listen?"

Would she? Laila, who was so stubborn, so hardheaded, she would argue until she ran out of breath. Laila, who possessed the unique ability to tune out anyone at any time. Nicola loved her, but she was highly aware of her faults.

"What you teach us, what we feel, will help us heal?" she asked.

"Yes. I have seen lepers cleansed. I have seen the lame walk and the blind regain their sight."

"I'll make her listen, then." Determination mixed with a heady dose of excitement. Over the years, she had been checked out by hundreds of doctors. A thousand tests had been run. A million procedures and surgeries had been endured. The prognosis had always been the same.

We're sorry, Miss Lane, but there's nothing we can do.

Now there was hope for Laila, too.

Koldo's expression softened as he gazed at her. He actually appeared proud of her. "The only sure way to fail is to give up, Nicola Lane. You aren't a quitter, I can tell."

A compliment from so blunt a man was sweeter than words of adoration from any charmer.

"Nicola?"

Nicola jolted at the sound of her sister's voice. A voice that was rough, the edges broken, but still unbelievably beautiful. "Laila! You're awake!"

Koldo stepped back, out of the way, and Nicola's gaze zipped in her sister's direction. First thing she noticed, the monkey hadn't returned. The second thing, Laila was glowing.

Though their features were identical, Laila had somehow always been the pretty one. The charismatic one. People had always gravitated to her, hanging upon her every word.

Even Nicola, the serious one, never willing to take a risk, had been enchanted by her.

"I'm thirsty," Laila mumbled. She was still on her side, with her head propped on her pillow, but now her eyelids were opening and closing slowly and repeatedly, as though she were fighting to stay awake. "I'd really like some water."

Nicola looked to Koldo. "Will you get—"

But he was no longer there.

Laila frowned, her gaze finally remaining open, and said, "Where'd the doctor go?"

Doctor? Yeah, the title fit Koldo very well, she thought. "I wish I knew."

CHAPTER EIGHT

LAILA WOULD BE COMING home today, far earlier than anyone had expected!

Nicola could barely contain her excitement as she puttered around her office, gathering the files and receipts she needed. Even the fact that Jamila and Sirena were the worst coworkers of all time and Nicola was carrying just as heavy as load as before failed to dampen her good mood. She could do the most pressing tasks tonight, after she had tucked Laila into bed and finished grocery shopping. Who needed sleep, anyway?

"Jamila," she called.

Silence.

"Sirena?"

Again silence.

Sighing, Nicola closed her bag. Between half-hour bathroom breaks and two-hour-long lunch sabbaticals, the girls barely had time to sit at their desks.

"Your forehead is healing nicely. I'm pleased."

Nicola's head snapped up, her gaze colliding with the golden brown of Koldo's. Instantly her heart sped into a frenzied beat. "You're here."

Last night she'd lain in that hospital bed thinking about him, wanting so badly to hear his voice, to draw in his scent, to feel his heat, to lean on his intensity. His honesty. His strength.

Now he was standing just in front of her desk, wearing a black shirt and pants, the dark shade the perfect contrast to the bronze of his skin, making him more beautiful than any model and sexy in a way that should have been illegal. Seriously. Giant warrior man had her drooling. He was total Drogo hot.

A scar bisected the side of his forehead, adding an air of danger. His lashes were thick and black. His nose was aristocratic, regal, and she'd never been one to think beards were a male must-have, but Koldo changed her mind, the dark shadow accentuating the masculine purity of his jaw.

His head tilted to the side, his study of her intensifying. "You're a strange mix of emotion and energy today. Happy yet anxious, enthusiastic yet fatigued." Expression stern, he added, "You must take better care of yourself, Nicola. That's an order."

She cleared her throat and shifted in her seat. "Yes, well, I'm waiting for you to teach me how. Hint, hint." That was the safest response.

He remained stoic as he turned and walked to the far wall, where he traced his finger over the peeling paint.

Hands trembling, she smoothed the wrinkles from the white cotton button-up she wore. Yes, he'd said he wasn't interested in her romantically, and that was fine. Really. She hadn't wanted to pout about it or anything like that—or try and change his mind. Therefore, she wasn't sure why she'd raced home from the hospital to shower and dress, spending a little extra time on her makeup and hair, just in case he showed up. *Really.*

"That's what I came to discuss with you," he said. "I hoped to begin your training today, but that's proven impossible. I have just returned from a mission, and have been unable to prepare."

"A mission? Oh. What kind?" she asked, trying for a casual tone.

He rolled his shoulders, saying, "The kind that involves an army."

Fighting some kind of enemy? "Using guns?"

"No."

"Daggers?"

"Of a sort." He strode to the only window and checked the lock. "Beginning tomorrow, I'll require half an hour out of your day, every day. You'll devote yourself to me, and only to me."

Just half an hour? Surely that wasn't disappointment swimming laps in her veins. "It's yours. But are you sure that's enough? I mean, don't we have a lot of ground to cover?"

He stiffened, saying, "We do." He massaged the back of his neck. "I'll give you forty-five minutes and—" He shook his head, narrowed his eyes. "That's not enough, either, is it? I'll give you…an hour." The last was gritted from him, as if granting her an hour was a hard decision to make.

Half of her was insulted. The other half of her was too excited to care. "Thank you."

"And when we're apart," he continued, as if she hadn't spoken, "you'll not worry. You'll not stress, as you humans say. You'll do only the things that make you happy."

"Great in theory, but how do you suggest I go about that?"

He faced her, his brow furrowing as he considered her words. "Perhaps you should listen to jokes."

A stellar idea from Mr. Serious, she thought drily. "That's all you've got? I thought you had all the answers."

"Spend time with your sister. She's better, I'm guessing."

"She is." Nicola had told her sister about Koldo and his claims, and her sister had laughed, thinking either the drugs or the concussion or both were messing with her mind. Nothing she'd said had been able to convince the girl otherwise. "She might need some convincing to take you seriously, but don't worry. I'll convince her." The alternative was to watch her sister die, and she simply wasn't going to allow that to happen.

Koldo closed the distance and flattened his hands on her desk. She had to fist her slacks to stop herself from reaching out and tracing her fingertips along his jaw. Just how would he respond to something like *that*?

"You'll do everything I tell you?" he asked sharply.

"Everything." No hesitation. "We've gone over this."

"Never hurts to double-check." His gaze dropped to her lips and stayed. "So pink," he whispered, and frowned. "So pretty."

Her palms began to sweat. He was peering at her as if she were splayed on a buffet table, a sign that read All You Can Eat for Free flashing overhead. As if he were starving.

Had he changed his mind about wanting her in "that" way?

He inhaled deeply, and blinked. His nose wrinkled as if he'd just encountered something unpleasant. "Why do you smell like that?" His tone was cutting.

"Like what?" Toxic waste?

"Jasmine and honeysuckle."

"Uh, it's from a new soap and lotion." The one Sirena had given her.

"Never use them again. That is your first order. In fact, throw them out."

No, he hadn't changed his mind.

A knock echoed through the room, and Nicola somehow managed to tug herself from the beastly magnetism of his face to glance toward the left.

The door was open, allowing Sirena to peek inside without any prompting from her. "Hey, Nicola," she said with a wide, toothy grin—a grin that slowly faded as her gaze swept through the office. "I thought I heard you talking to someone, but never saw anyone come in."

Nicola's attention darted to Koldo. Or rather, to where Koldo had been standing. He was gone, leaving only a waft of his sunshine scent in the air. He'd taken his heat with him, and Nicola shivered, suddenly cold and, well, somewhat bereft.

"I thought you were on a break," she said.

"I was, until I realized you'd be lost without me." Admitted unabashedly and with total conviction. "Of course, I hurried to return."

Lost? Seriously? That's what the girl believed? Three times this morning Nicola had heard Sirena misdirect a caller. The other four times the phone had rung, the girl had let it roll to voice mail. "What can I do for you, Sirena?"

"Just wanted you to know Mr. Turner is here to see you." She cupped her hand around her mouth and whispered, "And he's looking mighty fine. You should totally tap that."

Dex was here? Why? "Thanks for letting me know. Please send him in."

Sirena winked, and turned with an exaggerated sway of her hips. "You can go in now, Mr. Hot Stuff."

Annnd Nicola jotted down "Chat with Sirena about sexual harassment" on her to-do list. She underlined, circled and starred.

A few seconds later, Dex soared inside. His dark hair was combed, not a strand out of place. His eyes were bright, despite their dark color. He wore a gray button-up shirt and black slacks. Very businessman. Very attractive. But had he been standing next to Koldo, he would have paled in comparison.

He would have also probably peed his pants in fear. *Stop that.* "Hey, Dex," Nicola said. Now that Koldo was gone, her earlier rush to leave resurfaced. Her attention returned to her bag. Files were sticking out the top. "What can I do for you?"

"I hear your sister is all better."

"Not all, not quite yet, but she's on the mend."

He sat down, leaned back and relaxed, fitting his hands over his middle. "That's good, right? You'll have more free time now."

"Actually, I'll have less." She would be spending every spare second with Laila—and an hour a day with Koldo.

What the heck *was* he?

She needed a sensitive spirit to discover the answer, he'd said. Well, that seemed way complicated—so she'd given in and tried the internet. But a search for an invisible warrior who could heal with happiness had mostly yielded articles about soldiers suffering from post-traumatic stress disorder.

"—this weekend?"

Dex's voice pulled her out of her head. "I'm sorry, what?"

His cheeks reddened in the slightest degree. "I was wondering if you had any plans this weekend?"

"Oh. Yes. I have paperwork," she said. Plus, there was her second job at the grocery store.

"Yeah, but you also have to eat."

Actually, food was optional. "I've got Laila, and that means—"

"She'll need a date, too. Good news is, I have a friend," he interjected. "I'm sure you heard that Blaine and his girlfriend broke up a few months ago, and even though he forced me to eat that crap in the fridge after our race, I still like him."

Blaine. Blaine, who Laila would find too cute to resist.

Would Laila be strong enough to leave the house, though? And if so, could Nicola actually deny her sister a little fun before she…before she… *Anyway.* What if that fun led to the necessary happiness?

Maybe Dex sensed that she verged on capitulation. Boasting a half grin, he leaned forward and wrote something on a piece of paper. "Here's my number. Call me if you change your mind."

"Thanks," she whispered.

He stood and strode to the door, only to pause and say, "By the way, you smell really nice." He kicked back into motion.

"See you later, handsome," Sirena said from the reception area.

"Uh, sure thing," Dex replied, clearly uneasy.

So…Koldo thought she smelled terrible, and Dex thought she smelled nice. Who was right?

Koldo the Honest, no question.

She sighed. The phone rang as she was gathering the rest of her things.

The phone was still ringing when she stepped out of the office. Sirena and Jamila were standing in the gap between their desks, their noses touching as they glared and huffed and puffed at each other. Hands were fisted; limbs were trembling.

"I know what you are," Sirena snapped.

"I can't say the same," Jamila hissed, "but I know you're bad news."

"You want to survive this? You'll leave and never come back."

"This time, I *can* say the same."

The two clearly had history. "Is someone going to get that?" Nicola asked, the weight of the files already causing her to pant.

The women jumped apart as if she'd prodded them with hot pokers.

Sirena tossed her a smile, all hint of rage gone. "Sure thing," she said, strolling to her desk to pick up the phone. "Accounting." As she eased into her chair, she twirled the cord between her fingers. "Well, don't you just have the sweetest voice." A girlish giggle caused Nicola to cringe. "Yeah. I am. Wait. Tell me slower so I can be sure to transcribe every riveting word."

Nicola faced Jamila, who was still standing in place, still struggling to control her darker emotions. "I won't ask what that was about, and I also won't be back until late tomorrow. All I want is for the two of you to refrain from eating kittens, kicking puppies and boiling rabbits just to strike at each other."

"Where are you going?" Jamila demanded, ignoring

the insult. "You're not scheduled to leave for another three hours and eight minutes."

How cute. The girl most likely to be voted Useless was questioning her ethics. "Not that it's any of your business, but I'm going home. And I've already gotten permission, thank you."

"*Why* are you leaving? And why are you taking those files?"

"Again, it's none of your business. And because someone has to do them." Forget her bubbling excitement for her sister's homecoming. Resentment radiated from her.

That golden gaze narrowed. "I know how to crunch numbers, and that's what I'm here for, isn't it?"

"I don't know. Is it? You haven't so far."

Jamila popped her jaw. "Just give them to me." She grabbed the strap of the bag before Nicola could respond. "I'll make sure they're done. Properly," she spat at Sirena, who was still on the phone, giggling.

"No, I—" Nicola pressed her lips together. Per Koldo's orders, she needed less stress in her life. "Fine. Just…please don't let me down."

"I'm not unreliable," the girl snapped.

Was she unaware that there were other ways to speak to people?

"Thank you," Nicola said, and soared from the office.

"Wait. Nicola," Sirena called, stopping her. She slammed the receiver into place.

Impatient, Nicola backtracked. "Yes?"

"I'm happy to help Jamila out." Sirena smiled sweetly at Jamila, who clicked her teeth in anger. "Since you're the senior member here, I'd like your permission to take half the files."

"Sure, that'll be fine."

As Jamila sputtered in outrage, Nicola made her escape.

The building was set in a circular pattern, with winding hallways, multiple offices and very few exits. The elevators were always crammed, and she hated being squeezed inside like a pickle in a jar, conflicting perfumes battling it out for the title of Most Annoying Scent, but she couldn't take the stairs. She was twenty floors up and would pass out halfway down.

When she reached the parking garage, a quick walk took her to her old, beat-up sedan, a car out of place among the newer-model vehicles surrounding it. Bucket, she'd named the rust heap better suited for scrap metal than travel. She started the engine and, after the expected blast of backfire, pressed the gas—only to slam on the brake.

A monster stood just in front of the hood.

She yelped, her hand flattening over her thumping heart. He was a study of terrifying ugliness, with the body of a steroid-loving man, and a horn curling from the right side of his head. At one time, he must have had two. There was a stump on the left side. He had fur rather than flesh, and eyes as dark as the worst kind of nightmare.

His lips pulled back from his teeth in a parody of a smile, revealing long, sharp fangs. "You're mine, and I always kill what's mine," he said—just before vanishing.

KOLDO SHUT HIMSELF in the luxurious bedroom Thane had given him at the Downfall, and sprawled atop the massive velvet-draped bed. Thane, Bjorn and Xerxes were in their suite of rooms with the day's chosen females, and he knew he wouldn't see them again until morning.

That was probably for the best.

His too-short visit with Nicola had left him raw.

Her smoke-and-dreams voice still caused every muscle in his body to tense and hum. Once again he'd been able to sense her underlying scent of cinnamon and vanilla, an intoxicating fragrance no longer masked by the taint of the demons. Instead, it had been overlaid by the malodors that reminded him of his mother. Jasmine and honeysuckle. Far *worse* than sulfur.

And yet, he'd forgotten that fact when he'd peered at her lips. His own had softened in preparation for… something. A kiss, perhaps. A swift pressing together, or maybe a slow melding.

And what if he'd given in? He knew nothing about the art of kissing. He could have pressed too firmly, and hurt her. He could have pressed too gently, and left her wanting.

He would have made a fool of himself.

She might have laughed. And if she'd laughed…

Another rejection, he thought, his hands fisting. It would have been one of thousands—and thousands more to come. He was never good enough, and couldn't ever be. He was never what the people he most wanted to love him needed, and couldn't ever be.

He sucked in a breath as a portion of his words registered. *I don't want Nicola to love me.* He didn't need her love.

He didn't need anyone's love.

Whatever Nicola made him feel, it had to stop. The heat. The tingling. The craving for the unknown.

He jolted to a sitting position. He would exercise until he shook too badly to stand. That would stop *everything*.

Thane burst through the double doors. The warrior's hair stuck out in spikes and his skin was scratched and laden with bite marks, but his robe had morphed into battle armor.

"There's higher than usual demonic activity at a building in Kansas," the soldier said, not taking time for preliminaries. "We're being sent to investigate."

"Kansas?" Where Nicola lived. Koldo leaped to his feet, his own robe shrinking, tightening and thickening, becoming a lightweight metal that would shield him from the poisonous claws of his opponents. "We just came from there." He glanced at the clock. Three hours ago, he realized with a bead of shock. How quickly time had passed. "Where in Kansas?"

"Downtown Wichita. Estellä Industries."

One of Nicola's employers, housed in the building Koldo had just visited. This couldn't be a coincidence. Had Lefty and Righty returned with their friends?

"I'll fly you," Thane said, and motioned him over.

"No. I'll meet you there." Koldo flashed. He had a sword of fire palmed and at the ready the moment his feet hit the sidewalk outside, but...

There was nothing. No evidence of a demon attack.

Frowning, he stalked around the perimeter. All around him were red buildings, white buildings, tall buildings, short buildings and even a chapel. There were multiple cars on the road, some parked, some meandering. Trees, patches of grass. Birds in the air and on the ground. The singing of insects. But no hissing, cursing, or scraping to signal demonic activity. No caresses of evil.

He inhaled sharply. No hint of sulfur.

Whoosh. Whoosh. Whoosh.

He spun, finding Thane, Bjorn and Xerxes had just landed, their wings outstretched, each male alive with anticipation over the coming kills.

Whoosh. Whoosh. Whoosh.

Again he turned. Zacharel, Axel and Malcolm had just landed. The only one missing from the "inner circle," as he'd heard Thane describe the warriors Zacharel relied on most, was Magnus, Malcolm's brother.

"No humans are to be harmed," Zacharel said. They were the same six words he announced before every battle. Sadly, the repetition was a necessity. Humans wouldn't be able to see Sent Ones, or feel the sting of their weapons, unless the warriors purposely manifested in the natural realm.

In the past, several warriors *had* manifested, caring little for collateral damage, too desperate to make a kill.

What would happen if one of the warriors harmed Nicola?

Just in case anyone thought to override Zacharel's instructions, Koldo found himself adding, "If a single female is harmed today, I will remove the head of the culprit. And I'll take my time doing it. And don't think for a moment a fear of consequences will mean anything to me."

Six sets of eyes darted to him, some wide with confusion, some narrowed with aggression. He refused to waste precious seconds explaining and stalked into the building, misting through the brick walls rather than dealing with a door. Humans of every race and size strolled through the foyer and hallways. Males, females, anywhere from eighteen to seventy it seemed.

Some were demon-oppressed, as Laila had been. The creatures had created a stronghold.

Some were demonically influenced, as Nicola had been. The creatures were *trying* to create a stronghold.

A smorgasbord of temptation for the warriors, he knew. Already *he* fought the urge to appear and strike everyone in his path. *Calm. Steady.*

Koldo searched every inch of the place, but found no sign of Nicola. Her office was empty. And she'd left no notes on her calendar.

"What are you doing, going through Nicola's things?" a female demanded from behind him.

He recognized the voice and slowly turned, coming face-to-face with the woman who had been trapped in hell with his mother. The woman he had rescued and brought back from the brink of death.

The woman who had yet to thank him, and who had instead run to Zacharel, outing the fact that Koldo had locked another Sent One away.

Once a joy-bringer, she was now a warrior. One of Zacharel's warriors, to be exact. Jamila. Arabic for *beautiful.* And she certainly was. She was beautiful and elusive, but she was as sharp as he was. They were two blades and constantly sliced each other to ribbons.

"You know Nicola Lane? Where is she?" he demanded. Fury… A dark, terrible fury was boiling inside him, threatening to spew out. If she had been harmed, he would…what? Tear this place apart? Probably. Kill everyone inside? Maybe. He still couldn't bring himself to care about the consequences.

Calm down. Get your answers first.

"She went home." Jamila's chin lifted, a show of irritation. "Now it's your turn to answer my question. What are you doing here?"

If she was home, she was safe. "I could ask you the same," he said, relaxing.

"But it's not your turn."

"So?"

"So." She folded her arms over her chest and glared at him. "Zacharel told me to report what happens to Nicola while she's at Estellä. I tried staying in the spiritual realm, watching her, but I'm pretty sure she sensed me. She tensed every time I drew near."

She was always tense. But they would work on that.

"I decided to give the natural realm a shot," Jamila finished.

"Why would Zacharel want you to spy on Nicola?"

"He didn't offer an explanation, and I didn't care enough to ask."

Well, Koldo cared. He would ask. He had to know. This couldn't be a coincidence.

"Now," Jamila said, "you're not getting another answer from me until I get one from you."

What was he doing here? "An alarm was raised, and we were told there was an increase of demon activity."

She frowned, saying, "The alarm wasn't issued by me. The place has been crawling with evil since day one, but it hasn't increased."

"Then why were we called?" he demanded, a burst of frustration making him what the humans would call *cranky.* Already he could feel his knuckles preparing for contact with a wall. The more jagged the better. "And who would have issued such a report?"

"Like anyone ever tells me anything," she spat bitterly. "Ever since my—" The angry sparkle dulled in her eyes, and her shoulders hunched with defeat. "Never mind."

Ever since her…what? Her capture and rescue? People had treated her differently? Gently? As if afraid she would break? Probably. That's how they'd been with him, and he'd hated it. "You don't have to dread such treatment from me. You annoyed me before, and you annoy me now. Treating you sweetly is the last thing I want to do."

Her expression softened, but only slightly. "Thanks. That's kind of you to say."

Footsteps echoed behind them, clomping and hard, the culprit clearly not even trying to be stealthy. "We've never had a false alarm before," Axel said as he snaked a corner and sauntered into the room. His hair was disheveled, three bleeding claw marks in his cheek. "But word is, this one came from a giggling female."

All females giggled—all but Nicola. They would work on that, too. "You killed the demons without harming the humans, correct?"

"Actually, no killing was done on my part." A shimmer of humor danced in those electric blues. "I found a date for Saturday night." His gaze slid to Jamila, and his lips quirked up at the corners. "I was planning an evening for two, but say the word, princess, and I'll make it an evening for three. You, the other girl and my camera phone."

"You're disgusting." Jamila pushed him out of the way and stomped from the room.

"Is that a yes?" Axel tossed out.

"Argh!" was her only response.

Axel chuckled. "Feisty little thing, isn't she? I think I'll tame her just for grins and bragging rights."

He hoped to have sex with her, walk away and never look back? "You won't go near her," Koldo found himself barking.

"Why?" Axel asked, blinking at his vehemence. "You want her?"

"No."

"But you don't want me to have her?"

"Exactly."

A pause. A shrug. "Fair enough. But what about the girls from the hospital? Are they available?"

The name Axel was Hebrew for *peaceful*. In the warrior's case, the name was a flat-out lie. Koldo grabbed him by the collar and tossed him through the wall.

"Was it something I said?" Axel grumbled, his voice drifting through the untouched wood and plaster.

Wiping his hands after a job well-done, Koldo followed in Jamila's footsteps. He knew Axel had the necessary skills to fight him, savagely and without mercy—and he wasn't exactly sure who would win. So the male's easygoing attitude toward him mystified him.

He rounded the corner, only to see Thane pacing. The blond appeared harried, his usual I-want-a-little-wicked-with-my-breakfast-lunch-and-dinner facade gone. Had something happened?

As Koldo closed in, the entire building shook, and a rumble ripped through the air. Human voices rose in sudden panic. Koldo stopped, frowned. The shaking continued, intensifying. A chorus of pained shouts sounded from above, in the sky.

Then, everything stilled, quieted.

He kicked back into motion. An earthquake? Here?

Now? And one that affected the skies? But…that couldn't be right.

Thane spotted him and paused. "What was that?"

"No clue."

"Well, it doesn't matter anyway. Zacharel's trying to find out why we were sent here, when clearly there wasn't a real threat. In the meantime, we're to go home. My home."

"I'll meet you there." He would first check on Nicola, just to be sure all was well.

Because…a demon could have followed her home, he realized. There was a time Koldo would have done something like that. He would have followed his intended victim. He would have struck at the perfect time, away from the person's protection.

A demon could have harmed her. And here Koldo was, standing in a hallway, doing nothing. Punching the walls hardly seemed violent enough. He wanted to strangle himself!

The screams of the innocent…all the people he'd hurt…all the people he'd killed…suddenly rose in his mind.

Thane eyed him suspiciously. "You're planning an extra stop, aren't you?"

Koldo vanished without another word, appearing in the small, run-down house with threadbare carpet and well-used furnishings so dreadful he wouldn't have put them inside the cage with his mother.

He heard a sound—other than the screams.

He stomped forward and found Nicola in the bedroom closest to the living room. She was humming under her breath, tucking her sister into bed. And she was lovely in a way that should have been impossible.

"Do we have any chocolate?" Laila asked, the words slightly slurred, either from exhaustion or medication.

"Not yet, but we will. I'm headed to the store."

"You're the best, Co Co."

"That's because I got all of Mom's and Dad's good DNA," Nicola teased. "You got stuck with the leftovers."

Laila laughed, even as her eyes closed. Koldo's lips twitched at the corners.

"Love you."

"Love you, too."

He should leave. He had no right to stand here, watching, amused, while the blood of the past dripped from him and onto the floor. Splattered here, splattered there, staining every place he looked.

His fists found their way to his eyes, and he stumbled backward. He flashed to his bedroom in Thane's club, and collapsed on the floor, laboring for every inhalation. He was dirty; Nicola was pure. He was ice; Nicola was fire.

And he was in big trouble. Once again, he wanted to kiss her.

Argh! He shouldn't want anything from her. He *couldn't* want more from her. He wasn't good for her. Wasn't good enough.

He would help her, but he would have to be sure to keep her at a distance. He would help her—and then he would cut her loose.

How he would react to that, he wasn't sure. But it wouldn't be pretty.

CHAPTER NINE

BEFORE LEAVING THE DOWNFALL, Thane had asked his lover to remain in his bed, so that she was where he wanted her when he returned. She had acquiesced. Now, upon his return, he looked her over. Hair of gold and scarlet spilled over his pillows, the strands reminding him of living flames. Thin chains forged by an immortal blacksmith encased her wrists and ankles.

They were slave bands, the metal compelling her to obey whatever commands her owner issued. He despised slavery, and had tried to remove them. He'd failed.

And he was still angry over that fact.

He'd had to listen, helpless, as demons had violated Xerxes. He'd had to watch, helpless, as demons had hung Bjorn over him, peeled the skin from the warrior's entire body and danced around the room in the "flesh coat." He'd had to lie on the floor, chained, unable to fight, as those same demons had licked the warrior's blood off his chest and legs.

To scream was to make the demons laugh.

To beg for mercy was to make the demons laugh.

Laugh, laugh, laugh. That's all they'd done.

He hadn't gotten to hurt the creatures as he'd so desperately craved. But what was worse? They hadn't harmed him as they'd harmed the others. His only pain had been mental, emotional.

He would have preferred the physical.

"Hurry," she beseeched, writhing atop the mattress. "I've been thinking about all the things you're going to do to me, and I need you."

"You need my money," he said, disrobing. Kendra had been found in the sex district and purchased by Bjorn. The warrior had intended to set her free, but she'd desired a keeper—and the coin that came with him. A job Thane had welcomed.

"Maybe at first." She slid her fingertip along an indecent trail. "But I've grown addicted to your touch. I need *you*. Only you."

That was good. Wasn't it? He might take a thousand different lovers in a week, it sometimes seemed, but he always came back to this one. She wasn't ashamed of what they did, and never looked at him with horror in her eyes afterward. So why did he feel sick to his stomach?

He settled his weight on the bed and crawled up... up. Every inch closer to her, the desire to wound intensified. The desire to *be* wounded intensified.

The things he'd been denied inside that prison cell.

He wasn't foolish. He knew that was why he felt this way. Knew that was why he lashed out. And he would have hated himself for the desires, but the results pleased him far too well. For a moment, only a moment, he would bask in a satisfaction he couldn't find anywhere else.

It was fleeting, but it was enough. At least, that's what he told himself.

"You need me, too," she added. "I'm the only one who can please you."

No. That wasn't true.

He didn't want it to be true. Females were too mercurial. They loved one minute, and hated another. They smiled, and then they cried. He couldn't allow himself to depend on what he couldn't control.

She bit the end of his chin. "You'll never be satisfied with anyone else. They're too tame."

His blood heated with anger—and arousal. "Anyone can please me. Anytime. Any way." And he would prove it.

With intense focus, he set out to do the things normal males did to their women. Kissing tenderly, touching gently. She couldn't resist and melted into the moment, whispering encouragements, moaning, but...half an hour passed with more of the same, and while her excitement intensified, his dwindled.

Why? Why couldn't he like this?

"Oh, Thane," she breathed, wiggling underneath him. "I never knew you could be this way."

"I...can't," he replied through gritted teeth. A thin sheen of sweat covered his skin. The urge to do things to her...horrible things...bombarded him. She would cry and she would beg. But he would show no mercy. Afterward, she would make *him* cry and beg. But she would show no mercy. He wouldn't let her. Then...then he would feel.

He should be ashamed. Bjorn and Xerxes were. They hated what they did to themselves. Hated more what they did to their women.

With a shout of frustration, Thane severed contact with Kendra and rose from the bed—before either of them found satisfaction. He was shaking as he jerked his robe over his head and covered his nakedness. The material conformed to the tendons in his wings and fell softly to the floor.

"What's wrong with you?" she gasped out. "That was good."

No. No, it wasn't.

A sharp gleam entered her eyes. "Are you planning to hook up with another woman and try again?" Bitterness blasted from her.

"That's none of your concern." She had known what she was getting with him before she'd agreed to stay.

"You should be nicer to me," she huffed, punching at the comforter. "I might decide to leave you."

"I might show you to the door." And he wouldn't mourn the loss of her. He would miss her utter lack of inhibition, yes. But the woman herself? No. He was attached to Bjorn and Xerxes, and there was no room in his life for another.

He stepped from the bedroom, and as she screeched his name, he shut the door, cutting her off. He entered the parlor he shared with his boys. They were perched in the red velvet recliners he'd found in India, their feet propped on the crystal table one of the club's patrons had lost in a poker game.

The two had already finished with their women and were drinking. Ambrosia-laced whiskey, in Bjorn's case, and...he sniffed...vodka in Xerxes'.

Both were trembling and pale. Xerxes' cheeks had hollowed, and Thane knew the warrior had recently vomited. Bjorn's eyes had dulled from corrupted memories.

The touch of another always reminded the warriors

of the horrifying things done to them down in that hell-ish dungeon. And yet still they plowed through as many females as Thane. Perhaps trying to prove they were normal, he realized now. He'd always assumed they hoped to punish themselves for what they'd once failed to stop.

He poured himself a shot of vodka and eased into the chair across from his friends.

"Koldo is looking for you," Bjorn said after draining what remained in his glass.

A man could only deal with so much in one day, and as stubborn and intractable as Koldo was, Thane had to be at his best to emerge from an interaction unscathed. He wasn't. "Let him look."

Xerxes rubbed two fingers along the scars in his jaw. "He doesn't seem like the type to give up."

"Too bad." Zacharel suspected Koldo teetered at the brink of falling. He also suspected Thane teetered. So, he'd decided to pair them up, thinking they would look after each other, provide some sort of balance. At least, that's what Thane had surmised.

It was either the wisest thing Zacharel had ever done, or the stupidest.

"What's Koldo's deal, anyway?" Bjorn asked.

Xerxes raised a colorless brow. "If I know Thane, and I do, he did a little digging before he ever approached Koldo."

Thane shrugged. "I discovered our guest spent a little over a decade in a Nefas camp when he was younger."

Rainbow eyes glittered dangerously as Bjorn said, "What was done to him?"

"According to one of the Sent Ones who rescued him, nothing Koldo would admit to. He was filthy, feral, and had just slaughtered the inhabitants of a village. All human."

"Why would he do such a thing?" Xerxes asked.

"My guess? He was without hope." A man without hope was a dangerous weapon. The three of them knew that very well. "I've heard the Nefas lock their young in a prison with innocent humans, only allowing one of them out—whoever kills the others. If no one's willing to commit murder, they all starve."

Xerxes scraped his nails against one of the scars on his arm. "He couldn't have been raised that way. I've never heard him curse. I've never seen him drink. And we all saw how he treats females."

But they hadn't seen what Koldo did behind the scenes. They hadn't seen the holes in his walls. Holes the size of his fists. He was as screwed up as they were.

A beep sounded from his intercom, saving him from having to try to form a reply. "Sir, Cario tried to sneak in again," a male voice said.

Cario. The foolish girl. This was her third attempt to reach Xerxes in the past three weeks. For some reason, she was obsessed with the male. The warrior, however, had no idea who she was or why she wanted anything to do with him. Her origins were unclear, but one thing they did know. She could read their minds and knew about their pasts.

A past they were determined to keep secret.

"Tell me you caught her this time," Xerxes demanded.

A crackle of air over the speaker. "Uh, well…"

The warrior pounded his fist into the arm of his chair. "That woman needs to be put down."

"Double the number of guards at each of the doors,"

Thane said. Then, to Xerxes, he added, "We'll get her. Don't worry."

"What does she want with you, anyway?" Bjorn padded to the bar and poured another drink. A drink he quickly downed and chased with another.

"I haven't a clue." Falling against the back of his chair, Xerxes scrubbed a hand down his face. "The first time I met her was when she came to the club and Thane offered her my sexual services."

"I thought I was doing you a favor."

"You thought wrong, my friend. And now, I have to go." Xerxes pushed to his feet, clearly uncomfortable with the topic of conversation. "McCadden has yet to be fed."

McCadden was a fallen Sent One who had attempted to murder one of Zacharel's charges—and still planned to murder the man. Xerxes should have ended the male and saved himself the trouble of babysitting, but killing their former comrade wasn't an option. So, they kept him locked away.

Xerxes strode from the room without another word.

Bjorn peered into the bottom of his empty glass, his shoulders slightly hunched. "I should be going, too."

No, Thane wanted to say. *Stay with me.* But he wasn't needy. "I'll see you tomorrow, then."

"Tomorrow." His friend's reply was empty, his back ramrod straight as he strode from the room.

Silence immediately enveloped Thane.

Silence. How he despised it. It left him alone with his thoughts, his memories. Scowling, he stood and stepped toward his bedroom, only to stop. The Phoenix was still in his bed. He could go to her, could have her and finally finish them both…but no. He was going to end their association. He wouldn't welcome her into his arms again.

He strode from his private wing in the spacious building, down the elevator and into the bar. He would find another lover here, and he would forget his concern for his friends and keep his mind off his past.

The moment the doors opened, revealing the darkened cavern with velvet-lined walls, black couches and glass tables, noise assaulted him and he was able to relax.

He prowled through the darkness, patrons in every direction. Some sat at the tables, drinking, snorting ambrosia, while some lounged on the couches in back, leaning as closely as possible into their desired playmate for the evening. Some danced in the center of the room, their hands wandering. He listened to whispered conversations.

"—you'll like it, I promise. Just try."

"—relationship material. Seriously. All of the gorgeously hot ones are scum."

"—really think I'd go for someone like you?"

His gaze scanned…scanned…until finally homing in on the little blonde Harpy Koldo had rejected.

She would do, he decided.

Thane sauntered closer to her. As pink-and-blue light spilled from the strobe and onto her, he could see that she had opted not to cover her luminous skin with makeup. Jewel tones radiated from her, a feast for his eyes.

A feast for all the other males, as well. They gathered around her table, peering at her with abject fascination as she told a story about…the hazards of car exhaust?

He stepped up behind her. "Go," he told the men

with a curt tone that promised severe consequences if he was disobeyed.

Most scrambled away. A few lingered, glaring at him—until he turned the full force of his gaze their way. They hopped up and ran.

The girl rounded on him, frowning. "What'd you do that for? Now my experiment is ruined. Ruined, I tell you!"

"What experiment?"

"To see just how boring I could be and *still* rock the house."

She was an amusing little thing, wasn't she? He leaned down and whispered into her ear, "How about you rock me instead, hmm?"

"Uh, that would be a no."

"Why?" She'd been willing to give Koldo a lap dance because he had the face of a killer. Thane had the actual instincts.

"You're just not what I'm looking for."

A true refusal—or a game? "I can change your mind, female."

"Don't take this the wrong way, but no. No, you can't."

Hmm. As he straightened, he caught tendrils of smoke wafting through the air. Smoke that didn't curl from cigarettes or cigars but from charred wood and fabric. He studied the bar, searching for evidence of a fire. He found Kendra stalking toward him, wearing nothing more than a bra, a pair of panties and the slave bands.

"Thane!" she bellowed. "I knew you'd come down here."

The crowd parted to clear a path for her.

Bright red hair stood on end, as though her fingers were hooked to an electrical outlet. Her eyes crackled with blazing jade fire, and her skin sparkled enough to rival the Harpy's appeal. Her arms were lowered, spread, her claws extended and shooting little golden flames onto the floor.

Flames that didn't die, but grew.

She bared sharp little fangs and spat, "You left me in bed to come down here to play with some dirty street skank?"

"Hey!" the Harpy snapped. "I totally showered today."

He motioned to the head of security, and the male knew to clear out the room.

Angry voices rose from the crowd, but the Fae he'd hired was good at his job and footsteps soon pounded toward the doors. Thane despised public displays like this, and he wouldn't stand for it.

Soon, only he and the Phoenix remained.

"I never promised fidelity, Kendra," he said softly. "In fact, I promised the opposite. You claimed to be happy with our arrangement."

Her chin lifted in a show of pique. "I was. Things changed."

"Why?"

She thought for a moment. Obviously she couldn't come up with an answer that satisfied her, because she stomped her foot and said, "If you think there's another female out there who will do the disgusting things you need, you're wrong. I told you. I'm the only one who will ever be able to satisfy you."

Disgusting, she'd said.

And she was right. But she'd always made him think she enjoyed it.

She'd lied, and he hated liars. "I told you," he replied smoothly, even as rage kindled. "There are many who can satisfy me. And they have. They will. But not you. Not ever again." He closed the distance between them, grabbed her by the neck and squeezed just hard enough to make breathing difficult but not impossible.

Her eyes widened with fear.

"You shouldn't have pricked my temper, female. I *will* punish you—and I promise you, you'll wish I had killed you instead."

CHAPTER TEN

SHE HAD SEEN a monster.

Nicola had beaten back the fear percolating inside her since speeding out of the parking garage long enough to pick up her sister from the hospital, ensure Laila was settled in at home, take a shower to wash off the lotion Koldo despised and walk the aisles at the nearest grocery. Fear she wasn't supposed to entertain. But as she turned her car into her neighborhood to return home, it finally spilled over—and she couldn't stop it. Or if she could, she didn't know how. In seconds, she felt as though she'd downed the most toxic of champagnes, all of the possible side effects converging: light-headedness, upset stomach and ringing in the ears.

As her vision blurred, she parked at the nearest curb and leaned her head against the steering wheel, breathing with slow deliberation. *I'm still dealing with the aftereffects of a concussion. That's all.* Surely.

Hopefully.

Either that, or Koldo had brought something nasty into her life.

But…no. He was a (famous) warrior to his very core. He was observant. He would have known if he'd ushered in something malevolent. And if he had, he wouldn't have left her to fend for herself. He wasn't the type to run. He couldn't be.

He'd helped her when he could have remained invisible. Or whatever. He'd helped Laila when he could have washed his hands of her.

That left the concussion—but she wasn't satisfied with that explanation. She had no peace about it. So… what if Nicola wasn't hallucinating? What if the creature she'd seen had been real? After all, Koldo could arrive and leave in the blink of an eye, and *he* wasn't a hallucination. Why couldn't something else do the same?

So, if the warrior hadn't led the creature to her door, then…what had? And what was it, exactly?

When she was younger, she'd heard little girls whispering together at school, afraid of the monsters in their closets. Until that moment, Nicola hadn't known anything about such monsters. Her parents had never allowed her and Laila to watch TV, and they had carefully chosen every book they read. She'd been so wonderfully innocent in regard to the evils out there, afraid only of what her body was doing to her.

But of course, everything had changed after that overheard conversation.

She'd stopped sleeping. She'd looked for monsters around every corner—and she'd begun to see them. A furry, fanged monkey on her mother's shoulder. Two on her father's. One following Laila. One following Nicola.

The increase of fear and the constant stress had damaged her heart further. But after months of therapy and new medications, she'd managed to find a small measure of peace. Fickle peace, that is, that had come and gone. But she'd never seen another monster. Until recently.

The past few days, she'd seen two. One with Laila, and one at her work.

Maybe she hadn't been lost to paranoia back then. Maybe the monsters had always been there, and she had simply shut her eyes. But now…now her eyes were open again.

Her stomach twisted into hundreds of little knots, the edges sharp enough to cut. And cut they did, making her cringe.

She couldn't think about this now, she realized. Worrying—more than she already had—would violate Koldo's rules. And besides that, she had too much to do. Laila was at home, waiting for her. Nicola had the chocolate her sister requested, as well as a few other necessities, like ice-cream sandwiches and chips, and the groceries were probably baking in the heat of her car, since Bucket had no working air-conditioning.

Deep breath in…deep breath out. She forced her mind to focus on calming thoughts. Laila, happy. Koldo, telling her those jokes he'd mentioned. She could even imagine what he'd say.

Why did the warrior cross the road?

That's easy. To kill the guy on the other side.

A bud of amusement had her smiling.

Knock, knock.

Who's there?

Donut.

Donut who?

Donut run from me, puny girl.

The amusement bloomed the rest of the way.

Her vision cleared. Her stomach settled. After checking the road and finding it empty, she motored forward. Her gaze snagged on the depressingly run-down area anyone with half a brain would have avoided. Most of the lawns were tall and filled with weeds—to hide the evidence of recent crimes, she was sure—and most of the houses had a few boarded-up windows. *All* of the houses had graffiti spray painted on the brick, hers included.

Police sirens could be heard throughout the night, every night, and she was pretty sure the neighbor on her left had a meth lab in his basement. But this was all she could afford, her parents' house having been sold to pay a few creditors from their atrocious stack of bills.

Enough. Nicola had one hour before she had to clock in at Y and R Organic Market. A place she couldn't afford to shop at, even with her employee discount. She planned to spend every minute with Laila.

Only, after she put away the groceries, she discovered her sister had moved from bed to the couch, empty food wrappers all around her as she slept, the TV playing an old episode of *Castle*. Nicola grinned. This was what she'd wanted for so long. Laila, here. Laila, relaxed.

But her grin faded when she spotted two fanged monkeys perched on the top of the couch, both glaring at her, their fur raised aggressively. Like the creature in the hospital—in fact, the one on the left had to be the very one she'd seen—they had tentacles rather than arms, the appendages slithering around them like hungry snakes ready for a meal.

As a child, Nicola would have run screaming.

Only a few hours ago, she had burned rubber in her car.

Now, she would learn the truth one way or another. Trembling, she marched forward and reached out.

One of the creatures unleashed a shriek of rage, either to scare her off or to warn her that she was about to lose her hand. The other swatted at her with one of those tentacles, and the contact burned, leaving a red welt behind.

That meant...that meant the monsters were real.

Before she could panic, both creatures jumped off the couch and disappeared beyond the wall.

Her knees gave out and she sank to the ground, trying to steady her throbbing heart. Sweet mercy. What did this mean? And what she was going to do about it?

SHORTLY AFTER MIDNIGHT, Nicola closed her register at the Y and R Organic Market, and she'd never been so happy to finish a day. Not just because she was eager to return to Laila, but also because every coworker to cross her path had insulted her. For no reason! Every customer to come through her line had yelled at her. And, okay, yes, they'd had good reason.

The monkeys with tentacles had followed her. Them—and around twenty of their dearest friends. But at least they weren't hovering around poor Laila.

Ten minutes after her arrival, the horde had congregated inside the market, crawling up the walls, along the ceiling tiles, dropping upon the shoulder of everyone she encountered, unbeknownst to them, and laughing and pointing at her.

She had screamed.

She had stared.

She had almost passed out.

But no one else had seen them. No one else had reacted. Well, not to the demons. They *had* reacted to her high-pitched terror fits.

About twenty minutes ago, the creatures had left the same way they'd come.

She wanted to talk to Koldo. And maybe climb him like a tree and hide up there in the upper stratosphere of Giantland where, hopefully, no one would be able to see her and she wouldn't have to deal with this kind of stuff.

"Nicola, I need to speak with you in my office."

The voice pulled her from her thoughts, and she turned to see her boss standing at the end of her stall. He was five-eight, with sandy-colored hair, hazel eyes and olive-toned skin. He would have been a decent-looking guy if not for his skeevy ways.

He was the type to massage the shoulders of every female he encountered, "just to help with the strain." That wouldn't have been so bad, she supposed, but he also liked to whisper, "Now, doesn't this feel nice?" as he did it.

"Sure," she said, and gulped.

The instinct to run suddenly rose from deep within her. To run from this place and never look back.

Oh, no, no, no. He was going to fire her, wasn't he?

Only six other cashiers had worked this shift, and all quickened their pace, gathering their belongings and leaving the store. The front lights had already been turned off, but the parking lot was illuminated by several streetlamps, and she watched as the men and women entered their cars and drove away, careful not to glance in her direction.

Yep. Mr. Ritter was planning to fire her, and they knew it, too.

There had to be a way to change his mind.

Palms sweating, Nicola made her way to the back of the grocery, bypassing the oranges and apples. She needed this job just as desperately as she needed the other one. One paid her house payment, utilities and car insurance, while the other paid for food and gas. In this economy, she would have a difficult time finding another job with late hours and wages above the minimum.

Mr. Ritter's door was propped open, and she forced her feet to take her inside. *Run!*

He was already behind his desk, reading a file. She stayed.

"Shut the door," he said.

She reached back and tugged on the knob, and the thick metal swooshed closed. As always, the lock engaged automatically. The room was small, filled with metal cabinets and an oversize desk. There were two chairs. His, which was cushioned by a pillow, and hers, which wasn't.

"Sit."

As she obeyed, she said, "I'm sorry about my performance today. I'll do better, I promise. And I won't make any excuses." How could she? *I saw monsters no one else could see, Mr. Ritter.* What could he possibly say to that? "I'll just—"

"How's your sister?" he interjected, at last looking up at her.

A shudder nearly rocked her out of the seat. A monkey had just appeared on his shoulder. It was smaller than any of the others, and far hairier, and it glared at her with the same hate-filled eyes. And as she watched, it…it…couldn't be doing what she thought it was doing.

But it was. It was peeing.

"It" was obviously a "he," and he was aiming at Nicola. Trying to…mark her? Like a dog with its territory?

She scooted as far back in her chair as she could, successfully avoiding any splatter. Mr. Ritter and his papers weren't so lucky.

"I asked you a question, Miss Lane."

How could he not know his shirt was now soaked? How could he not see the sogginess of the papers? How could he not smell that…her nose wrinkled…disgusting aroma? "She's, uh, doing better. She's home."

"That's good." His tone lowered, and so did his gaze, landing on her breasts and staying. "That's *very* good."

Nicola's hands curled into fists. "Was that all you wanted to see me about?"

A moment passed before he remembered she had a face. He leaned back in his seat and folded his hands over his middle, his expression stern. "Your performance today was subpar, but you know that. You angered several customers by ringing up their items two or three times—"

"But I always fixed the mistakes."

"Nevertheless," he continued smoothly, "I'm sure you'll soon be asking me to take some time off to spend with your sister, and as you know, we don't have anyone who can take your place. I'll need to hire someone new. And if I hire someone new, why can't that person just take *all* of your hours?"

A tide of dread washed over her, followed quickly by an intensified urge to run. But why run? she wondered now. The threat had already been issued, and this was her chance to offer a counter. So, once again she stayed put.

"I can promise that I'll never have another day like today." From now on, she would ignore the existence of the monkeys. That's what the therapists had told her to do as a child, and it had worked. Right? "I won't be asking for any days off, you have my word."

The monkey began hopping up and down, screeching, and she had trouble distinguishing Mr. Ritter's next words. "What if your sister gets sick again? What then? What if *you* get sick again?"

"It won't matter. I'll work."

Lips pursed, he reached out and traced a fingertip over the photo of his wife and three children. "How badly do you want to keep this job?"

"Badly," she said, leaning forward. "Is there something I can do? Take extra hours? You name it!"

His hand fell to his side. He grinned.

The monkey went quiet—and he, too, grinned.

"I was hoping you'd say that," Mr. Ritter said, a disgusting gleam flickering in his eyes. "I want you to start by telling me how you'll use your mouth on me, and end with how you'll bend over my desk. Then I want you to do it."

A moment passed in silence as her mind processed what she had just heard. He hadn't… He couldn't have… Oh, but he could, and he had. "You don't have to fire me. I quit." She stood and marched to the door. The knob held steady when she twisted. Anger mixed with frustration as she barked, "Let me out. Now."

"I rigged the lock. I hope you don't mind." Smiling, Mr. Ritter pushed to his feet, walked around the desk. The monkey jumped to the floor and followed him, the pitter-patter of clawed footfalls resounding. "I've wondered what you're like in bed, you know."

She tried the knob again, but again, it held. Fear squeezed the air from her lungs, expunging all other emotions. She was trapped in this small room, and no one was out there to hear her cry for help.

"Let me out, Mr. Ritter." There was a tremor in her voice, one she couldn't hide. "If you try anything, I'll fight you. You'll be punished."

"I want you to fight. Not that it'll do you any good. But no...no, I won't be punished. That I promise you."

Heart pounding, she rounded on him. The action left her dizzy, but she managed to remain on her feet.

He was so close he had only to reach out to pinch a lock of her hair between his too-thin fingers. "I told everyone I planned to fire you tonight. Tomorrow, if the cops come knocking on my door, I'll let them know you offered me your body to stay on, and of course, in a moment of weakness, I succumbed. And oh, the sick things you let me do to you. Afterward, though, you were still fired. Horrible of me? Yes. But deserving of your malicious lies about rape?" He tsked under his tongue. "No."

Rape. The word echoed hollowly in her mind. *This* was why her instincts had wanted her to run, she realized, not because he'd planned to fire her. Why, why, why hadn't she listened?

"N-no one will believe you."

"Won't they?" He inched ever closer to her. "I know what I'm planning to do, but even I believe me. See, you told me you fell at the hospital and banged your head. I'm guessing you have bruises from that. What's a few more? How will anyone be able to tell the difference?"

The doctors would be able to tell the difference. And she was sure the authorities would be able to tell the difference...but what did that matter right now? By the time they discovered the truth, his awful deed would already have been done.

The fear magnified, opening welcoming arms to panic. *Can't yield to it.*

Must fight. Nicola swung out a fist, intending to punch him in the nose and buy herself a few minutes to find a weapon, but he jumped out of the way, avoiding contact. Before she could swipe out another fist, he kicked out his leg and knocked her ankles together. She jetted backward, her skull hitting the door. A sharp pain wrung a gasp from her, even as pinpricks of light dotted her vision, and she slid to the concrete floor.

Another concussion? she wondered distantly.

Grinning all the wider, Mr. Ritter bent over her. "I put a camera in the women's bathroom, you know. Your panties have always been my favorite."

His image swam, blurring with that of the monkey. The creature was once again preparing to pee. Somehow, she managed to find the strength to turn her head and bite Mr. Ritter's ankle.

Howling, he ripped from her hold. Blood instantly coated her tongue. Good. She'd taken a hunk of skin and muscle.

Temples throbbing, she pulled herself up and spit whatever was in her mouth at the monkey, causing him to lurch away. "I won't let you do this."

"You won't be able to stop me." He leaped on her, shoving her back down, staying on his knees to straddle her waist. The monkey laughed and pointed at her, just as his friends had done earlier.

"No!" she screamed, bucking to dislodge him. Failing. "No! Stop!" She punched and punched at him, nailing him in the shoulder, the chest and the side, but weak as she was he was able to withstand the abuse and eventually catch…her…wrists….

"Gotcha."

And he did. He had her, and worked quickly to tie her arms over her head and latch her to the door. Though she could barely draw in a breath, though her heart was fluttering painfully and her vision was dimming, she contorted her body to kick at him. He soon had her legs corralled and her ankles tied to his desk, leaving her stretched out, open to attack.

Tears beaded in her eyes. She'd lost, she realized. As easily as that, she'd lost. And—no, no, no—she was going to pass out. Any moment now, she would fade, utterly vulnerable, even more helpless.

"Now, now," he said. "I'll make sure you enjoy yourself. There's no reason for you to be upset."

"I said no!" she gritted out.

"And I said oh, baby, yes." He began unbuttoning his shirt.

This wasn't happening. Was it? This couldn't be happening. Could it? Her boss, a man she had known for three years, had not just threatened her, bound her with his necktie and rope. He wasn't stripping. And she wasn't fighting for every breath, holding on to her state of awareness with every fiber of her being.

"The things I'm going to do to you…" He discarded the cotton with a shrug of his shoulders.

"Please, don't do this," she pleaded.

He ignored her words, looking her over. "I'll be very careful with your clothes, so that there's no sign of a struggle." He reached down, tugged her shirt and bra over her breasts, baring her to his view, and licked his lips. "Well, well. I never expected you to be so pretty here."

The tears cascaded down her cheeks, burning. "Please." The room was growing darker by the second.

"Hmmm, I do like when you beg." He unsnapped the waist of her jeans, slowly lowered the zipper.

"Why are you doing this?" she whispered, fighting sobs. Darkness…so much darkness…

"Because I want to. Because I can." She heard the slide of *his* zipper.

A ferocious bellow suddenly ripped through the entire room, scraping at her ears. Mr. Ritter stiffened—just before his weight was thrown off her.

Boom!

Nicola blinked, light returning. She saw her boss across the room, plaster and dust forming a cloud around him.

"I grant you battle rights to the demon," a familiar voice snapped, and then Koldo was leaning over her, cutting her loose, righting her clothing. His big, strong hands were gentle, comforting. "But the human is mine."

He was here.

He had saved her.

The sobs finally battled their way free, and she threw her arms around his neck, holding him as tightly as she possibly could.

"Are you all right?" he asked in a soft voice.

She tried to reply, but she was choking, gasping, and couldn't work out a single word.

He lifted her against his chest, anchoring her with one hand and righting the chair she'd vacated with the other. He placed her in the seat and tried to straighten, but she maintained her grip.

He knelt in front of her and cupped her cheeks, forcing her to face him. "What was done to you, Nicola?"

Somehow, she found her voice. "He…he…tried to… was going to…"

A hard gleam in his eyes as he said, "But he didn't?"

"Not yet."

"I know you gave me rights, but I will bow to your desires. What would you prefer I do?" an unfamiliar male asked. "Capture or destroy?"

"Destroy," Koldo replied, and with the word, whatever tether he had on his control must have snapped. He straightened, every inch of him vibrating with aggression, and stomped over to Mr. Ritter.

One punch. Two. Three. Four. There were no pauses. No stopping to issue a taunt. Koldo simply unloaded, his fists pounding into her boss's face. Blood sprayed in every direction. The sound of breaking bone echoed.

The brutality of the act stunned her. She'd never seen such focused rage.

Her gaze slid in the other, unfamiliar man's direction. He was the same size as Koldo, and sweet mercy, he was beautiful. So blond and tan and, wow, he had some big baby blues. But what truly snagged her attention were the huge, feathery wings arching over his shoulders and swooping all the way to the floor.

He was…an angel?

I grant you battle rights to the demon, Koldo had said.

Angels fought demons. Right? So…yes, he had to be an angel.

The winged male picked up speed as he chased the

monkey—the demon—through the room, his image blurring. He swung two menacing swords, papers floating from the desk to the ground. Files scattered, and furniture was toppled over. Finally, though, his blades slicked through the monkey's fur—right across his throat. The head separated from the body, and both toppled to the ground. Black mist rose from the pieces… pieces now sizzling, burning to ash.

Ash that danced through the air, curling up, up and away.

He tossed the blood-soaked swords behind him, and as they vanished, frowned at Koldo. "Hey, that's enough," he said.

But Koldo continued.

Mr. Ritter was too busy dying to weigh in with his opinion.

The winged male threw his arms around Koldo's middle, trapping him against his chest. Koldo jerked free and spun, his expression cold and menacing, his teeth longer and sharper than she'd ever seen them. He clearly intended to bite the other man, perhaps even to rip his head off.

Somehow, he caught himself in time. Just before contact, he shut his mouth. But he was moving too quickly to stop altogether, and his cheek slammed into the other guy's chin, sending him stumbling backward. When the blond straightened, the two faced each other.

"You can't kill him," the blond snarled. "I did us both a favor."

There was something about his voice…something that caused Nicola to flinch. A purity she'd never before heard. A compulsion to believe him, whatever he said.

"I know," Koldo spat. "But I can hurt him."

"You've done that."

"Not enough."

Otherworldly blue eyes narrowed with determined calculation. "Fine. You finish with the male, and risk ruining us all, and I'll take care of the female."

A second later, Koldo was standing in front of her, yet he'd never taken a step. His heat quickly enveloped her, and his comforting scent followed suit. "You won't touch her."

The blond nodded as though disappointed, but he couldn't hide the twitching of his lips. Clearly, he was now amused.

He leaned down and wrapped his big hand around Mr. Ritter's neck and lifted him off the floor. Her boss was unconscious, his face nothing but blood and pulp. His eyes were swollen shut, his nose flattened against his cheek, and his lip slit in multiple places.

"What are his crimes?" the blond asked her.

Koldo reached out and placed his hand on her shoulder, offering comfort.

"He videos girls going to the bathroom," she whispered, wrapping her arms around her middle. At least she could cross *concussion* off the list. Her eyesight was fine, her stomach calming. "He tied me up. He touched me. He was going to… Was happy about…"

A growl erupted from Koldo. Those too-sharp teeth were once again bared. His nostrils flared with his every breath, and his muscles knotted, seeming to expand. "You will give him to me and walk away, Thane."

"Hardly," the male—Thane—retorted. "I told you. You've done enough. I'll take him to the human authorities."

Nicola studied Koldo more intently. He might skirt

the edge of savage right now, but his image was her lifeline to sanity. He wore a long, white robe, just like the other guy, but there were no wings stretching from his back.

He couldn't be an angel, then. So…what was he? And why wasn't he covered in Mr. Ritter's blood? There wasn't a single crimson speck on him.

"I can't allow you to break Zacharel's golden rule," Thane added.

"I will *gladly* break the rule," he snarled, every word edging closer to murderous.

"Koldo," Nicola whispered. She didn't want him in trouble over this.

Instantly the warrior spun back to face her, flickers of concern in his golden eyes. "Yes?"

"I want to go home. Will you…please open…the door?" Her chin began another round of trembling, not from tears, not this time, but from cold. Despite the warrior's heat, ice was crystallizing in her veins, shock giving way to a heavy realization. After this, her life would never again be the same.

"He somehow locked the office from the inside," she added, "and I couldn't get the door to budge."

Rage contorted his features, but his voice was tender as he said, "I'm sorry I wasn't here sooner."

"Please, don't be—" She pressed her lips together, and her heart skipped a beat as she remembered the words she'd offered to Mr. Ritter…. *Please, don't do this*…. Yet he had spurned her. Laughed.

"I'll take you home," Koldo replied, and she almost slumped over with a new tide of relief.

"Thank you."

"Find the proof of the cameras," Koldo told Thane,

"and make sure the authorities learn of his crimes. *All* of his crimes. If he isn't locked up by morning, make no mistake, I'll return and finish what I started."

"Of course. By the way," the other male said, "Zacharel just spoke inside my head."

Koldo nodded stiffly. "Mine, too."

"So you know we're free of each other."

"And that the girl is now my charge. Yes."

She was?

"Makes sense," Thane said. "You know when she's in trouble."

He did?

Koldo popped his jaw.

"Until the next battle, warrior." Thane spread his wings and catapulted through the air with Mr. Ritter clutched at his side.

CHAPTER ELEVEN

His charge, Koldo thought. Nicola's actions were now his. If she killed a human, he would be held accountable. If a demon killed her, it would be as if he had delivered the deathblow himself.

Their lives were now irrevocably tied together.

As Koldo's commander, Zacharel had the authority to place someone, anyone, in Koldo's care. Just as Germanus had the authority to place Koldo in Zacharel's care. But why had Zacharel done this to him? What could the Elite warrior possibly hope to gain?

Whatever the answers, Koldo would have to question Zacharel later. Right now, he wanted the shell-shocked Nicola tucked safely away. And he *reeeally* needed to rein in his temper.

As gently as possible, he tugged the trembling Nicola to her feet and into his arms. "Close your eyes." He could flash whatever he held, and was thus able to take her home with only a thought. One moment they were in the office, the next they were in the center of her living room.

His arms fell from around her, and she stumbled backward. When she righted, her gaze caught on the familiar surroundings of her living room and her jaw dropped.

"I'm home. But how did… We never took a step and…only a second passed!"

"It's called a flash. It's what I've done every time I've arrived and left you. This time, I brought you with me."

Her hand fluttered to her neck. "Where I'm from, flashing means exposing your naked body to someone."

He wouldn't touch that statement. Not after everything she'd been through today. "But we aren't from the same place, are we?"

"I—I guess not."

He'd been here before, but still he looked around, taking in details he'd previously ignored. The house was small and on the verge of collapse, but it was clean. The walls were yellowed with age and peeling, but scraped. Where the carpet had been ripped out, the floor was stained to blend.

The dwelling would never be worthy of her.

He should move her into one of his homes.

Yes, he thought. He'd never invited anyone to one of his homes, though some of the warriors had invited themselves, yet he suddenly longed to flash Nicola to the beach house or the ranch by the volcano, to surround her with velvets, silks and luxuries of every kind.

If she protested, he could remind her of their bargain. For however long he deemed necessary, she was to do what he said, when he said it, with no argument. But…

He wanted her agreement.

"Sit down. I'll make tea."

"You're staying?" she squeaked.

Was the squeak a sign of relief? Or disappointment?

"I'm staying." *Just try to get rid of me. See what happens.*

She gulped, nodded.

He didn't like how pale and shaky she was, and though he hated to walk away from her, even for a second, he did just that. In the kitchen, he searched until he found the required items. She had one pot, one pan and two of everything else. There were a few boxed dinners, a few cans of soup, but very little else. How long had she been living like this?

Too long, he decided.

He had to fix the pilot light in order to boil the water, but soon had a steaming cup of chamomile tea in her hands. She rested on the couch, her legs tucked under her and a blanket draped around her shoulders. Some of the color had already returned to her cheeks, and the more forceful of her trembles had subsided.

"Thank you," she said, proper and polite and so adorable his chest ached.

"You're welcome. Drink while I check on Laila."

"I checked on her before I sat down," she admitted.

He should have guessed. "And how is she?"

"Well. She's sleeping." After blowing on the surface of the liquid, Nicola sipped from the cup. "In fact, that's all she's been doing lately. Is that normal?"

"Yes." Her body was playing catch-up with her spirit. "Don't worry. She won't spend all of her remaining time in bed."

Nicola flinched at the reference to the ever-ticking clock. "But if she's better now, why can't she stay that way?"

He heard the longing in her tone and knew this was the perfect time to introduce her to the spirit world around her.

Koldo crouched in front of her. Several curling locks of hair had escaped the confinement of her ponytail and now tumbled at her temples, framing her face. Dark bruises marred the tender flesh under her eyes, and her lips were swollen. Had she chewed them in fear? Or had she been struck?

Calm. "You'll cease working for the grocery store. Understand?" It wasn't what he'd planned to say, but the words escaped anyway.

"Well, duh. I already quit." The waspish statement failed to hide the flood of vulnerability and humiliation suddenly consuming her features. "I'll need to find another job as soon as possible, though."

"No." He wanted the first fruits of her time and energy, not what was leftover.

"But, Koldo, I have to—"

He cut her off, saying, "Recover. Yes."

Nicola's gaze lowered. "I shouldn't have to recover. I knew better than to go back there with him. I had a feeling I should run."

Her spirit had picked up on things the mind could not and had tried to warn her. "Why did you disregard the feeling?"

"I convinced myself he only meant to fire me, and I wanted a chance to talk him out of it."

A mistake so many made.

A mistake *Koldo* had often made.

"Why did this happen to me?" she asked softly.

Because she'd gotten a taste of hope and happiness, the demons had sought to squash the beautiful emotions before they could bloom into spiritual weapons. "The world is populated by beings with free will, and free will allows for absolute good…and absolute evil."

She nodded as he spoke. "Evil. Yes. There was a demon in the room. The other warrior said so."

"Yes. Demons seek the destruction of mankind."

"Why?"

"Because they despise the Most High, and He loves you. They cannot strike at Him any other way, so they destroy what He wants kept safe."

"Why?" she asked again, then blushed. "Sorry. I sound like a four-year-old child. Who is the Most High? Why does He want me—us—kept safe?"

Rather than answer her just yet, he said, "Have you figured out what I am?"

She peeked at him through the thick shield of her lashes. "Well, I know your friend is an angel."

"But not me?"

"You don't have wings."

She had meant no insult. He knew that. She had merely stated a fact. He knew that, too. And yet still a razor seemed to scrape against his chest. "I'm going to remove the top portion of my robe. Not to harm you, or tempt you—" if such a thing were even possible "—but to prove what I am. All right?"

"A-all right."

He stood and, suddenly trembling, tugged the robe from his shoulders, then turned to reveal the scars and tattoos on his back.

She gasped with…disgust?

"Oh, Koldo. You're so beautiful."

No, not disgust. Wonder.

How could that be? Wings were prized, not pale imitations. Yet still he'd spent six days having the back of his body inked, all but his spine colored by images of feathers and down.

By the time he'd had it done, his regenerative powers had been activated, and ambrosia had had to be added to the ink to ensure the colors remained vibrant. Ambrosia, what his mother used to add to her wine. Ambrosia, the flowers he'd picked for her.

Ambrosia, a drug for immortals.

Cornelia had hated her life with her unwanted son so much she'd drugged herself to endure it.

"You were injured," Nicola said, seeing the scars beneath the tattoos. "How?"

"Torture."

"Oh, Koldo. I'm so sorry."

He wasn't sure how to reply. He only knew he longed for her to stand, to reach out, to ghost her fingertips over the raised tissue.

But she didn't. And that was probably for the best.

Probably? No. Definitely. He was unsure of his reaction.

She said, "You're an angel, too, then?"

He shrugged back into his robe and slowly turned to face her. She'd set the teacup on the table beside her, the steam rising, curling around her, creating a dreamlike haze.

Must be near her.

Any other time, he might have fought the urge. But after what she'd just been through, he allowed himself to return to the couch and crouch between her legs. "I'm like the angels in many ways, yes, but I'm not an angel. I'm a Sent One."

"A Sent One," she parroted. "What does that mean?"

"I'll explain as best I can, but I must start from the beginning."

She nodded, eager. "Please do."

Here goes. He hoped she was ready. "Long ago, the most beautiful of all the cherubim was Lucifer, and he was given charge over one-third of the Most High's angels. One day, he entertained a glimmer of pride…then another…and another and another, until he was nursing his self-importance as a babe at a mother's breast."

"I know that word. *Cherubim,*" she said, her brow furrowed. "*Cherub* is the singular version, right? An actual kind of angel. And the Most High is your leader, I'm guessing."

"Right on both counts."

"But I thought cherubs were small, like toddlers. And okay, I'm just going to say it—don't they wear diapers?"

"Lucifer is taller than I am, but I do like the image of him in a diaper."

Her jaw dropped, but she managed to breathe out, "Wow. Anyone taller than you must be… I mean…uh, I like your height. It's just right."

A wonderful recovery, he thought as he continued his story. "Ultimately, Lucifer became so convinced of his own power that he decided to exalt his throne above the Most High's. He gathered the angels under his charge, convincing them they would have a better life under his reign. Together, they attacked. The Most High defeated and denounced the treacherous angels, tossing them out of the heavens."

She reached out, as if she meant to toy with the beads in his beard. Just before contact, she froze. Her hand dropped to her lap. "Were you part of the battle, helping the Most High?"

He hated that she'd changed her mind about touching him—and hated that he hated. "No. I wasn't yet born."

"Wait. Angels are born?"

"No. They were created."

"But… Oh, I remember," she said with the half grin he so admired. "You aren't an angel."

She was beginning to understand.

"So, what happened after the bad guys got spanked?"

"Back then, the earth was different than the place you know it to be, and home to another race of beings. And no, they weren't human. Lucifer was so angry with the Most High, he infected these beings with his evil. They became so vile, the earth was destroyed—but the beings survived in the core, in hell, because nothing of the spirit can die. Not in the sense you know the word, at least."

Her eyes widened as he spoke.

"Time passed. The Most High re-created and repopulated the world, this time with humans, and it was a veritable paradise. And to answer your earlier question, He loves your people and wants you kept safe because He created you. He created you because He longed for fellowship. You were to be His beloved children, to rule the earth as kings."

He paused, waiting for her reaction.

She nodded to encourage him to continue.

"Lucifer decided there was no better time for a counterattack and, through trickery and deceit, stole the reins of control of the earth. The humans began to seek fellowship with *him,* cutting the Most High from their lives." Hope had seemed lost.

Once again she reached out. This time, she was so distracted by his story that she failed to catch herself. Her fingertips glided over his jaw.

At the moment of contact, he sucked in a breath. It felt so right. So perfect. No wonder humans touched each other whenever they had the chance. A handshake. A pat on the shoulder. A hug. Each action offered comfort. He leaned into her, seeking something deeper, more intimate.

How many years had he yearned for something like this? Dreamed of it? Once, as a child, he'd even cried for it. And now, here it was. Offered freely.

Never stop, he thought.

"I'm so sorry," she gasped out, and dropped her arm. "I didn't mean to maul you."

That gentle caress was considered mauling? What did she think *he'd* done to *her?* he wondered, a bit sick to his stomach.

"I liked it." Koldo took her hand in his as tenderly as possible and brought it back to his face. Bit by bit, Nicola relaxed—and so did he. Soon, she was stroking his beard of her own accord, mesmerized by her actions. He had to swallow a purr of approval.

"What happened next?" she asked.

"Lucifer and his fallen angels introduced sickness, suffering, poverty and even physical death to the world. As for the beings living in the earth's core, they were disembodied, desperately seeking a host. Some came to the surface, searching. They are the creatures you know as demons."

A shudder of revulsion rocked her. "They all sound terrible."

"They are." More so than she realized. "For a while, the fallen angels lived among the humans, called themselves gods, stalked the land at their leisure and tormented whomever they desired. Some even mated with your females, and the offspring became known as the Nephilim. They were horrible creatures filled with hate and driven by greed. They were giants, savages, brutal and…" How to explain? "Different cultures have given them different names."

"In mythology," she said, her eyes widening.

"Exactly. Greek, Titan. Egyptian. Norse. Any, all. The fallen angels were punished for contaminating the human race, and chained beneath hell, where they couldn't be freed by their comrades. The Nephilim were wiped out—at least for a little while."

Her arms wrapped around her middle, severing contact, and her tremors intensified again. Not to the same degree as at the grocery store, but enough to hurry him along.

As he tucked the blanket more firmly around her shoulders, he said, "There are also demons in hell, there to torment the spirits cast there. They refer to themselves as high lords and minions, but they have many different names, many different ranks. Some prefer to stay here."

"Seeking a host, you said."

He nodded. "And someone to torment, to feed from."

"Is that what they want with me?"

"Yes. They want to pump you full of their poison, weakening your defenses against them, allowing them to slip past your skin and into your body. Once there, they fight to control your thoughts, your actions, all the while feeding off your negative emotions, infecting you with sickness."

"Sickness," she echoed.

"Yes, but there is a cure. To obtain it, the Most High fought and defeated Lucifer all over again." That's when the first of Koldo's kind was created, tasked with escorting humans out of Lucifer's darkness and into the Most High's light.

Over the centuries, Sent Ones like Koldo had lost sight of their goal. But not anymore, he decided. He *would* help Nicola.

"What's the cure? And why am I still sick?" Nicola asked.

"Every cure comes with instructions. You have yet to follow the right ones."

A long while passed as she absorbed his words. Finally she said, "Well, tell me the instructions. I'm ready to follow them. Honest."

Koldo was pleased by Nicola's words. He might not wield the ring of truth as other Sent Ones, but even still, she heard the certainty of his claims. She believed. She accepted.

She wanted to act, and action was power.

"I gave you some of the instructions already," he said. "The demons breathed their poison into your ear, sparking fear. You embraced that fear, and it strengthened the poison, and all too soon your emotions were feeding the demons. Calm, peace and joy cause the poison to weaken."

"Hence the reason you want me to feel them." She nodded as she spoke. "So…the poison is like a parasite. Or a virus. Like influenza or E. coli. It can grow, but it can also die."

"Yes. If the demons cannot feed, they'll flee. That's why guarding your thoughts and words is so important." Koldo lifted slightly and twisted, making room for his big body on the couch.

Nicola snuggled against him, surprising him— thrilling him. Her cheek rested against the quickening beat of his heart. He breathed her in, all that cinnamon and vanilla and honey.

And oh, heavens above, he was hot and cold at the same time. He trembled. He...wanted more. He wasn't what she needed; he'd already realized that. His past being what it was, he had no right to console a female. He'd hurt too many. He deserved a whipping, a beating, not a caress. But he just couldn't bring himself to move away.

"You're so warm," she said.

You're so soft.

She reached up, her fingers again toying with the ends of his beard. "So even my thoughts matter?"

"Of course. Your thoughts can create a fiery storm or a peaceful sea."

"But I can't control—"

"You can. If the wrong thought comes, force yourself to think of something else." *That's good advice—why don't you follow it, too?*

She sighed. "What about the water you gave Laila?"

"It healed her body and cast the demon out of her, but what will happen if she's attacked by other demons? Will she once again cave to the toxin and fear?"

"She had a demon *inside* her?"

"Yes." Perhaps he should have broken that particular piece of news more gently.

Several moments passed in silence. "I had no idea. Was so ignorant." A tremor raked her body, and warm tears soaked the fabric of his robe.

Tears? He had to see her face. Koldo palmed her waist, lifted her and parted her legs with his knee. She gasped as he settled her on his lap, and only then did he realize the sheer intimacy of the position.

He bit back a groan. Of pleasure. Of pain.

Of need. And regret.

"Frightened of me?" he rasped. *Of this*. He would rather die than cause the same reaction as her boss.

"No." Her eyes were watery, glassed over, but the tears had stopped. "I've just… I've never been in this position before."

Never?

A sense of possessiveness filled him, hotter than fire, more lethal than a flood. "Do you have any other questions for me?"

"I do." She hooked her fingers over the collar of his robe and rubbed, as if she experienced the same compulsion to touch. Her skin brushed against his, cool where he was overheated, soft where he was calloused.

Must wrap my arms around her and urge her closer…closer still…then mesh my lips against hers… kiss her…savor her. Devour her.

He didn't. One thought stopped him. He couldn't put his filthy, ugly lips on so innocent a female.

But…what if he did it anyway? What if he gave in? What if she liked it?

Temptation had arrived, he realized, whispering so prettily.

He resisted. Her fragile heart would give out from too much stimulation in one day. And maybe, just maybe, so would his.

"I'll answer one," he croaked. "Just one. I don't want to overload you."

She thought for a moment, nodded. "Do the demons look like little monkeys?"

Two circuits seemed to connect in his mind, and he frowned. There was only one way she could have known what one of the lowest-ranking demons looked like. "You saw the one in the office?"

"Him and many others. Two have even been hanging around Laila," she admitted shakily.

Yes, he'd seen those two. One had been inside her. The other was his "friend." They ran away every time Koldo neared. "They'll continue to return to her as long as she feeds them."

Tension radiated from her. "And if we're attacked by others?"

Koldo would sense it. But…what if he didn't…or what if he couldn't get to her? "Call upon the Most High. He'll send whoever's closest to help you." Germanus would never be as powerful as the Most High, and wouldn't hear a human's cries. More than that, he was limited in the number of troops he could send.

"How do you know that for sure?"

"He promised to rescue every human who calls upon Him, and He always keeps His promises."

"Every human. Even me?"

His brows furrowed into his hairline—or what had once been his hairline. "Are you human?"

"Har, har. You know that I am. Wait. I am, right?"

Do not smile. "You are. And now, I'm ending this conversation." For both their sakes. "There are chores to be done, and hopefully I'm man enough to do them."

CHAPTER TWELVE

NICOLA WATCHED as Koldo stalked through her entire house, fixing everything that was broken, reinforcing the locks on the windows and doors, and even flashing in and out to stock her cabinets and refrigerator with food. All the while, she reeled.

The monsters she'd seen as a child were real.

Demons had poisoned her and her sister.

The guy she couldn't stop thinking about wasn't even human.

She focused on him—the least complicated. Was he naturally bald or had he shaved his head? There was no hint of stubble on his scalp, which led her to believe there were no follicles. But that hardly mattered. As beautiful as he was, he had no need of hair.

And now that she knew what his back looked like under his robe, she found him more than beautiful; she found him breathtaking. Running parallel to both sides of his spine was scar tissue about twelve inches long and four inches thick. At one point in his life, he'd had wings. Something or someone—a demon?—had cut them out. Now, crimson ink branched from both scars, forming glorious wings. The design was so amazingly detailed, each individual feather accounted for. And the muscles underneath those tattoos…sweet mercy.

How could a man who looked as fierce as he did

be so kind? Or were the man and the Sent One intertwined? Could there not be one without the other?

And what about the smoldering fire in his eyes? Did it spring from a place of danger? Or desire?

He finished stocking her cabinets and leaned against the half wall between her kitchen and living room. He folded his arms over his chest and nodded. "So you *do* know how to relax."

Har-har. "If you want to pamper me, I'm going to let you pamper me."

"Actually, I want to question you. Why do you work so hard?"

What he was really asking: Why do you work so hard, yet live in such squalor? "Medical bills" was all she said.

He opened his mouth, closed it, then pushed out a heavy breath. "I want to pay your bills," he said hesitantly, probably expecting her to fly off the couch and attack him for daring to suggest such a thing.

As if such a kind proposition would offend her. "I wasn't hinting or anything like that," she said with a smile. "And wait a second. You have money?"

"*A lot* of money. Sent Ones are rewarded for our work. And I would like nothing more than to do this."

"But—"

"I'd planned to pay your bills one way or another. This way, I can take the past-due notices stacked in the basket you've labeled Doom with your knowledge rather than stealing them and perhaps earning myself a punishment."

To have such a huge financial weight lifted from her shoulders…to no longer live in fear of losing her house, having her utilities turned off, to be able to afford real Hostess Twinkies rather than a dry knockoff…

"Oh, Koldo." She leaped from the couch and threw herself against him. At first, he was stiff. After a few seconds, however, he softened and wrapped his arms around her. "Yes, yes, a thousand times yes. I accept. You're welcome, by the way," she teased in an effort to mask her trembling chin. "I mean, I'm such a giver, unwilling to allow you to be punished."

He snorted, and it was such a gorgeous sound. "This pleases you, then? Makes you happy."

"It does." Her heart thundered in her chest in a *boom, boom, boom* rhythm. "I know I should feel guilty, too, like I'm using you for your money or something, but I just can't summon the emotion."

He stiffened all over again, saying, "If you feel a shred of guilt, I will rescind my offer."

"You heard the part about being unable to summon the emotion, right? And you're loaded, aren't you? That's what 'a lot' means, right?"

"Yes, I'm loaded," he said, the stiffness leaving him.

Of course he was. A dreamy sigh left her. "You have to be the sexiest male I've ever met." Beauty, brains and megabucks.

He stilled.

Her words echoed in her mind, and she almost groaned. No. No, no, no. She hadn't just said that aloud. She couldn't have said that aloud. "I mean, you have to be the *sweetest* man I've ever met."

He peered down at her, silent.

"You consider me sexy?" he finally asked.

She had. She really had said it aloud. Heat filled her cheeks. To hide, she buried her face in the hollow of his neck. "What would you do if I said yes?" He might have touched her today, might have held her close, but she hadn't forgotten what he'd said. *I don't want you in that way.*

"I would tell you…that you have had a very eventful evening, and that you will have to wait until tomorrow." His voice was gruff. "I would show you my reaction then."

And just what, exactly, would he show her?

Her heart fluttered as he set her away from him and strode to her kitchen table, where the Basket of Doom waited. He lifted it high—and it disappeared.

She blinked, saying, "Uh, what just happened?"

"I placed the items inside a pocket of air."

She closed the distance between them and reached up, trying to feel the spot where the basket had last been seen, but she was too short. Even when she jumped. And jumped again.

His lips twitched at the corners. "Is there a problem?"

"Do *not* crack a short joke, Gigantor."

"Very well. Allow me." Koldo wrapped his big hands around her waist.

The strength of his grip wrung a startled gasp from her, though he was nothing but gentle as he lifted her off her feet. She palpated the air. "There's nothing solid," she said, amazed.

"The pocket is a small doorway between the spirit realm and the natural." Slowly he set her back down.

"Realm?"

"One for your world, and one for mine."

"That's so cool." She turned, intending to return to the couch.

He reached out and cupped the back of her neck,

forcing her to stay. No, doing more than that. Tugging her deeper into the hard line of his body. Heat rolled through her, and she gave another gasp.

"Don't be afraid. Am I strong enough to force myself on you? Yes. Will I? No." His gaze pierced all the way to her soul. "I'll never hurt you, Nicola."

"I know," she said, and shivered. He was so intense. She flattened her palms on his chest, on the softness of his robe, the hardness of his muscles.

"I told myself I wouldn't do this while the memory of what happened today is so fresh. But then I got my hands on you." He leaned down, coming closer and closer, his lips soon a whisper away from hers. "Now I have a desire to replace the bad with the good. It's a desire I no longer want to resist."

Can't quite catch my breath. "I like…the way you think."

"Then we should start over. Do you find me sexy?"

She gulped, softly admitted, "Yes."

Just like that, his pupils expanded, black consuming gold. "Very well. My reaction." He lowered his head and pressed his mouth against hers, the contact soft at first, noninvasive, and yet still her head spun. Then he lifted his head and peered into her eyes. Whatever he saw must have encouraged him because he once again lowered. This time, his tongue flicked out, tasting her, and he moaned. Eager for more, she opened for him.

He swooped in, angling his head, hesitantly rolling his tongue against hers. At the moment of contact, a cascade of heat melted her bones, and she sank into him, her body suddenly smashed against his.

The force of the kiss increased, quickened.

This was… This was…

"Good," he rasped, and she wasn't sure whether he was asking a question or commanding her to like it.

"Perfect." But *perfect* hardly seemed adequate.

Magnificent. Heady. Exquisite. No, they weren't good enough, either.

Her tongue met his, thrust for thrust, her fingers sliding through his beard, locking behind his neck, kneading of their own accord.

The horror of the day faded. Mr. Ritter ceased to exist. There was only this moment and Koldo. He'd been right. She'd needed something good to wipe away the bad.

"Am I hurting you?" he asked, and there was something in his tone. Something she'd never heard before. Vulnerability, perhaps.

"No. Promise."

"Not giving you enough?"

"You're giving me plenty."

He lifted his head. Lines of tension branched from his eyes and mouth, and a bead of sweat rolled down his temple. "My blood is heating, practically in flames already."

"Mine, too."

"You were pleased?"

"Very." Was he…unsure of his performance? Was that the problem?

Back down he went, not just kissing her but consuming her. His big hands roved over her back, up and down, up and down, then rode the ridges of her spine. As strong as he was, he managed to keep the touches light.

"Koldo, I want… I need…" More.

"Nicola," Laila called, her voice cutting through the tension.

Koldo jolted, then set her away from him, looked away from her and rolled his shoulders, as if he had wings he wanted to flare.

"I'll be back," he said tightly.

Wait. What? No! "Where are you going?"

He ignored her, saying, "I'm commanding you to take the day off tomorrow. To rest."

"I will. But—"

"No. No buts. There will be no arguments. Remember?"

He was using their bargain against her, she realized. So, what else could she say, but, "Don't worry about me. I'll remain calm, be at peace and sow joy." Her voice was trembling. "And thank you. For everything."

He nodded, but the action was stiff. "Do us both a favor and guard your thoughts, your words."

"I will."

"Good." He nodded again, glanced at her lips, stepped toward her—took another step and vanished.

Her heart skipped a beat.

"Co Co?"

What am I going to do with that man? "Coming, La La."

She raced into the bedroom on unsteady legs, only to grind to a halt, everything else suddenly forgotten. The sight that greeted her brought a fresh round of tears to her eyes. Her beautiful sister was here, home, and totally lucid. She was sitting up, with blond hair tangled around her delicate shoulders. Her color was healthier than before and bright, her gray eyes sparkling.

Nicola had never thought to have this again.

"Who's here? Because, whoever he is, I like his voice. Very rough, very intense," Laila said, rubbing the sleep from her eyes before wiggling her brows. "Very hubba hubba."

Just how much should she tell her? Nicola wondered. How much could Laila take right now, when she had believed nothing else Nicola had said on the matter?

Did the answers really matter? If Koldo was going to teach Laila how to survive, and he was, the two would have to come to an arrangement.

Nicola drew in a deep breath. "What do you know about angels and demons?" she asked.

KOLDO FLASHED TO the cave where he'd stashed his mother, remaining on the outskirts of the door to the cavern. He listened. Along with a drip and flow of water, he could hear Cornelia muttering about how much she hated him.

"—rotten to the core, just like his father. Lives only to make me suffer."

He ground his teeth together. How could she see him that way? Not now—she had every reason now—but before, when he'd been such an innocent little boy, so desperate for her affection. After all these centuries, he'd still never figured it out.

He'd made the mistake of asking her only once.

Everything about you disgusts me! You're evil. An abomination. But you know that already. I've told you.

A thousand times or more. But I'm innocent. Blood of your blood.

You carry my shame, nothing more.

His hands curled into fists. What would Nicola think of him now, standing here as a woman suffered at his hands? Nicola, who had enjoyed touching him. Nicola, who had looked at him as if he were worthy. Nicola, who had kissed him with such passion and asked for more.

He'd had her in his arms. He'd had her body pressed against his and her scent in his nose. He'd felt the thunderous pound of her heartbeat. Need had created a wild tempest inside him, undeniable, nearly uncontrollable.

His hands had begun to burn just as fiercely as his blood, as if coming to life for the first time. Rather than sinking into a pit of despair—*bloodstained hands on a woman who deserved better*—he'd reveled in the knowledge. Sent Ones produced essentia, a fine powder that waited underneath the surface of their skin. Koldo's had never broken free.

Soon, that would change. If he continued along this path, it would soon seep through his pores, leaving a bright glow on whatever he wished, a gold only those in the spirit realm would be able to see. It would be a warning to demons. *Touch what's mine, and suffer.*

Had her sister not interrupted…

Well, he wouldn't think about that now. He flashed to Nicola's home, landing in the backyard. His mother had enough food and water to last a week. He wouldn't abandon her that long, but he would give her another few days to herself. How many times had she left him in the palace, taking the servants with her? Countless. At six years old, he'd had to hunt and kill his own food to survive. She deserved this abandonment and more.

And he wouldn't feel guilty for the way he was treating her. He wouldn't!

He searched the yard for any sign of thieves—either human or demon—and thankfully found none. As he walked past the bedroom window, a crack in the curtains allowed him a peek inside. He paused.

Nicola and Laila were sitting on the bed. Both females had their hair wound into a thick bun, and green goop covering their faces. They were talking and laughing and painting each other's toenails. They paused every few minutes to pick up a pillow and smack each other.

The males he'd overhead throughout the years had been right, then. Every time two human females got together, they had a pillow fight.

Such a circumstance had never before intrigued him. Now his attention remained riveted on Nicola. She was as relaxed and happy as he needed her to be. And she was utterly enchanting. The storm had settled in her eyes, leaving a bright morning light. A perfect, cloudless sky.

He'd held her tiny waist in his hands. He'd come close to fisting her hair. To taking everything she was willing to give. Perhaps he would one day. How would she react, though? As eagerly as she had tonight? Or would a little time and thought convince her of the truth—that she deserved someone better?

The rattle of a snake's tail reverberated behind him, claiming his attention. A sulfur-scented waft of smoke filled his nose.

Dread pricked at Koldo as he spun and drew a sword of fire. Two serp demons had closed in on him, one at the left, one at the right, and sank their fangs into his thighs. In less than a blink, an undiluted surge of venom shot through his system, valiantly attempting to weaken him.

You'll have to do better than that.

He released his sword, causing the weapon to disappear, and latched on to the creatures.

"Your father sssaysss hello," one hissed.

"And goodbye," the other laughed.

Koldo tied the two together and tossed them to the ground. They were long and thick, like snakes, with gnarled antlers growing from their heads, glowing red eyes and fur interspaced throughout their scales. There wasn't a more hideous creature. Their bodies writhed as they fought to escape each other—and thereby him.

Too late. He reclaimed his sword long enough to slice, slice, removing both of their heads. Then he stood there, dumbfounded.

His father had said hello?

His father had said goodbye?

Serp demons were his father's allies, yes, but Nox couldn't have ordered an attack. He was dead. Koldo was sure of it.

They had to have lied. Demons always lied. Perhaps they'd hoped to distract him. Because…why? They had friends nearby?

And sure enough, they did. As he straightened, two other serps flew from the shadows. The two were followed by another. And another. And another. Each converged on him.

The creatures had been following him, he realized. They had known where he would come, had left no tracks and had waited for the perfect moment to act.

Koldo grabbed as many writhing bodies as possible and tossed them into the grass. Once, twice, three times. Yet all the while still more came at him, biting him, shooting more venom inside him.

He formed the sword of fire. Hisses erupted at the

first flare of light, and the vile creatures backed away from him. He stepped forward, prepared to give chase… only to stop. His knees collapsed, his legs no longer able to support his weight. He watched, horrified, as the demons slithered toward the house.

They would attack Nicola and her sister, and the girls, weak as they were, would crumble.

Can't let that happen. Koldo summoned every ounce of his strength and labored to his feet. He'd never used his ability to send his thoughts into the mind of one of his fellow soldiers. He hated the idea of mental contact, a link, someone able to breach the barriers in his mind, as Zacharel often did, and perhaps read his innermost musings. But, to protect Nicola…

Need…help, he projected to a specific warrior.

He expected a thousand questions. Instead, the reply was simple. *Where are you?*

He rattled off Nicola's address, even as he struck out, flaming two demons to ash. Others crawled up the bricks, some branching left, some branching right, others going straight up. Koldo flashed one way, then the other, then to the roof, always striking out with his weapon.

"Whoohooo!" a familiar voice suddenly exclaimed. "Daddy's here, and it's spanking time."

Axel landed in the front yard, his wings snapping against his back. He ran forward, drew his sword of fire and hacked, hacked, hacked at the enemy. Demons darted away from him, but he followed, spinning and striking, not allowing a single enemy to escape. He moved up, he moved down, he moved all around…all around… The world was spinning, spinning, spinning so quickly, Koldo thought. Faster and faster.

Panting, weakening still, he flashed to just behind Axel and fell to his knees. He would guard the warrior's back.

"Dude! I thought you needed help scoring a chick," Axel said, patting him on the shoulder and nearly drilling him neck-deep into the grass. "I think that was the last of 'em but I'll do a double check around the perimeter."

Or just wait here. He ached terribly.

He heard footsteps. Whistling.

Hours later, or perhaps minutes, Axel returned and loomed over his prone form—*I must have tumbled the rest of the way to the ground*—his electric blues glowing with a strange, otherworldly light. "You stalking Chesticles or something? 'Cause, dude, this is totally her house."

"No, and don't call her that." His throat was swelling, and he could barely force out the words.

"My bad. I didn't realize you'd staked an official claim."

She was his charge, but had he staked a claim, even though he had yet to cover her with essentia? Maybe. He despised the idea of another male thinking about her, looking at her, or touching her.

"Thank you. For coming, I mean."

"No problem. I was just doing someone unimportant."

Someone. Nice.

Sadly, that was the last thought Koldo had before his mind went blank.

CHAPTER THIRTEEN

"Your ugly face disgusts me," his mother shouted.

"You hesitated over a kill today," his father growled. *"You must be punished."*

Love me. Why can't you love me?

"I wish you had never been born!" His mother.

"I'll make you regret the day you were born." His father.

Be proud of me. I just want you to be proud of me. For once.

"You're not a Sent One. You don't deserve to breathe the same air as me." Again, his mother.

"I'll make a soldier of you yet." Again, his father.

Please…please…

Koldo came awake gradually, his head a heavy block, his muscles sore and knotted. When full light at last dawned, he blinked rapidly, then gazed around. A barren cave with jagged, bloodstained walls greeted him. The air was cold, the warmth of his breath creating a thick haze in front of his face. He lay upon a stone dais, no blanket beneath him.

This wasn't one of his homes, he thought, jerking upright. Dizziness struck him, but he pushed through it, inhaling, exhaling.

"Easy now," he heard Axel say.

Axel. Familiar. He relaxed, but only slightly, his attention cutting through the gloom and finding the warrior crouched in the corner, razing a stone against a short, broad stick to create dangerous spikes at the ends.

"Where am I?" he asked.

Eyes of crystal blue flicked up and stayed on him for only a second before returning to the weapon. "Only the best place ever—my place. I carried you here. And by the way, you'll be getting the bill for my new back brace. Anyone ever tell you that you weigh, like, ten thousand pounds?"

"How long?" he croaked.

"The bill's only one, maybe eight, pages long, you have my word. The good doctor said—"

"No. How long have I been here?"

"Oh. Three days."

Three days? Nicola had been on her own for three days. After he'd promised to spend at least an hour a day with her. But now he could spend far more than an hour, couldn't he? Zacharel had placed her in Koldo's constant care.

He might have failed her on day one.

He threw his legs over the side of the dais, and despite the return of the dizziness, stood. He waited until his vision cleared, then looked down at himself. He wore a long white robe, the material as clean as he was. In fact, he was as clean as if he'd just taken a couple hundred showers.

"Don't worry," Axel said, holding out the stick, closing one eye and zeroing in on one of the ends of the weapon. "I checked on your girl. She's fine. And I mean that in every sense of the word."

He left that last part alone. "The serps stayed away from her?"

"Of course. They were too dead to move. But she does have two minions hanging around."

Two minions were hanging around Nicola? Had Lefty and Righty returned? If so, they would have to be dealt with—permanently. "And the other girl? The blonde?"

"Wait." Frowning, Axel set the weapon aside and peered over at him. "You mean the redhead is yours?"

"Yes. Why? Did something happen? Did she see you?" Want him?

Rage blossomed...

"Uh, no. Nope. Not at all. She's fine, too."

...receded. "You're sure?" he asked, watching for any sign of a lie. The smacking of his lips. The wrinkling of his nose. A deeper frown. Axel displayed none of those.

"I am." Easily stated. Expression relaxed.

Very well. The demons were hanging around Laila, then, and he'd already known that. "Thank you," he said, only slightly grudging.

"I'll be collecting, don't worry."

Koldo would have said the same, and couldn't blame him. "Collect from me. Not her." He'd promised to pay her bills, not to add to her tab.

Axel rolled his eyes. "As if there was ever any doubt. She's got nothing I want." He wiped his hands on the towel draped over his thigh before digging a piece of melon out of the bowl beside him. "Here. Eat."

Koldo caught the fruit and bit into the juicy center. Sweet flavors exploded on his tongue, and his body purred gratefully. Sent Ones could die in a number of ways, and starvation was a big one.

Thank the Most High, Koldo had had the foresight to stock Nicola's cabinets before leaving her. She had been well fed during his absence. And thank the Most High forevermore, Axel had been willing to see to her defense.

But Koldo wanted to do more than rely on another Sent One for such a thing. If anything like this ever happened again—not that it would, Koldo never made the same mistake twice—Axel might be too busy to check on Nicola. He might lose interest, or decide Koldo had nothing of value to offer in trade.

I'll have to mark her, Koldo thought. Not just with the essentia, but with ink. He would code her.

The Most High had made a blood-covenant promise to the Sent Ones. In exchange for obeying His laws, they were given protection. Koldo hadn't been kicked from the heavens, therefore the promise still applied to him, and the code was still etched into his heart. And because Nicola was his charge, his responsibility, the promise now extended to her. But he would have to give her an outward sign of it.

He would etch the code into her flesh, and that code would be able to create a barrier between her and any demons that dared approach her. All she would have to do was concentrate on the numbered sequences during an attack. The more she stared at her tattoos, the stronger the power of the code would become, until finally expanding, covering her entire body and shielding her.

But if a demon managed to distract her...

Not going to happen, Koldo assured himself. He would train her for that, too.

"So why were the serps after you?" Axel asked.

"I'd like to know the answer to that, as well." Was his father still out there or not?

Koldo hadn't seen Nox's body, had only watched as

grenade after grenade soared toward him, the unsuspecting male not knowing to flash away. There'd been multiple booms and an intense wave of heat, flames drenching the ground and bouncing into the sky.

Should have killed him up close and personal. But Koldo had had a choice. Destroy Nox face-to-face—or destroy the man and everything he'd worked for in one swoop. Koldo had chosen the latter.

When the fires eventually died, he'd dug through the rubble and found too many bones to count.

If Nox had survived, why was he making himself known now? How had he tracked Koldo to Nicola's home?

"So, what do you plan to do with the redhead?" Axel asked.

"Why do you live in a place like this?" Koldo retorted. "You clearly thrive on what you probably consider adoration from your peers, and yet you seclude yourself."

A pause.

"So we agree not to question each other," the warrior finally replied.

"We do." They both had their secrets. Koldo finished off the fruit. "And now I must go."

"Okay, but uh, hey," Axel said, standing. "You might want to hunt down your girl and give her a stern talking-to. Normally I wouldn't tattle, even on a human, but if I keep quiet this could really come back to haunt me. Meaning, you'll want to punch my pretty face."

Rambling? Now? "Just tell me!"

"She's planning to go on a date with another guy."

FUMING, KOLDO FLASHED to Nicola's home. He wasn't sure what he'd do when the two of them were face-to-face. He only knew he had to see her. But she wasn't there, and another flash proved she wasn't in her office. Jamila and another girl, the blonde with the mysterious origins, *were* in her office, and the two were hurtling curses at each other—while the girl had a male pinned to Nicola's desk, her fingers curled around his neck, his pants and underwear pooled at his ankles.

"Sleeping with every guy here?" Jamila spat. "Really? That's your master plan?"

"Part of it," the blonde smirked. At least her clothing was in place. "So why don't you do me a solid and get lost? And next time knock before you enter an office."

"Sure, I'll go. By the way, your plan is stupid."

"Yeah, well, your hair is stupid."

Females.

Jamila bared her teeth in a scowl. "What does this accomplish?" she asked, waving a hand in the male's direction. "I mean, really."

"When the girlfriend finds out what he's done, she'll be hurt, want to cry."

"He doesn't have a girlfriend."

"Fine. He has a love interest."

"And you want to hurt her, why?"

The blonde grinned evilly.

The male's cheeks were bright red as he struggled to sit up, but the girl was obviously stronger and managed to hold him down without any effort.

Koldo stepped into the natural world. "Where's Nicola?" he demanded.

All three gazes swung to him.

The blonde paused for a moment, momentarily rendered speechless. Then she shook her head, blinked and smiled slowly, wickedly, an invitation and a declaration. "Well, hello, handsome. What can I do to help you?"

The male increased the fervency of his struggles. He would have spoken, but his tie was stuffed into his mouth.

Jamila scowled at Koldo, as if her predicament was his fault. "You! Even though Little Miss Human is your responsibly, Zacharel told me to stay here."

A detail he didn't care about. "I'll ask again. Where is she?"

"Her sister showed up and they went to lunch. They mentioned a park."

"Forget about her," the blonde said. "You'll be better off with me. I'll take care of you in a way she never will. Just give me a chance."

A park. Very well, he would search every one nearby.

Without a word, he stomped from the office. The human had been too distracted during his arrival to notice his sudden appearance, but he certainly wouldn't miss Koldo's departure.

The blonde called out a protest, and she actually sounded angry. Not that he cared about that, either.

Once he cleared the reception area, and knew no prying eyes were locked on him, he flashed to the park closest to the office. Searched. Found no sign of her. Next, he tried the one closest to her house. Searched. And—

Spotted her.

Laila was beside her, the two walking along a cobbled path, talking and laughing and eating chocolates. The pair of demons perched on Laila's shoulders spotted him, hopped to the ground and darted away.

Some of the tension faded from Koldo's shoulders.

This kind of interaction was good for both of the females. They were relaxing, enjoying themselves, purging the poison. He would leave them to it, he decided. *Without* yelling at Nicola for making a date with another man.

He flashed to her house and began to box up her things. He wanted her installed in one of his homes by the end of the day. There would be no discussion, no debate. And this had nothing to do with her decision to turn to another man for her joy.

Nothing at all.

Nicola would probably cry because of Koldo's actions. He would have to calm her down, do something to make her happy—but he would also have to harden his heart. The move was for the best. He would be able to protect her better.

But he would have to bring her back for the date, wouldn't he? Because...what if the male did indeed bring her joy? What then? She would need him. He would help her purge even more of the demon toxin.

Flickers of rage danced through Koldo, and he found himself breathing far more heavily, battling the urge to punch the walls.

If he gave in to his temper, Nicola's home would topple.

He was a little rough with the boxes in the back of her closet, the things inside clinking together. He checked to make sure he hadn't broken anything and found a box of photos. The more he flipped through the prints, the more his actions gentled. There were shots of Nicola and her sister, and the two of them with their parents, as well as a redheaded little boy. He looked just like them, had to be a relative, but...who was he? A brother? Nicola had never mentioned him, and he had never come around. In all the information Koldo had uncovered, nothing had been mentioned.

Intrigued, Koldo dug deeper into the box. He found articles about her parents' death and learned a drunk driver had slammed into their car, killing the couple *as well as* their young son, Robby, and that the driver had been released from prison last year.

Nicola had lost more than Koldo had ever realized. She had lost a healthy six-year-old brother with a bright future, a boy who had most likely owned prime real estate in her heart.

She must despise the man who had ruined her life. She had to dream of his painful demise. She had to crave revenge. She just hadn't been well enough and hadn't had the time or resources to do anything about it.

Perhaps Koldo would hurt the male on her behalf. Punishment or not. Perhaps then she would like him more than this other—

He shook his head violently, stopping the thought before it could fully form. Koldo wasn't interested in earning anyone's affection. He'd tried that before, and he'd failed miserably. He'd vowed never to do it again, and it was a vow he would keep. And paying Nicola's bills wasn't an attempt to earn anything, he told himself. He needed Nicola relaxed, that was all.

Finish this.

Yes. He would keep her in…Panama's Chiriqui Province, he decided, and flashed most of her things to one of his more opulent homes. There were lush green mountains in every direction, and a blue sky filled with puffy white clouds. The weather was springlike and constant all year round. The food was fresh, organic and homegrown, and would nourish both Nicola and her sister in the best of ways. They would thrive here—whether they liked it or not.

Unpacking her belongings took very little time. She owned so little. Well, he would buy her and her sister a new wardrobe. And the clothes wouldn't be an attempt to win their affections, either, but a simple gesture of kindness. A welcome-to-your-new-home gift.

But what did he know of human fashion? Nothing.

He knew someone who did, however.

Koldo flashed into the foyer of Zacharel's home and called out a greeting. A few seconds later, the mist thinned and Annabelle stepped into view, wearing a T-shirt and jeans. Her blue-black hair was swept into a ponytail, reminding him of Nicola, and her golden-brown eyes gleamed merrily.

She smiled when she spotted him. "Hey, Koldo. Zacharel's not here."

"I'm not here to see him."

Her smile fell into a frown of confusion, and she glanced behind her. When she refocused on him, she tapped at her chest. "Me, then?"

"Yes. I need a favor."

"A favor?"

Would she question everything he said?

"But we're out of Water," she added.

"I know that. I need…" Ugh. Was he really going to do this? he wondered, then pictured Nicola in a lacy pink top and a pair of tiny shorts he'd once seen a human female wear. A strange burning ran from his nose to navel. Yes, he was really going to do this. "I need to take you shopping."

Annabelle rubbed at her ears. "Wait. Did you just

say *mopping?* Is your home dirty and you want a maid? Because I know a warrior like you would never say my favorite S word."

"Did someone say the S word?" a female called out. "Because I couldn't help but overhear your conversation as I was eavesdropping."

Excited twittering echoed. Footsteps followed. Then four of the women in Zacharel's army stepped through the mist. Charlotte, Elandra, Malak and Ronen.

He would rather have battled a horde of demons than face these women. They were trained soldiers, monsters on the battlefield, cold, callous killers, and yet they liked to twitter incessantly about nothing.

"What are you shopping for?" asked Charlotte, a lovely brunette with bold features and dusky skin. "A new sword? Well, good news. I've got one I know you'll love, and with my friends with benefits package, it'll only cost you a portion of your soul."

"I told you guys to stay back and stay quiet," Annabelle scolded.

"You mean that wasn't just a suggestion?" said Ronen, a black-haired vixen with an addiction to popcorn.

Elandra was the shy one of the group, and she looked down at the floor, where the hem of her robe swirled. She was, by far, the most beautiful female Koldo had ever seen. Or had been, until he'd met Nicola. From the top of her head to the soles of her feet, Elandra reminded him of a living diamond. Her long white hair sparkled. Her silver eyes sparkled. Her pale skin sparkled.

Malak was the only one in the group with a flaw, though she hid it well. There was a large round scar in the center of her forehead, probably from an injury she'd received when she had been too young to regenerate. Her hair, which had been dyed a bright green, sported thick bangs to hide it.

"Give the man a chance to explain," Annabelle said.

The females stared at him, expectant.

Koldo had no idea what they'd done to land in Zacharel's Army of Disgrace. Unless their irritating personalities had been the deciding factor.

He looked to Annabelle, saying, "My...woman—" Wait. Was that what Nicola was to him? He wasn't sure, considering she would soon be going on a date with another man. And were his teeth elongating like his father's when the man was enraged?

He would have to be more careful.

"I have a friend," he added a little more harshly than he'd intended, and stopped himself from going on. She wasn't that, either. "I have a human, a female, and she's in need of new clothing."

The Sent Ones exclaimed excitedly. Ronen even jumped up and down and clapped. "Juiciest gossip ever," she said. "Koldo has a *gurl*-friend."

"I bet she's ten feet tall and six hundred pounds of muscle," Charlotte exclaimed.

"Get. Give us some privacy," Annabelle told them, shooing them away.

Though they frowned and pouted, they obeyed.

"Okay, so let me get this straight," Annabelle said. "You want to take me, rather than your woman, friend, human, female, to pick and buy these clothes?"

Yes. He would hurt her feelings right now. He might ruin her newfound happiness. "I don't wish to wait," he said through gritted teeth. Truth. He wanted this done, out of the way. "And…I don't know what females prefer."

Her hand fluttered over her heart, and she grinned. "Zacharel once had the same problem with me. So why don't you buy her what *you* would prefer to see her wear?"

"I will buy her what I like, yes—" because he wouldn't be able to help himself "—but I would like her to have choices." He had to get this right. That way, she would have no reason to refuse the gift.

"Do you even know her sizes?"

He held up his hands. "She's tiny, like this. Delicate."

Annabelle laughed, the sound carefree. "Oh, you are in so much trouble, buddy. But yeah, okay. I'll help you."

Relief was as potent as a drug. "For a price, of course."

"Nope. Not at all. I know that's how you guys like to operate, but this one's free of charge. Just invite me to the wedding, and we'll call it good."

CHAPTER FOURTEEN

"You've got to try this." Laila shoveled a piece of chocolate into Nicola's mouth before she had time to form a reply.

Chocolate contained caffeine, so very rarely did she allow herself to indulge. But when she did… The gooey goodness delighted her, and she closed her eyes to savor. A mistake. She and her sister were in the process of strolling along the cobbled path winding through the park, and she bumped into a trash can.

The thud brought Laila's attention around, and her twin burst out laughing. "Kooky Co Co kicks a carton."

Empty wrappers, half-eaten sandwiches and Starbucks cups spilled onto the concrete, yet Nicola smiled as she cleaned the mess. How wonderful to hear her sister's amusement. When she finished, she dug the antibacterial gel from her purse and slathered her hands.

"You've got chocolate on your chin," Laila said, trying to be calm but failing. The gray of her eyes glimmered gorgeously. The sun cast bright, golden rays over skin that hadn't seen the outdoors in months, illuminating her, making her radiate health and vitality.

Nicola wiped her face with the tips of her fingers. "Better?"

"Much. Now you're almost as pretty as me." Pretending a vanity she'd never possessed, Laila studied her decimated cuticles. "Notice I said *almost*."

"Someone needs glasses. Your hair is blond but your roots are red," Nicola replied, giving her ponytail a flip. "It's quite hideous."

Laila gasped with mock outrage. "I'll have you know this look is all the rage right now. Total style and sophistication."

"I don't follow trends. I make them."

Grinning, her sister held out her hand. "You are so totally lame. Come on, walk with me."

They linked fingers and resumed their stroll. The tranquillity of the moment helped diffuse the memories of the attack—something she hadn't shared with her sister. Memories kept trying to rise to the surface of her mind. While she was in the shower. While she selected today's underwear. While she cooked breakfast.

Once, she'd almost broken down and cried. But then she'd remembered Koldo's kiss, his sweet, sweet kiss. His uncertainty. His vulnerability. His desire to make sure she was enjoying herself. And everything had changed.

He was such a big, strong warrior. There was a time she would have bet nothing could shake his confidence. But then *she* had.

As if her opinion mattered to him.

"I could hear you at the hospital, you know," Laila said, delving into a subject they had previously avoided.

"Really?" She'd always wondered. Had always hoped.

"Yes, and you kept me there longer than I wanted to stay. Anytime I would feel myself drifting away, you were right there to tug me back."

"That makes me happy."

"But not me. I was ready to go."

The words were like a fist to the gut. "Well, I'll never regret holding on to you, La La. I love you."

"And I love you, too." Laila's smile was sad. "But, Co Co, if we're ever again in that situation, I want you to let me go."

Nicola stopped, forcing her sister to do the same. They faced each other, right there in the middle of the path, causing the people behind them to trip to the side in an effort to avoid slamming into them.

"No," she said with a shake of her head. "I won't. I'll fight for you with every bit of my strength." And Koldo would fight with her. Right?

She wanted to believe it, but he'd seemed to abandon her. He'd promised to give her an hour a day, to teach her, to train her, and then he'd vanished for good, leaving her to believe he regretted showing her so much vulnerability.

And why shouldn't he? She had nothing to offer him. He was tough, fierce and knowledgeable. She was weak, defenseless and ignorant of the truth.

Exasperated, Laila spread her arms. "Be practical about this."

Expecting a twenty-three-year-old girl to die of heart disease was *practical?* "Koldo says we have to—"

"Ugh. Koldo this, and Koldo that." Laila anchored her hands on her too-tiny waist. She'd gained weight since her release from the hospital, but not enough. "He's all you ever talk about anymore. Whoever he is, he's lying to you, my love. Why can't you see that? He's not an angel any more than I'm the tooth fairy."

"You're right. He's not an angel. He's a—"

"I know, I know, but it doesn't matter. If he's so concerned with our health, where is he?" Her sister's tone gentled as she added, "Why isn't he here, giving me this information himself?"

Her shoulders drooped. "I don't know."

A mother pushed a stroller around them as Laila reached out and tugged at the end of Nicola's earlobe. In the background, a dog barked. "He's not a Sent One, whatever that is. He's a con man."

"I've seen him pop in and out of thin air."

"You've seen an illusion."

"Just wait until you meet him."

Laila tsked with a mix of exasperation and pity. "Darling, he's only looking to sell you a miracle cure."

"No. He's *giving* me a miracle cure and paying our bills."

"So you think."

Nicola swallowed a sigh. No matter what she'd said, or what angle she'd tried, her sister had rejected all things Koldo. She'd called Sent Ones "a romantic idea." She'd scoffed at the concept of demons.

Frustration and upset had tried to take up residence inside of Nicola—neither of which she welcomed, per Koldo's orders. She just… She *had* to get through to her sister. Laila's life was in danger. She needed saving, and Nicola would do whatever was necessary to save her.

Laila shook her head, saying, "You only believe him because you have a crush on him. Your eyes go dreamy every time you talk about him."

"Do not."

"Do, too."

"Not!"

"Too!"

Laila dropped the empty box of candy and they began a slap fight, giggling like the girls they used to be, before sickness and fear and loss had taken such a vicious toll. But Laila sobered all too soon, too busy fighting for breath.

Nicola picked up the box and tossed it in the nearest trash can, then reclaimed her sister's arm to urge her forward. She'd missed this kind of interaction. A few years ago, she'd gone to the local community college and Laila had opted not to "waste what little time she had." Then Nicola had gotten a job at Estellä and Laila had focused on her art. *Then,* Laila had gotten sick. Well, sicker. After that, Laila had stopped painting and had started spending every free minute inside a doctor's office or in bed.

"I promise you," Laila said. "There isn't a demon following me around."

"Not right this second, no."

Another sad smile was cast her way. "You're seeing things again, that's all. That'll stop, just like before."

No, it wouldn't. Not this time. Nicola's spiritual eyes had been opened, and she would never shut them again. But she didn't want to spend her lunch hour arguing. "So, listen. I already said yes to this, and I'd love for you to join me. Just…promise you'll keep an open mind when I tell you about it, okay? Please."

Laila's brows drew together with confusion. "What are you talking about?"

"A guy at work asked me out. Asked the two of us out, really. On a double date, not anything weird," she rushed to add. Some men heard the word *twins* and their minds went to strip clubs and tag teaming.

"I'm intrigued so far. Go on."

"Yesterday I called him and accepted. For me, not for you." And she'd only debated three hours before picking up the phone—and another hour after that. She'd just gotten tired, and maybe a little resentful, of waiting for Koldo to appear, of hoping for something more than a conversation and a kiss with him, of dreaming of what might have happened if Laila hadn't interrupted them, of wondering how he would look at her the next time he saw her. Tenderly? Fiercely? Or as coldly as a teacher with his student?

And what if he wasn't allowed to date? Or, what if he was already committed to someone and forever off the market?

A fiery fog rolled through her mind, and she experienced what she suspected was a killing rage. If that sleazebag had a girlfriend...

"Uh, Co Co?"

"What?" she snarled.

"Nothing. Nothing," Laila said, holding up her hands, palms out. "You just tell me when you're ready and not a moment sooner, and I won't wonder what this little mini makeover is all about. I mean, one second I was talking to my big sis, and the next I was staring at a serial murderer."

Calm down. Just calm down. Already her heart was pounding erratically, and if she wasn't careful she would pass out. Or worse, strengthen the demon toxin. And really, this was silly. She was raging for nothing. Koldo wasn't the type to cheat. He was the type to just flat out tell you he was done with you.

"There's the sis I know and love," Laila said. "So... continuing our previous convo. You accepted a date with a coworker."

"Yes. And I'd love to call him back and accept on your behalf. The other guy's name is Blaine and he's—"

"Stop right there. The rest of the deets don't matter. I'm in!"

After Laila's last disastrous relationship, Nicola had expected a little resistance. "Really?"

"Really. I'm not sure how much longer I've got to live, so yeah, I'll be doing anything and everything I possibly can."

"That includes listening to what Koldo has to say, I hope."

Laila stuck out her tongue. "We'll see. So, what'd this guy at your office have to do to get you to say yes? You've always been oblivious to the male population."

"I have not. I just didn't want to have to deal with all the complications." And, okay, yes, the argument fell a little flat considering Koldo brought more complications than most.

A shirtless guy in blue shorts grinned as he jogged past Laila. "Hey, beautiful."

"Hey." She returned the grin with one of her own, and even waved, causing him to slow and then stop, clearly determined to approach. Her sister saved him the trouble and closed the distance.

Sighing, Nicola stepped off the path to wait. Another five minutes, and she'd have to head back to work.

She sidestepped a man walking his dog and—

Saw a shaved Koldo?

No, not Koldo, she realized with disappointment. A few yards away stood a male with the same body type as Koldo, with a bald head and bold features almost eerie in their similarity. This male wore a black shirt and black leather pants, and both were molded to his skin. He was, perhaps, ten or twenty years older than Koldo, the skin around his eyes and mouth lined. He was handsome, but he was without a sexy, beaded beard.

They had to be related, though. There was no way two guys could look so much alike and not spring from the same family line.

She waved, only to freeze in place when he reached up to stroke…a snake. A large snake with fur sticking out from underneath sickly green scales and the long, multipoint antlers usually only seen on deer. The rest of the creature's body coiled around the man, the tail shaking and rattling. Its eyes were as red as rubies— and watching her intently.

Not a snake. That thing couldn't be a snake. A… demon?

Evil wafted on the breeze, a hint of sulfur in the air. Oh, yes. A demon. And demons caused sickness, Koldo had said—and probably a thousand other things she wanted no part of.

No way this man was any kind of Sent One.

"Laila," she called hollowly.

"Just a sec," Laila replied. "I'm currently memorizing a very important number."

The jogger chuckled.

The bald man grinned at Nicola, but it wasn't a nice grin. A gaze as dark as the night perused her from head to toe, reminding her of the leering Mr. Ritter. Her heart, already amped up from the chocolate, kicked into an erratic beat.

Nicola raced forward and grabbed her sister's hand, tugging her a few steps backward. "Come on. We have to get out of here."

"But—" the jogger began.

"Why?" Laila said, turning her back on him to concentrate on Nicola. "What's wrong?"

"Do you see that man over there?"

Laila glanced to the right. "Baldy? Yeah. So?"

"What about his pet snake? Do you see it?"

"Uh, he doesn't have a pet snake. Or a dog or a cat or a bird. Honey, are you okay? You're pale and shaky."

Her sister still couldn't see the demon, then. "Come on." She pivoted and quickened her pace, dragging Laila with her.

"What's going on?" her sister demanded.

"I'll tell you later." The park was crowded with moms and their kids, dads and their dogs, as well as businessmen and women out on their lunch break like her, hoping to soak in a little sun before crawling back inside the shadows of the daily grind. She maneuvered around them, but wasn't quite at her best and ran into a few.

She heard "Hey!" and "Watch it!" multiple times, and had to mutter a few hasty apologies. Her blood chilled to a dangerous level, even as her skin threatened to overheat. Sweat rolled down her spine.

"Slow down," Laila huffed.

She cast a glance behind them. The man was still there, still grinning at her, and still stroking the demon. But he wasn't following her. Relieved, she slowed… slowed…and finally halted.

Panting, Laila pressed her palm over her heart. "Can you tell me what that was about now?"

She opened her mouth to do just that—only, another demon slithered from the tree beside her, baring long, sharp fangs with dripping ends, and the words formed a jagged knot in the center of her throat, only a few gurgling sounds escaping.

Nicola stumbled to the right, tugging Laila with her. "What are you—"

A woman stepped from around the thick trunk, and Laila closed her mouth. The newcomer was bald, just like the man. Her skin was as pale as milk, which was a striking contrast to the black mist seeping from her pores.

"Do you see that?" Nicola demanded of her sister. "The mist?"

"No. But the woman…"

The corners of the woman's lips lifted in a slow grin…revealing fangs of her own.

Nicola's heart skipped a beat as she once again launched into motion, heading in another direction. "They're after us," she rasped. "We have to get out of here!"

"Who…are they?" Her sister could barely get the words out. Neither one of them was used to this kind of activity. "What…do…they…want?"

Nicola glanced back. The woman remained just under the tree, but the demon had opted to follow Nicola and was closing in fast, its scaled and furry body dragging over the ground, its antlers shaking.

What did it want with her? What would it do to her if it caught her?

Another bald man stepped in her path, grinned evilly, and she screamed. She jerked Laila to the left, heading in the only uncharted direction. A second…third… fourth demon followed this time, slithering, slithering so quickly, as if they'd just scented the afternoon meal: two gimpy mice.

"Nicola, please," Laila pleaded. "I can't…take much… more."

She wanted her sister to see what was happening around them, to finally believe, but she also *didn't* want her sister to see. Fear would probably consume her, and fear would do her no good right now.

No one else seemed to realize what was happening. People went on with their day, smiling and laughing and flying kites, completely unaware of that other realm currently teeming with malevolence.

"I can't…" Laila ripped from her hold and hunched over, gasping for breath. "You have to…"

Nicola backtracked, leaped in front of her sister and spread her arms, expecting the demons to attack. But they surprised her. They skidded to a stop a few feet away, gravel and twigs settling around them. Vile red gazes locked on her.

She fought a wave of dizziness, her eyesight dimming. *Not now. Please, not now.* The creatures circled her, but she couldn't move with them and continue protecting Laila's back; there were too many of them to watch all at once.

"Go away," she demanded.

One hissed at her. Another spit at her, spraying whatever dripped from its fangs. The others flashed razor-sharp teeth stained crimson, as though blood was a morning obsession.

"Go away or…or…I'll ask the Most High for help." Yes. That's what Koldo had said to do.

To her utter shock, the hissing and the spitting morphed into whimpering, and the creatures began to back away from *her*.

Already, it was working. "Most High," she shouted, hit by a sudden wave of confidence. "If you can hear me, I could really use your help right now."

The demons froze in place—before slowly backing away from her.

It was working, she realized.

"Most High," she repeated more loudly, and terror fell over the creatures. They quickened their pace, desperate to get away from her. But they weren't fast enough. Two warriors unfamiliar to her shot from the sky and swooped into the park. Their wings were the color of cerulean and they wore robes of the most brilliant white.

Nicola threw her arm around her trembling sister, who was still hunched over, gasping for breath. "Everything will be okay now. I know it."

"My heart…"

"Just breathe in…out… Good girl." She watched, wide-eyed, as the Sent Ones—angels?—unsheathed double-edged swords and attacked. The demons darted in different directions, too many for the two warriors to contain. But she should have known they would find a way. They flashed to one and hacked, then to another and hacked, then to another and another, their opponents swiftly decreasing.

"Do you see them?" she asked.

"See who?" Laila said through gasps.

Well, that answered that.

At last the battle was over, and no one on the other team was spared.

The warriors returned their weapons to their sheaths and looked to Nicola. They inclined their heads in greeting, flared their wings and, without a word, shot back into the sky.

CHAPTER FIFTEEN

THE FRONT DOOR of Nicola's home swung open, the hinges moaning in protest. The two females marched inside.

"—almost killed me," Laila was saying.

"No, I was protecting you," Nicola retorted.

"Yes, but from what?"

Finally. They had returned.

Koldo rose from the couch, the only piece of furniture he'd left behind since he'd had no room for it. A little while ago, he'd sensed that Nicola was in trouble. But he'd flashed to the park and she hadn't been there. He'd flashed to all the other places she liked to visit, but had had no luck.

He'd returned to her house, where he'd waited. And waited.

Now, relief failed to overshadow his anger. Where had she been? What had happened to her? He needed to know. Not because she was his charge. Not because he would be penalized if something happened to her. But because. Just because.

He searched her in a single glance. Her color was higher than usual, and worry glazed those storm-darkened eyes. Her hair was a mess, tangled and sporting several pieces of grass.

Nicola ground to an abrupt halt, and Laila slammed into her from behind.

"Koldo," Nicola said, exasperation giving way to nervousness. She ran a hand down the length of her ponytail. "You're here."

A moment passed in silence. He wanted to demand answers, but he held his tongue. He would shout, and she would fear him, and that would only strengthen the demon toxins.

"*You're* Koldo?" Laila asked, her tone incredulous. She had zero color in her cheeks, and fatigue dulled her eyes. "But you look just like—uh, never mind. There's no way I can say that and *not* insult you. And I'm rambling. I'm sorry. It's just that you're so big and…well, never mind."

He had been mentioned by name. He wondered what all had been said.

"Wait. Hold everything." Frowning, Nicola turned in a circle. "I think I was robbed. My pictures are gone. And so are my vases and blankets and pillows. Everything but my couch."

I can have a conversation without raising my voice. I can. A tiny human female could not anger him more than his mother and his father ever had. "You weren't robbed. I moved everything to my house in Panama. Now, I want you sitting at the kitchen counter in the next two minutes. Or else." He didn't wait for her reply, just stomped into the desired room.

To his surprise, she dogged his footsteps, even caught his wrist. He could have easily tugged from her grip. Instead, he reveled in his first contact with her in three days. Far too long. He had to feel this soft, soft skin, and those hands—no longer cold, but warm—every day or he would not be content.

"Or else, what? And what's going on?" she demanded. "*Why* did you move my stuff to Panama?"

He swung around and anchored his hands onto her waist. He lifted her up, swung back around with her as she yelped, and placed her on the nearest chair. There. He had her where he wanted her, the tattoo equipment on the counter and ready to use.

As he put the pieces of the gun together, he said, "I don't want you living here any longer. It isn't safe."

She searched his face, and sighed. "Apparently, it isn't safe anywhere."

Not the reaction he'd expected. "Why do you say that?"

"We were at the park and several demons chased us."

His instincts had been right. She *had* been in danger. And he had failed to protect her. He could have lost her. Stupid, foolish, unwise, ignorant man! Yes, that's what he was. He should have searched more diligently. Should have done something. Anything. "Did they hurt you?"

"No," she replied, and he was able to relax. "You told me to call upon the Most High, and I did. He sent in the troops. Whoever was closest, I guess, just like you promised."

Thank You, Most High.

"Alleged demons." Laila strolled into the kitchen. "All I saw were giants. And I'm the twin sister, by the way. Just so you know, I'm not quite as gullible as my darling Co Co. Sorry, honey," she said. "I don't mean any offense."

Nicola offered a small though genuine smile. "I

know. I also know that you'll come to eat those words one day."

"Demons are very real, I assure you," Koldo said, opening the packages of ink.

"Yeah, and you're a Sent One." Laila anchored her hands on her waist. "Listen, you're taking advantage of an innocent—humph!"

He'd dropped the gun and grabbed her, tugging her into the hard line of his body. With a final look at Nicola, who jumped from the chair, possibly to attempt to free her mouthy sister, he flashed to the roof of a training facility in Germanus's realm of the skies.

The huge building was perched atop a mile-long cloud, the edges of that cloud dipping into an aqua sky, stars twinkling even during the day. Laila looked down, down, down at the earth so very far away, and screamed with bloodcurdling fear.

"Still think I'm taking advantage?" He didn't wait for an answer but flashed the girl inside the building, to the room where Sent Ones were taught how to fight demons. Once there, Koldo remained in the spiritual realm, forcing Laila to open her inner eyes and finally see.

A young trainee swung a sword of fire as two envexa darted from floor to ceiling, ceiling to wall. The warrior had wings of white with thin strips of gold, an indication of his warrior status. Joy-bringers possessed wings of solid white. The Elite, like Zacharel, possessed wings of solid gold.

Though fully grown, the demons were the size of ten-year-old boys, with thick humanoid bodies and skin as green as toxic slime. They had hooks rather than hands, and long, thin tails with barbs.

Laila trembled against Koldo, her mouth opening and closing, small gasping sounds emerging.

"They're real," he said, "and they're evil. They roam the earth, stalking humans like you, and would love nothing more than to ruin your life and cut it short. And you have been letting them."

"I—I—"

"Can overcome them, yes. I'm here to help you." Taking pity on her, he flashed her back to Nicola's living room and gave her a little push toward the hall. "You may go to your room now."

"R-room. Yes. Thank you." With her arms wrapped around her middle, she tripped her way around the corner. A door clicked shut.

"What did you do to her?" Nicola demanded, stomping forward and banging her fists into his chest.

As slight as those fists were, he barely registered the impact. "I proved that demons do, in fact, exist."

"You should have eased her in. She had a tough day, and that kind of stress couldn't have been good for her toxin levels."

"Some people can be eased. Some must be shoved. Now we will return to the kitchen. I'll tattoo your arms and you'll tell me everything that happened at the park."

"Wait. What? Tattoo my arms?" she squeaked.

He urged her forward. "For your added protection against the demons."

A little dazed, she flopped into the chair. "I'll tell you about the park," she said quietly, "but first you're going to tell me about this move. *Then* we'll talk about the tattooing."

"My home is fortified against evil." He owned a cloud of defense, and that cloud now surrounded the property, acting as a barrier against the rest of the world. "Yours isn't."

"But—"

"No buts. I was attacked the last time I was here. That's why I've been gone. I was recovering."

A gasp slipped from her. "You were hurt?"

"Yes."

"Oh, Koldo. I'm so sorry. I had no idea." She placed her hand over his, a gesture of remorse, kindness.

A gesture that caused his blood to flash-heat to white-hot.

"It wasn't your fault," he said, his voice rough. He was responsible for his own distraction. "Now, what happened at the park?"

She propped her elbows on the counter, ending the contact, and he wanted to howl.

He was *that* needy for her?

Pressing his tongue against the roof of his mouth, he finished with the ink. He'd chosen a deep, rich red that, at first glance, would cause most people to assume she was bleeding. But he didn't exactly care what other people thought. He wanted her tattoo to match his.

She was his charge, after all. There was no more to it than that.

For the first time in his life, he thought he tasted a lie and grimaced.

"These demons…" She shuddered. "They weren't like the monkeys. They were worse. They were snakes! They slithered from the trees and on the ground and chased after us, and—"

"Snakes?" he interjected, his stomach twisting.

"With antlers! And fur! They cornered us, surrounded us, and that's when I called out to the Most

High, and He sent angels—or maybe Sent Ones. They had large blue wings. A blue like I'd never seen before, radiant and sparkling, almost like a waterfall of glitter. And their robes were the brightest white I'd ever seen."

"Real angels." He nodded. "Continue."

"There was a battle, and then, boom, the angels had won, the demons were gone and Laila and I were able to walk out of the park uninjured."

So. The serps had returned for Nicola the very day Koldo awoke from their poisoning. That couldn't be a coincidence.

"You'll never regret being inked," he told her. "What I put into your flesh will protect you, as the angels protected you today, but it will also do what they can't. It will strengthen you when you're at your weakest. Let me. Please."

"But…but…"

"Have I ever lied to you? Ever steered you wrong?"

"No," she admitted softly.

He reached out and traced his finger along the curve of her jaw. "Let me do this," he repeated. "Please."

A moment passed. Finally, determination hardened her features and she removed her sweater, rolled up her shirtsleeves. "Very well."

Relief and satisfaction collided, and he wanted to pound his fists into his chest. She trusted him fully, nothing held back. That was a first, and he would do everything in his power to earn what she'd bestowed upon him. "I wish I could tell you otherwise, but this will hurt, Nicola."

"I had a feeling," she said drily.

Before she could change her mind, he got to work. At first, as the needle pounded into her skin, she cringed and she gasped. Twice he almost stopped, but both times he reminded himself that this was for her good. This was necessary.

"Distract me." Her voice was strained. "Please."

"How?"

"Tell me...how you age. Or if you ever will."

"I was a little boy once, a child to my parents." Now, he and his mother looked to be the same age. "I matured normally, like a human, until reaching the age of thirty. After that, my appearance remained the same. And as long as I live, my appearance will stay this way."

That was true of most supernatural races. The Nefas, however, aged to fifty before stopping. He supposed it was because the vileness of their deeds rotted their souls, and rotted souls produced rotted flesh.

Koldo was glad the characteristics of the Sent Ones were stronger than those of the Nefas, allowing him to have hair, diffusing the black smoke.

"So...one day I'll be an old lady but you'll still look like a young, virile Viking?"

A Viking? *That's* how she saw him?

And...she was right about the age thing, he realized. He'd never given the notion any thought because he'd never imagined himself with a human. But there *was* a way to prevent such an outcome. Zacharel had tied his life to Annabelle's, ensuring she no longer aged. But if one died, the other would immediately follow. Koldo couldn't make that same commitment to Nicola. He would have to share a piece of his tainted soul, and that he would never do.

And why should he bother sorting out his feelings on the matter now, anyway? She was interested in another male.

"Yes" was all he said, and left it at that. "Is there anything else you'd like to know?"

Nicola sucked in a breath as the gun glided over a sensitive tendon. "Will you do this to Laila?"

"If she will allow me." He leaned back, studied the etchings. The scripted numbers began at her elbows and coiled all the way to her wrists.

161911213327.
219113215122231.
2209131520825418.

"Done," he said, pleased.

Nicola's head tilted to the side as she looked over the red, swollen flesh. "Is that some sort of code?"

"It is."

"And what does it mean?"

"That you are protected by the Most High, and His strength is yours."

"Very cool." She traced a fingertip over several of the numbers. "There's something so mesmerizing about each one, isn't there? Almost as if they're alive, holding my gaze captive."

That's because they were, on both counts. "The next time you see a demon, simply stare at the numbers as you're doing now."

"Stare? Really? And that will…what?"

"Save your life."

"Well, all right, then."

The cinnamon and vanilla scent of her wound around him, melding with his skin, claiming his attention. "Nicola?" he rasped.

She glanced up at him, licked her lips. "Yes."

Whatever he'd meant to say, he forgot. He found himself stalking around the counter, standing just in front of her, between her legs. His hands tunneled through her hair, the strands soft, silky, tickling his skin.

She closed her eyes and leaned into his touch.

He wanted to kiss her. But he couldn't. Not again. Every time he neared her, the desire grew. He wasn't sure how he would react if it grew any more.

Throw her down and take her? Kill the man she actually wanted?

"Will you move to Panama with me?" he asked.

She licked her lips. "You'll be there with me?"

"Yes." He dared anyone to try and pry him away.

"And you'll be happy to have me, even though I have nothing to offer you?"

Nothing to offer him? She was the gentle touch he'd always craved. The acceptance he'd never before had. And when she looked at him, he never felt as if he was a nuisance, as if he was beneath her. He felt…empowered.

But all he said was "I'll be happy."

"Then I would love to," she replied without a single beat of hesitation.

"Good."

"On two conditions," she added, blinking open her eyes.

He stepped back, increasing the distance between them. "And those conditions are?"

She gulped and shifted uncomfortably in her seat. "You have to bring us back on Saturday. We, uh, well, we have a double date."

He'd known, but hearing the words from her lips caused every ounce of his earlier fury to return—times ten. "You'll not be going on any date, Nicola."

Her mouth fell open, snapped closed. "I already said yes."

"And now you'll say no."

A moment passed in stilted silence.

"Is that so?" she said with a quiet fury of her own.

"That's so. You must do what I say, when I say. Remember?"

She drummed her fingers over the counter. "You once told me to do whatever was necessary to remain calm. You once told me to do whatever was necessary to find peace and sow joy. Well, the date seemed like my best bet at the time. So which would you have me do? Please you, or save my sister and myself?"

He clenched his jaw painfully. It was just as he'd suspected—and no matter his feelings, he couldn't take this away from her. "Very well. Go on your date." The concession scraped his throat, left it raw and burning.

Perhaps, while she was out with the male, Koldo would return to the Downfall. Perhaps he would allow the Harpy to dance for him. Perhaps he would kiss and touch *the Harpy,* and forget everything Nicola had ever made him feel. He wouldn't ruin the Harpy, and the Harpy wouldn't blame him for her troubles.

Yes, that's what he would do, even though every cell in his body rebelled at the thought.

"What's the second condition?" he demanded.

She exhaled with force. "You have to take me to my job at Estellä every weekday morning, and pick me up every evening."

Yet another blow he was unprepared to deal with right now. "You won't quit?"

"No. I have to make a living."

Was that all? "I'll pay you to live with me."

Again her mouth fell open. "No. You won't."

"I'm paying your bills. One is the same as the other."

"Actually, no, it isn't. I won't be dependent on you for my future."

Understanding took root, and it didn't sprout a pretty flower patch. It had gnarled limbs and dripped with blood. She would allow Koldo to clean up her past, but she was afraid he would muddy up her future—the one she planned to share with another male.

"Very well," he said stiffly. "I agree to your terms." And he would do more than take the Harpy. He would take others. So many others! As many as it took to find someone who made him feel the way Nicola did. Or had. Right now, the only thing he wanted from her was distance. And, all right, an apology.

"Now I *know* you're related to the guy in the park," she said snippily. "You look just like him when you glare like that."

Guy at the park? He didn't allow himself to leave. "What guy?"

"Well, the demons were with some very scary people. People as tall as you, with bald heads, even the girl, and fangs and a terrible black mist that rose from their bodies. And the first one I saw looked like an older version of you."

At first, he was too stunned to react. But as he breathed, his thoughts aligned and the shock gave way to dread.

His father *had* survived the bombing.

His father was here in Kansas.

His father, he thought, dazed—the vilest male he had ever encountered.

"Did any of them touch you?" he demanded.

"No. They just looked at me and smiled the meanest of smiles."

He should be relieved, but his emotions were simply too volatile. His father had approached Nicola. His father could have harmed her in the worst of ways. He could have absconded with her, and Koldo wouldn't have known what had happened to her until too late. But Nox hadn't done any of that. He'd wanted Koldo to know of his return.

How like the man, to deliver fear before the battle. And there was no question there would be a battle. Nox was here for revenge. After all, Koldo had destroyed the male's entire camp. His harem of lovers, both slave and free. The best of his warriors. The bulk of his allies. Now, he hoped to hit Koldo where it would hurt most. Destroying the first female Koldo had ever taken under his care.

Well, I won't let him. Koldo would have to find a way to strike first. To end this. Now. Forever.

He tugged Nicola to her feet. "Get your sister. I want you installed in my home within the hour."

Koldo flashed Nicola and Laila to the living room of his ranch. "Look around," he said, doing his best to mask his growing tension. Probably failing. "Change whatever you want. Eat whatever you want. I'll be back."

He hated to leave them so abruptly, without any more of a welcome, but his next task couldn't wait.

As Nicola sputtered out a protest, he flashed to the cavern where his mother was stashed. This time, he didn't hang around outside but stalked inside. With a single glance, he had the details memorized. Cornelia was dirtier than before, her robe stained with mud and blood, the hem frayed. Her short hair was matted at the sides. She sat in the corner of the cage, and there was a rat perched on her hand—a rat she was feeding a piece of grain.

She spotted Koldo and cursed. "Can't you just leave me alone?"

"Your precious lover is stalking my woman."

"I have no lover," she spat.

"Oh, but you do. My father, the man you've pined for all these years, thinks to strike at me."

Cornelia stiffened as she absorbed his words. The moment she accepted them as truth, she actually tossed the rat at him, the creature screaming along the way. Koldo caught him, set him down and watched as he scampered away.

Your first mistake was assuming she had a heart, little guy.

"Cruel even to your pets," Koldo said.

She trembled, visibly fighting to keep her temper under control. If he wasn't mistaken—and he had to be mistaken—there was a gleam of regret in her eyes.

"I thought he was dead," she whispered.

"As did I. We were both wrong."

Watching him intently, Cornelia stood on unsteady legs. "If he's after you, you're doomed. He's crafty, and there's nothing you can do to stop him."

"I can kill him."

"And that worked so well for you before?" she mocked with a hard laugh. "Especially now that you have a woman, did you say? I'm surprised one can actually stand to look at you."

His woman. That's what he'd called Nicola, wasn't it?

He would have to better guard his words, for the human was not his, not in that way, and now, she would never be. She had chosen another male. And Koldo couldn't really fault her—even though he was still so angry he could tear this cavern apart rock by rock. She would be better off with one of her own kind.

"You should probably say goodbye to her." Cornelia traced her fingertip along the bars beside her and grinned happily. "He'll do the most horrendous things to her, and he'll force you to watch. But you share his blood—maybe you'll like that, huh?"

Koldo punched the cage so forcefully the reinforced steel bent backward.

Cornelia paled, backed away.

He *had* been forced to watch such behavior while chained inside Nox's tent, and he had vomited every time. Had even tried to behead the man the first hundred times he was allowed to walk freely through the camp—and he had always been disciplined for his efforts. He would never—never!—enjoy watching such treatment.

"I protect what's mine," he gritted out. "But you protect no one. Did you witness such events when you were with him, huh, *Mother?* Did the two of you discuss it while you were snuggled in his arms?"

"Shut up!" She changed course, stomping forward. When she reached him, she gripped the very bars he'd harmed and attempted to shake them.

"I bet you did. I bet you were eaten up with jealousy when he turned his attentions to another."

"You know nothing about me!"

"I know you're exactly like him, a pretty face hiding rotten bones. And just so you know, I *will* kill him before he hurts the girl." He should shut up. He should leave. His temper was overtaking him. If he wasn't careful, he would erupt. But his feet felt anchored in place. "You'll help me. Not because you love me, but because you want him to suffer for abandoning you. Isn't that right?"

She popped her jaw, some of the anger leaving her. "I do want him to suffer."

"Then tell me. What are his weaknesses?"

"You spent the most time with him. You should know."

He should, shouldn't he? But then, to him, Nox had been the pinnacle of strength, an unstoppable force. Koldo had been surprised to deliver the deathblow, especially from a distance.

Should have chosen up close and personal, as I craved.

Then, he should have taken the time to identify all of the remains. But he'd assumed Nox had been burned to ash—had wanted to believe it so badly.

Mistakes, he realized now. He wouldn't make another.

"Will you help me or not?" he demanded.

Cornelia lifted her chin, haughty despite her circumstances. "I will not."

"Not even for a human?"

"Oh, I'll help a human. Any but yours," she added.

Koldo tried to calm his raging nerves. A thousand times these past few weeks, he could have killed this woman. But he'd never even bruised her.

As a child, he'd only ever wanted her love. Offered freely. And when it was clear he wouldn't be getting that, offered through bribes. Yet time and time again she had rejected and denied him.

In that moment, peering into her defiant, hate-filled face, his restraint vanished. His control finally snapped. He'd had enough.

For once, she would know the pain he'd experienced at her hands. For once, she would understand the depths of betrayal. For once, she would fear the things Koldo could do to her.

"Let's see if I can change your mind, shall we?" He withdrew a razor from the air pocket at his side and flashed into the center of the cage—the only way in or out. "I look like my father, even though I despise him. I think it's only fair that you look like him, too, since you're clearly still in love with him."

Her eyes widened, and she backed away from him, as far as she could possibly get. "You wouldn't dare," she cried. "My hair has only just begun to grow back."

Her words merely proved how little she knew about him. "Just like you wouldn't dare to take my wings?"

She leaned toward the left, then darted to the right, trying to avoid him as he closed in. "You disobeyed me. You had to be disciplined."

"Not that way." Koldo flashed to just in front of her and latched on to her upper arms. It was their first contact since he'd carried her out of the depths of hell and brought her here. She was thinner, practically skin and bones, reminding him of Laila. Laila, the very image of Nicola. But that didn't soften him, either, and wouldn't stop him. In fact, it made him far angrier.

"Your only goal was to make me suffer," he said, shaking her. "Why?"

He shouldn't have asked. He regretted the question

immediately, and knew it revealed the hurt he'd never been able to shed.

"I couldn't allow you to turn out like him," she said, and all the fight vanished from her. She peered up at him with more of that hatred. "I should have known it was a useless cause."

I'm nothing like my father! "So you despised him."

"Yes," she hissed.

"Yet you slept with him."

"Yes! All right? Yes. I could tell you he tricked me. I could tell you it was a moment of weakness. What do you want to hear?"

His grip tightened as he gave her another shake. "The truth."

Utterly calm, she said, "You were a mistake. That's the truth."

With her words, she ripped a scab off his heart, and the wound bled into his soul. "You're right," he said, wishing he were emotionless. Instead, he was so torn up inside he wasn't sure he would ever be able to put himself back together. "I was a mistake. And now I'll show you why."

He pushed her face-first into the ground, held her down with a knee in the center of her back and, while she screamed and tried to fight her way free, removed every strand of her hair, until he scraped her scalp clean.

The sound of a woman screaming, the sight of her struggling, caused so many terrible memories to rise. But even when he closed his eyes and shook head, the images wouldn't leave him.

He'd never stopped being the man his father had made him, he realized. And he never would.

CHAPTER SIXTEEN

"SENT ONES, CO CO. Sent Ones," Laila whispered as Nicola tucked her into bed.

"I know."

"Demons, Co Co. Demons."

"I know, sweetheart. But we don't have to fear them, and Koldo assured me they won't be able to hurt us." And now, having witnessed what happened in the park, her confience in Team Good was untouchable.

"How did I not know they were out there? Why could I not see them?"

"Your eyes were closed. Now they're open."

"I…I…I'm not sure I can deal with this."

Nicola remembered when they were little girls and Laila had tucked *her* into bed after she'd seen her first monster. How gentle and patient and kind her twin had been. "You've always been the strong one. You'll find a way."

A soft, humorless laugh left a sense of sadness behind. "You always thought that. You always thought I was strong. But, Co Co, it was you. Always you." Laila stuffed her ears with the buds from the iPod Nicola had given her for their last birthday. She'd scrimped and saved for months to afford such a little piece of technology.

Sighing, Nicola kissed her sister on the cheek and

left her to her rest. Not knowing what else to do, she explored Koldo's home. Awe continually struck her, and she felt as though she had entered a fairy tale rather than a third-world country. The house itself was built of pine, and smelled rich and clean, but the furniture was what really stunned her.

There were velvet couches and chairs, ornately carved tables. Glass figurines, and bowls filled with diamonds, sapphires, rubies and emeralds as big as her fist. There were tapestries on the wall, and plush carpets on the floor. And that was just the living room!

Koldo really was loaded.

The kitchen boasted gold-veined marble countertops, copper pots and pans hanging from a sterling silver rack, and a large refrigerator that blended with the cabinet woodwork. Nothing was out of place. Not a speck of dust had settled onto the surface of the hand-carved table.

There were four bedrooms. Laila had claimed the one closest to the kitchen, and Nicola picked the one at the far end of the hall. There was a huge monster-size bed in the center, the rails draped by sheer pink lace. Pink? Lace? In a warrior's home?

Had a female decorated?

Nicola bit the side of her cheek, fighting a tide of jealousy. The comforter was a lighter shade of pink, but no less brilliant. And this must have been where Koldo had wanted her to stay because the blankets her mother had sewn a few weeks before the car crash were folded and resting at the edge.

A bejeweled ceiling fan whirled slowly overhead. A mural of the heavens had been painted on all four walls, with a bright sun in the right corner, shining upon clouds of every size and shape.

At the left was a large bay window overlooking a thriving grove of orange trees. And behind the lush green leaves and plump pieces of fruit, she could see several mountains and even a volcano blowing thick smoke through the air. There were three breathtaking ponds, with fish that jumped up and cleared the surface.

Nicola stood there, amazed by the beauty, watching as the sun set on the horizon, reds and pinks forming, creating the perfect contrast to the lush greens and blues of the sloping land. Birds sang.

How long would Koldo want her to stay here? She'd thought…hoped…well, it didn't matter anymore. Koldo hadn't wanted her to go on the date—a wonderful sign—but she'd gotten so angry she'd insisted. How silly. Especially considering the fact that she'd only accepted the date because he'd disappeared those three days.

Now he was back…but she was stuck.

What was she going to do?

A rustling of clothing behind her had her spinning. Koldo stood a few feet away from the bed, with his head down and his hands clenched. Strands of hair stuck to his face and chest, both dark and light. Dirt streaked his skin. He had bite marks on his hands. His breathing was deep and even, but he was using too much force, as if the hold he had on his calm facade was tenuous.

"What's wrong?" All thoughts of the dating disaster left her, and she raced over to him. "Were you attacked again?"

Silent, he just sort of fell back into the plush chair behind him.

Worry filled her as she crouched in front of him and rested her palms on his rock-hard thighs. Heat radiated from him, enveloping her, and she shivered for a reason that had nothing to do with temperature.

"Talk to me," she prompted. "Please."

Golden eyes beseeched her to…what?

She'd never seen him like this. So torn up. So tortured.

So broken.

"Koldo." What else could she say?

He leaned back, his head thumping against the wooden arch. "I…did something. Something terrible. It was deserved. I should be thrilled with the results, but…but…"

What could he possibly have done to cause this kind of reaction? "Tell me."

He scrubbed a hand down his face. "And watch hate fall over your features, too?" Like Laila, he laughed without humor. "No."

The strands of hair floated from him and into the air, twirling to the ground. *He likes jokes. Tease him.* "You gave someone a mullet, didn't you?" she asked with a small smile.

He closed his eyes, pushed out a breath and lifted his arms up and back with fierce force, punching a hole in the wall. The sharp boom jolted her.

Such a reaction… Had he actually given someone a mullet? "Koldo—"

"I'm sorry," he croaked, focusing on her. "I shouldn't have done that."

Okay, so maybe not a mullet, but his doom and gloom definitely had something to do with the hair.

"Make me forget," he pleaded. "Just for a little while. Tell me a story."

She would do anything to bring him peace. But what could she tell a centuries-old warrior to entertain him? *Oh, I know!* "One time, a girl in my class called me and Laila freakazoid Frankensteins because of the tubes coming out of our clothing—and I know, I know, it's a very original name, but I digress. It made Laila cry. Notice that I said *Laila*. Not me, just so we're clear. I did *not* spend twenty minutes in the bathroom, leaning against a very unsanitary toilet, sobbing so hard snot was bubbling from my nose."

The slightest measure of pain faded from his expression, and he ghosted his hand over the line of her jaw. "What happened next?"

She shivered as she said, "You have to guess what very polite, very mannerly thing I did to pay the little wench back."

"What?"

"Guess."

"You, hard-core punk that you are, called her a very naughty name."

"Nope. I punched her in the face and broke her nose. No one calls my twin sister a freakazoid Frankenstein and gets away with it. Let that be a lesson to you. You might want to write that down and circle it."

He barked out a laugh. A very rough, very hoarse laugh, leading her to believe he hadn't laughed in years. If ever. And *she* had been the one to bring him to that point, pushing him past his upset, drawing him out of miry darkness and into light. And oh, he was beautiful like this.

So badly she wanted to rise up, crawl into his lap

and kiss him. Just press her lips into his, taste him, relearn him and offer comfort in another way. But after their fight...

"Another story," he said.

"I'll give you a question instead." And probably sound needy, but she didn't care. "Do Sent Ones date?" Obviously they kissed, but...

His brow furrowed, as if the change of subject confused him. "Some do."

Don't do this. Don't press. "Do you?"

"No."

Oh. The very disappointment she'd denied crashed through her. "Never?"

"Never." He looked at her, really looked at her, his golden gaze boring deep. His arms lowered to his sides. His hands gripped the fabric of the chair, as if he had to force himself to be still.

To keep from punching another hole in the wall—or from doing something else?

"If I told you I had tortured another Sent One," he said, "would you think I was a monster?"

Would she? "Did you?"

Silence.

Yeah. He had. And he'd felt the action, whatever it was, had been deserved. Wasn't that what he'd said a moment ago? But still he regretted it, whether he realized it or not.

"What I've learned over the years is that people shouldn't be defined by a single mistake. Everyone messes up," she said. "You have to forgive yourself and move on."

He ran his tongue over his teeth. "What makes you think this was my first mistake?"

She sighed. "You're missing the point, Koldo."

"Doesn't matter. Whatever the point, I can't forgive myself."

"You can. It's not a feeling, but a choice—and then acting on that choice. And I know *I'm* supposed to be the one seeking joy, but it's clear you need it, too. I think your unwillingness to let go of this, whatever this is, is as much a toxin as what the demons cause."

Another round of silence.

Well, wisdom hadn't worked. She would try humor again. "I mean, seriously. All the best therapists on TV say that focusing on the past causes stagnation. And diarrhea."

He barked out another laugh, then quickly sobered. "Did you ever do anything to hurt—" He pressed his lips together.

"Hurt who?"

He cleared his throat. "Where's your sister?"

Nice dodge. But as upset as he was, she allowed it. "Sleeping in her room." Nicola stood, held out her hand. "I know what'll make you feel better. We'll go to the kitchen and I'll fix the most mediocre meal you've ever had the pleasure of tasting, since my specialties are cereal and microwave dinners. Meanwhile, you can give me another lecture."

"I don't lecture. I teach." He placed his hand in hers, his calloused palm causing goose bumps to rise. He paused for a moment, never allowing her to help him up. Then, he shook his head as if he'd just made a decision and tugged her down.

Yelping, she tumbled into his lap and her ponytail slapped him in the face. She put her hands on his big, strong shoulders for balance—and lost her breath as he meshed his lips into hers.

Oh, sweet mercy. Just like last time, her bones instantly melted. It didn't matter that he was too rough at first, then too soft; he branded her, claimed her, delighted her. And his taste, oh, his taste. It was decadence, pure and simple, like the summer and the winter, the spring and the fall, every season, every day, carrying her straight into eternity.

She wrapped her arms around him, holding him close. He groaned, and then…*then,* he figured out exactly how he wanted to kiss her, and the pressure evened out. He tilted his head, deepening the contact. Taking, giving. Demanding, beseeching. Owning.

It became more than a kiss, and on some level, it scared her. He was giving her something precious. And she was giving him something precious right back. But she didn't know what that thing was—her trust? A piece of her heart?—and wasn't sure she wanted to know.

What would happen if she fell for him? If she gave him everything?

Would he welcome her softer feelings? Or run from them?

Whatever the answers, they scared her, too. All she knew was that every point of contact reminded her that she'd never experienced anything like this—and probably never would again. How could she? He was the light in the darkness. The harbor in the storm. The hope she needed in the middle of the war.

There was no other man like him. He was one of a kind. And she wanted him to find as much pleasure with her as she was finding with him. She wanted to be what he needed.

To delight him, and not disappoint him.

His hands roamed the contours of her back…then lower. He caressed and he kneaded and…and…she was consumed, shaking, needy. Gasping, desperate. And he was…shaking, too, she realized, as affected as she was, his fingers rough, a little desperate, and the knowledge shattered her.

"Koldo." Frantic, she tunneled her fingers under the collar of his robe. The fabric ripped away with a simple touch, granting her skin-to-skin contact, the sizzle of his flesh heating her up. And when his muscles jumped underneath her touch, as if seeking closer contact, the heat got worse—and a thousand times better. He was so soft, so hard, so…exactly what she'd always craved without ever knowing she craved it.

"Nicola," he gasped out.

"More," she demanded, the word escaping of its own volition. She continued to rip at his robe, finally baring the full breadth of his chest.

Sweet mercy. He. Was. Magnificent!

Bronzed and toned, stacked with muscle and sinew, chiseled by the hand of a master artist. His chest… That stomach rippled with iron bars… That perfectly dipped navel. A scar here, a scar there, but still, nothing about him was flawed. He'd been honed on a battlefield, every mark a badge of strength.

She kissed his neck, and his head fell against the back of the couch, allowing her better access to him. She kissed his shoulder, his collarbone, reckless in her bid to show him just how deeply she accepted him, whatever he'd done, whatever the future held. His grip tightened on her hips, and she lifted to once again fit their lips together. He moaned into her mouth, and took over, dominating her in the most amazing way. And she was…she was…

Struggling to breathe, she realized, trying to suck in a single gasp of oxygen but failing. Her mind fogged.

"Nicola?" he demanded. "What's wrong?"

"I'm…okay…will be…" No, no, no. Not this. Not now. She would ruin the moment—maybe even his feelings for her.

He tugged his robe together, the material somehow repairing itself. He cupped her face in his big hands. "Inhale slow and easy, all right? Now exhale just as slow, just as easy." His thumbs traced her cheeks, his skin so hot she could have been pressed against the sun. "That's the way. In. Out. Yes. Good girl."

A minute passed. Then two, three, before she finally regained her composure. And then she kind of wished she hadn't.

She *had* ruined the moment, she realized. Worse, she'd revealed the depths of her weakness and proven just how worthless she was in the relationship department.

A strong man like Koldo had to despise people like her.

"I'm tired," she muttered. "I should go to bed."

His gaze locked with hers, unwavering. "You're upset. Why?"

"Just forget it, okay?"

"I can't. Are you angry about something I did?"

"No." She couldn't let him think that.

"Then what?"

"Just let this go. Please."

"I can't. Talk to me."

"Look, I—" Wanted to leave the room and his penetrating stare. Wanted to leave and hide and forget this had ever happened.

But she wouldn't be able to forget, would she? This was burned into her mind—and every cell in her body.

"Knock, knock, is home anyone?" Laila asked, stumbling past the door and into the room, the scent of alcohol accompanying her. She giggled when she spotted them, wavered on her feet. "Uh-oh. Did I something interrupt? Wait. That came out wrong. I something interrupted." A nod. Another giggle. "Much better."

Nicola climbed off Koldo and stood, nearly toppling over herself. Stupid legs. "I thought you were asleep," she said, happy for the reprieve. Only, she jolted backward.

The monkeys—the demons—were perched on Laila's shoulders.

"Koldo," she whispered, and pointed. "Look."

Laila spun in a full circle, nearly fell. "What?"

Koldo pushed to his feet, the beads in his beard clanging together.

The monkeys squeaked out a protest and darted from the room.

"I'll pretend I know what's going on," Laila said with a stern tone ruined by a goofy expression.

Why hadn't she seen the demons? Her eyes had been opened—she should be able to see them now. Right?

"I was in the kitchen and found this." Grinning, Laila raised a bottle of vodka.

Koldo stiffened. "Where did you find it?"

"In the hands of one of your friends. And a good thing he brought it, because I almost died of a heart attack when I spotted him and needed a little something to calm me down."

"A friend? What friend?"

"The kind that will stab you in the chest just to hear you scream."

Nicola's gaze snagged on the chair Koldo had abandoned. There were two glowing palm prints on the cushions, with flecks of golden glitter the exact shade of his eyes. Prints that hadn't been there before. What...how... odd, she finished.

Standing by her side, he reached out, settled two fingers under her chin and forced her to face him. "Stay here. And remember what I told you about the tattoos." With that, he stormed from the room, shutting the door behind him.

CHAPTER SEVENTEEN

KOLDO WOULD NEVER FORGET the exquisite feel of Nicola's lips against his or the softness of her body pressed against him, or the sweetness of her taste and a thousand other things that had set his blood on fire, causing him to ache, to reach the razor's edge of desperation.

The entire time he'd had her in his arms, he'd forgotten the horror of his earlier actions. His inner brokenness had been eased, and he'd felt whole. Happy. At peace for the first time.

The future had seemed bright. Problems? What problems? There'd been no anger, no dread, no sense of hopelessness. He'd been…normal.

But he'd done something to upset her, no matter what she'd claimed. First, she had melted. Then, after she'd come out of her faint, she had stiffened, preparing to bolt.

Had she regretted what had happened?

Probably. He'd mauled her, and she'd been prepared to leave him. Had she succeeded, he would have chased her and…what? Demanded she still desire him?

He wouldn't be so pathetic. Would he?

Maybe her desertion was for the best. He wouldn't always have her, and so he couldn't allow himself to come to rely on her. He had himself, and only himself, and that's the way it had to be. That was safe. That's what he knew.

Stalking into the kitchen, he summoned the sword of fire. The flames crackled, light spilling in front of him. What he expected to find, he wasn't sure. Zacharel didn't know this place existed, nor did any other Sent Ones. His father didn't, either, but the male was out there, actively hunting him.

To his astonishment, he found Axel sitting at his kitchen table, eating the food Koldo had bought for Nicola and her sister.

Anger ignited. "How did you find me?"

With cheese dust on his chin, the warrior said, "I can find anyone, anywhere, anytime. A little talent of mine." He lifted a bag of chips. The only source of junk food in the entire house. "Do you have these in Tabasco?"

The anger instantly subsided. If Axel could find anyone, he could find Koldo's father before Nox found Koldo.

The battle could be over before it ever began.

"You shouldn't have come, and you shouldn't have brought alcohol." A single drink and Koldo's Nefas side would come rushing to the surface. His teeth would elongate. His nails would curl into claws. His temper would overtake him. *Yeah. Alcohol is all that's needed for that.* "But since you're here, I'll put you to work. Whatever your price, I need you to hunt down a… Nefas." He waited for a reaction. Most people shuddered at the mere mention of the race.

Axel ignored him, popping another chip in his mouth. "You should have a chat with the blonde about sharing her drinky drink with guests—especially when said drinky drink belongs to the guest! It was way impolite to threaten to bash me in the head with the vodka bottle when I tried to steal it back. And by the way, did you know your hands are glowing?"

"What are you—" Koldo's gaze locked on his palms. His glowing palms. The essentia had at last begun to seep from his pores.

He'd wanted Nicola *that* much, his body instinctively seeking to mark her as his exclusive property, even though she wanted someone else.

He should be ashamed, considering he'd never bond with her.

But he wasn't.

"How did you bypass my cloud?" The warrior should have encountered a solid barrier.

"If I told you, blah, blah, blah."

He arched a brow. "You'd have to kill me?"

"Don't be silly. I'd only cut out your tongue to keep you from talking, and cut off your hands to keep you from writing or signing." Axel dusted his hands together and stood. "I'd love to help you with your little Nefas problem, but I'm actually here because Zacharel called a meeting in the heavens. And what do you want with the Nefas, anyway? Those suckers are hard-core."

"So are we." Was the meeting the one Zacharel had mentioned when Koldo had visited his cloud? When the warrior had been covered in blood and injuries? "Where does he want us?"

"Deity's temple in the heavens."

Deity. Germanus. Koldo looked forward to seeing his mentor again. They hadn't spoken since Koldo had been told he belonged to Zacharel. And that was all Koldo's doing. He'd been so irate to learn of his fate, he'd kept his distance rather than yell. However, Germanus would have welcomed him at any time.

"I'll meet you there," he said pointedly.

"Like I really want to stick around and carry you again. Did I mention you weigh more than a building?" Axel stood, flared his wings and leaped into the air, misting through the ceiling and disappearing.

Koldo stalked down the hall and into Nicola's room. Laila was jumping on the bed, singing off tune, losing her breath.

"—something, something, something, you love me. Yeah. Yeah. Something, something, together."

Nicola lounged on the couch, a blanket strewn across her legs. One of his books about heavenly battle strategies rested in her lap.

"There are nightclothes in the dresser," he said, and she glanced up. Meeting those stormy gray eyes was always a pleasure and a pain. They were always direct—

Except this time.

She looked away. Her cheeks flushed.

He shifted uncomfortably and added the words Annabelle had told him would be necessary. "These garments were purchased for you and you alone. No other female has ever worn them."

"Thank you," Nicola said stiffly.

That hadn't been the problem, then.

Laila continued to sing.

"I've been called away," he explained.

"Hey, Cool-e-oh," Laila said, falling back on the mattress and bouncing. "Guess what? I'm going to have your house's baby. I just love it so much!"

He…had no idea what to say to that.

"When will you return?" Nicola asked, toying with a loose thread on the blanket.

"I'm not sure, but I'll make sure someone is here to escort you to work if I can't return by morning."

"No worries. I don't work at Estellä over the weekend."

That's right. Tomorrow was Saturday.

"But we do have our double date," Laila said. "And it's gonna be fun!"

His hands fisted at his sides as he waited, hoping Nicola would speak up. But she remained silent, clearly still desiring to go, even after everything that had happened between them.

For the best, he reminded himself.

"I'll make sure you get there, as promised," he gritted out.

And now, he should go. He knew he should go. Yet still he hesitated. "I bought you a cell phone," he told Nicola. Annabelle had insisted. "It's in the top drawer of the nightstand. I bought one for myself, as well." It currently rested in a pocket in his robe.

"What's your number?" she asked.

"It is already programmed into the device." And it was the only one in there. The only one he would allow her to put in there. "Call me if you need me. For any reason." *Or even if you don't have one.*

She nodded, opened her mouth, closed it.

"Don't worry about anything. Stay calm."

"And sow joy," she said with a sigh. "I know the drill."

He didn't bother telling her to stay within the bounds of his property. The cloud would ensure that she did.

Without another word, Koldo flashed to the garden

of Germanus's temple. As many times as he'd been here throughout the centuries, he knew the area by heart. Two rivers flowed out of the alabaster columns in front and wound through the flowers, cascading over the sides of the cliff in the clouds to shower the stars. For the first time, however, the entire expanse was covered with Sent Ones. Hundreds of males and females surrounded him, the noise level utterly out of control.

Koldo flashed here, and he flashed there, searching for the soldiers belonging to Zacharel. He found them at the far left, in front of the alabaster steps and ivy-rich columns that led to the towering double doors of the temple.

Charlotte and Ronen winked and waved at him.

Elandra turned her back on him.

Malak was too busy staring at Bjorn to notice him.

Bjorn was too busy talking to Thane and Xerxes to notice Malak.

Jamila spotted him and frowned. She shoved her way over and said, "Things are going down at Estellä. Sirena has it out for your girl. Hates her, in fact. The things she does and says when Nicola's back is turned…" She shuddered.

The news surprised him. How could anyone find fault with such a gentle human? "I'll deal with her." Whoever—whatever—she was. "Do you know what Sirena is?"

"Yes. Evil."

"So you aren't sure?"

"No," she grumbled.

Monday, when he flashed Nicola to work, he would find a way to question this Sirena. She wasn't Nefas, and she wasn't demon. But she was something. And if she hated Nicola, she could be working for his father.

At this point, Koldo had to suspect everyone.

Axel sidled up to his side and patted him on the shoulder. "Glad you could leave Chesticles long enough to make an appearance."

"Call her that again, and I'll cut your heart from your chest and give it to her as a trophy." As he spoke, he spotted Malcolm and Magnus.

The two looked to be of Asian descent. Malcolm had dark hair dyed green at the ends, the strands sticking out in a single spike along the center of his head. He had eyes so pale they were almost white, and bones tattooed on his neck.

Magnus was as serious and clean-cut as any human businessman. Well, if "any" were six foot eight and three hundred pounds of muscle.

Axel waved the threat away. "May I recommend you peel my skin from my body, too?"

What could you say to a male like this?

His gaze landed on Thane. The warrior nodded a greeting.

Bjorn and Xerxes frowned as they looked up, up the steps at…Zacharel, who was walking onto the dais alongside the six other members of the Elite.

There were four males and three females, each representing one of Germanus's armies. Though they possessed the same wings of solid gold, that was their only similarity.

The blond and dark-eyed Lysander stepped forward, held up his hands, and the crowd instantly quieted. Expression serious, he said without any hint of emotion, "It pains me to be the bearer of bad news, but the time has come. You need to know the truth. You need to know that our king...our king is dead."

KOLDO REELED. He wasn't sure how much time had passed since Lysander had made his pronouncement, he only knew that time had indeed passed. Shouts of denial and despair had resounded, and, emotions high, chaos had ensued. Fights had broken out, Sent One against maniacal Sent One. Tears had been shed and the future of their kind had been bemoaned. Eventually, things had calmed enough for the meeting to continue. To end. Then, one by one, the armies had flown away. All but Zacharel's.

Zacharel had commanded them to stay, and so they had stayed.

Koldo paced back and forth, his body moving of its own accord. His leader was...their king was...Germanus was...dead. *Dead.*

Gone.

He never should have allowed his anger to override his affection for the male and keep him away from the temple. And not just his anger, but regret. He'd known Germanus would disapprove of his plans for his mother, and he hadn't wanted to give the male a chance to express his displeasure, to warn Koldo against his actions.

Now he would never again have the opportunity to sit with the Sent One who had fostered and nurtured him and soak in his many words of wisdom.

After everything Koldo had endured in his childhood, Germanus had been the only one to give him hope for the future. And now his body was dust, his spirit in the heavens with the Most High.

When could this have possibly...happened? The an-

swer slid into place before the question finished forming. The shaking of Nicola's office, he thought. At the
time, he'd guessed the shaking sprang from some kind
of isolated earthquake. But no. A great and powerful
being had died, and even the entire world had felt it.

But Koldo hadn't known, hadn't suspected. Had continued on, as if nothing was wrong.

Zacharel waved the soldiers closer. They stomped
forward, and Koldo fought for calm.

"We had planned to tell the armies this news at the
same time, but after such a strong reaction to our first
order of business...well." Zacharel cleared his throat.
"I want you to know that the Most High didn't want us
lost, even for a moment, and so He has placed a new
king in charge of this realm. His name is Clerici, and in
the coming months he will be summoning each of you
individually to meet you and reassure you."

Clerici. Meaning, *the clergy.* Koldo had never met
the male, but he had heard of him—heard he was fair,
just and driven to succeed.

But he wasn't Germanus.

"Z just gets right down to business, doesn't he?" Axel
muttered in his ear. "He's a man with balls of brass."

"We're warriors, not babies," Koldo snapped. "We
don't need any coddling." But oh, all he wanted was to
return to Nicola, tug her into his lap and bury his face
in her hair. He would sob like the baby he'd just said
he wasn't, mourn for the father figure he'd turned his
back on.

She would wrap her arms around him and tell him
the pain of this loss would pass. And he would believe
her.

"*Someone's* on their period, isn't he?" Axel said.

A growl rose from deep in his chest. "Do you not regret the loss of Germanus?" Was he not torn apart inside?

"I didn't know him. Not really."

"Then you should regret *that*."

Zacharel continued to talk, but not about what Koldo most wanted to know. "How was he killed?" he finally interjected, able to stand it no longer.

Zacharel frowned. "That was explained during the—"

"Explain again!" A call from the depths of his bleeding soul.

At any other time, Zacharel would have struck him down, he was sure. Instead his jade-green eyes radiated sympathy. "Lucifer decided to make another power play for mankind and sent six of his best soldiers to kill our king. They didn't kill him right away, but absconded with him and tempted him to evil before delivering the deathblow. These demons are the worst of the worst, and they aren't through with their plan for destruction."

Demons.

Fury burned his chest. Fury and sorrow. Guilt and remorse.

"Why didn't you summon us sooner?" Thane growled, his own restraint bursting. "We could have hunted the attackers. Killed them before they delivered the final blow."

"And we would have liked it," Bjorn snarled.

Zacharel's expression was grim. "You know as well as I that the only way the demons were able to reach Germanus was because he allowed it. For whatever reason, he allowed it. There was nothing you could do that we weren't already doing. But we *shall* employ your skills now, for the demons are on earth and in hiding. We have reason to believe they're planning to build armies of possessed humans, making it impossible for us to fight effectively."

Because the humans weren't to be harmed. Because the humans couldn't be possessed unwillingly. They had to fall to the toxin or welcome the demons with open arms.

"They must be found," Zacharel continued, "and they must be stopped before their evil spreads like the disease it is. And you, my soldiers, are the ones charged with this task."

CHAPTER EIGHTEEN

ZACHAREL DISMISSED EVERYONE except Koldo and Axel.

Thane, Bjorn and Xerxes flew up and darted west. The females stepped from the cloud and arrowed down, toward the earth. Each person wore a similar expression: a blend of shock and horror, fury and determination.

Koldo wanted to curse. There was only one reason to keep him here—an assignment that would prevent him from hunting the demons responsible for Germanus's death.

"A horde of Nefas and serp demons did some damage to a park in Wichita, Kansas." Zacharel rattled off the coordinates. "Clerici has asked that I send the two of you to clean the mess and find the culprits, since you each have a personal stake in this."

"Because we fought the serp scum a few days ago," Axel said, a statement rather than a question.

Zacharel's piercing green gaze locked on Koldo. "That's one of the reasons, yes."

He didn't know. He couldn't know. Not even Germanus had known about Koldo's origins. Zacharel had to be referring to the fact that Nicola was involved. "I'll take care of this. Alone." His father's people had done the damage, and so Koldo would be the one to fight the battle—and finally wipe out the entire clan. "And then I'll hunt the demons responsible for this travesty."

Zacharel arched a brow, amused rather than irritated. "Actually, you'll do it together. I've decided to make your partnership permanent. And no, you won't be hunting the demons responsible for the king's demise. You're too busy guarding the human."

"I can do both."

"But you won't. You singled her out, and I allowed you to bring her into our world because I wanted to see you happy. I know how drastically love can change your—"

"I don't love her," he said in a rush. He couldn't.

Zacharel patted him on the shoulder. "You agreed to look after her, and you cannot do that if you're never with her."

Bottom line: he had to choose between helping Nicola and avenging his dearest friend. "If your men haven't found the demons by the time Nicola is healed and able to defend herself, I'll take over the hunt."

"Take over? No. One day, however, I might allow you to *join* the hunt. One thing you need to learn, Koldo," Zacharel said tightly. "You can't do everything on your own. Sometimes you have to accept help. It's a lesson I had to learn, as well." With that, the Sent One flared his golden wings and shot straight into the night.

"Should we get rings to seal this deal, life partner?" Axel asked, stroking his chin.

"One day I'll probably remove your head," Koldo replied, and flashed to the park in Wichita.

The change in time zones brought him to a sun-drenched paradise. Humans strolled through the grass and along the cobbled walkway. Mothers pushed strollers, men walked their dogs. Trees stretched high, casting shadows. He knew this was where Nicola and Laila had spotted his father, but where was the mess Zacharel had mentioned?

He dug the phone out of his pocket and dialed Nicola's number. After three rings, she picked up.

"Hello?"

The sound of her voice soothed the roughest edges of his emotions—and the knowledge irritated him. "Where did you see the bald man?"

"Oh." She described the area.

"Thank you." A pause. "I'll be late."

"No worries."

He cleared his throat. "Are you wearing the pajamas I got you?"

"I am. But, Koldo—is everything okay? You sound upset."

Do you care? he wanted to ask.

Axel landed beside him, wings snapping into place at his back.

"I must go," Koldo said, shifting from one booted foot to another. "I'll speak to you soon." He closed the phone and stuffed it back in his pocket.

"So...no rings?" Axel asked, as if their conversation had never lagged.

Koldo picked up where he'd left off, as well. "One day might be today." He walked until he reached the location Nicola had described. There! Tracks. He pounded forward and crouched in front of a pair of footprints. The soles of the boots had been spiked with serp venom, leaving the grass singed. It was a pattern he knew well. His father or one of his men had stood in this very spot and—

He sniffed. And infected the bark of the tree, as well.

Frowning, Koldo studied the trunk. Several areas had been scraped and left jagged by sharpened claws. The sulfur-scented black smoke the Nefas projected covered the wood. There appeared to be hundreds of tiny bugs crawling from the damage.

Already the tree bore signs of impending death. The leaves were withering. The grass around it had yellowed. Several dead birds lay in its shade. A nearby dog had attempted to mark the tree but was now hopping around next to its owner and whimpering, its paws probably burning.

"What's the damage?" Axel asked, stepping up beside him.

"Have you ever been exposed to Nefas smoke?"

"Well, yeah. Who hasn't?"

Almost everyone still breathing. But all right. Axel knew what to expect if he allowed himself to so much as brush against the stuff. "Check all the other trees. Any bearing the taint will have to be uprooted, the entire area cleansed."

"So you plan to be the boss in our little partnership?" Axel asked casually.

Koldo ignored the question. "Do you have a cloud?"

"Is this silly-question day? Of course I have a cloud."

"Summon it."

Axel nodded, and a split second later, white mist enveloped them.

"Let the humans see the park," Axel told the cloud, "but don't allow them to come near us."

As the mist cleared, becoming translucent to the eye and somewhat solid to the touch, forming a bubble around them, Koldo jumped into the necessary work. The venom and smoke wouldn't kill him, but it would weaken him. Still, he wrapped his arms around the tree trunk and, using all of his strength, ripped the roots from the ground. He tossed the entire thing into an air pocket to be burned later. He also scooped up every grain of dirt bearing the sharp, telltale aroma of the smoke. He picked up every fallen leaf, even the dead birds.

"There were five others," Axel said, returning to his side.

They spent the next few hours on cleanup, Koldo leaving pieces of the cloud around each of the sites, preventing any humans from seeing what had been done. Tonight, when the people were tucked safely in their beds, Axel could remove the barrier. The humans would arrive tomorrow morning and assume what they would about this "travesty."

"What do you know about the Nefas?" he asked Axel as they picked up the last of the infected leaves.

"They like to attack humans, Sent Ones, or anyone, for that matter, and they think rules, compassion and generosity are stupid. Oh, yeah, and they're as bad as demons."

Koldo nodded. "They're planners. They do little things at first, to see how their opponent will react, as well as to elicit as much fear as possible, since fear confuses, weakens and makes you do things you wouldn't normally do."

"Your mother took your wings, but I'll take your heart and feed it to the dogs," his father said. The silver glint of a blade he held waved in the light. "Do you want me to take your heart, boy?"

Why not? You've already broken it. "I want you to

die." He sat in the far corner of his cage, dirty and blood-caked from his many failed attempts to escape.

A mocking laugh boomed. "Too bad. I'm here to stay. And I've given you five days to do what I commanded you to do. Now, you have five seconds to do it. Kill the human or else. One."

"Someday I'll make you suffer for this."

"Three."

"Someday soon."

"Five." Hinges squeaked as the door to a cage he could not flash in and out of was thrown open.

Koldo jumped to shaky feet, stalked over to the trembling human that had been shoved into the cell and struck.

In the present, he ground his fists into his eyes to disrupt the sickening crimson-soaked images behind them. If he could go back... He so wanted to go back.

You have to forgive yourself, Nicola had said.

He doubted she would have uttered those words if she'd known even half of the things he'd done. He should have died rather than cave to his father's demands. He should have—

Concentrate. Distraction killed. Right. So. An old war had now been renewed. Strike one, Nox had appeared to Nicola. Strike two, the decimation of this park. The third would happen all too soon—but it would be by Koldo's hand.

He would bet his father had left a man behind, someone to watch the area to report Koldo's every reaction. He gazed around, and sure enough, he spotted a tall male with a bald head and the dark eyes of a predator at the pretzel stand, buying a midday snack and peering at the right area.

Even though the contact with the smoke had left him a little shaky, Koldo stepped from the protection of the cloud, allowing the Nefas to spot him.

The male grinned a wide, toothy grin, his fangs gleaming bright white as he approached. The smoke wasn't seeping from his pores. The bodily function was something all Nefas could control; most days they simply opted not to.

"We're doing this, are we?" Axel asked, sounding excited. "Well, okay, then. Good thing I strapped on my big-boy panties today."

Anticipation buzzed through Koldo. He met his enemy in the middle, studied him anew. They'd never met before. Either the male was younger than Koldo by several centuries, or his father had stolen him from another Nefas clan.

He munched on his treat, as if he hadn't a care in the world, assuming Koldo would do nothing in front of human witnesses. "Took you long enough to gather your courage and show up," said the Nefas in a too-deep voice. "I have a message for you, Koldo the Terrible."

Koldo had no desire to hear the rest. All Nefas could flash and he had to act quickly. In one fluid motion, he withdrew his double-edged short swords from the air pocket he used to store his weapons and struck, crossing his wrists to form a giant pair of scissors.

"Cloud," Axel said, as the man's head detached from his body.

The cloud was there in an instant, shielding the happenings as both pieces thudded to the ground and a pool of black blood formed.

"Well, the pretzel's ruined," the warrior added conversationally. "So you weren't curious about his message?"

"No. I knew what he was going to say." A hello from Koldo's father, as well as a threat to Nicola, all in an attempt to draw out Koldo's apprehension.

"Mind sharing with the rest of the class?"

"I do."

"Fair enough, since I wasn't really interested. But I gotta say, I am *so* proud right now." Axel flattened his hand over his heart. "You borrowed my patented move, proving I'm made of more than awesome. I'm awesalicious. Is that a word? It's probably a girl word, but who cares! Seriously. Do you see a tear in my eye? Because I'm pretty sure I feel one."

Koldo didn't understand the man's humor, and yet, he realized he was coming to like Axel despite that. He was strong, courageous and never backed down from a fight. He never allowed Koldo's moods to affect his own, and he was happy to do anything Koldo asked. Or demanded.

What was the male's history?

"You're very weird," Koldo observed.

"Nah. I'm mysterious. There's a big difference."

"You're definitely weird."

Koldo placed the body and the head in the air pocket with the trees and dirt, and searched for any other spiked footprints. He found none, but then, he hadn't expected to. Had only hoped his father would have left a trail behind, thinking to lead him into a trap.

A trap you knew about wasn't actually a trap—but a weapon.

"So, where do you want to go from here?" Axel asked.

"I need to burn the air pocket and check on the females. Let's meet tomorrow night and go hunting for the Nefas."

"Color me there."

MORNING ARRIVED, sunlight seeping through the crack in the curtains covering Nicola's bedroom window. She stretched muscles gone tight, and sat up. After she'd tucked Laila into bed, she'd reclaimed her spot on the couch and read. After a while, she'd closed her eyes, thinking to recharge, and then…nothing until now.

She hadn't made it to the bed, but she was there now. She hadn't covered herself up, but she was wrapped in the comforter. There was no way Laila had carried her, so that could only mean Koldo had returned. He just hadn't woken her up.

Argh! He was too sweet for his own good. Now she couldn't avoid him forever and pretend the kiss had never happened. Now she had to face him and thank him for his kindness.

She grumbled as she lumbered out of bed, grumbled as she brushed her teeth and showered, being careful of her new tattoos, and even grumbled as she pulled on an adorable pink top and glittery jean shorts.

The moment she looked at herself in the mirror, the grumbling stopped. She had worn hand-me-downs most of her life. Her parents had shopped at thrift stores, and then, when she had been in charge of her own finances, so had she. Now…look at her. It was… It was… amazing.

A groan bubbled from her. Once again, Koldo was responsible for something wonderful in her life. And really, for a little while during the kiss, she'd made him feel this same sense of awe. She'd made him feel special. She knew it, would never forget the way he'd trembled.

Maybe...maybe she wasn't such a bad choice for him, after all. Yes, she'd passed out during their second intimate moment together. And yes, she could pass out next time, too. But cutting him from her life rather than facing the infirmity and the embarrassment that followed? How silly could she get?

She might be weak—but she was stronger than that, she thought, anchoring her hair in a ponytail while the strands were still wet. It was her mother's hair, and she'd almost cut it a thousand times. But every time she'd grabbed the scissors, she'd remembered the way her mother used to brush and braid it, the way her father used to call her Mini Kerry, after her mom, and the way her brother used to tug on the ends.

Her brother. Her beautiful Robby.

We're sorry, Miss Lane, but your brother was thrown—

Nope, not going there. Thinking about him opened wounds that had never really healed. So, she always removed him from her thoughts before they had time to form.

Raising her chin, she marched out of her room and decided to check on her sister first. But Laila's bedroom was empty, the bed unmade and clothes strewn across the floor.

She moved through the living room—still no sign of her sister—and into the kitchen. Nicola breathed a sigh of relief when she spotted Laila at the table, her head resting in her upraised palm. A cup of tea steamed in front of her.

"Don't talk," her sister croaked. "Just...don't."

"Hangover?"

Laila groaned. "Co Co! Please."

"Sorry," she whispered. Nicola fixed a cup of tea for herself, and sipped at the hot, sweetened liquid.

"You should eat the fruit," a male voice said, and Laila issued another groan.

Nicola's heart sped into a faster beat as she twisted to face Koldo. He wore the same flowing white shirt and pants he'd worn at the hospital. There were lines of tension branching from his eyes. A tension that matched what she'd heard in his voice last night.

He paused to look her up and down, and his jaw dropped. He began a more leisurely perusal of her, his pupils expanding. "You...you..."

"Yes?" she asked hopefully. *Are beautiful? Stunning? Worth trying to kiss again?*

"Are wearing the clothing I picked for you." A croak.

"Yes." She waited. He said nothing more.

Seriously? That's all she got? The obvious? "I'll eat if you eat," she grumbled.

He thought for a moment, nodded stiffly and sat at the table. Nicola eased into the chair beside him. There was a plate piled high with oranges, strawberries, bananas and melon. She selected a strawberry and bit into the center, the juice running down her throat and making her moan.

"Oh, that's good." Almost enough to make her forget Koldo's lack of appreciation for her makeover. Almost.

He reached out and swiped a droplet that had dribbled onto her chin. Her eyes widened as he brought the finger to his mouth, and tasted. "It is," he agreed, a husky note to his voice.

Her skin tingled where he'd touched her, burning in

the most delectable way. And when his gaze lowered to where his finger had been, a gleam of satisfaction glowed in his eyes.

Okay, so she finally forgot.

"You're in better spirits today," he said.

She liked that he was so attuned to her. "I am."

"Why?"

Her unease with yesterday's kiss was private, something between them, not something to be shared even with her beloved twin. "So," she said, changing the subject. "Who decorated your house?"

There was a pause before he shrugged, and said, "I did," surprising her. What, no pushing for an answer? No deep concern for what had bothered her?

You're a mess. "Just so I'm clear, you decorated every room?"

"Yes, every room."

"But…there's so much pink in mine."

"And I can't like pink?"

Her eyes widened. "The room is yours?"

"No. But when I was younger and foolish, I hoped my moth—" He pressed his lips together. "Never mind."

Hoped his…mother would stay with him? What had made him think such a hope was foolish?

"Sorry, guys, but I'm in desperate need of a thousand profees." Laila stood, pushing back her chair. "And maybe a total body massage, a nap, an hour-long shower and a TV marathon of *How I Met Your Mother.*"

"Profees?" Koldo asked.

"Ibuprofen," Nicola explained.

"Once they kick in, I plan to get ready for my date. By the way, I'm sorry I busted into your room last night.

It won't happen again. Probably." Laila shambled out of the kitchen.

Koldo held Nicola's gaze. "Why the change?" he asked, pouncing the moment they were alone.

He'd known why she'd avoided the question. He'd cared. *Melting...* "I was embarrassed that I'd passed out."

A breath gushed from him, and she thought she caught threads of relief. "I never want you to be embarrassed with me, Nicola."

"Good, because I'm over it," she said. Mostly.

"So, you didn't regret what we had done? Didn't think I was too rough?"

"Not at all. You were amazing."

"Then why did you dress this way for your date?" he asked softly. "As if you crave another man's desire."

She gulped, then answered honestly, "I—I didn't." *I did it for you.*

A pause. Then, in a strained voice, "I don't want you to go. I...need you here. With me."

Nicola's stomach performed a series of flip-flops. The way he'd said the word *need*—he *did* care. And he'd issued a request this time, rather than a demand. Her own relief was palpable, her elation hard to tamp down. But... "I wish I could cancel. I really do." Just then, more than anything. "But you heard Laila. She's excited, and she won't go without me. And she's been so upset, and I've been so worried about the toxin inside her. I need her calm, peaceful and joyous."

"You can control your emotions, not hers."

"I know, but I have to try *something*." *Please understand.*

His hands were on the edge of the table, and his

knuckles began to bleach of color. Finally, the side of the table snapped off, wood chips raining on the floor. Koldo jumped to his feet and stomped from the room.

Leaving her alone.

So heartbreakingly alone.

CHAPTER NINETEEN

THANE LANDED IN THE CENTER of Teaze, a salon and dance club on earth that catered to immortals. Eleven women of varying species bustled around the small building, each prettier and more scantily clad than the last. The only male on the premises was William of the Dark, aka the Ever Randy, aka the warrior who refused to reveal his origins, and he was currently sitting in a swivel chair with sheets of foil in his hair.

"I know you're here," William said, sipping at a glass of what looked to be ambrosia-laced red wine.

Tensing, Thane stepped into the natural realm to fully reveal himself to the warrior. Immediately he smelled the sweet scent of the wine, the sharp odor of hair products, the pungent aroma of nail polish and the familiar fragrance of sex. Lots and lots of sex.

William must have bedded every single one of the stylists.

"How did you know?" No one could sense him when he had no wish to be sensed.

"He's been saying that every two minutes for the last hour," said the girl stepping up to William to remove the foil.

Electric-blue eyes glittered as William handed his glass to a female strolling past him—electric-blue eyes that reminded Thane of Axel. But then, there was a reason for that. "Did you have to ruin it, Lakeysha?"

The gorgeous black girl grinned widely. "Well, yeah. You ruined me for other men, so I thought I'd return the favor somehow."

Thane studied the building, halfway expecting their easy banter to be a trick, for an enemy to be waiting in the shadows, ready to attack him. He saw bricks and mortar, open indoor spaces with fifteen beauty chairs, or whatever they were called, and a row of round hair dryers and sinks. No menacing shadows. No swish of a weapon.

In the back was a big red door. If he were to walk through it, he knew he would enter the club, where there were small cages hanging from the ceiling, and poles stretching from individual tiers. A *thump, thump* of rock music shook the very foundation of the building.

"I should be offended," William said, having noticed Thane's darting gaze. "I've done nothing to earn your distrust."

"You live. You breathe. That's enough."

William had shacked up with the Lords of the Underworld—immortal warriors fighting to free themselves from the dark urges of the demons that oppressed them. He had spent centuries locked inside the prison Tartarus, both for his philandering ways and his savage temper. He would kill anyone at any time for any reason.

Without a doubt, he wasn't the most trustworthy of males. But intel was intel, and Thane wanted to know what he knew.

Thane had asked some of his shadier connections at the Downfall what they knew about the six demons responsible for the travesty in the skies, and while he had learned several interesting things, he hadn't learned anything of value.

"Clearly I got your message," William said. "You wanted to meet, so here we are. What do you want?"

Many things. They would start with information. "You are Lucifer's brother."

For a moment, the affable mask William sometimes wore fell away, revealing the vicious warrior at his core. "He's my adopted brother. Adopted. We're not blood."

"You were both fostered by Hades, the keeper of Sheol."

A pop of his jaw. "Yeah. So?"

So they both thought the same way. Surely. "Where are his minions? The six demons responsible for my king's death?"

"How should I know?"

An evasion. One that wouldn't be tolerated. "The demons are now living among the humans. You are now living among humans. They are evil. You are evil. They came from hell. You spent many centuries in hell. You should know where they went."

Far from offended by the description, William puffed up. "They could be anywhere. Everywhere. You'll have to draw them out."

"How?"

"Do I really need to do your job for you?" William shrugged wide shoulders. "Fine. I will. There might be a whole pack of you guys on their tails, but that doesn't mean you'll find them. So, put a bounty on their heads. Even their mothers would turn them in—if they had mothers, of course."

Every warrior instinct he possessed rebelled. "And take the kill out of my own hands?"

"But the job will be done, so I don't really see the problem."

Of course William saw no problem. He thought only of the goal, not the collateral damage. "The job may be done—but it may not. I wouldn't know for sure, since I had no part of it. And demons lie. They are never to be trusted."

The girl finished with the foil, and William waved her away.

"If I fail to destroy their forces," Thane added, "someone else will step into their role. Their plans must be stopped at the root."

William snickered like a teenage boy. "You said *root*."

This is one of the many reasons I kill demons. This right here. No, William wasn't actually a demon. He'd even fought and escaped hell, allowing light to shine in the darkness of his soul. But he'd since begun to race down the road that led back into the darkness. So, he qualified.

"Look. I have a feeling you'll be a little too busy shopping for bras to set a trap for the demons you want killed," William said. "You're a what? Forty-two C? Lakeysha over there will give you hers, I bet, freeing up your time and allowing you to do as I suggested."

Thane had to admire his courage. "As I said, demons lie. Demons cheat. I will never trust them to do the job for me. I or someone I trust will make the kill. What can you do to aid me?"

"Nothing."

Perhaps the warrior would reconsider. "I know you have always desired to know who your real parents are."

William stilled, and for a moment, he appeared to stop breathing.

"I can help you with that," Thane said. "Aid for aid."

A sharp inhalation of breath, proving the action hadn't malfunctioned permanently. "Fine. I'll set a meeting with Maleah. You've heard of her, I'm guessing?"

Maleah. Who *hadn't* heard of her?

Once a Sent One, she had been the most decorated soldier in their realm of the skies. She had been so decorated, in fact, that scheduling a meeting with her had been harder than scheduling a meeting with the king. Then, one day, she was gone, fallen, and no one had known why or what had happened.

"Set the meeting," Thane said. "As for the information I owe, check with the Sent One named Axel. I think you'll discover something very interesting during your first conversation."

THANE, BJORN AND XERXES armed themselves for war.

The meeting with Maleah was scheduled to happen in half an hour. William had worked fast—and the childish male would have snickered had he heard Thane's thoughts on the matter.

Thane had returned home with just enough time to bed a new female in an effort to clear his mind and ease the growing pressure to succeed. Afterward, he had alerted his boys. At least Kendra wouldn't be bothering him again. Yesterday, he'd done the unthinkable.

He'd given her to her people.

The number of Phoenix had severely declined over the centuries, since very few of their women were able to conceive. That was why the males continually hunted the females. If one was ever found, she was immediately whisked to a Phoenix camp—and kept there forevermore.

By now, Kendra had been wedded to a warrior. By now, she was once again a slave.

Thane should feel guilty.

He didn't feel guilty.

He probably never would.

"I've felt the tension in this realm of the heavens, as well as the earth, and knew it was a prelude to the coming war," Bjorn said. "I knew an enemy was planning some kind of attack, but I assumed that enemy would spring from the Titans trying to overtake and rule the world."

"Titans…demons…what's the difference?" Xerxes said.

Not much. "I wouldn't be surprised to find out they're working together."

Thane finished snapping the metal on his arms, each etched with number after number to represent the Most High's promise for strength, then tugged on his gloves and smacked his friends on the shoulder. He preferred this armor over that formed by his robe. "No one comes to our territory and hurts our people. The demons wanted a war, and so we will give them a war."

"To the king," Bjorn said.

"He hadn't yet finished his course," Xerxes said, "but he's now at peace, his spirit in the Most High's realm of the heavens. A far better place."

They shared a moment of silence, each remembering the good the king had done them over the years.

Together, they stalked out of their suite and to the

roof of the club. Thane flared his wings. A darkened sky stretched all around him, stars glittering prettily.

"And now we will finish *our* course." Thane dived into the night, heading down, down, down, and angling west. Air whipped against his skin, tangled his hair, becoming warmer the closer he got to the ground, even when the snowcapped Sierra Nevada came into view. There was a wealth of pine trees, and a lake as clear as crystal. Human ski huts. Humans trudging through the snow.

And there was Maleah's place. A cabin comprised of stone and ice, hidden in a cliff. Sent Ones liked to dwell in the elements, and the fallen female must have clung to the habit.

Thane misted through the walls and found himself inside a room lacking any sort of comfort. There were computers, TV screens, radios and all kinds of other equipment, but no couches, cushions or blankets. No photos.

A female he'd heard about but never seen manned everything with a sharp eye and a constant tapping on a keyboard. She looked like a Goth princess, with her white skin, long white hair, multiple tattoos and piercings. A thick sweep of bangs hid her forehead and framed her big blue eyes.

Bjorn and Xerxes landed beside him.

"Pretty," Bjorn said, looking her over. "I hadn't heard that fact."

If she cooperated, perhaps he would take her to the Downfall for a few days of fun. If not...

He couldn't kill her. That would be against the rules. But he could do other unpleasant things.

"I expected you sooner," she said suddenly. Her chair

swiveled around, and she pinged Thane with an unwavering stare.

She shouldn't have been able to sense him. Just then,
she was human.

And *pretty* failed to do her justice, he realized. Her
features were bold, sensual. She had a thick fan of white
lashes, and heavy-lidded eyes. A strong nose, with a
piercing curling from both nostrils. Well-defined cheekbones. Lush lips, with two barbells beneath the lower.
A stubborn chin.

He stepped into the natural realm. "Impossible," he
said. "You knew exactly when I would come."

"I knew when you were *scheduled* to come. I thought
you'd be in a bit more of a hurry." Her gaze swept over
him, taking him in. Whether or not she liked what she
saw, he couldn't be sure. Her hardened expression never
changed. "William said you were a cocky one."

She hadn't heard of him while she'd lived in the
skies. He was somewhat offended. "Are you his lover?"

She chuckled with genuine amusement—but she
never confirmed or denied.

Bjorn and Xerxes joined him in the natural, and she
gave the warriors the same once-over. Again, her expression remained blank, unreadable.

"Armed for war, I see," she said. "Against me?"
There was no fear in her tone. Only acceptance.

"Why did you fall?" Thane asked.

Another chuckle bubbled from her. "Yeah. Watch
me as I *don't* talk about that."

Very well. He would find out later. "What do you
know of the six demons—"

"Now hiding here on earth?" she asked, one brow
arched.

He stepped toward her, hands fisting. "Yes."

"I'll show you." She turned back to her monitors, began typing. "New York is a high crime area, right, but it ebbs and flows, and there's very rarely a huge and sudden spike. Things usually build. Well, last night there was a spike unlike any I've before seen. Murders, rapes, thefts, beatings, but most happened in the privacy of human homes and have gone unreported. And it wasn't just in a select area, but widespread."

"That proves nothing," he said.

She snorted. "As you know, the mere presence of a demon causes the very atmosphere and energy of a place to change."

"True, but that doesn't mean the spike was caused by demons."

"Whoever killed your king would now be weak. Germanus would have fought, and fought hard. The demons would have known you guys would soon be on their heels, and so they would have wanted to rebuild their strength quickly. As they fed on evil, they would have sent their minions to do the most damage possible."

Stunning and smart. Yes, he wanted her. "So they have spread out."

"Definitely." She pointed to a map of the world on a separate screen, tapping her finger against the reddened areas. "Each of these places had a similar spike."

"There are twelve places," Xerxes said, "yet only six demons."

She rolled her eyes, saying, "You know as well as I that we aren't unwise to the schemes of the enemy. They would have known we could track them this way, and they would have wanted a way to circumvent that. Hence the minions I mentioned."

We, she'd said, as if she were still part of an army. "You think they're commanding their forces to attack other areas, away from them, to divide our efforts."

"Exactly."

He, Bjorn and Xerxes shared a look. She was probably right—and they should have figured that out on their own.

So where do we start? Xerxes asked, his voice whispering through Thane's mind. They could communicate with every member of Zacharel's army this way—if they so chose—but they preferred to speak only with each other.

I don't think it matters, Bjorn said. *No matter where we go, we'll be destroying part of a demon army.*

True. *But the six leaders will be concentrating their efforts on gaining control of the humans. The more humans they recruit, the less we can do to fight back.*

So again, where do you want to start? Xerxes asked.

"Hasn't anyone ever told you that it's rude to mind-talk in front of a girl?" Maleah muttered.

Thane ignored her. He thought for a moment. *We'll split up, each take an area. If one of the six is discovered, the finder will alert the others and we'll go in together.*

Bjorn nodded.

Xerxes stiffened. *Very well.*

Since their rescue from that demon dungeon, they had spent no more than a single night apart. They had always had each other's backs. But to stay together now was to slow their search, and they owed the former king more than that.

I'll take New York, Bjorn said.

I'll take the Highlands, Xerxes said.

Las Vegas was the second-biggest red dot, but...

I'll take Auckland. I have a house there. Thane protected what was his.

He clasped Bjorn's hand and pulled him in for something the humans called a chest bump. Then, Bjorn flared his wings and was off. He did the same with Xerxes, and he, too, darted away.

"Thank you so much, Maleah," the girl muttered with a shake of her head. "You helped us tremendously, Maleah, and we couldn't have done this without you."

"That has yet to be proven," Thane told her.

She tossed him a scowl. "You better learn some manners before you approach me again. Otherwise, I won't give you any new information."

"A promise?"

"A threat."

He fought a grin. He had yet to meet a female who could resist him for long. And that wasn't pride talking, but truth. Too many ladies had a weakness for a pretty face, and he had a face prettier than most. He would have been saddened by the fact that so few cared to look beyond the surface at the man inside if he'd ever actually wanted a female to see the man inside.

"Why do you do this, anyway?" he asked Maleah. "You cannot buy your way back." No one could. Some Sent Ones *had* returned to the heavens after falling, but actions had had nothing to do with it. They'd had to approach the Most High and ask.

"I know I can't," she said softly.

"Then why do you do this?" he asked again.

She didn't face him, but he could see that her smile

was sad. "You're probably intimately acquainted with my answer."

"And that is?"

"Regret."

CHAPTER TWENTY

NICOLA WANTED TO BE anywhere other than a fancy steak house with two men she barely knew. But she was determined to have a good time for her sister's sake. And so far, everyone at the table believed she was.

"—and so, about two years in, I realized she'd been cheating on me with my brother for most of our relationship. And you know what? That wasn't even the worst thing she did!" Blaine, Laila's date, told another story about the woman who'd broken his heart, ruined his life and left him tangled in all kinds of emotional wreckage, only stopping long enough to gulp the rest of his fifth beer.

Laila placed her hand over her heart, her eyes watery as she listened raptly and tried to offer comfort.

Dex rubbed the back of his neck.

Nicola forced a smile and shifted in her seat. She'd ditched the comfortable, pretty clothes Koldo had given her in favor of the black dress she'd worn to the triple funeral for her mom, her dad and her brother. It had seemed like a good idea when she'd pulled it out of the closet. After all, it was probably better to look outdated than to wear what one man had bought her while spending the evening with another. But she'd put on a little weight, and the material was constricting, making it difficult to breathe.

Koldo had taken one look at her and scowled. "*That's* how you want the human to see you?"

How could she have responded to that?

After that, he'd lectured her about safety, ending with, "Do you have your phone? You had better have your phone. Call me if he does anything you don't like. Or if he doesn't like something you do. And don't forget you have the tattoos on your arm. And don't forget you can call upon the Most High."

"I won't. Daddy."

His scowl had darkened before he'd flashed her and Laila to her house. Then, he'd commanded her to stand still while he ran his burning-hot hands all over her face, her arms, even her legs—smearing every inch of exposed skin with some kind of glittery lotion. *Then,* without an explanation, he'd vanished. She hadn't seen him since. But at least he hadn't taken his warmth with him. For the first time in her life, she wasn't wearing a sweater, wasn't pressed up against the living furnace known as Koldo, yet her body temperature was properly regulated. She wasn't shivering.

Dex and Blaine had arrived soon after that, and here they were, at Kodiak. They sat at a small table illuminated by candlelight, the thrum of a harp playing softly in the background.

Laila looked gorgeous in a red satin sheath dress Koldo had purchased, with her pale hair tumbling down her shoulders. Blaine wore a dark suit and tie, both of which were askew. Dex also wore a dark suit and tie, the perfect complement to his lean build. He'd been nothing but solicitous, eager to please, and had hung on her every word. Every woman needed to date a man like him at least once. But, despite all that…she still wanted Koldo. Only Koldo.

"So," Dex said, tracing her knuckles to pull her into a private conversation probably meant to tune out Blaine.

There was no heat in their touch, no tingles. "So," she said.

He frowned, even paled, and drew back his hand. He looked down, studying his fingers in the light.

"Is something wrong?" she asked.

"No. No. I just… I thought I felt a terrible… Uh, never mind." He forced a laugh. "So you got tattoos, huh?"

"Yes."

"I never would have guessed."

Her, either.

"Why numbers?" he asked.

"Why not?" she said, because she had no other believable response.

He shrugged, saying, "Fair enough. So did I tell you that I haven't been on a date in months?"

"But why?" The moment the words left her mouth, she realized her mistake and blushed. "I'm so sorry. That was such a rude question. And I have no room to judge. I haven't been on a date in years."

He sipped at his wine, studying her over the rim of the glass. "That's impossible. Every man at the office is halfway in love with you. And if you had ever shown the slightest bit of interest, they would have been *fully* in love with you."

In love with *her?* There was just no way. "Why would they want…" Another rude question, and one she wouldn't finish.

"Why would they want you?" Dex asked, completing the sentence for her. He gave another laugh, this one relaxed. "You're so composed, so quiet, and you've been so sad lately. It's become a compulsion to make you smile. You're more beautiful every time I look at you, yet you have no idea. And I could go on and on."

"Thank you," she replied softly. If she didn't change the subject she would burst into flames. "So...have you spent any time with Jamila and Sirena?"

He'd been in the process of swallowing another sip of wine and choked. He coughed, beat at his chest.

"Are you okay?"

"Fine, fine," he wheezed. "Uh, what makes you ask about those two?"

"I was just wondering how they seem to be doing to the rest of the office."

"Oh, uh, great I think. I...haven't really cared to find out about them."

The waiter arrived with the food, set the plates on the table, and Dex released a relieved breath. The sharp scent of the spices hit her, and her stomach twisted with hunger, a voracious appetite demanding attention. Just then, she wished she'd ordered a juicy rib eye rather than a bowl of fettuccine.

"Tell me more about your recovery process," Laila said—and Blaine did just that.

"They're sure getting along," Dex said, again reaching out to pat Nicola's hand.

The table never shook, and yet his wineglass suddenly tipped over, the dark red liquid quickly spilling over his jacket and pants. Yelping, he jumped up.

"Excuse me," he gritted out before hurrying to the men's room.

"You're acting like a child," Axel said.

"That's funny, coming from you," Koldo replied through clenched teeth.

"You threw alcohol at a puny human male."

"He's lucky to still be alive. I could have thrown daggers."

"Wait. Did you think I was complaining? I was actually cheering."

They'd stood beside the foursome's table for the past twenty minutes, watching the couples interact.

Koldo had arrived in a bad mood, and that mood had only grown worse. He'd tracked his father, and it'd been easy to do. Every flash left an imprint in the air that was vacated, and Nox had done a lot of flashing. But the trail had led to Nicola's house and grown cold, a fact that had enraged Koldo. A rage he wouldn't allow himself to express. He had a woman under his care now. No longer could he give his temper free rein. What if he scared Nicola? Or inadvertently hurt her?

Axel, who could find anyone, anywhere, had had no luck with the Nefas. So, they'd given up for the time being and come here.

Koldo had nearly dialed her number a thousand times. He wanted to tell her how beautiful she looked— so beautiful he hadn't wanted the other male to see her. He wanted to tell her that he was sorry for snapping at her.

He wanted to tell her that her date was a liar and a sex fiend.

Dex was the one Koldo had seen having sex with Sirena right on top of Nicola's desk, that time he'd visited her office. And now the male was pretending not to know the girl.

With every second that passed, one fact had become stunningly clear. Koldo should have gathered Nicola in his arms and staked a real claim. Another kiss. Only longer. Deeper.

She belongs to me.

And it was time he proved it.

A moment passed. He nodded. Yes, it was indeed time he proved it. Poor Nicola.

He was half-Nefas. He was dangerous. He was disgusting. He was evil. Already his past had risen up to threaten her. He had no wings. He'd never been with a woman, wasn't sure how to please her in that way and wasn't sure how he would feel afterward.

She'd had so little joy in her too-short life. Everything she'd ever loved had been stolen from her. If Koldo kept her, romantically speaking, she would be no better off. His time would be divided between her, his mother, his father and ultimately his duties. And what would happen to Nicola if ever he fell from the skies?

Still, that hadn't stopped him from spreading his essentia all over her little body today, marking her and warning all other males away.

Now there was a radiant, golden sheen to her skin.

Koldo could see it, and he knew Axel could see it. But not Dex. And yet, the human had felt the heat of it when he'd dared to reach out and touch what belonged to Koldo. An action that had nearly gotten him killed. Koldo had snarled and launched forward, determined to remove the human's head from his body—and would have, if Axel hadn't tackled him to the ground.

She deserved better than Dex. Better than Koldo. But…she wasn't going to get it, and that was that. She was getting Koldo. All the other details could be worked out later.

Blood might stain his hands, but he would only ever treat her with tenderness. And she wasn't like Cornelia and Nox; he'd already realized that. She would never treat him with hatred and cruelty.

She'd made him laugh while he was at his worst. He loved having her in his arms. He loved having her in his lap. He loved talking to her, teaching her, listening to her wit and her observations, simply breathing her in. He loved tasting her, and now wanted all of her.

Why try to find another woman, an imitation, when he had the real thing already? Nicola was the most beautiful creature he'd ever beheld, and he wanted… everything from her. He wanted to hold her. He wanted to see her with her hair flowing down her back. He wanted to hear more stories about her childhood. He wanted to avenge the wrongs done to her.

He just…wanted.

And he would have those things—and more.

One day you'll want a woman, Nox had said in one of his "teaching" moments. *You'll do anything to have her.*

At the time, he'd scoffed. Now? He realized the truth of those words.

But once you have her, you'll be done with her. Your curiosity will be assuaged, the obsession will fade, and you can turn your eye to the next conquest.

Is that what happened with my mother? Koldo had asked. *You wanted, you had, and you no longer desired.*

Nox had belted out a deep, rumbling chuckle. *Exactly. But oh, I did enjoy her in the meantime.*

Maybe Koldo would lose interest in Nicola, too, but maybe he wouldn't. His father's word wasn't exactly trustworthy, though Koldo *had* seen evidence to support his claim. Thane, Bjorn and Xerxes certainly seemed to think females were disposable.

But that didn't matter. Koldo would fight the attraction no longer. He wouldn't worry about what could go wrong, what Nicola might want or what might happen in the future. He'd told her not to fret about her illness or anything else, that it would only harm her, and now he was going to take his own advice.

He just had to figure out how to proceed.

"You look like you're ready to have the redhead for dinner," Axel said, as though reading his thoughts. "Just reveal yourself, flash her home and do your business. That way we can get back to tracking the Nefas."

"And if she fights me in public?"

"There's only a 49 percent chance she'll actually win, so you should be safe."

"Can you not be serious?"

"When it comes to math, I'm always serious. Just do something or leave," Axel said, buffing his nails. "I'm bored. Bad things happen when I'm bored."

"The Nefas trail went cold," he reminded the warrior. "All we can do is ask around, and try to find their nest. And if that fails, all we can do is wait for their next attack. You have nothing better to do."

He looked at Nicola, who was now picking at her food, watching her sister. Before Dex had raced away, she'd peered at the pasta with a hunger Koldo had wanted directed at *him*.

He looked at Laila, who had pushed her food away without taking a single bite and propped her elbows on the table. While Blaine shoveled in his pork chop and told her another story about his former lover, she dabbed at her watery eyes, sympathetic to his pain.

Dex came around the far corner, his jacket hanging over his arm. His plain white shirt bore a few splatters of red, and there was a damp spot on the left side of his pants. He was sullen as he reclaimed his seat.

"We can leave," Nicola offered.

"That's all right," Dex replied stiffly. "My vanity took a hard knock, that's all."

"Well, maybe there's something I can do to help." Nibbling on her lower lip, Nicola grabbed her water glass, drew in a deep breath and poured half the contents into her lap.

Dex's jaw dropped as she gasped and grinned—and Koldo hated that another male was seeing her so relaxed, so happy, and that she was striving so diligently to entertain, to please.

"Now we both look like we peed our pants," she said.

A bark of laughter boomed from the male.

Laughter that should have been Koldo's.

"Okay, *I* might have to fight you for her," Axel said. "That was seriously cool."

Koldo flashed to outside the restaurant, mentally commanded his robe to become a black shirt and black pants, and marched back inside, this time in the natural realm, where everyone could see him.

The hostesses spied him, and could only gape. Several groups were waiting for a table, and they gave him a wide berth. Gasps sounded. Murmurs arose. He didn't bother speaking to any of the humans, and marched straight to Nicola's table. Conversations ceased. He could imagine Axel laughing, but thankfully couldn't see or hear him.

Dex spotted him, and his fork paused midair. His eyes widened. "You!"

Blaine caught sight of him and straightened in his seat with a snap.

"What—" Laila began, only to look up and groan. "Oh, no."

Nicola glanced up, and performed a double take. "Koldo. What are you doing here?"

"You know him?" Dex asked with a wheeze.

Koldo peered down at the table's occupants. He should have thought this through a little more, he realized. He had no idea what to say. "Nicola," he began.

"Yes?" She tossed her napkin on the table and stood. The bottom half of her dress was soaked, water droplets trickling down her bare legs.

He towered over her, and that should have dissuaded him. He could hurt her without ever realizing it, and could damage her badly enough to kill her. But their eyes met, and his blood heated, and he knew he couldn't go another night without having her in his arms.

"Your sister has had her fun, yes?"

"Uh, not really," Nicola said, looking at Laila's tear-streaked face. "If anything, she's sadder than ever. Sorry, Blaine, but it's true."

"That can be fixed." To Axel, who he still couldn't see, he commanded, "Take care of the sister. Make her happy." He took Nicola's hand and tugged her toward the exit.

"Koldo," she gasped, though she offered no resistance. "Seriously. What's going on? Has something happened?"

In the background, he thought he heard someone ask if she wanted the police notified.

He tossed her a glance over his shoulder. "You're mine. And I'm keeping you."

CHAPTER TWENTY-ONE

THE MOMENT THEY CLEARED the doors, the night air enveloping them, Koldo wrapped Nicola in his arms and peered down at her. The rest of the world faded from her awareness. He was all that she saw as her mind churned with possibilities and problems. He was keeping her? They were innocent words, yet his tone had been intense, as if he was making a life-altering vow in front of a judge.

Was he trying to say they were an official couple now?

"What's going on?" she asked, really liking the thought. Except…

What if she wasn't enough for him? What if her heart never recovered, and she could never satisfy him physically?

Threads of yesterday's panic returned, weaving into new threads of fear, forming a noose around her neck and squeezing. *Come on, girl. You hopped off this road already. Don't jump back on.*

"Your circumstances have changed," Koldo said.

"I know, but…" *But? No buts!*

A sizzling pause as he searched her face. "Breathe."

"I'm trying."

"Try harder."

In. Out. Innn. Ouuut. There. Getting better, evening

out. Whatever happened to her, they would get through it together. She knew that. Could count on that—on him.

"Are you frightened?" he asked.

"Not of you," she replied truthfully.

"Of you, then. But I can fix that." He looked at her with the same intensity she heard in his voice, and with such heat. "Close your eyes."

"Why? Are you flashing me—"

He did. He flashed her. She blinked, and found herself standing in her bedroom in Panama. He released her...only to back her against the nearest wall.

Nicola gulped. "Laila—"

"Is being taken care of."

"Well, I have to apologize to Dex."

"You can. Tomorrow. You can mail him a card." He braced his hands at her temples, his heady scent wrapping around her as certainly as his arms had done. She breathed in deeply, her heartbeat careening out of control.

"You can't be with another man," he growled. "Not ever again. For any reason."

Despite the too-fast rhythm of her heart, the rest of the panic faded, both old and new. "I don't want to be with another man," she admitted.

He nodded with conviction. "You belong with me. Only ever me." Again, he sounded as though he was making a vow.

They *had to be* a couple.

"Do you understand the kind of girl you're getting?" She flattened her hands on his chest, the heat of him seeping through his shirt and brushing against her skin. "I'm just me, and I come with a few challenges."

He smiled, pleased. "I know that. What I don't know

is how to be in a relationship, but I'm going to learn. Along the way, I'm bound to make mistakes. You'll simply tell me when I mess up, and I'll fix it. Agreed?"

Melting faster... "Agreed."

He said no more. He simply pressed his lips into hers.

It wasn't the brutal kiss she expected from so determined a man, or the sweet and tender kiss they'd first shared. It was heat and electricity, need and want and obsession. Addiction and desire. A taking and a giving. An unwavering claim.

She moaned at the pleasure of it, and he lifted his head. He peered into her eyes, searching.

"I wasn't complaining," she said. "Promise."

Back in he went, kissing…kissing so deeply, surrounding her with the fever-heat of his skin. She could hardly believe this was happening. It was surreal. It was wondrous. He belonged to her—and there was no one here to stop him prematurely. They were alone.

Her heartbeat fluttered. Her limbs shook.

"All is well?" he rasped.

"Mmm-hmm."

He cupped her cheeks, his palms searing brands as he angled her however he desired. His pupils were blown, his lips red, swollen and moist. "You'll tell me if that changes?"

"Yes. But don't be surprised if I'm embarrassed by it."

"I told you. I never want you embarrassed with me. What happens happens, and we'll deal with it. We're in this together."

He'd taken the words from her mind—words of hope, now confirmed. *I'm more than melting. I'm falling for him. Hard.*

Back in he went, taking, giving. Her hands slid along his spine, her nails scraping over the fabric of his shirt.

"Under the clothing," he rasped. "I want your skin on mine."

A low growl rumbled from him as she obeyed, reaching under the hem of his shirt. Her fingertips stroked over his hard-won strength, and she marveled all over again. He was velvet over iron, perfection over perfection, and he smelled so good, all that sunshine reminding her of summer. Summer reminded her of blooming flowers and blooming flowers reminded her of colors, so many colors, and life, such vibrant life.

Life. Yes. That's what Koldo was. Around him, she was stronger, happier...freer. Like the flowers, she bloomed. He'd become the peace she'd never had.

"More," he said, and released her long enough to rip the garment over his head.

She reached for him. He grabbed her by the waist and lifted her off her feet. She wound her legs around his waist, and white lightning zinged through her veins.

"Did I tell you that you're mine?" he demanded.

A thrill stole through her. "You did. And you're mine." He was a gift, created with her every secret desire in mind, and she wanted so badly to be perfect for him. To be everything he needed. She *had* to remain aware, couldn't allow the infirmity to win. Not this time, and embarrassment had nothing to do with it. Only Koldo mattered.

His hands glided up, up, and kneaded her softly, then more tightly, wringing another moan out of her.

"This is good," he murmured.

"Beyond."

Their breath mingled, short panting rasps. He kissed

the corner of her mouth, along the side of her jaw, sometimes nibbling. Lower still, he licked at her neck, at her hammering pulse, her collarbone. Always he treated her as if he couldn't get enough of her, as if he wanted to taste every inch of her at once.

"But it's not enough," he said, coming back up to kiss her mouth.

She wrenched away with a moan. "I thought you just said—"

He pulled the top of her dress down, revealing more and more skin to explore. The protest died as he pressed her against the wall. He hadn't been insulting her. He'd been demanding more of her.

More she would happily give.

He slid his magnificent hands down...down, until finally reaching the *bottom* of her dress. He raised the hem higher and higher, until the material pooled around her waist. Cool air brushed against her, and sensation after carnal sensation shot through her.

He dragged his fingertips back down her thigh, eliciting one shiver after another. Then...he dragged those fingertips back up, leaving a trail of fire in his wake, and oh, this was...this was...so good, too good, too much after the stress of the evening, and...the fog formed in her head, just like before.

"Koldo," she tried to say, but his name was nothing more than a breath. He kissed her again, stealing what little she had left, and all the while those decadent fingers continued to give her the softest of caresses, taking her body to heights it wasn't ready to reach.

Her world tilted, and darkness descended.

Time ceased to exist. Noise faded. Sensation left her....

Suddenly, something patted at her cheek. Something cold swiped over her brow.

Frowning, Nicola tugged herself from the darkness and blinked open her eyes. Koldo loomed over her, and she—she was lying on the bed, her head resting on a plush, soft pillow. Her dress was in place, smoothed down her legs.

Oh, no. "It happened again, didn't it?"

"Yes. You passed out." His self-castigation was palpable. "I carried you to bed."

Even though she'd come to the realization that he would want her anyway, despite something like this, embarrassment still heated her cheeks, just as she'd suspected. "I'm so sorry, Koldo."

"Don't be. I pushed you for too much, too fast." His shirt once again covered his magnificent chest, and that was, perhaps, the greatest tragedy right now. "Next time, I'll go slower."

"Next time," she said, and wanted to purr with satisfaction.

He frowned. "You don't want a next time?"

More than anything. "What makes you think that I don't? Unless you don't want me to want a next time," she added in a rush. "Are you trying to hint that you want to go back to being just friends?"

He flattened his hand against her jawline, his thumb caressing her cheek. "Did you hit your head? Of course I don't want to just be your friend. And you should know me well enough to know I've never hinted at anything."

So true. She smiled at him. "Could you be any sweeter?"

His lips twitched at the corners. "First, I don't care if you pass out every time we do this. You are worth *any* effort. Second, I make you happy. Therefore, I'm aiding your healing."

Not just happy, she thought. *Delirious.*

"Do *you* wish to remain just friends?" he asked, and this time his tone was so sharp it could have cut her. His expression, however, was tortured. "I'm not a man willing to buy your affections, but perhaps I could do other things. Is there something you want that I haven't given you?"

Her heart lurched. "No," she admitted. "I don't want to be just friends. And you've given me everything." He was the man she'd thought about all evening. The man she'd wanted to be with. The man she'd craved.

He relaxed, nodded and moved his touch to her neck, where her pulse hammered wildly. "I like the kisses we share."

"I like them, too."

"I like the taste of you, the feel of you."

"Yes."

"I want the toxin out of you." His tone was layered with determination. "Forever."

Her, too. More than ever. And they had to change the subject before *she* pushed for too much too fast. "Say something to distract me. Please."

He peered at her for a long while before nodding, decided. Rolling to his side, he said, "The first time I saw you wasn't in the elevator."

"It wasn't?"

"No. The day before I was sent to the hospital to help a human male, and I stumbled into your sister's room. The Most High showed me that she was in the condition she was in because she'd entertained a demon of fear for so long, the demon was able to worm its way inside her body. He showed me because He wanted me to help her. Her, yes, but also you I think. You were in danger of succumbing the same way."

Nicola rested against him, finding comfort, companionship and acceptance, all wrapped into one tantalizing position, despite the topic. Or maybe because of it. Knowledge was power. "I was entertaining a demon? I mean, I know I had the toxin, but I just thought... I don't know what I thought."

"There were two of them hanging around you."

A gasp lodged in her throat. "But I never knew. Never saw them."

"If I have my way, you never will." He draped his arm over her neck in a gentle choke hold—gentle, but a choke hold nonetheless. He was as new to this kind of thing as she was, and she was suddenly fighting a smile.

"Tell me something about you," she said. "Something you've never told anyone else."

A long pause. He gulped. "When I was a child, I lived in constant fear. My mother hated me, and my father...abused me."

"Oh, Koldo. I'm so sorry." Had his father caused the scars?

"I never knew what horrors I would have to face next, only that I would, in fact, have to face them."

No wonder he was so fierce, so standoffish—so vulnerable and unsure. He had built a shell around himself, desperate to protect a fragile heart that had been trampled by the people who should have loved him most. People who instead had rejected him with their abuse.

She traced her fingers along the ridges of his stomach, wishing the shirt would disappear, then chiding herself for wishing.

"Ask me a question," he said. "Any question. I like sharing with you."

She thought for a moment. "Why were you so upset when we spoke on the phone after yesterday's meeting?"

"I had just found out a man I loved was killed."

"Oh, Koldo," she repeated. He had endured one blow after another, and the knowledge saddened her.

He took her hand, brought her knuckles to his lips and kissed. He next rubbed her hand over his cheeks, his jaw, his beard tickling her skin, before once again kissing her knuckles. "It's a punishment I deserved." The same guilt and shame she sometimes saw in his eyes now dripped from his tone.

"I'm going to say something, and I don't want you to be offended, all right?"

"All right," he said reluctantly.

"That's the most ridiculous thing I've ever heard! You did *not* deserve to lose a friend."

He relaxed the tiniest bit. "I haven't always been the man you know."

"And I haven't always been the girl you know."

He shook his head. "You've always been sweet, kind and caring, and that's that."

No. He didn't know the full truth—that she and Laila had once planned to murder the man responsible for the deaths of their parents and brother. And she would be forever grateful the plan had failed. A moment of rage would have changed the entire course of their lives, and not for the better.

But all she said to Koldo was, "You're making a mistake," and kissed his chest. There was no reason to spoil the moment. "And notice how wonderful I am, pointing it out just like you asked."

"Wonderful. Yes."

There'd been no sarcasm in his voice. Darling man. "Say-la," she interjected, recalling the way he'd once used the word with her.

He fell silent.

She traced an X over the heavy beat of his heart. "What does the word mean?"

"To pause and think about what was said."

Well, well. From now on, she might be using the word after everything she said. "So now that we've bared our souls, and I've blown your mind with my intelligence, what do you want to do for the rest of our date?"

"Rest. For what I have planned tomorrow, you're going to need it."

CHAPTER TWENTY-TWO

FOR THE FIRST TIME in his entire life, Koldo spent the night in bed with a woman. His woman. Something he'd wanted. Only, what he'd truly wanted was to strip Nicola, strip himself, kiss her, have her, have her again—and maybe again—and fall into a deep sleep. Then wake up and have her again. Physically, however, she wasn't ready for that.

Maybe he wasn't, either.

Next time, he needed to slow down, get them both ready. He'd loved the sensations coursing through him so much he'd verged on losing control. If that had happened, he could have taken her too forcefully. Hurt her the way he'd always feared.

A sobering thought.

A horrifying thought.

What a man feared came upon him. He knew that. So it was time to stop giving in and start fighting these worries the moment they came. To practice what he taught.

As they'd talked, and she'd snuggled into his side, he expected the rest of his arousal to fade. But it hadn't.

It had only gotten worse.

As she slept, her warm breath fanned over his neck in a decadent caress. Her heart beat in sync with his, connecting them in the subtlest of ways. Their scents blended, male musk with feminine sweetness, and all he'd wanted to do was pick up where they'd left off.

Can't. Won't.

Everything had to be perfect for her. He never wanted her to look back and wish or regret. He would rather die. He wouldn't be another tragedy in her life. He would be something else.

I have to be something special.

All of his strength was needed to remain still, ignoring the achiness of his body.

By the time the sun rose, he was trembling—and sweating and panting and far more desperate. He untangled from Nicola, and even though she was the source of his torment, he hated leaving her. She muttered a soft sigh and rolled to her stomach, strawberry hair still in a ponytail and spilling all over the pillows.

Can't dive on her. Really can't. He didn't bother with a shower before he flashed to a nearby lumberyard and gathered what he would need to build a second, smaller home in the backyard of the ranch. His clothing cleaning him inside and out.

Next, he got to work. He'd decided to move his mother to Panama.

She was a part of his life. A part he no longer wanted to hide from Nicola. Last night, telling her about his past, he'd discovered a peace unlike any other. He'd liked it. Now, he wanted her to know everything. He wanted to be completely honest with her. He wouldn't just tell her, though. He would show her.

One hour sped into another as he worked that morning, sawing and hammering. Eventually he removed his shirt. Sweat rolled down his chest and back, and the sun beat against his skin. His muscles welcomed the strain.

"Would you like something to drink?" Nicola called from the kitchen doorway. "I made lemonade."

He glanced up—and wished he hadn't. The arousal returned full force, as if he'd never moved away from her. She'd taken a shower and pulled her damp hair into another ponytail. Those storm eyes were bright, her cheeks rosy. Her lips were still plumped from his kisses. She wore a tight white T-shirt and jeans with rhinestones around the waist. So young. So fresh.

So his.

"No, thank you," he replied. If she came out here, he would grab her and never let go.

"Are you sure?" She held up a glass filled to the rim. "You look really, really hot. And I mean that in every way."

He paused, the hammer raised midair.

"What are you doing out there, anyway?" she asked.

"Building a cage."

He expected her to throw another question at him. She didn't. She said, "I bet you're working up quite a thirst."

I am. For you. "You don't want to know."

"I'll bet I do...."

Oh, no, you don't. "Are you flirting with me?"

"I am."

Confirmation. *Killing him.* "Go back inside, Nicola. Now."

A dreamy sigh left her. "*So* commanding. I never thought I'd have a snarly handyman fantasy, especially after I got mad at you for snarling just the other day."

He almost ditched the tools and stomped after her. Almost.

She walked away. A few seconds later, Axel strolled

out the door, his dark hair disheveled, his blue eyes glittering as he drank the lemonade that had been meant for Koldo. His wings were tucked into his back, and he wore the customary angel robe, the white gleaming in the sunlight.

"Hey, you know anything about an immortal named William of the Dark? He also goes by the alias Ever Randy. Because all of a sudden, for no reason, he's decided to track me down," Axel said between sips. "It's really getting to be annoying."

"No." The moment the warrior reached Koldo's side, Koldo snatched the glass and drained the contents. "Mine," he said.

"*So* not cool. Someone needs to learn the meaning of *hospitality*. And *sharing*. And *kindness*. And *brotherhood*. And *friendship*. And *selflessness*."

"I'll be sure to look the words up later." Koldo handed him the empty glass. "Thank you for taking care of Laila last night."

Axel tossed the glass into the bushes behind him. "Dude, that girl's got problems."

"I know."

"I probably shouldn't have slept with her."

Koldo was in the process of hammering another nail and on his next downward swing, hit so hard the end of the board snapped. Surely he hadn't just heard what he thought he'd heard. "You slept with her?"

Blink, blink. "What? I'm not a he-slut or anything. She was only my third lay of the day. And you told me to make her happy, right?"

Three. Three women. In one day? Koldo wanted Nicola and only Nicola, and couldn't imagine sharing his bed with anyone else. Yes, he'd entertained the idea of returning to Thane's club and taking the Harpy, and others, but he never would have been able to go through with it. He knew that now.

No other woman would be able to assuage the ache. No other woman would taste the same—sweetness and light. No other woman would be as soft. No other woman's moans would be as intoxicating. Oh, yes, only Nicola would do.

"Why is that vein throbbing in your temple?" Axel asked. "Laila's not your woman, right? Or is she? I've asked before but you've never said. Are you thinking about doing a sister-wife thing? Because it's totally not the party in the box you think it will be."

"No," he gritted. "Laila isn't mine." But he wasn't sure how Nicola would feel about her sister being with a Sent One that wouldn't keep her. "If you hurt her..."

"Hey," the warrior said, palms up. "I deprived her of Blainey Boo Bear, or whatever lame nickname humans like to give each other, and I owed her big fun—and no, that's not the name of my penis, even though it fits. They'd swapped so many stories about their exes they were both depressed. I did her a favor, and she kicked me out afterward, not the other way around. She just used me and ditched me, and made me feel all dirty inside. So *of course* I'm hoping we can do it again."

Koldo wiped his brow with the back of his hand. "And she didn't pass out?" he found himself asking.

"Well, yeah. Yours did, too, eh?"

He shouted, "And you took her anyway?"

"Hello. I woke her up first."

Koldo shook his head. The male had no shame.

"So we're building a cage?" Axel asked, as he

claimed a hammer of his own. "That's what you told Nicola, right?"

"No more questions," he said, looking away. His gaze landed on Nicola, perched next to her sister in front of the kitchen window, gazing out. She waved, unabashed at being caught staring. He swallowed a curse.

Desire wasn't supposed to hurt. Was it?

THOUGH THE TIME ZONES were off, Koldo knew when Monday morning dawned in Kansas, and flashed Nicola and Laila to the rear of the Estellä building. The girls hadn't wanted to be parted, and he'd liked the idea of having them both in the same location.

He materialized in the natural realm and walked the pair from the alley to the front door.

"You won't grant my request and quit?" he asked Nicola. "Even though it's dangerous here?"

"I won't."

Frustrating woman. "Why?"

"Because she won't always have you, but she'll always need the job," Laila answered.

He...had no protest, he realized. He planned to keep Nicola, but he was as uncertain about his future as any human. Actually, his was more uncertain than most.

"Very well," he replied, because really, there was nothing else to say. He stomped inside and into the confines of the elevator.

There were two other males in the tiny cart, and they pressed themselves against the far wall, getting as far away from him as they could. He forced his scowl to ease before the pair began screaming for aid.

"Don't look at the women, and you'll be fine," he said.

Instantly they averted their gazes.

Nicola's sweet perfume wafted around him, and his anger with her was lost to another punch of arousal. At what point would his body just shut down, the desire for this woman too much to endure? How was he supposed to ease her into making love without killing himself?

She leaned into him and whispered, "The last time we were in an elevator together, I wanted to sniff your neck."

He sucked in a breath. She really was going to kill him.

"I wonder how you would have reacted."

Laila gagged. "If you guys get any more lovey-dovey, I'm going to puke."

Nicola slapped her on the arm. Laila slapped her back, and the two erupted into a childish fight and a fit of giggles.

The elevator dinged, and the doors slid open. The men raced out, and the girls ceased their antics, acting as if they'd never attacked each other. Silly humans. But their play lightened his mood. Oh, to have a playmate.

He wasn't sure whether or not Axel had slept with Laila again last night, but either way, her color was better, and there was a bounce to her step.

Koldo wanted to put that same bounce in Nicola's step.

He took her hand—soft, delicate—and ushered her to her office. Jamila sat at one of the desks out front, dressed in a tight black dress, her dark hair piled on top of her head. Sirena was nowhere to be found.

Guard her, he projected into the Sent One's mind. An ability he was more and more comfortable using, he realized. Anything for Nicola's safety. *With your life.*

Jamila blinked in surprise, but nodded.

He yearned to kiss Nicola goodbye, but couldn't allow himself the luxury. At the moment of contact, he would convince himself it would be okay to take things further. Already his muscles were knotted. His blood was fever-hot. His palms itched.

"I'll be back," he growled, and didn't wait for Nicola's reply. Her expression was one of confusion, but now wasn't the time to explain his thoughts—and if he tried, he would only make things worse.

The moment he cleared the doorway, he entered the spirit realm. He stalked through the entire building, searching for unattached demons and lurking Nefas. He found neither.

He should have forced Nicola to quit, but…he couldn't bring himself to argue with her. He didn't want her mind on his stubbornness, didn't want her to think he was mean. How ridiculous was that? He *was* mean.

He just, he wanted her focused on her healing.

And that wasn't an attempt to buy her affection, he told himself. Even though, every time she looked at him with those big stormy eyes, he experienced a desperate urge to hand her the world.

He materialized in the natural before pushing through the door to the accounting offices. Jamila was exactly where he'd left her, but now, Sirena was also in place. Sirena, meaning *temptress*. And she was certainly that— for other men. She was the girl who had slept with Dex. The girl of questionable origins.

It was time to talk to her, and find out what she had planned.

When he loomed in front of her desk, she glanced up from polishing her nails. "Well, hello there, gorgeous."

Her bold gaze perused him from head to toe, lingering on his chest, between his legs, making him feel like a piece of meat. "You decided to return. I'm glad."

He flattened his hands beside her keyboard and leaned forward. "What are you?"

A sultry grin revealed a mouthful of pearly whites. "What do you want me to be?"

The pale haired, blue-eyed vixen failed to tempt him in any way, even though she would have been a more appropriate choice for his mate. Though she was small, she was stronger than a human, with a greater muscle tone hidden underneath her bulky clothes. He wouldn't break her, and her health wouldn't fail.

"What are you?" he repeated.

"Why, I'm Nicola Lane's coworker. What else?"

"You know what I mean."

She bopped the tip of his nose with a fingernail. "Do I?"

He'd always resented the fact that he couldn't taste another's lies. "You do."

"Maybe I do." A pause as she returned the lid to the polish. "You're Koldo, aren't you? The Sent One with a will of steel and a fist as hard as iron. I've been hoping to meet you for a very long time."

She was here for him, then, not Nicola. Sent by his father? he wondered again. To…what? "I'm a Sent One, yes, but I'm also Nicola's protector, and I'll destroy anyone who thinks to hurt her to get to me."

"Well, you're not doing a very good job with your protecting duties," she announced, and tsked. "I could have killed her at any time. And I wanted to, I admit it. Resisting has proven difficult."

A flicker of rage practically burned a hole in his

chest. He could feel his teeth and nails elongating. *Control*. "You've done something to strike at her, haven't you?"

She flicked her tongue over one overlong canine. "I have, but before I start bragging, you should know I'm the one who raised the false alarm about the demons. I knew you'd return again and again to investigate. And guess what? You have."

"And you wanted to see me…because?"

"Because we're destined to be together." She leaned back and traced a finger between her breasts. "As for what I did to Nicola… I stole her petty cash and doctored a few of her accounts. And she would have been arrested if your precious Jamila hadn't found out and fixed everything. But don't worry. I'll get her next time."

Destined to be together? He reached out and grabbed the girl by the neck, jerking her into the air. As she yelped, he flashed her to the cavern where he'd kept his mother. Cornelia was now in the other cage he'd built for her, though he hadn't yet explained things to Nicola.

He'd tried, but had stopped himself. What if she was unable to understand?

He dropped Sirena in the center of the cage and flashed out, behind the bars. She whirled around to face him, her eyes narrowing. "What do you think you're doing?"

"Think? No. Know? Yes. You'll stay here for a few days. On your own, with nothing to do but ponder how best to appease me. I'll return and you'll tell me everything I want to know and probably a thousand things I don't."

She raced toward him, trying to reach through the bars and grab him.

Grinning coldly, he flashed back to the office.

But he wasn't given a chance to speak with Nicola. Axel was there with Jamila, and the two were arguing.

"Whatever you're planning to do needs to wait," the warrior said when he spotted Koldo. "I've found Nefas tracks just outside this building."

CHAPTER TWENTY-THREE

THE LIGHTS IN NICOLA'S OFFICE flicked off—yet no one stood at the switch.

Laila stopped dancing. "Power go out?" she asked, her voice louder than it should have been as she listened to her iPod.

"No. My computer's running."

The lights flipped back on.

"A momentary short in the wires, maybe?"

"You're probably right." Laila started dancing again.

Nicola returned to the work piled up in front of her. Jamila and Sirena had only done half of what they'd promised, and nothing that had come in since. *So utterly useless,* she thought.

An instant message popped up on her screen.

Dex Turner:

What happened Sat? Who was that guy?

Her palms grew damp as she typed:

I'm sorry! Koldo is a guy I met a few weeks ago. We had never dated, but we had—never mind. It's complicated, and I know that sounds cliché, but it's true nonetheless. I'm sorry, though. I really am. But now I'm together with him. For sure.

Even though he'd acted like a jerk today, snipping and snapping at her before marching off without any explanation.

The lights flicked back off. On. Off.

Sighing, she propped her elbows on her desk and rested her head in her upraised hands.

On. Off. On. Off.

"Seriously, this is annoying," Laila said with a tremble to her voice. "And okay, fine, a little scary."

Nicola never moved, but her phone was suddenly thrown across the room. The device slammed into the wall and shattered, little pieces raining to the floor. Laila yelped and darted in her direction.

Demons, Nicola realized. Dread slithered through her.

"Get underneath the desk," she commanded. "And stay calm."

Her sister obeyed, gasping out, "What about you?"

The sound of hissing and giggling filled her ears. Dark shadows crept along the walls. Definitely demons. Her heart skipped a beat, the first sign of oncoming fear, but she resisted.

I'm not helpless. I'm protected.

That's right. She was. She leaped up. In the corner, a shadow thickened, solidified into a hazy blob and scurried across the desk, reaching out to brush her hair. A light breeze dusted her skin, the scent of rotten eggs clinging to her nose.

On went the lights.

Off.

On—and as brightness flooded the room once again, five demons came into view, and they resembled the snakes from the park. Their scales were the same shade as blood, and their temples were flared. They had glowing green eyes, and jaws open wide, revealing fangs sharper than any knife, with a yellowed substance drip, drip, dripping onto the floor and burning, causing the carpet to sizzle and steam to rise.

Forked tongues slithered out, waving in her direction. *I'm not helpless. I'm really not. I'm protected. I really am.*

"I'll enjoy having you for breakfassst," one taunted.

"Your sssister will be desssert," another added.

More giggles.

She opened her mouth to shout for the Most High, but the door burst open, silencing her. Sirena raced inside, pale hair flying behind her. She brandished a long, thin sword, and the snakes jolted backward, cursing at her.

"Get out of here, fiends! Now," she shouted. Metal whistled through air, and the creatures darted left and right, desperate to get out of her way.

One of the creatures disappeared in a puff of black smoke. Another soon followed.

There was a wild light in Sirena's blue eyes, one that said she was just crazy enough to fight the demons with her bare hands if necessary. Those remaining must have sensed her determination, because they tossed one last hiss in Nicola's direction and vanished.

Panting, Sirena dropped the sword on the floor. "You're safe."

Laila peeked out from underneath the desk as Nicola raced over to her. "Are you all right, Sirena?"

"I'm fine." The girl brushed her fall of pale hair over one shoulder. "Promise."

"How did you do that?" Inside, Nicola's instincts

were churning. Something wasn't right. "How did you know we needed help?"

She flashed a quick smile. "I'm like Koldo. He asked me to look after you."

Koldo! He hadn't abandoned her, after all.

"I'm just glad I got here in time," Sirena added a little tightly. "Those things are dangerous. They're the foul offspring of serp demons and Nefas."

Nicola placed her hand on her stomach to ward off the oncoming ache. "Thank you. Thank you for helping us."

Laila stood, swaying. Her skin had taken on a sickly cast, and her eyes had glassed over. "Are you okay, Co Co?"

"I am. You?"

"F-fine."

"If you both want to stay that way, we have to get out of here," Sirena announced. "Koldo wants you with him. Come on. I'll take you to him."

"I DON'T LIKE THIS," Koldo said. It was too easy. The Nefas had never been this obvious with their tracks.

He and Axel had gone from point A to B to C and now D, without ever having to search for a clue. The breadcrumbs had just been here and there, obvious to any Sent One. A trail from the flashes. A glaze of venom on a door. A spiked footprint. A hint of sulfur-scented smoke. A scattering of serp demon scales.

"Want to get a mani-pedi and discuss our options?" Axel asked.

"No." They were aware of the fact that this could be a trap, and so they could turn the plan against the Nefas.

Koldo darted through the back alley, Axel a few

paces behind him, each hidden in the spirit realm, their swords of fire at the ready. But the further he followed the newest trail, the clearer Koldo remembered the times he'd helped his father provide false tracks for others, even though they'd known the searcher would suspect it was a trap. Nox had never cared about that— had only wanted the males distracted.

Distracted, so that Nox could steal something of value without any opposition.

Koldo stopped, and Axel slammed into his back. "This isn't a trap, it's a distraction. He just wants us away from Estellä."

Teeth grinding, Koldo released the sword of fire and flashed to the building, into Nicola's office. He found the phone shattered on the floor. He found a discarded weapon—one he recognized. Long, thin, the metal stretching from a hilt that appeared to be the wide jaw of a snake.

His father's.

The first spark of rage hit him. Nicola's perfume created a soft sweetness in the air, but that sweetness couldn't cover the taint of sulfur. Serp demons had been here. And Nicola was...was...

No! He punched the wall. She was alive, he told himself. He wouldn't believe anything else. His father wouldn't kill his only ace.

But still the rage magnified, such dark, dark rage. His teeth elongated; his nails sharpened.

Control. He needed answers. What had happened here? Where was Jamila? How had the demons gotten Nicola out of the building?

They would have had to trick her or take her by force. With the destruction in this office, he had to go with force. So…why hadn't she asked the Most High for help? Why hadn't she peered at her tattoos?

Or had she?

Had she acted too late?

Had both force and trickery been used?

This time, the rage grew like a tree, sprouting branches, budding leaves, until he couldn't see past the thickness of the foliage. Koldo swiped the papers and files from the desk and onto the floor. The computer was next, the screen cracking. He picked up the desk and slammed it down, the wood splitting. He ripped the chair into pieces. Punched another hole in the wall. Then another and another.

Stop. You have to stop. This isn't you. Not anymore.

He paused, panting, sweating—wasting time, he realized.

He breathed in and out, forcing himself to become the calm, rational man his woman needed. Nicola couldn't have been gone long—Koldo had seen her an hour ago. But then, he knew how much damage could be done in that amount of time.

Steady.

Axel landed beside him, took one look around the room and understood what had happened without having to be told. "Our new plan?"

The human authorities might decide to delve into Nicola's disappearance, and he didn't need their interference—they would only slow him down. "Clean this."

"Uh, that would be a no. I have people for that."

"Call them."

"Already done. They'll be here in five."

Koldo nodded stiffly, the only kind of thanks he could manage.

"So what do you want to do?" Axel asked.

He scrubbed a hand down his face. Where would Nox have taken her? His father was a braggart, a showman and big on vengeance. Every misdeed was punished. Koldo's most recent crime was the killing of the messenger in the park—

Yes. The park. The scene of the crime.

"The park," he said, and flashed to the very spot where he'd decapitated his father's man. Too late, Koldo realized he should have demanded Axel stay behind. The warrior could find out about Koldo's past, his lineage, and tell the others in their army.

No. It didn't matter. Koldo wanted Nicola safe, whatever the cost.

He cataloged the area—and when his gaze landed on a male who should have been dead, his breath caught in his chest.

Nox. His father. Alive, all this time. There was no question about that now.

Koldo stumbled backward with the force of his shock. Yes, he'd suspected. But seeing the evidence was a blow he'd been unprepared to take. This should have been impossible.

Nox stood in the center of a dirt pile, where a tree had once been, buffing his nails, allowing Koldo to study him. The male responsible for so many years of torment. Nox was everything Koldo remembered. Tall and strong, with dark, evil eyes.

He was tattooed from the neck down, with gruesome images that told stories of pain and suffering. They were marks of victory. Some for those against enemies. Some for his female conquests. Some for acts of revenge. Blood appeared to drip. Heads seemed to roll.

He also had several piercings in his eyebrows, two in his lip, one in his chin.

Koldo stepped from the spirit realm to face his worst nightmare and save the sweetest woman he'd known. "Where is she?"

His father looked him over, triumph twisting his features and revealing the ugliness of his core. "Aren't you a pretty thing?" His voice was deep. Husky.

Hated.

The only reason Nox had never forcibly shaved Koldo's head, pierced Koldo's face or tattooed Koldo's body was because the traits were considered admirable among the Nefas and Koldo hadn't yet earned the right.

"You should be dead," Koldo said.

A smug smirk, one of thousands Koldo had received over the years. "Oh, you mean that pathetic attempt you made to kill me all those years ago? I saw you coming and flashed away. Your rain of fire failed to singe a single part of me."

He raised his chin. "Your people can't say the same. You abandoned them, choosing to save yourself rather than to stay and issue a warning."

In a snap, the smugness gave way to fury. "*You* are responsible for their deaths, not me. You're the reason I've had to spend all this time rebuilding. Planning. Waiting. I knew I couldn't hurt a man who had nothing to lose."

Having Nox's intentions stated so plainly—to hurt Nicola in an effort to hurt Koldo—doused his rage with fear. Nox never made an empty threat. He only made promises.

"Where are the girls?" Koldo demanded.

"We'll get to that," Nox replied smoothly.

A whoosh of air, and then Axel was beside him, wings tucked into his back.

Nox grinned slowly. "You made a friend. How nice. But all that means is that more blood will spill today."

Humans walked past, spotted them and picked up the pace.

"Aw. The ugly Nefas thinks he's going to win." Axel placed a hand over his heart. "It'd be cute if it wasn't so stupid. I bet you're a crier, aren't you? Yeah, you'll cry when you're spanked. I can tell."

"The girls," Koldo insisted.

"Here."

The new speaker had him turning to the left. He watched as Sirena stepped from a puff of black smoke, dragging Nicola and Laila behind her.

The girls were bound, pale and shaking. Sirena gave a vicious tug of her wrists, yanking at their ties, and they tripped forward, falling to the ground. Nicola had a split lip and a bruised jaw, but Laila was otherwise unharmed. There was a clear strip of tape covering both their mouths, and tears had stained red tracks down Laila's cheeks. Nicola radiated anger and determination.

She would fight. Till her dying breath, she would fight.

Koldo's rage returned full force, guilt fast on its heels. He should have protected her. But he hadn't. He had failed. And he would punish himself for it, he vowed. No one would have to do it for him. He would make sure he suffered for this.

"How?" he demanded.

Sirena preened, fluffing her hair. "Like you, I can flash. I'm surprised you didn't realize. But I do appreciate the suggested stay at Chez Caveman."

She could flash. She wasn't bald, but she could produce black smoke when she flashed. She was definitely Nefas, though she must be of mixed race, like him. Her other half wasn't Sent One, that was for sure. She had no wings, hidden or otherwise. No sword of fire.

"Look at that," his father said. "My only children are getting along so well. How delightful."

Axel, who had moved, but had remained at Koldo's side, stiffened.

But then, so did Koldo. Nox's only…children? Koldo's study of Sirena intensified. She was short. He was tall. She was blonde, her eyes blue. He was dark-headed, his eyes amber. But…their features were somewhat similar, he realized. They had the same strong cheekbones, the same proud nose and stubborn chin.

He…he had a sister.

"I'll give you one chance," Nox said. As he spoke, five serp demons rose from the dirt and slithered to his sides. "Just one to make things right between us. Bind yourself to Sirena and continue my bloodline, or die here with your woman—after I play with her a little."

A trick, surely. "You expect me to wed a blood relation?"

"Expect? No." Nox laughed with evil intent, the sound chilling. "Demand? Yes."

Koldo popped his jaw, not allowing himself to so much as glance at Nicola and catch her reaction to this.

"Sirena's a tasty little treat," his father added, reaching out to pat her bottom. "You'll quite enjoy her. I did."

Disgusting male. *And I sprang from his loins.* "Are you agreeable to this?" he barked at Sirena.

"I am," she said, and bent over Nicola. She placed a kiss against the tape covering her mouth as the girl tried to turn her head away. Sirena's intentions were clear: she wanted Nicola's soul. All the while her gaze remained on Koldo. "You've been promised to me since my birth, and I *will* have you. One way or another. What happens to the human depends on you."

Four other Nefas strolled over to their group, one eating from a bag of popcorn, another biting into a caramel apple and another drinking a cup of coffee. But he could see the guns and knives stashed at their wrists, waist and ankles. They were warriors.

Worse, there were two demons with them. Lefty and Righty. Lefty's arm had been reattached, though it hung limply at his side, but Righty's horn was still missing. Both males were grinning.

I'll flash to the girls and throw them at you, he projected into Axel's mind. *Catch them and fly them to safety. I'll stay behind to fight.*

He expected resistance. After all, a Sent One had just found out that Koldo was half-Nefas, the vilest race to walk the earth.

Instead, Axel said, *Dude, you better keep yourself alive. There's no way I can deal with those two ladies for long…without throwing a shagging party.*

"What's it to be?" Nox demanded.

The serps slithered to the girls, mouths hovering near their ears, ready to breathe their toxin all over them. The girls would experience intense waves of fear, and that fear would open their minds to harsher attack. Were they strong enough to resist? To overcome?

Sirena gave Nicola's taped mouth another kiss, and grinned.

"I'll have her," he said—though he failed to specify which one. And the word *have* had many different meanings, didn't it?

Nicola flinched. Laila sobbed into the ground.

Sirena straightened.

Nox nodded with satisfaction, but said, "I don't actually believe you. But that's okay. You won't leave this spot until it's done. Then, you'll have to be punished for killing my people."

"No. That's not how this will go down." He flashed to the girls, dislodging Sirena as he covered both humans with his own body. The serps immediately bounded into action, exhaling their toxin before sinking fangs into his arms.

A burning in his veins, a release of the venom.

The moment the creatures pulled back, intending to make another play, he tossed both females at Axel, as planned. The angel's wings whipped out, and he darted into the air, leaving Koldo alone with a horde of enraged Nefas.

CHAPTER TWENTY-FOUR

"YOU SHOULDN'T HAVE done that," Nox said, reaching up to grab the hilt of a sword he'd strapped to his back. "I was willing to be nice. Now, not so much."

Sirena withdrew two short swords.

The four Nefas warriors dropped their food and withdrew guns.

Lefty and Righty unsheathed their claws.

"We should take this somewhere private," Koldo said.

One word from his father. "No."

Very well, then. Koldo extended his arm and summoned the sword of fire. The flames burst forth, a mix of yellow and blue, crackling. He would be battling his enemies in both the natural *and* the spiritual realms. It wasn't ideal, but it also wasn't impossible.

Most of the humans in the park gasped at the display of aggression and weaponry. Some ran. Some sat down as if they were about to be entertained with an after-dinner theater performance.

The Nefas flashed to Koldo's sides as the demons converged. He swung the sword left and right in quick succession, going for his father first, but the male flashed a few feet away to avoid being hit. At the same time, the others lashed out at him. He dodged one, two, three, but not the rest, and took the impact in his arm, side and leg.

A bullet grazed his shoulder. A sharp sting caused him to hiss. Bleeding, he flashed behind Nox, and swung his sword. But his father sensed him and also flashed, leaving three of his men vulnerable. The sword slicked through their bodies. Two of the Nefas went down face-first, dead. The other whipped around as he fell and squeezed off another shot. This time, Koldo flashed before the bullets could nail him.

Lefty realized he was close enough to strike and swung, his wing slicing out, reaching…missing. Koldo flashed to the other side, struck—decapitating a Nefas. But Lefty and Righty were familiar with his brand of fighting and anticipated his landing.

The moment he was busy swinging his sword at someone else, they flew up and over, kicking him in the face. He stumbled backward. A chorus of "ooh" and "aah" erupted from the growing crowd.

Sirena flashed behind him, catching him before he could straighten, but rather than stab him, as he expected, she pressed her body against his, and dug her nails into his neck. Nails that seemed to leak a boiling liquid straight into his veins. Her grip was strong. Impossibly strong.

Hot breath fanned over his skin as she said, "I'm going to relish cutting your female to ribbons and sucking out her soul." She jumped up to lick his cheek with a long, hot stroke. "You're mine, and don't you ever forget it."

As she spoke, the serps wrapped their tails around his ankles and jerked. He slammed his elbow backward, drilling Sirena in the stomach as he fell. They both went down. As breath exploded from her in a pained rush, he tried to turn, determined to end her. But the demons still locked around his ankles gave a vicious tug, and he skidded away.

Lefty and Righty were there, kicking and punching at him. All the while, the remaining Nefas flashed in and out, punching and vanishing, punching and vanishing. Sharp stings erupted over every inch of him. He rolled over, and the demons clawed at him as he tried to sit up. He let them, wanting them close enough for contact—with his weapon. They scratched and bit at him, lost to their need for revenge, unaware he was raising his sword of fire.

He killed three before Sirena regained her composure and approached him alongside Nox. But when Sirena raised her arm, as if to strike him, putting herself in harm's way, Nox shoved his daughter out of the way. She slammed into the two demons approaching his other side, the three tumbling to the ground, away from the strike of Koldo's sword. Still Koldo carved through the demons at his feet. Fetid steam rose, and black blood spilled. The grass sizzled.

A booted foot propelled into his side. Nox's.

He rolled to avoid another kick, and saw a glint of metal in the corner of his eye. One of the Nefas was lifting a sword, preparing to behead him. Again, Koldo rolled, the tip of the weapon slamming into the dirt, dark grains flying in every direction. He flashed to a stand a few feet away, just behind his father. He swung, and the fiery tip slicked just above Nox's shoulder, headed for his heart, before the male flashed away.

A whoosh of wings penetrated his ears, followed by another. Malcolm and Magnus landed a few feet away from him, Jamila behind them. Grunts began to split the air. Metal slammed against burning metal, clanging. Koldo spun, and saw that the Sent Ones were engaged in a fierce battle. Malcolm and a Nefas. Magnus and a Nefas. Jamila and Sirena. The Nefas could have flashed away for good, but Koldo knew their mind-set. Knew they liked to remain in a battle as long as possible, inflicting as much damage as they could, only leaving at the threat of death.

The serps were in the process of slithering away as quickly as possible.

Nox hadn't returned.

Malcolm attacked with hands gloved in spiked metal. The Nefas warrior he fought had leaking holes all over his body. The male staggered backward, and Malcolm eagerly chased. But Magnus beat his brother to the prize and used a whip to decapitate the creature before he could flash away.

The two nodded at each other in a job well done.

Jamila was obviously weaker than Sirena, and was tripping more than she was swinging. Koldo pulled a dagger from an air pocket and flashed behind his sister—his sister!—and grabbed her just as she had grabbed him.

He lifted the weapon, determined to plunge it deep. He wouldn't waste time with threats. Growling with frustration and rage, Sirena performed her final flash before he could strike. The only other remaining Nefas disappeared a second later.

The sound of police sirens caught Koldo's attention.

The crowd looked around, their smiles giving way to frowns. The clapping tapered off as the onlookers realized the authorities wouldn't have come for a performance.

Acting quickly, Koldo and the other Sent Ones picked up the pieces of the deceased and tossed them into air pockets, then stepped into the spiritual realm. As policemen rushed into the area, the crowd bolted with confusion, and the Sent Ones faced each other.

"How did you know where I was and what I needed?" Koldo asked.

"Axel told us," Malcolm said, rubbing the spikes in his hands together.

And what else had Axel mentioned? He waited, but no one informed him of anything more.

"Thank you," he said. He wouldn't tell them he'd had no need of them, that he would have pulled through on his own, because he still couldn't bring himself to lie. And they would have tasted it, anyway.

To Jamila, he stiffly said, "Why weren't you at Estellä?"

Her chin lifted. "That little witch Sirena flashed me to a cage in a cave and locked me inside. I can't flash and couldn't leave. I had to summon help."

"I needed you with Nicola," he said, even though he knew he couldn't fault her for how things had gone down. They'd both been taken by surprise. But he wasn't exactly rational at the moment.

"Well, too bad," she snapped. "Nicola Lane is your responsibility, not mine."

She was, wasn't she? "She will never again set foot in Estellä Industries." He would make sure of it. And if she protested, she protested. He would deal with the fallout, as he should have done before this happened. "I'll take things from here."

Koldo flashed to the house in Panama—or rather, tried to. He remained in place. He frowned, and once again tried to flash. But once again he remained where he was.

What was wrong? He'd been bitten by the serps. He'd been stabbed, shot and scratched by the Nefas. But he'd endured all of that before—and worse—with no such consequences. Only difference was…Sirena, he realized with sickening dread. She *had* leaked something into his veins.

If he'd forever lost his ability to flash—

He couldn't finish that thought without howling. No. Her poison would fade. He would recover.

He had to recover.

But he'd wanted to be punished, and this certainly fit.

At least now he knew Nox's game plan. He knew Sirena's purpose. He knew the Nefas and demons were working together. And he knew Lefty and Righty were back in the picture, more determined than ever to reclaim Nicola.

"Fly me to Panama," he told Malcolm, his cheeks heating with embarrassment. He hated that he had to rely on another being for his transportation.

"Wow. Aren't you a big bag of polite," Malcolm muttered, but still the warrior strode over to him and wrapped him in his arms. "You'll owe me for this."

"I know." That was the way of the world. He only wondered if Nicola found him as aggravating as he now found Malcolm.

White wings laced with gold flared, and a twinge of envy lit a fire in Koldo's chest. Then they were airborne, the wind whipping against his skin, and he found himself closing his eyes and pretending he was soaring on his own. That he was healthy and whole.

That he had an untainted future.

KOLDO ARRIVED AT the ranch cradled in the arms of another man. A beautiful Asian man with a green fauxhawk, weird silvery eyes and tattoos of bones on his neck. Just...wow, he was beautiful, but he was also seriously scary.

Desperate to figure out a way to return to the park and help Koldo, Nicola had been pacing in front of the couch, where Axel and Laila sat. If anyone could win with ten-against-one odds, it was Koldo.

Koldo, who had promised to marry Sirena. His horrible troll of a sister.

Koldo, who never lied.

"He lost consciousness halfway here," the newcomer said.

"Put him—" Axel began, standing.

Nicola cut him off. "Put him in my bed." She rushed forward to show the new guy the way, surprised her heart wasn't pounding more forcefully and that she wasn't light-headed.

"Don't leave me here, Co Co!" Laila shouted.

She glanced back to watch Laila shrink to the edge of the couch in an effort to get as far away from Axel as she could.

"And don't you dare touch me!" Laila yelled at him. "I don't want anything else to do with any of your kind!"

Axel shrugged and strolled to the kitchen. "You want something to do with a muffin? I'm starved."

Nicola was torn between rushing back to her sister to offer comfort and staying with Koldo. In the end, she shouted, "No one's going to hurt you, La La, I promise," and raced to the bed to jerk the comforter and sheets out of the way. Then she moved so that the newcomer could easily place Koldo in the center.

"What was done to him?" she asked, heading into the bathroom to gather a washrag drenched in hot water and all the creams and cleansers Koldo had brought from her house.

"War."

Well, duh. She would ask Koldo, then. When he awoke. And he would. She wouldn't believe otherwise. "Give me a knife," she said when she next stood beside the bed.

Fauxhawk frowned. "Why?"

"So I can cut away his robe and doctor him. Why else?"

"So you can kill him," he stated simply.

"I would never hurt him!" She placed all of the supplies on the mattress. "We're dating." Or rather, they had been, BS. Before Sirena.

"Good for you, but that doesn't help your case. Just so you know, I'll hurt you worse than you've ever been hurt if you injure him further." That said, he handed her a blade. Rather than leave the room, he rocked back on his heels and crossed his arms over his massive chest, as though waiting for her to mess up.

Nicola worked the tip down the center of the fabric, careful not to nick Koldo's skin. By the time she got to the hem of the robe, the top part had already woven itself back together.

"Help me," she commanded.

The warrior pursed his lips, as if he wasn't fond of

being told what to do. "Your male will owe me another favor, I think."

Another? "I'll pay for your favor. How's that?"

"You have nothing I desire." He bent down and ripped the robe in two, then yanked the material out from under Koldo.

"So why did you just help me?" She dropped the blade and grabbed the robe before the man could discard it, then draped the fabric over Koldo's naked waist. He was littered with bite marks, cuts, bruises and scratches. At his neck, four tiny wounds in the shape of half-moons had turned black and now festered.

"I told you. Your male will owe me another favor."

He was a great listener, wasn't he? "So what's your name, anyway?"

"Malcolm."

Nicola cleaned each of the injuries, taking extra care with the ones on his neck. Even still, the skin broke open and pus oozed out. Couldn't be an infection, she thought. Not enough time had passed. Had to be… poison?

She reached for the blade.

Malcolm latched on to her wrist, stopping her. "I knew you would make a play."

Then why hadn't he stashed the weapon away from her? To test her motives? "Look, I'm going to slice the wounds open the rest of the way and—"

His grip tightened painfully, nearly cracking bone.

A cry parted her lips.

Footsteps pounded, and then Axel was there, ripping Malcolm away from her.

"What do you think you're doing, my man?" the warrior demanded.

"She wants to cut into his neck!"

"For a good cause," Nicola said with a sigh. "I want to drain the wounds, and to do that, I need to widen them. I'll be careful with him." More careful than she'd ever been. This man had come to mean a lot to her. More than he probably realized.

"You haven't seen him panting after the female," Axel told Malcolm, pushing him toward the door. "If you had, you'd know he wants her hands all over him— whatever she wants to do."

Panting after her? *I wish.* "Will you guys just get out of here? You're distracting me, and I need to concentrate. I may not be a doctor, but I've watched every episode of *House.* I'm pretty sure I know what I'm doing."

Whether they obeyed or not, she wasn't sure. She settled beside Koldo's waist, leaned forward and raised the knife.

CHAPTER TWENTY-FIVE

KOLDO TUGGED HIMSELF from the darkness and into the light. Though he was paralyzed, his mind blank, he wasn't unaware. He felt gentle hands stroking over him, easing the stings that plagued him. The moment the stroking stopped, a wave of anger stormed through him, giving him the strength he needed to jolt into mobility.

He opened his eyes, but his vision was hazed. Blink, blink. Bit by bit, things began to clear. Blink, blink. He saw the glint of a knife. Saw a female stretch that knife toward him, aiming for his neck.

His mother. His mother had escaped, was here, was determined to kill him while he was too vulnerable to fight back.

Growling from the depths of his being, he lashed out, hitting the knife and the arm that held it. A feminine moan of pain filled his ears.

A moan he recognized. Not his mother's.

Nicola?

He tried to sit up, the gentle hands suddenly replaced by strong calloused ones, applying more pressure to push him down.

"He didn't mean to hurt me," the woman said.

Yes, Nicola. His Nicola.

Had she been speaking to him? Or was someone else in the room?

Of course someone else was in the room. The hands that restrained him belonged to a male. He recalled his father's threats against Nicola....

Koldo fought against the one keeping him in place. He managed to get his fingers wrapped around hard steel bands—arms? He tossed with all of his strength. There was a crash, a cloud of plaster in the air.

"Easy now," a male said.

Another voice he recognized. Not his father. But it wasn't Nicola, so he didn't care. Koldo wanted to get to her, and would do anything to succeed. He punched and punched and punched, until finally the male stopped trying to subdue him and started fighting back. But Koldo quickly got hold of something soft—feathers—and ripped.

A howl rent the air.

A soft weight landed on Koldo. He reached up to dislodge it, but caught Nicola's sweet scent.

"Calm down," she said, fingers brushing over his jawline. "You have to calm down now. All right?"

"Safe?"

"You're safe. I'm safe. We're at your home in Panama."

Trusting her, he relaxed against the mattress, wound his arms around her and held her close, breathing her in, savoring the scent of cinnamon and vanilla.

"I have a bald patch now," one of the males said. Axel. "Do you know how bad that sucks?"

"I have a broken spine," the other growled. Malcolm.

"Like you've really got it worse. You might never walk again, but at least you look pretty."

"You think I'm pretty?"

"I think you're about to get a dagger in your gut."

Footsteps. Two sets, receding from the room. Malcolm must not have lost the ability to walk, after all.

"Stay," Koldo said to Nicola.

"I will," she whispered. "Rest now."

Unable to deny her anything, he sank back into the darkness.

SHARDS OF LIGHT penetrated his consciousness. Koldo was glad, even though the light was accompanied by pain. He was used to pain. But the moment he worked his way to full consciousness, where Nicola's voice soothed and delighted, he was tugged back into the waiting darkness.

How much time passed, he wasn't sure.

The light tried again, lifting him up, higher and higher.

"—you're sure he's not marrying her?" Nicola asked.

"Positive," Axel replied.

"But he doesn't lie."

"He wasn't lying."

"Argh! How can that be?"

"Ask him."

Darkness.

Light.

"—and all of these Sent Ones have been showing up to check on you. I've been cooking for them, and I'm getting better." A soft chuckle caressed his ears. "There's never a crumb left, and I..."

The volume was cranked down before she could finish, the darkness returning.

No! No, he wanted to hear her words...everything she had to say....

The next time the light made an appearance, he

heard, "I'm learning the most interesting things about you. You used to have hair, but then, one day, fairly recently, in fact, you didn't. You used to not talk very much at all. Magnus said the words had to be yanked out of you with pliers, but now you talk more than is wise. Their words, not mine. Elandra says you're fond of shopping for bras and panties. I'm pretty sure she was joking."

He gritted his teeth and, with an internal roar, tore the rope binding him to all that darkness.

His eyelids flipped open.

Unlike the first time, there was no haze. He saw Nicola sitting beside him, her features smooth rather than bathed in worry as she looked down, her hair caught up and gleaming, her clothes neat and tidy. And she utterly took his breath away.

He smacked his lips together, tasting mint. She must have brushed his teeth for him. Though his arm was weak, shaky, he managed to reach up and pinch the ends of her hair. She gasped in surprise and met his gaze. He lost his breath all over again. Those eyes…a summer storm, heat rising, steaming up the flower gardens.

"You're awake." She leaned over him to flatten her palm against his brow. "And your fever is gone."

The position pressed her body against his, delighting him. Then she settled back into place, ending the contact, annoying him.

"How long have I been out?" he asked, a rough quality to his voice. He took stock. He was naked, a sheet draped over his middle.

"Three days."

Once again, he'd lost three days to his father. He remembered…fighting the Nefas and the demons, winning when the Sent Ones arrived, but not being able to flash away. Had the ability returned? He wanted to try, but didn't want to leave Nicola. More than that, he knew it would be better to wait until he was stronger. If he failed right now, just because he was weak and hadn't fully fought off the poison, he would waste precious time and energy fretting.

"Oh, and before I forget, Axel told me to tell you he's been taking care of your dirty little secret in the backyard."

His mother, he realized, his tension increasing.

"I wanted to stay as close to your side as possible and haven't yet investigated the yard—which I totally plan to do, I won't lie about that. So you might as well fess up and tell me what your dirty little secret is," she said.

He'd wanted her to know. Just…not right now. He'd tell her when he was stronger. "Nothing that concerns you," he croaked.

"You don't trust me?" A wealth of hurt in her tone.

"I trust you more than I've ever trusted another, but one has nothing to do with the other." To distract her, he said, "What have you been doing all this time?"

A moment passed. She sighed and said, "I've been taking care of you, entertaining your friends. Staying calm, happy. And guess what? Deep down, I knew you would heal. Just like me! I've been getting stronger, too. Isn't that wonderful?"

"Wonderful," he parroted. If she was better…

She set his hand back at his side, reached toward the nightstand and lifted a cup of water. "You talked in your sleep, you know."

He tensed, saying, "About what?"

A gleam of sadness in her eyes as she quietly said,

"About a mother who ripped out your wings and a father who tossed you into a pit of snakes. You'd told me they were awful to you, but I hadn't imagined how bad." She placed the straw at his lips. "Drink."

He obeyed. He didn't know what else to do. His stomach twisted, nearly rejecting the cool, sweet liquid trickling down his throat. Perhaps now was the time to tell her about his mother, after all.

"Why don't I tell you something about my past?" she suggested. "That way, we'll be even."

Perhaps not. He nodded, intrigued, hungry for more information about her. Any information.

"Well…several years ago, my mother, father and little brother were killed by a drunk driver."

He'd known that, but hearing the pain in her smoke-and-dreams voice affected him deeply.

"Robby wasn't supposed to be with them that day. He was supposed to stay with me and Laila." Guilt joined the pain. "But she wanted to go out with friends, and I wanted to tag along to make sure she didn't get sick, so we convinced our parents to take him on their dinner date."

"You couldn't have known." But she blamed herself, he thought, and it was a heavy burden to carry. One he wished he could lift from her shoulders. But he couldn't. Only she could. And if she didn't, if she failed, the weight would eventually crush her.

That, he knew firsthand.

"That's just it. I did. Deep down, like with you, I had a feeling. I knew I should keep him with me. And I think Laila knew it, too. That's why she's like she is, so determined to live in the now and not look back. She doesn't want to remember our part in Robby's death."

"And neither do you."

"I know. For years we tried to pretend he never existed. It was easier, I think. But it was also a disservice to him, and he deserves better. I know that now."

That might be why Koldo had found no record of Robby in the heavenly archives. What you denied down here, you lost up there.

"You must forgive yourself. Isn't that what you told me?" Koldo reached up, the actions easier now, his strength returning bit by bit, and cupped the back of her neck. He applied pressure, tugging her toward him, but for the first time in their relationship, she resisted.

"I know you didn't marry that girl," she said. "Axel told me. But you told tattoo guy you'd have her, and you never lie."

Was she jealous? He kind of hoped so. He actually liked the idea. "You're right about my words. I said I would have *her*. He assumed the one I was talking about was Sirena—but I was talking about you."

Her eyes widened. "You want to…marry me?"

Did he? No. No, he couldn't. He was tainted, he reminded himself. "Having a woman isn't the same as marrying one."

"Oh," she said, her shoulders drooping.

He pulled her the rest of the way against him. She settled atop his chest, her head finding the hollow of his neck, just the way she liked. "You're disappointed?" Why? And why was he happy about her reaction? Did he *want* her to want more from him?

"Me? I'm glad things worked out."

"Because I'm better than your other date?"

"Immensely." She toyed with the end of his beard. "I wish I could ask *you* about a last date."

"Why?"

"So I'd know how I rank."

"I don't need experience to tell you that. Simple observation proves you are the only one for me."

"And just what have you observed?" At least her tone was lighter now.

"Over the centuries I've heard many a woman tell her friends that a man has to accept her just as she is or he doesn't deserve her. But if she's a lying, cheating gossipmonger, cruel to those around her, often angry, often hateful, of course he cannot accept her. He's better off without her."

A choking little laugh left her. "That's a good point, but the same is true for men."

"Yes."

"So…how do you know I'm none of those things?"

Was she serious? "I've watched you interact with your sister, always placing her needs above your own. You've spent time with Axel, but haven't killed him—a feat for anyone. And the way you are with me…kind, caring, sweet, thoughtful, helpful, considerate, compassionate, loving—"

She gave another laugh, saying, "Basically, all of those words mean the same thing."

"Beautiful, exquisite, stunning, gorgeous, lovely, stunning, striking—"

"So you want me, huh?" she asked huskily.

"I do." So badly.

"Good, because you've got me. *All* of me." She lifted her head, met his gaze directly. "I quit my job, and you're now my official keeper."

He liked that, too.

A lot.

"Well, then, I had better start keeping you properly."
He cupped her cheeks and angled her head back, his
hands heating up. A shiver rocked her as he pressed a
soft kiss into her lips.

Immediately she opened, welcoming him.

He kept the pressure light, relearning her, reacquaint-
ing himself with her sweetness, going slowly, trying to
fortify himself against the burning flood of desire rushing through him.

This was Nicola. Every moment had to be perfect.

But then she moaned, a heady, titillating sound, and
her hands returned to his beard, and he lost the battle of gentleness versus need—not that he'd fought all
that staunchly. He kicked the sheet away from him and
rolled, half pinning her slight weight to the mattress.
Her legs parted, allowing him to sink against her. Hardness to softness. Need to need.

He reached up, tore the elastic from her hair and
watched as strawberry curls tumbled over the pillow,
spilling around her. All he could do was stare at her.
He'd wanted to see her like this for so long, and now,
here she was, far more beautiful than he ever could
have imagined.

"What?" she asked, shifting underneath him.

"You are…" There was only one word that fit. "Mine.
You're mine." With the claim ringing in his ears, he fed
her another kiss.

She met his intensity all the way. Her hands explored
his chest, his shoulders, his back, her nails scraping.
"Sorry. Sorry," she gasped out. "You're hurt, and I—"

"Don't stop."

She kissed the length of his neck. "'Kay."

"Do you have a special attachment to your shirt?"

"No."

He ripped the material down the middle, revealing a white lace bra and soft, flat belly of the most luscious cream. A smattering of freckles dotted her skin.

He'd always hated freckles. These? He thought he... loved. On Nicola, they were a road map he longed to follow, to lick his way from one to another.

"The bra?" he rasped.

"You have a thing for destroying clothing, don't you?"

"The bra?" he insisted.

"Get rid of it."

He did just that, baring her to his view. And oh, the newest flood of desire to wash through him nearly undid him. His muscles shook. His bones vibrated. His soul shouted, *Yes. Yes, this is the woman I was created to enjoy.* The one who would lift him up, never tear him down.

He could only drink her in, every one of his senses humming a lullaby he'd never heard. The intoxicating song surrounded him, caressed him, *owned* him. He was lured, not to a place of slumber but to a place of shattering change.

He would never be the same.

The cinnamon and vanilla that was so much a part of Nicola clung to him, embedding in his pores. She branded him with her very own essentia—he was hers. A half to a whole.

Those stormy eyes watched him, glassed with a hunger-charged yearning. Light trickled over her, complementing pleasure-flushed skin.

"You're staring at me," she whispered.

"I'm sorry." Then, "No. I'm not sorry. I like doing it."

"Well, then, I'm glad."

He couldn't hold in his next words. "I want to be with you, Nicola."

"I want that, too."

He moved the back of his hand along the length of her neck, soft, light. "I'll be careful."

She shook her head, all that fiery hair dancing over the pillow. "I don't want careful."

"But that's what you'll get." And he would make sure she liked it. Whatever he had to do.

He explored her, and every new point of contact sent him deeper and deeper into a pool of need, until he was drowning, desperate. But he knew, in the depths of his core, that his every action was a declaration of his feelings for her. She was someone of value. She was someone worth saving. She was the woman he wanted at his side. Everything he'd needed, nothing he'd known.

He stripped her of the rest of her clothes, marveling at every new revelation of this woman who had so captivated him, and spread his essentia all over her, leaving no inch untouched, causing all that flushed skin to glow so much more brightly.

"Koldo," she breathed. "I feel so hot…burning."

"That's the essentia, sweet Nicola."

She looked him over, saying, "Flawless," before closing her eyes and moaning. "Essentia?"

"A powder my body produces just for you." The tension inside him expanded…and he no longer wanted, he realized—he needed. Every muscle he possessed was clenching on bone. His blood was molten in his veins.

"Oh. That's nice."

Nice?

But then she was gasping, writhing atop the mattress, and he was gasping out word after word of approval and praise, a deluge he'd kept trapped inside far too long. They clutched at each other and they kneaded at each other and he could feel the fast beat of her heart as they kissed each other desperately. A beat that was faster and faster with every moment that passed, as if she neared the edge of a ledge.

"Koldo," she said on a moan.

Such a heady entreaty. Nearly more than he could bear. "Yes?"

"I need…"

"I need, too." But his concern for her well-being suddenly overshadowed everything else. He wouldn't take her, no matter what she said and no matter what he felt. Not until she was ready for him.

No matter how desperate he was, her health was more important, and nothing would change that. Because he didn't want to take from her, he realized. He wanted to share with her. And it would be difficult to stay this course, he knew. All his life, he'd been denied the things so many others took for granted. Acceptance, softness. Affection. He finally had them. And now he had to wait for them, when they were so freely offered?

"Nicola," he said.

"Koldo," she moaned.

"One day we'll be together."

"Yes. Today. Now. We already said so."

Sweet mercy. "No. There's been a change of plans."

Her hands tightened on him, her nails digging into his back. "I can take it. I can!"

Maybe. Maybe not. But he couldn't. The thought of hurting her, even in so small a way, *destroyed* him. If ever he gave her reason to look back and think of him with disappointment, regret or anger, he would willingly fall on his own sword.

"Can't...continue like...this," she said. "Please."

Never beg, he wanted to say. But he liked it too much to stop her from doing it again.

"Pleeease."

"I'll help you with these feelings." Somehow. Someway. Though he lacked experience, he touched her here, there, seemingly everywhere at once, but it was never enough, not for him, yet she began crying out, gasping so hard, straining against him, begging, begging, begging for more.

The pressure inside him increased. It reminded him of the times he'd gone to his cave and exploded, the rage too much for his body to contain. But this wasn't rage. This was raw, animal hunger. She was just so exquisite to watch, her eyes closed, her lashes casting spiky shadows over her cheeks, her lips red and plump, her scent intensifying, the fragrance of her honey eclipsing all that cinnamon and vanilla, and his mouth watered, and his insides...his insides...shattered.

And then she was shouting his name. And he was roaring at an exquisite agony that consumed him, utterly stunned, gasping, sweating, perhaps even babbling.

Yes, babbling.

"What happened? That was... I can't describe... I've never... What we just did... Did you feel that... How could..." The realization left a film of embarrassment and a desire to flee, but he remained in place.

Nicola was hugging him.

He collapsed on the mattress. He was shaking, and... smiling despite his emotions. "Did you experience what I experienced?" Finally. A coherent sentence.

"Yes, and I didn't pass out," she said with a smile of her own.

"Neither did I." He hadn't lost control, hadn't taken what he shouldn't. Had stayed the course and taken another step on the path to claiming her. He had given her pleasure, and had, apparently, taken his own.

Soon, he told himself. Very soon, he would take the next step—take her fully. And they would fall off the ledge together.

CHAPTER TWENTY-SIX

AS THE DEMON SCREAMED in pain, Thane removed the horns on its head.

As the demon cried and sobbed, Thane plucked out its eyes.

As the demon mewled, Thane peeled away huge hunks of the creature's flesh.

Black blood ran down his arms in tiny rivulets, stinging, leaving welts. The scent of sulfur coated the air. At his sides, the walls to the cavern dripped with bodily fluids from the other victims. At his feet was a pile of organs he'd removed.

"If you refuse to talk," he said, "I'll remove your tongue before I kill you."

The creature babbled, but all Thane heard was, "Blah, blah, blah, please. Blah, blah, blah, better than me."

"You think you're better than me?" he lashed out. "Or that I'm not any better than you?" Either way...

Giving in to the rage, Thane sawed at the demon's tongue, as promised. But that wasn't violent enough, and he ended up sawing through the creature's throat. The body slumped against the chains binding it.

Perhaps the next one would be— There was no next one, he realized. He'd killed them all.

He scrubbed a blood-soaked hand through his hair.

He had arrived in Auckland two days ago, tracked a path of evil to the slums and found a group of homeless men and women that had turned on each other. They'd fought over the rights to a trash can, killed each other by sheer physical brutality, and the only survivor had then turned on the patrons of a nearby coffee shop, slaying three innocents before the cops arrived and gunned him down.

Thane had shown up as the remaining patrons were being questioned. Two had displayed tempers that hadn't fit the situation, and he'd ended up following the worst offender to an office building. The male had yelled at everyone he encountered, and the employees had huddled around the watercooler to discuss how odd his behavior was.

That was when Thane realized the truth. Demons of strife were here, infecting humans. Probably obeying their leader—one of the six that had killed Germanus.

So, Thane had gone out, hunting the minions. Within half an hour, he'd found eleven, roaming the streets like hungry lions searching for gimpy prey. He'd initiated battle and immediately killed two. One had gotten away. The other three he'd managed to injure so severely that they weren't able to run. He'd scooped them up and brought them back here, to his cave.

He'd spent the past few hours doing things that had once been done to his friends. Terrible things. Horrendous things. The only things that brought Thane any measure of peace. But no matter what he'd done, he'd gotten no answers.

Where was the leader?

Frustrated, he flew up, up, up to the opening of the cavern, then flattened out to dart through the narrow passage. Light spilled inside, chasing away the darkness and showing the way to the surrounding forest. Within minutes, he was outside, in the air, soaring above the rushing river, the tall, lush trees and the snowcapped mountains.

The scent of sulfur dissipated and the crimson stain of blood vanished from him, his robe cleaning itself as well as his body. The heat dropped off him like a winter cloak, cool air slapping against him. But nothing could wash away the feel of defeat.

A rustle sounded behind him.

He summoned his sword of fire as he turned—but there was no one there. The sun was in the process of setting, casting rays of pink and purple, the sky a darkening blue. The clouds were thick and white, the stars just becoming visible. He hovered in the sky, wings lifting and falling slowly, gracefully, his gaze tracking the surrounding area. But…again, he found no one.

"Come out, coward," he commanded. "Fight me."

Silence.

Irritated, he darted higher at top speed. Then, he leveled out and searched the clouds for any sign of movement. To his right he heard a whoosh…. He frowned. What was that? Whatever it was, the sound of laughter quickly followed. He changed course, only to find four winged warriors playing ball in the clouds. One threw the ball, while another tried to stop him. One caught the ball, while another tried to stop him.

Football. In the skies. Who would ever have thought? But…how happy they appeared. How content.

They weren't part of Zacharel's army, but Lysander's. Thane recognized one of the males. Brendon was his name, and he had frequented Thane's club on many occasions.

Thane stopped, hovering in the air some yards away. Perhaps they had heard something about the highly ranked demon that he had not. He called out a greeting.

The game paused, and all four looked over at him. At first, they smiled. But those smiles quickly faded as his identity was discerned.

"You're part of the Army of Disgrace," one said.

Thane was beginning to despise that name. "I am."

"What are you doing here?" another snapped. "This is *our* territory."

"Your kind isn't wanted," Brendon said, peering down at his feet.

The fourth remained silent, but his glare spoke volumes.

Judgment and disdain, from his own kind, when they had no idea what had shaped him into the man he was. They had no idea what he'd had to do to survive. They had no idea the pain and guilt and shame that constantly stalked his every step—even though he told himself he enjoyed his life, that he liked what he was. And he did.

He did. Because he had to.

The four closed in around him, forming a circle, blocking him in. He could have mentioned Brendon's own proclivities and called him a hypocrite, and the others would have believed him. Like all Sent Ones, his voice possessed the ring of truth. But he remained silent. He had many, many faults, but he would never ruin another man's standing with his friends.

He knew how important those friends could be.

"You don't want to fight me," he stated calmly.

"Oh, yeah?" The leader raised his chin, all aggression and assurance of success. "And why's that?"

"I have no honor, and you won't like what I do to you." To prove it, he kicked out his leg, nailing the leader in the stomach and making him hunch over for breath. At the same time, he twisted his upper body and, grabbing a sword from the air pocket at his right, swung out. He clipped the bottom of one of Brendon's wings.

The warrior dropped from the sky, forcing the others to dart after him to prevent him from ultimately going splat. Thane wanted to laugh, but couldn't force a rise of amusement. He hated that he only received respect inside his club. He hated that everyone outside it mocked him, and drove him to such violent behavior.

As if he needed to be driven.

They're better than you. They can do whatever they want. He couldn't even remember what it was like to be untainted by the evils of life.

Whatever. He sped back into motion.

Any luck? he projected into Bjorn's head. They were bonded so surely, so solidly, distance never mattered.

None. You?

None.

Any luck? he projected into Xerxes' head.

Yes. Bad. You?

The same.

He had to find and stop Strife before any other human lives were ruined. Unlike some of his brethren, he understood the humans. He sympathized with their weaknesses. He wanted to protect them from the very pain he had endured.

Thane increased his speed. He needed to figure out his next plan of action. To clear his head. To think. Sex was his usual method, but he was used to finding his women in the club. They knew a little about him, what he expected, and he knew they were already on the road to ruination. He didn't have to worry about destroying their innocence.

But he didn't have time to fly to the club and fly back here. He would have to risk going to a human club, then. Yes, he decided. He would go to a human club. He would find a woman, the wildest one, have her and figure this out. Surely.

CHAPTER TWENTY-SEVEN

"—CAN'T FLASH," Nicola heard Koldo say, his voice dripping with all kinds of rage. "You have to continue the hunt on your own."

He couldn't flash? She'd just turned the corner into the kitchen, where the men were located, but hearing him say that, she froze in the doorway.

"I don't mind doing that," Axel replied. "But I gotta tell you. I'm getting nowhere. Your father leaves zero tracks."

"He's been planning this a long time. Before approaching us, he would have come up with a way to avoid detection."

Neither man noticed her. They sat at the table. And how odd they looked. Two primal warriors, seated so domestically at a hand-carved table, white-and-black-checkered curtains covering the bay window behind them.

"But he's not smarter than me," Axel said. "Or is it 'than I'? I always forget. Anyway. I'll find a way to draw him out."

"Hungry?" she asked, finally earning their notice.

Axel squared his shoulders, at attention. Koldo raked a hand over his scalp, as if he were embarrassed. How adorable.

They were wearing identical white tops and pants,

the material loose, and they both looked adorable. Like best friends who had made a pact to always do everything together—even dress.

Say that aloud. I dare you. "Well?" she prompted.

"We can feed ourselves," Koldo said at the same time Axel said, "I'm ravenous."

"Well, my answer matches Axel's," she said. "Therefore, I'll make something." These past few days she'd spent a lot of time puttering around in the kitchen, trying new recipes brought to her by Koldo's friends, and it had been wonderful. She'd discovered a blooming talent she hadn't expected. Lack of time and money had never allowed her the luxury of even trying.

Axel smirked. Koldo scowled. She gathered dishes and cutlery and the appropriate ingredients for an avocado-and-strawberry salad, and all the while she could feel Koldo's gaze on her, two white-hot pings drilling into her back.

Was he thinking about last night?

She was. With every glance, every touch, she'd felt the depths of their connection. Something deep, inexorable.

"I'd like to hire you at my place, Miz Nicola," Axel said. "I have a benefits package I know you'll love."

A shuffle of clothing, the squeak of a chair. The pound of bone against bone.

Nicola turned and watched as the two men slammed together and propelled to the ground.

A growl from Koldo. "She's mine!"

A laugh from Axel. "And I can't tease you about her?"

"No."

"Children! Enough," Nicola said, clapping to claim their attention.

They broke apart, Koldo huffing and puffing, Axel grinning.

"Your jealousy is so cute," Axel said.

"Just try to leave me," Koldo threw at Nicola.

I won't roll my eyes. "Sit."

Instantly the men obeyed, reclaiming their chairs at the table.

She tossed all of the ingredients in a large bowl, then set smaller bowls in front of the guys. When she attempted to ease into the seat between them, Koldo took her by the arm and tugged her onto his lap. The warmth of his body and the sunshine scent of his skin instantly enveloped her, holding her captive.

He glared at Axel.

Axel grinned.

"So…you can't flash," she said to Koldo.

He stiffened. "No. I tried again this morning. I failed."

"What's wrong?"

"Something was done to me during that last fight." Koldo finished his meal in a hurry, stood, moved aside and urged her back into the chair. "Stay here. Eat." He gave her a swift, hard kiss and tugged Axel from the room.

"But I'm not done with my food," she heard the black-haired warrior whine.

"You are now."

The back door slammed behind them, cutting off any reply.

What am I going to do with that man?

She padded to the window and watched as he led

Axel inside the small building they'd erected last week. Was Koldo's dirty little secret in there? If so…what could it be? Another woman?

No, he wasn't the type to cheat. He had far too much honor.

Refusing to dwell, she fixed Laila a bowl, rinsed the rest of the dishes and placed them in the washer, then strode to her sister's bedroom. Her twin was pacing in front of the bed, her hands wringing together.

"I made brunch," Nicola told her.

"I'm not hungry." Laila's skin was pale, her motions stiff.

"Well, you need to eat."

There was a tinge of desperation to her sister's tone as she said, "We were almost killed, Co Co."

"But we weren't. We survived."

"What if we're attacked again?"

"What if we're not? You shouldn't worry about what's going to happen, La La, but you *should* expect to be protected when something does." So far, her sister had wanted nothing to do with Koldo, the tattoos or anything he'd said—despite knowing he was right!

"You really believe that?"

"I do."

"And I want to be like you. I do. I just… I have trouble trusting it all. I mean, staring at a bunch of number tattoos is going to help me? Please!"

"Trust is a decision, not a feeling." Just like forgiveness. "Give it a shot."

"I just… I'm sorry. No. I can't."

Nicola could have curled into a ball and cried. But instead, she rallied, determined. "You'll continue to worry and that worry will kill you. Is that what you want?"

"No." Her sister's shoulders drooped.

Nicola reached out, squeezed her hand. "Let's do something to distract you." Something to improve her frame of mind. Books wouldn't cut it, and TV might exacerbate the problem. All that left was… Ugh. Something that sounded like torture. "We can, I don't know, work out or something. Get our bodies in shape."

"I don't know. I—"

"Please. For me."

Laila massaged the back of her neck. "I'm not in the mood."

"Neither am I, but we could both use the exercise." Before her sister could issue another refusal, she added, "I'll be in the workout room. Join me, okay?"

A pause, a sigh, then, "Okay. Maybe."

"Definitely." Nicola clomped into her bedroom and changed into a sports bra, tiny skintight shorts and running shoes. Her first pair. Well, the first pair she would actually put to use.

She entered the workout room and looked around. Machine after machine greeted her. All large. All intimidating. The only piece of equipment she recognized was the treadmill.

That would have to do.

Nicola set a slow pace—at first. But the sweat began to roll, and her heart began to pound, her muscles to burn, and she liked it, so she raised the incline and kicked up the speed. Soon she was jogging. And jogging and jogging! Shock filled her, but the exercise felt so good, too good to stop, invigorating her, and she thought she could go on forever, and that if she were outside, she could run across the entire world. There was so much oxygen in her brain, her thoughts were actually fizzing, her blood popping and crackling and her ponytail swinging back and forth, slapping her in the face, and oh, even that felt good, because she was free and she was healthy and nothing could stop her, and—

"I'm pleased."

Her attention jerked to the left. Koldo stood in the doorway, his expression satisfied, his hands fisted on his hips. The action jolted her, and she missed her next step. The treadmill was unforgiving, and she stumbled, flying backward and slamming—

Into Koldo.

His body was big and hard, and she lost her breath—breath that had already gone thin and raspy. Suddenly light-headed, she hunched over. Or would have. Koldo's arms banded around her, holding her upright.

"I'm sorry," he said. "I didn't mean to startle you."

"Don't worry about it," she wheezed. And okay, wow, the workout had affected her more than she'd realized. "You should probably let me go. I'm sweaty."

His pupils expanded, gobbling up the golden color of his irises. "I like you that way."

The huskiness of his tone… "Are you flirting with me?"

He blinked with surprise. "I think that I am."

The world spun—but not because she was feeling faint. Koldo had taken her by the waist and maneuvered her around to face him. She teetered forward, and had to balance her palms on his chest. His heart beat as hard and fast as hers.

"Is it working?"

"It is."

"Prove it."

He hoisted her up. Her legs wrapped around him

as he lowered his head. Their mouths met in an explosive kiss that offered no preliminary exploration, only passion.

Just like that, she was a study of movement, her hands on his face, no, on his neck, no, kneading his shoulders, her nails digging into his skin. It was such a beautiful moment, so charged, two pieces of a puzzle being fit together.

Desire burned through her, and need, so much need. Want, so much want. As if she hadn't found satisfaction last night. The two drives were intertwined, indistinguishable, as tangible as Koldo's body.

"I have to have you," he said. "All of you. If you're well enough to run the treadmill, you're well enough to be with me."

"Yes."

"Here. Now."

"Yessss." This was happening. Finally. They would be together, and they would belong to each other, and they would stop worrying about what could go wrong—even though they weren't supposed to be worrying about anything.

"Uh, that's going to be a bit of a problem," another male said.

Growling, Koldo swung his head toward the door. Nicola followed his lead. A grinning Axel stood next to another male of equal strength. This one had black hair and blazing green eyes that utterly contrasted with his lips, which were set in an ice-cold line.

"Zacharel," Koldo said, nodding his head in stiff deference. To Nicola, he added quietly, "He always looks that way. Fear not."

Nicola's legs dropped to the floor. Her heart was

hammering, but the beat was now steady, strong. Her clothes were in place, nothing disheveled, and yet she felt as though she were a teenager caught with her pants down.

The new guy looked her over. "You're thriving. That's good."

"You know me?" she asked, surprised and confused. She'd never met this man. He wasn't the type of guy a girl would ever forget. No, he was the type of guy a girl dreamed about for the rest of her life—either sighing dreamily or sobbing with fear.

"I noticed a certain warrior's interest in you, and made it my business to learn everything possible." That glorious jade gaze slid to Koldo before she could comment. Not that she knew what to say. "Your presence has been requested in the heavens."

A tense pause slid into a long, uncomfortable silence before Koldo gave another nod.

Axel and Zacharel walked away, leaving her alone with her warrior.

"I must go," he said.

She reached up and cupped his cheeks, the soft hair on his jaw tickling her skin. "I understand. Just make sure you hurry home. I'll still be here, and we can pick up where we left off."

He leaned down, placed a soft kiss against her lips. "You've just guaranteed I'll return at the soonest possible moment. And don't worry about evil invaders. Axel ensured other Sent Ones can come and go, but no one else can get through my cloud."

A second later, he vanished, startling Nicola. Then he reappeared, a look of wonder on his face.

"I flashed," he said.

"I know. I just watched you." He hadn't lost the ability, after all.

"But I did it twice. Not just now, but before, to catch you when you fell off the treadmill. I was too consumed with what we were doing to realize I had done it until I appeared in the heavens."

His lips lifted in a slow, sensual smile, revealing perfect white teeth, lighting his entire face. She could only stare in amazement, her head practically spinning, her limbs definitely shaking.

"I can protect you," he said.

"I knew that, too."

"I'm not helpless."

Hoping to tease him, she said, "Are we playing the Obvious Game? If so, guess what. I can run on a treadmill. I can wear my hair in a ponytail. I'm a girl."

Laughing, he placed another kiss on her mouth. And then, for the second time that day, he flashed away. This time, she reeled. That laugh…it had been rusty, but hearty. Ragged, but gorgeous.

Would she ever get used to his magnetism?

Nicola snagged a glass of water before heading into her sister's bedroom, where she found Laila pacing. Still.

"You didn't come to the workout room," she said.

"Sorry, sorry," Laila replied. "I lost track of time."

Nicola opened her mouth to respond—but caught sight of two little monkey faces peeking over Laila's shoulders. They spotted Nicola and grinned smugly.

She strode forward, but they ducked down. Laila seemed to have no idea. Nicola walked a circle around her, searching, but there was no longer any sign of the creatures.

A sense of urgency hit her. "Pick something to do, La La. Anything at all. I'll do it with you. The constant anxiety has to end *now*."

"I just… I need to think."

"About what?"

"Everything! We're so weak, Nicola. Both of us."

"I'm stronger every day, and you could be, too. I mean, we're on the winning team. We have warriors fighting for us. We have the power and protection of the Most High."

"You say that, but…." Laila scrubbed at her face. "What if He doesn't respond next time?"

"He will."

"How can you be so sure?"

"I just know it, deep inside." Somehow, Nicola maneuvered her sister into the bed and tucked the covers around her. "If you won't do something with me, I want you to rest and give your mind a break. And if you insist on thinking about anything, think about everything I've said. It's the truth."

"All right."

"Promise?"

"Promise." Laila closed her eyes, and Nicola stroked her face the way their mother used to do to them. At first, her sister's expression was pinched, her body restless, unable to settle. But as one minute drifted into another, she settled down. When her breathing finally evened out, Nicola stood and strode to her own room.

She showered and dressed in a pink tee and jeans, wanting to look her best when Koldo returned—and give him a few new pieces of clothing to rip off her. But she waited…and waited…and he never showed up.

After a while, the rays of sunlight seeping from

the windows lulled her into the backyard. The air was warm, perfect and scented with wildflowers, citrus and pine. She breathed deeply, savoring.

Bang. Bang.

A muffled female voice rang out. Frowning, Nicola hurried to the little shack Koldo and Axel had built. There were no windows, and seemed to be no doorway.

"Help me. Please."

There was the voice again, clearer this time—coming from inside the shack. Her tone was…pure. Strong. Enough to give Nicola chills. It was a purity she recognized, since both Axel and the one named Zacharel possessed it.

Was this female a Sent One? The lover Nicola had been so certain Koldo didn't have?

"Who are you?" she called, palpating the walls for any kind of seam.

"Help me. Please! Let me out."

Why had Koldo placed the woman in the shack? He wasn't a cruel man. Was he?

Nicola stilled, her mind whirling. He was a man who had never hurt her—had even beat the man who had. He was a man who had despaired over the fact that he might not be able to protect her. He was a man who made her feel safe in his arms.

He was a man she trusted.

But she didn't know or trust the woman.

"What's your name?" she asked.

Once again the woman ignored her question, saying, "Just let me out. All right? Yes?"

The desperation was warranted. The evasion was

not. Could she be a serial killer? Or working with the demons?

"Let me out!" Fists banged into the wall. "Now!"

Nicola nibbled on her bottom lip…and backed away.

CHAPTER TWENTY-EIGHT

KOLDO WATCHED as Zacharel landed at the edge of Germanus's cloud—no, Clerici was the owner now.

Golden wings tucked into the warrior's back, and an unexpected pang of envy hit Koldo—as always. He had to stop feeling this way, but oh, what could have been. He wasn't someone who believed everything happened for a reason. Bad things happened because people had free will.

Of course, he did believe something bad could be worked to a person's good. The loss of his wings, however? He couldn't imagine anything good ever coming from that.

And the loss of his ability to flash? No. Nothing good could have come from that, either. How would he have traveled? How would he have survived? He was grateful he had healed.

Either Sirena's poison had faded on its own, or his joy at being with Nicola had helped him overcome it. Probably the latter. Every day he was tied a little more firmly to the delicate human. Needed her a little more fiercely.

Zacharel flowed into motion, saying, "Clerici wishes to meet you."

Koldo kept pace with him, boots thudding against the cobbles that formed a path through the cloud to the temple's dais. Flowers bloomed at each side, rivers as clear as crystals winding throughout. The sky was a bright blue, the sun throwing rays of gold and orange and twining them like ribbons.

"You knew I wanted Nicola before you assigned me to guard her," he said.

"Yes. But you've known that for a while."

"I have. What I haven't been able to figure out is how you knew."

Never one to reveal a sense of being uncomfortable, Zacharel shrugged as if he hadn't a care. "The Most High opened my mind to a vision. I watched you return to the hospital. I listened to you speak to the girl in the elevator."

Koldo didn't mind having visions about others. But others having visions about him?

"He wants you happy," Zacharel added.

"I know." But did he really believe it? After everything Koldo had done... "Is that why you placed Jamila at her office?"

"Yes. I wanted her well guarded while you were away. You were so unstable, Koldo. You know you were. You were a bomb too close to detonation, and everyone in your path would have felt the sting of your explosion. The girl has calmed you, and I'm glad for it." Zacharel patted his shoulder.

Blue-winged angels pushed open the double doors.

"I'll leave you to your meeting now," Zacharel said.

"Very well. And thank you." Koldo stalked inside the building, his footsteps echoing. The corridor was empty. Before, it had been lined with antique furniture, and always burst at the seams with Sent Ones, movement and chatter. The demons must have defiled the furniture, and the Sent Ones must be waiting for a summons.

A summons Germanus should have been the one to make.

Hands fisting, Koldo stalked down the hall. The doors to the throne room were guarded by another set of angels and were already pushed open. Koldo passed, silent, and entered, noting that the walls were now bare, the murals of the Most High's realm of the heavens painted over.

Had they been defaced?

He should be out there, hunting the culprits. Instead, he was playing naughty cat and recovering mouse with his father.

"At last I meet the famous Koldo."

The deep voice came from the right, and Koldo turned. Clerici perched on the middle step of the dais, polishing a sword. He wore a flowing white T-shirt and pants, just as Koldo preferred. There was dirt on his hands, as well as his middle and calves.

Where Germanus had appeared aged, Clerici appeared young, even for their kind. He looked to be a mere twenty years old, with brown hair, brown eyes and an unassuming face. Plain, to be honest. But there was something about him that arrested Koldo's attention. A magnetism. A gleam of…love, perhaps, shining brightly in those dark depths.

And like Koldo, he was without wings.

"I'm not what you expected, I know," Clerici said, running a rag over the length of a weapon.

"I hadn't given you any thought."

A nod of that dark head. "Brutal honesty. I like that."

"You receive that from all of us."

"Ah, but you aren't bound by the ring of truth. You offer it willingly."

A defect all Sent Ones could sense in him. "You have an assignment for me?"

Clerici set the blade aside and looked up. "Not currently, no."

Confused, he said, "Why not?" He'd thought that was why he was here.

"You aren't ready."

A lie, surely! "How do you know that?" he gritted out. He was a first-round pick, and that was that.

The new king of the Sent Ones offered a half smile and tapped the center of his chest. His heart. "I just do."

And I'm now brewing a rage just for you. "I'm strong, capable."

"No. You're enslaved by your emotions."

He popped his jaw. He wouldn't discuss his mother. Not with this stranger. And he knew that's where the male was headed. "Why did you summon me?"

"Perhaps I wished to welcome you to my fold." Clerici's head tilted to the side, and he perused Koldo with the same intensity he'd received. "Perhaps I wished to ask you if you miss your wings."

More than anything else in the world, but all he said was, "Do you miss yours?"

"Who says I ever had a pair?" Clerici stood and closed the distance between them, and it was then that Koldo felt the power crackling from his skin, lightning strikes against his own, burning him from the outside in.

"Did you?"

"Ah, but that information isn't yours to collect, is it?"

Privacy. That, Koldo understood and respected. He shook his head.

"And now, on to our business," Clerici said. "I offered each of the Elite Seven a reward for their dedicated service to Germanus. I expected requests for riches, clouds and other tangible items. But every warrior astonished me, I must say. And your Zacharel most of all."

There was no time to reply.

"I have a gift for you," Clerici added. He lightly placed his hands on Koldo's shoulders, but then, strength wasn't needed. At the moment of contact, a warm cascade of honey began to wash over Koldo, bathing him, empowering him. "Not because you deserve it. You don't. Unlike the Merciful One, the Anointed One and the Mighty One, I cannot see into your heart and know the good you are capable of. Unless the Most High informs me otherwise, I can see only your actions. But Zacharel named you as the recipient of his reward, and I promised to deliver it."

But…why would Zacharel do such a thing?

Dark eyes pierced deep. "Right now, Koldo, you are filled with so much hate there's no room for love. I can feel it. And without love…well, you'll fall, and Zacharel has no desire to see you fall."

"I will—"

"Silence."

A simple command from the king, but one Koldo could not refute. His lips felt glued together as he nodded.

"The mouth can be a snare," Clerici added more gently. "Sometimes it's better not to say anything at all."

He knew that very well. He gave another nod.

"Do you know what Zacharel asked me to give you?" Clerici asked.

Before Koldo could guess at the answer, pain shot through his entire body. Pain like he had not endured even in his father's camp, when he was hung from the ceiling by hooks embedded in the muscles in his chest, each of the Nefas warriors allowed to strike him once, with the weapon of their choice.

His knees buckled, and he hit the ground with a hard thump. The shirt was ripped from his body, though no one touched him, the material floating to the floor. A sharp, agonizing lance bowed his back, and he fell the rest of the way forward. His chin slammed against the marble, the taste of copper coating his tongue.

A shout pounded against his teeth, split his lips apart. What had Clerici done to him? There was no way he could survive this. It was too much…it was…fading? Yes. Yes, it was, the pain ending as abruptly as it had begun. Panting and sweating, Koldo lumbered to his feet. Clerici was nowhere to be seen, and there was a heavy weight at his back, as if two warriors had jumped on him and refused to let go.

He reached back—and encountered the soft graze of feathers.

Heart slamming against his ribs, he jerked whatever he held forward. White feathers veined in gold greeted his eyes, the tendons thick, strong and unscarred. He lost his breath, again fell to his knees. He gave another tug, but the appendage remained attached to him, pulling tight, creating the most wondrous pain.

Wings. He had wings.

His mind reeled as he pushed to his feet. "Thank you. Thank you!"

He walked toward the door, dazed, but the moment he cleared the entrance he picked up speed. Soon he was running, bypassing the second set of doors, outside, racing along the cobbled pathway, hitting the edge of the cloud—

Falling.

Koldo spread the wings and they caught in a current, evening out his glide. He threw back his head and laughed with undiluted joy. He was flying! Up, down, up, down, flapped the wings. No, not "the" wings. *His* wings. His. They belonged to him. And no one would be able to take them away from him.

The wind whipped against his skin, his feathers. He shot as high as he could go, the air growing colder. He dived low to the ground, the air heating, before twisting his body and shooting back up. Clouds dusted over him, cool and moist, and birds flew beside him. He performed flips, laughing all the while.

Never had he been so carefree.

What would Nicola think when she saw him? He imagined her at home, in their room, on the bed, waiting for him. She would smile, and she would gasp. She would exalt over the beauty of his wings. And why not? His feathers were the purest shade of white and threaded by the most beautiful rivers of molten gold.

She would be the first person to touch them.

He flew until the forgotten muscles in his back burned from the strain, unable to take much more. Until his wings seized, refusing to move another inch, and he began to plummet. Just before landing, he flashed to the front yard of his ranch. He hit with more force than he was used to, and had to roll with the impact. Dirt and grass tangled in his beard, clothing and feathers.

The moment he stilled, he popped up and ran inside. There was no sign of Zacharel, no sign of Axel. Laila was asleep in her room. He burst through the door of Nicola's bedroom. She sat at the edge of the bed, and jumped up when she spotted him. She was…upset.

He lost his grin, his excitement. "What's wrong? Did something happen?"

She blinked, her gaze zeroing in on his wings. "We'll get to that. First, how…?"

"So you're not hurt?"

"Not physically, no."

The excitement returned and he spun. "The wings were a gift." Pleasure filled him as he clasped the ends of the wings and stretched them to their full length. "Touch them. They're real."

She reached out, her fingertips brushing the arch, flowing down the center. He closed his eyes and savored. Even as a child, no one other than his mother had ever touched his wings, and never this way. Never so gently, so tenderly.

"They're wonderful," she said. "But it's kind of hard to enjoy them when I know you have a woman locked in the shack out back, and I don't know why she's there."

He whipped around, his elation draining. She knew. He'd wanted this, he reminded himself. He'd wanted her to learn about this side of him. To know him, all of him. To want to be with him anyway.

"She demanded that I set her free."

"But you didn't," he confirmed. She couldn't. There was no door.

"I didn't." Her hand fluttered to her neck, rubbing. "Who is she?"

He watched a feather float through the air and land

on the ground, and fought a wave of fear. What if Nicola considered him a monster? What if she decided she was better off without him?

Find out now, before you come to depend on her any more than you already have.

"My...mother."

Nicola's jaw dropped. "What? Why?" she demanded, closing the distance and flattening her palms over his bare chest. "Because she removed your first pair of wings?"

His mouth went dry. "Among other things, yes." *Understand. Please.* "Afterward, she threw me into a nest of vipers. I was so weakened, I couldn't escape, and for years I was forced to do terrible things to survive."

Sympathy cloaked her features. "I'm sorry about that. I really am, but this isn't the way to make her pay. You need to take her to the judge of your people. There *is* a judge, isn't there?"

He nodded stiffly. "I don't know what her sentence will be, if it will be harsh enough."

Her brows knitted together. "That's not your call."

"She hates me. For no reason, she hates me. She isn't sorry for what she did. She's proud."

"And you, what? Want to inflict upon her every pain that was inflicted upon you?" she asked, clearly dazed. "Yes. You do. It was her hair that you cut that day, wasn't it?"

A pause before he nodded.

"And you were so angry with yourself, so torn up. Koldo, don't you see? The longer you keep her, the more likely you are to harm her irrevocably. And if you do, you'll never be able to forgive yourself."

He breathed in...out. "She deserves to suffer."

"Maybe so, but hatred makes *you* just as much a prisoner as she is. You can't even see past it."

"I don't care."

"Well, I do. Take her to your judge."

Stubborn female, just as he'd known she was.

Anger beaded in his chest. "You've been hurt by someone, too. Hurt horribly, and yet you had no means of fighting back. Well, what would you do if the opportunity to gain revenge finally presented itself?"

Before she could respond, he flashed to the apartment of the man who had killed her parents and brother. Oh, yes. He'd memorized the address. The male sat on his couch, watching TV and drinking beer. Scowling, Koldo materialized. The man spotted him, cursed and scrambled backward. Koldo grabbed him by the scruff of his neck and flashed back to the bedroom in Panama.

Nicola was pacing in front of the bed, and now stilled.

Koldo shoved the male to the floor face-first. "What do you have to say to the one who murdered your family?"

"Wh-what's going on?" the man in question cried. His eyes were wide, glassy, as they darted between Koldo and Nicola.

Finally, his attention remained on Nicola and he gasped. "You."

So. He recognized her, despite the years that had passed.

Nicola's hands formed a tent over her mouth.

"Do you truly have the strength to pardon him?" Koldo demanded.

She said not a word. Her gaze remained locked on the one responsible for her loss.

Tears rolled down the human's reddened cheeks. "I'm sorry," he cried. "I'm sorry. But please, let me go."

"You're sorry because you were caught," Koldo yelled down at him.

The male squeezed his eyelids together, his tears falling with more force.

Koldo looked to Nicola. "Remember your brother in his casket and then tell me what you want me to do to this man."

As the man tried to crawl away, Koldo pressed a foot into his lower back and held him down. "I'm sorry. So sorry," he repeated.

"Well?" Koldo insisted. *Stop. You have to stop this.* But he didn't. He'd started it. He would see it through to the end.

Nicola raised her chin and finally met Koldo's stare. Her eyes were cold, hard. "After the accident, Laila and I went to his house, intending to kill him while he was out on bail. Yes. That's right. We actually plotted a cold-blooded murder. We were so angry, so hurt. We figured we were dying anyway, and at that point, we *wanted* to die. So why not, you know?"

Koldo listened, dread replacing the anger.

She continued softly, "His wife answered the door. She was holding their infant daughter. We realized we couldn't hurt the pair of them the way he had hurt us."

The dread left him, too, leaving only despair and desperation. He had to make her understand his position. "I assure you. No one will be hurt by what I do to my mother."

"You will. You'll have to live with whatever you do, and we both know you can't do that."

This time, he had no response.

She laughed without humor. "All along we thought I was the one in need of healing, but it's you. You're wounded inside, and those wounds are festering. You're filled with a toxin of your own making," she said, and then she walked out of the room.

CHAPTER TWENTY-NINE

KOLDO HAD MADE a grievous mistake. He never should
have wanted Nicola to learn about his mother. He should
have kept the two women separated now and forever.
If he had, he could have continued on with his life, just
the way it was.

His mother...his to torment, to feed his need for vengeance.

Nicola, his to taste and touch, to feed his yearning
for affection.

Now, he had his mother, but not Nicola. She avoided
his gaze. Anytime he entered a room, she vacated it.

While he couldn't fix the problem he'd created, he
could certainly burn the reminder of it. Two days after
their argument, he moved his mother to the home he
kept in South Africa, and torched the cage in Panama.
He couldn't take her back to West India Quay. Sirena,
and now Jamila, knew its location.

When he finished, he returned to the cavern above
the waterfall.

He'd chained Cornelia to the wall. Her hair was
growing back, her scalp covered by stubble. She spit
curses at him, and tried to reach for his wings.

"You shouldn't have spoken to the female."

"Aw," she sneered. "Has she wised up and decided
you're too repulsive for her?"

His blood boiled, but he flashed away before doing something he would forever regret. As Nicola had said.

He spent the afternoon with Axel, hunting his father. They found several sets of tracks but each proved to be a dead end, the Nefas nowhere to be seen. As weak as the Sent Ones had left them, they had to be hiding, licking their wounds. But where?

He wanted this war over with, done.

He wanted to concentrate on Nicola. Nicola, whose heart amazed him. She had been dealt the worst, and yet light still shone inside her. He had been dealt the worst, and had allowed darkness to consume him.

She was right. He was wounded. But he had no idea what to do or how to heal himself.

He just knew he had to make things right with his woman.

"Get your head in the game," Axel muttered.

Koldo blinked into focus—and realized he was about to slam into Charlotte and her girls, who stood atop a cloud, discussing...Nicola.

"—need the redhead to make me another omelet. So good!"

"I know! Think Koldo would let me borrow her for a few years?"

He angled up and over, avoiding contact. Heard a shouted, "Hey!"

As the wind whipped against him, he looked to Axel. "I must go. I'll see you tomorrow and we'll continue this."

"Uh-oh. I recognize that look. Papa Bear's gonna do some groveling, isn't he?" The warrior laughed with smirking amusement. "Much as I'd like to see that, I've got some people to do. See ya."

They branched off in opposite directions. Koldo flashed as he flew, traveling from state to state and across an ocean in the blink of an eye, until finally arriving at the ranch.

The sight that greeted him nearly stopped his heart.

A dark cloud surrounded the entire ranch, rather than the white one he'd left behind.

Through the darkness, he saw multiple demons crawling over the walls. And that's when he knew. His cloud had been pumped full of demon toxin, sickening it. He'd heard of this happening only once, and had thought it a rumor. False.

He palmed his sword of fire and flashed to the top of the cloud, where he hacked through the gloom. The edges curled backward, sizzling, creating an opening. He jumped through and landed on the home's roof, keeping his wings tucked as close to his sides as possible. He'd never fought with them, and wasn't trained to do so. But that wouldn't stop him from fighting now.

The demons scrambled to move away from him, but he turned and swung the sword, turned and swung, slicing one after the other in half. Black blood sprayed in every direction. Bodies thumped against the grass.

Finally the roof was cleansed and he was able to drop into the house. Demons, demons, all around, each one bigger and stronger than the last, and all the more determined to wreak havoc.

Two leaped on him from behind, ripping handfuls of feathers from his wings. Koldo gritted his teeth and released his sword, then pulled the creatures off, broke their necks and threw them down like the garbage they were.

Where was Nicola? Laila?

He palmed his sword and worked his way down the hall, his wrist in constant motion. Demons dropped like flies. There were more inside Laila's room, but no sign of the girl herself. There was no sign of human injury, either, though the furniture was overturned, clothes strewn across the floor. If she'd been taken…

A demon spotted him and attacked, diving low, locking on to Koldo's ankles, tripping him. His balance was off, and he couldn't catch himself. The sword of fire disappeared as he crashed. He lost his breath, and the rest of the demons attacked, swarming him.

More feathers were pulled. His skin was bitten, scratched. Someone was attempting to chew through his Achilles tendon. Koldo grabbed the two creatures hanging on to his leg, ripped their spines from their throats and tossed them into the far wall. He grabbed two more and did the same, then two more, until he was able to jump up. The rest of the demons fell to the floor. He kicked them, the razor in his boot neatly slicing through intestines.

When he finished, he stomped down the hall. Nicola's door was shut. He burst inside, wood shards spraying in every direction. In the center he found Lefty and Righty grating their claws against a puff of white fog.

Nicola was inside that fog, kneeling, her body draping Laila's. She was staring at the tattoos on her arm. Tattoos that had come to life, forming a protective barrier around her.

The girls were here. They were alive. They were safe.

A potent flood of relief sent him marching forward. Lefty spotted him and backed away, dragging Righty with him. The pair picked up speed and careened through the wall, disappearing.

Koldo followed them, determined to end them once and for all, but they proved wily and slipped into the skies, hiding in the clouds.

Resigned, he returned to Nicola's side and dropped to his knees. He patted, felt the hard shell around her, and knew it was thinning, softening. Finally, nothing was left but air.

"Nicola," he said.

The sound of his voice jolted her, and she straightened in a snap. Wide, stormy eyes found him, and a mewl escaped her lips.

"I'm sorry," he said. "I'm so sorry."

She threw her arms around him and hugged him tight. Her little body was trembling.

Laila remained curled in a ball, her eyes closed, her breathing even. She'd passed out, he realized.

He leaned back, palmed Nicola's tearstained cheeks. "What happened?"

"I convinced Laila to come into my room so that I could read to her. All was well one second, and demons were swarming the next. I don't think Laila could see them, but she could feel them, and she screamed. They wanted to kill us, not just infect us with more toxin. They wanted you to find our bloody bodies. All I could do was throw myself at Laila, skid us both across the room and look at the tattoos, just like you told me."

A new flood of relief had him shaking. "You did the exact right thing."

She sagged against him. "I was so scared."

"But you cast that fear aside and acted." He ran his hands over her back, the ridges of her spine. "I'm sorry I yelled at you. Sorry I wanted you to hurt another living being. Sorry I tried to bring you down to my level, my pain. Sorry I left you. Sorry I wasn't here to help."

Warm tears wet his skin. "I forgive you."

That easily, he thought. Just that easily, and the knowledge caused tears to bead in *his* eyes. She could have thrown his words in his face. She could have sought some sort of revenge, and he would have deserved it. Yet, she embraced him.

"And I'm sorry I ignored you these past few days," she said. "I was trying to give you time to work through your problems without any pressure from me, when all I really wanted to do was kiss you. Or strangle you. I wasn't sure which."

And now *she* apologized to *him*.

He loved this woman, he realized. He loved her with all of his heart, all of his soul.

The knowledge hit him with the force of a jackhammer, leaving a big hole that finally allowed light to flood inside him, revealing thousands of creepy crawlers, evil things he'd stored. The crawlers hissed and scrambled to avoid contact with the brightness and warmth.

He loved Nicola Lane.

But he wasn't yet worthy of her.

Her heart was pure, unsullied. His was tainted. Her hopes and dreams were so sweet. His had always been dark, violent. She had seen a way past similar urges.

She wanted to travel the world, she'd once told him. Wanted to jump from an airplane, pet an elephant and dance on a skyscraper. And he could give her those things. Right now, that was his one saving grace. A saving grace he would take. He would earn her love— deserve it—one way or another.

And then, when he was worthy, he would wed her

in the way of his people and permanently join her life to his, twining their life spans. He couldn't bear to be without her.

I have to let my mother go.

Every muscle he possessed tensed, and his mind instantly rebelled. No, no. He couldn't. He couldn't abandon his need for vengeance. But it was either the vengeance, or Nicola. He couldn't have both. His mother would always stand between them, a wall he could never hope to breach.

So, yes, he had to let his mother go. He couldn't look back anymore. He could only look forward.

As the thoughts formed, the hole widened, widened still more, allowing the light to brighten and spread, eliminating the darkness altogether.

Koldo kissed Nicola softly, gently, and she welcomed him. But he knew now wasn't the time to reveal his plans. Their emotions were too high. And he hadn't yet romanced her as was proper.

"Let's get out of here," he said.

"Please."

He helped her to her feet before crouching beside Laila and scooping her into his arms. Her slight weight barely registered. "Tuck yourself into my side," he told Nicola, "and wrap your arms around me."

She obeyed, and he flashed to Zacharel's home in the heavens. The mist swirled at their sides as he called, "Zacharel? Annabelle?"

"I'm back here," Annabelle replied.

The mist parted, creating a dreamlike walkway as he surged forward.

Nicola gasped, reached out. "What is this place?"

Several tendrils of mist twined around her fingers, but he knew she also encountered a solid wall.

"The usual home for a Sent One," he said.

Annabelle was in the living room, once again perched in front of the coffee table, with books covering the entire surface. She glanced up, golden eyes soon catching and staying on Nicola.

"And who do we have here?"

"My female," he said, with a bloom of pride in his chest. "The one in my arms is her sister. They need a place to stay for a bit."

A grinning Annabelle spread her arms. "Well, welcome to the home of Zachy the Delightful."

He breathed a sigh of relief. No questions. No scrambling for answers.

"We're not interrupting anything, I hope," Nicola said hesitantly.

"Not at all. I'm studying the ways of the Sent Ones, and could use someone to bounce around a few ideas. I mean, I'm the wife of an army leader, and I need to know their laws, their strengths and weaknesses."

"I've been studying, too," Nicola said, and eased beside the Asian beauty. Her gaze remained on her sister. "I'm Nicola, by the way."

"I would say nice to meet you, but that would fail to convey my happiness. You're the first human female to enter this cloud in…ever. I've been starved for decent conversation. And besides that, anyone who can take on Koldo and live, well, I like her already."

Koldo placed Laila on the couch. A slight moan parted her lips, and she shifted to her side, but other than that, she remained in her sleeping state. He straightened.

"She'll be all right, yes?" Nicola asked.

Rather than answer, and spoil her mood, he said, "There's something I must do."

"What?"

"You'll be safe here," he said, sidestepping this question, as well. "Annabelle is just as much a warrior as Zacharel."

With that, he flashed to the cavern in South Africa. Though Cornelia was chained to the far wall, the thick sheet of moisture in the air had left her drenched. The dirty, human-made robe was plastered to her skin.

Her head lolled to the side in an attempt to rest on her shoulder. There were bruises under her eyes, her cheeks were gaunt and her skin wrinkled. Her lips were chapped.

He stepped in front of her. Despite the still-churning anger he had for her, he suddenly felt sympathy for her state—and remorse for being the one who put her in it.

She blinked open her eyes. The moment his presence registered, she spit at him.

He wiped the spittle from his cheek.

"All my hard work destroyed," she said, still fuming about his wings. "You've been given a gift you'll never deserve."

How right she was, though they weren't talking about the same thing. "I know."

"I'll pray every day that someone takes them from you."

And I'll pray every day you find a way to forgive me for whatever wrong you think I've committed. "I'm going to start a new life, Mother."

Her nostrils flared as she drew in a sharp breath. "Oh, well, good for you. I hope it kills you."

"You're not included in that life."

Her lips curved into a vile grin. "Finally decided to end me, have you? Well, well. It's about time. You'll be kicked from the heavens. You'll be disgraced, humiliated, forgotten. You'll be hunted by demons the rest of your life, but you'll be powerless to stop them. You'll suffer, and eventually, you'll die. You'll spend eternity in hell—where you belong."

All that hate, he thought. It lived inside her. Traveled with her, ate with her. Probably conversed with her. She was never without the faithless companion. And she never would be, as long as she nursed it at her breast. It hurt her, not him, just as his hatred had hurt him and not her.

Nicola was right. He'd been a prisoner.

But now he would be free.

He drew a dagger from the air pocket beside him and reached out. She raised her chin, stoic, waiting, ready. Rather than slicing her neck, as she expected, he slammed the tip into one of the cuffs at her wrists.

"Wh-what are you doing?"

"Seeing to your liberation. I threw the key to your chains in the farthest ocean." He had to work at the metal, grinding the dagger through the cylinder, but finally the two sides split. He did the same to the other wrist, then her ankles.

"Why are you doing this?" she demanded.

"Does it matter?"

A tense pause, her confusion saturating the air as surely as the water. "This doesn't change anything."

"I know that, too," he said.

The moment the metal fell away from her, she shoved him. She was too weak to put much power behind the move, so he stepped back on his own. Her gaze locked on him, as though she expected this to be a trick, and she hobbled to the ledge of the cave. She spread her wings.

The action must have pained her, because she grimaced. "When I'm stronger, I'll come for you."

"I'll be ready. But if you try to hurt me by hurting the girl, I *will* end you. I won't give you another opportunity to strike at her."

"As if I would hurt an innocent." With that, she leaped from the cave, falling down, down, down. He wasn't sure she would have the strength to pull herself up, until, a second later, he caught a glimpse of her rising. Her glide was stiff, slow, but still she managed to stay in the air.

It was done, then. Over.

He waited for regret to overwhelm him. He experienced only…peace. Such sweet peace. He'd done the right thing. He'd taken the matter out of his hands. He'd turned away from the temptation.

Now, for his reward.

CHAPTER THIRTY

THE CHANGE IN KOLDO confused, delighted and electrified Nicola.

Only half an hour ago, he'd arrived at Annabelle's to pick up Nicola for "a date." He'd given her a pink angel robe and waited for her to change.

Before they left, Nicola had gone to check on Laila, who had awoken from her faint, thrown herself at Nicola and sobbed. Eventually she'd calmed and promised to listen to everything Nicola had to say about good and evil, joy and fear—in the morning. She'd wanted a night to herself, to relax. To forget, if only for a little while.

Grateful for the change, Nicola had agreed and allowed Koldo to gather her in his arms and take her away.

And so here she was, out on her date. Part one? Flying. Koldo held her as they soared through the sky, the wind in her hair, caressing her skin. The scent of the clouds, morning dew and sunshine inundated her very being.

He was behind her, holding her tightly. The air pressure kept her legs glued to his, rather than dangling below. And the world… The world was lush and alive and glorious. Vibrant greens and blues melded earth and sea. Mountains rose, and valleys dipped. Winter here, summer there. A veritable feast for her senses.

"Everything is so beautiful," she said.

"There was a time I saw only the ugliness." He kissed the back of her neck, and she shivered. "But not today. Today is a new day, a fresh start. I...I freed my mother."

She tried to twist around and look at him, but couldn't quite manage it. "Oh, Koldo."

"You were right. I could keep her and worsen, or let her go and heal."

She wished she could hug him. "It was difficult, wasn't it?"

"The most difficult thing I've ever done, and yet, somehow the easiest."

She patted his hands, joined as they were over her middle. "I'm pleased," she said, as he'd often said to her.

"You're about to be more so." He angled their bodies, and began to descend.

"Where are you taking me?" she asked, breathless.

"You'll see."

Already she could make out...a jungle safari? A river wound through lush trees and patches of dirt. A lioness chased a pack of gazelles. Birds of every color scattered in the wind. Elephants drank at a pond.

He straightened just before landing and placed her feet gently on the ground. Familiar scents layered the air. Scents she'd encountered at the zoo, the few times her parents had taken her, but also things she hadn't encountered. Exotic flowers and flourishing ivy. Damp vegetation, and a startling purity.

"You're in the spirit realm with me. They can't see you," Koldo said. "Go on. Get close."

"Really?"

In answer, he gave her the gentlest of pushes.

Nicola moved forward hesitantly. Despite what Koldo

had said, she expected the magnificent creatures to bolt. Instead, they continued to suck water through their trunks and spray drops into their mouths. They even bathed themselves and splashed each other.

A laugh bubbled from her, but still the elephants remained in place.

Koldo stood off on the side, watching.

Finally she moved beside one of the few babies, an adorable thing that weighed more than she and Laila combined. His gaze lifted, seemed to lock on her. But… he couldn't see her. Could he?

"Touch him," Koldo said. "He won't hurt you."

"Will he feel me?"

"His spirit will, yes."

So…some animals could sense what happened in the spirit realm just as some humans could. She reached out. Her hand met warm, soft flesh, and ghosted through. From behind, a trunk brushed over her arm. Startled, she turned. And found herself face-to-face with the momma.

Apparently, Nicola's spirit could feel things, too!

The female wasn't scared of her, but intrigued. Momma touched her and sniffed her, and then attempted to play with her hair. Nicola laughed, carefree and overjoyed.

After a while, the creatures wandered off, bored with her.

Koldo approached and gathered her in his arms, tension and warmth radiating from him.

"Wait. I'm dirty. You don't want to—"

"You're not dirty."

She looked down. Of course she was—not. The dirt

and stains the elephants had left behind had completely faded.

"Wearing the robe is like walking around in a shower."

"In that case, I might never take it off."

"Let's see if I can change your mind about that," he said huskily.

Her blood began to fizz with the same charged need this man always ignited.

He flashed her to the top of a building. A reeeally tall building, with a flat roof. The sun had set, and the moon was high. The wind offered a gentle caress. There was a patch of grass, with jewel-toned flowers planted all around. In the distance, she could see multicolored, twinkling lights. Soft music played in the background.

Koldo turned her around, only to tug her closer to him. "Now we dance."

"Why would you—" He was giving her all the things she'd said she wanted, she realized suddenly. To travel the world, to pet an elephant. To dance on a skyscraper. What a sweet, sweet man. Tears burned the backs of her eyes and she rested her forehead against his chest. His heart hammered against her temple.

They swayed together, and though it was obvious neither of them knew what they were doing, the moment was perfect. His hands roved over her back, caressing. He played with the fabric of her robe. He combed his fingers through her hair. Every action seduced her, intoxicated her, leaving her trembling, aching.

"Koldo," she said.

"Nicola," he said, the sweetness of his breath fanning over her cheek. "I want you to know…have to tell you…I…love you."

She stopped, certain she'd misheard, and looked up at him. He peered down at her with hope and need and fierce possessiveness in his eyes.

"I want to marry you in the way of my people." He dropped to one knee, in the way of *her* people. "I want to protect you with my name, my status, my fortune and my future."

He…really did. He loved her. Her. Plain Nicola Lane, who'd spent her life in one hospital or another and endured one tragedy after another. And he wanted to marry her. By the world's standards, she was unexciting, not worth a second glance. And yet, this man loved her enough to give her the desires of her heart. He loved her enough to let go of his past. To want to build a future with her.

"But I'll age," she said, wanting to save him heartache later. "You won't. And—"

"No. Your life will be bound to mine, and as long as I live, you will live. As long as you live, I will live."

How…how…perfect. He was offering her a life she'd only begun to dream about.

"I love you, too, Koldo," she said, voice trembling. She did. She loved him. Loved the man he was, the man he was becoming. The man he would one day be. She loved his strengths and recognized his weaknesses. He was good for her, and she was good for him. "And yes. Yes, I will marry you."

His lips lifted in a slow grin. "You will?"

"I will." He was the other part of her, a necessary part.

He was on his feet a second later, flashing her to a bedroom she'd never before seen. He flashed her again, and this time she landed on the large bed, Koldo poised over her, a lacy canopy over him.

"So confident I would say yes?" she asked with a chuckle, sliding her hands up his chest.

"So hopeful."

Her gaze moved over the room. She saw dark velvets and light silks, Victorian furniture and an old-world aura. The scent of roses drifted on a soft breeze. "Where are we?"

"One of my favorite homes."

"How many do you have?"

"*We* have sixteen. I'll give you a tour of each one. Later."

He lowered his head, pressed their lips together, and…sweet heaven. The need they had for each other once again exploded. They were frenzied, eager for more. For all.

"We won't stop this time," he said.

"Not for a second."

"Not for any reason."

If they did, her heart would finally give out. Not from sickness but from frustration. They'd just admitted their love for each other. Now she wanted to show him.

She tugged at the collar of his shirt, saying, "I want your skin against mine." *Need it.*

He helped her out, jerking the material over his head. Her robe was the next to go, leaving her in a bra and panties. A growl rose from him.

"You are more dazzling every time I see you."

He made her feel that way. As if it didn't matter how she fixed her hair or whether or not she wore makeup. As if he would like her no matter how much she weighed. "I feel the same about you."

He lifted to his knees, hastily worked at the waist of his pants. But he had trouble and ended up yanking hard enough to send the fabric flying to the floor in pieces. Any other time, that would have made her laugh. Whenever they were in bed, clothes were destroyed. But one look at him, and she lost her breath. He was intense, determined.

"You make me happy, Koldo," she said truthfully.

His weight returned to her, pressing into her, thrilling her. "Hopefully as happy as you make me."

"Let's see if I can make you happier. Stay just as you are. Don't move."

"Why?" he asked, even as he obeyed.

"I want to learn everything I can about the man I love. Everything you like. Everything you want." They'd done things before, but this was different. This was a commitment, body and soul. She would give him all that she was, and he would know a satisfaction like no other. She would make sure of it.

Her hands roved over the muscles of his chest, even tunneled underneath his arms to the tattoos and the softness of his wings. Then she brought them to the front again, moved lower…lower still. The ripples of his stomach. The hairless calves. The smooth bottoms of his feet. Other than the feathers, there wasn't a yielding spot on him. He was rock solid, the strength she'd always craved for herself.

And he was silken heat, a smooth whiskey that intoxicated, melting away inhibitions. He was everything. He was light in the darkness. He was…hope.

"Nicola," he gritted out. "I don't want to stay just as I am. I want to move."

The jaggedness of his tone caused her to shiver. "So you like what I'm doing?"

"I love." A trickle of sweat slid down his temple. "I hate."

A breathless chuckle left her. "Then I'm doing something right."

"*Very* right," he said on a groan. "And very wrong." His features were strained, his lips compressed. His desperation was growing, just like her own.

How could she not love this man? He never tried to play it cool, never tried to hide the depths of his feelings or his pleasure or his need. And oh, the smell of sunshine he emitted, a smell her body had begun to associate with pleasure. Now was no different, and stunning need became incomparable hunger.

"Nicola. I can't... I must..." One second she was poised over him, the next he was poised over her. "This is all right, yes?"

With his weight pressing into her, forcing her to revel in her own vulnerability? "Yesss."

He was a flurry of movement, smoothing his hands over *her,* preparing her for what came next, singeing her with the intensity of his heat, wringing gasp after gasp out of her as he gave her what her body so desperately wanted.

"There won't be anyone else for you," he said.

"Nor you."

"Never. I'm so glad I found you, sweetheart."

Sweetheart. An endearment sweeter even than his touch. "Me, too."

A masculine purr of satisfaction. "You're so soft. So warm. So mine."

"So desperate for you." For all that he was. Rough or gentle, rushed or slow.

But he stilled and peered down at her, intense and determined. "I want to be man and wife before we come together."

"Here?" she squeaked. "Now?"

"This very second."

Melting all over again.... He was so eager to claim her legally, he was willing to put sex on hold. How many men would do that? "Okay," she breathed. "All right. But hurrrry. Please."

He kissed her before saying, "I belong to you, Nicola. I pledge my life to yours."

"I'm glad. Now, if you would just—"

"Say the words back to me."

Oh. "I belong to you, Koldo." She rubbed her knees against his waist, squeezing. "I pledge my life to yours. Now, do you need me to tell you what to do next or—"

"Now and forever."

"Now and forever. So can we just—"

Suddenly, though Koldo hadn't moved, she felt split in two, her back bowing off the bed. She hurt. She burned. And the terrible heat spread like wildfire, liquefying her bones, torching her organs. She was no longer one being, but two, and both parts of her were agonized. But as quickly as the sensations had arrived, they were gone, and she sagged on the mattress, panting.

"What was *that?*" she gasped out.

Koldo braced himself on his elbows. "We are wed now."

"Just like that?"

"Just like."

"How?"

"Our souls bonded."

"You mean we're…one?" Even saying the words filled her with a wild, bone-deep satisfaction.

"In that way, yes. Now, for the other way." He kissed her again—a kiss that affected every inch of her, making her forget the pain of before and remember the pleasure to come. "I'm glad we waited for this moment. Now you'll be mine in every way that matters."

"And you'll be mine."

"Nicola," he said and finally—*finally*—claimed her.

She screamed. He stopped, staring down at her. Concern and horror radiated from him.

"I'm okay," she panted. "I am. I'm sorry. I just didn't know what to expect, and then it was happening, and now I'm babbling, and you're not moving, and I'm really sorry. Please continue."

"How badly did I hurt you?" he asked, the strain of holding back evident.

"You didn't. Promise. Well, not much."

He wasn't convinced. "You'll tell me if I do?"

"I will."

Hesitantly, he leaned down and kissed her again. Softly, gently. It didn't take long to renew their passions, and then, oh, then, they wed in body, as well. She yielded to him without reservation, accepting him, burning for him, loving him, enfolding him in her arms, crying his name, begging for more, nipping at his lips.

"Never get enough," he rasped.

"Glad." It was the only word she could manage.

He kept a slow pace. Her gaze found his, and locked on. He could have looked away, but he didn't. He peered down at her as if there was no one else he'd rather see, as if he were utterly mesmerized by her.

No one had ever looked at her that way before.

And I get to keep him. Forever.

In that moment, something profound happened. The connection between them deepened, and her soul sang the most beautiful song.

He's mine. He'll always be mine.

Thank you. Oh, thank you.

This love will never die.

Her heart actually felt like it expanded, welcoming even more love for him. Love and joy and peace—everything he'd ever wanted her to feel, in the sweetest degree.

She gave him all that she was, all that she would ever be, her breath emerging choppily. He gave her all that he was, all that he would ever be, his muscles knotting underneath her hands.

"Love you, Nicola."

He felt the intensity, too, she thought. He must. "Love. Yes." Oh, sweet heat… More, more, please more… Her heart was pounding…her body seeming to expand, just like her heart, unable to contain her innermost being. "Faster," she begged.

He obeyed, his motions sharp and sure.

"Yes. Yes! Koldo, I'm going to…" Burst apart at the seams and fly away.

And that's exactly what happened.

She burst. She flew. And wherever she ended up, utter satisfaction slammed through her, at last assuaging the ache that had plagued her since their first kiss. She was suddenly complete, a woman who had survived the worst and found the best.

In the distance, she heard Koldo's loud roar echo, masculine contentment at its finest, drawing her back.

He collapsed on top of her, his heavy weight nearly smashing her lungs. But it was far more glorious than before. She was shaking and clutching at him, this man, her husband.

"How are you… You feel…" he said.

"Amazing," she sighed.

"Yes. That was… That was… I don't have words."

"I do." She kissed his neck, his hammering pulse. "That was worth doing again."

CHAPTER THIRTY-ONE

As THE MORNING SUN crested in the sky, casting rays into the room, Koldo's mind whirled. Nicola was draped over him, her chin resting on his sternum, her fingers petting through his beard, then along the planes of his chest. He had his hand flattened on her lower back, a possessive hold to be sure.

He opened his mouth to say thank-you—again—but he sang instead. He hadn't sung since his childhood, days before his mother removed his wings. He'd never thought to sing again. He'd never had reason. And yet, his low baritone emerged, filling the room, giving Nicola this final piece of himself.

I'm yours. I surrender all.

When he finished, she sat up to peer down at him. He'd once again covered her with his essentia, causing her skin to glow the most luscious shade of gold—and his heart to constrict.

"That was so beautiful." Her eyes were heavy with slumber, wet with tears, her lips swollen and red from his kisses. Beautiful strawberry curls fell in tangles, shielding her breasts. She was the picture of a well-loved woman—one he wanted to love again. "Such a serious expression, my famous warrior. What are you thinking about?"

He twirled one of her curls around his finger. Sex

wasn't what he had imagined. Oh, he'd known naked bodies would strain together. And because of the kisses and caresses he and Nicola had already shared, he'd expected the pleasure. But he hadn't expected to have every bit of his sense of self shredded by her. Had he, he would have thought he'd hate it. Instead, he'd loved every second.

"I would tell you, but I've satisfied you too intently for you to have a working brain. You wouldn't understand."

A pause. A gasp. "Did Koldo the Serious just crack a joke?"

"He hopes not," he said, trying not to grin.

She tsked. "I'm thinking someone needs assurance that he did a good job."

"He does." And he wasn't ashamed to admit it. Her feelings mattered to him.

"How very human of him," she said with a grin of her own.

"It's fitting. After all, he has a human in his heart now." He'd expected to go slowly with her, to savor every moment, help her gradually reach a climax so that her body wouldn't shut down. Instead, his own had urged him to go faster, to do more, to do everything she would allow him to do. He'd been lost in a world of carnality—committed carnality, that is. He wouldn't have liked doing this with anyone else. He'd suspected before, but he knew beyond a doubt now. He'd been too vulnerable during the act, all of his defenses down.

"If I had to describe our night together with a single word, I would say…hmm." She nibbled on her bottom lip. "Pleasant, I guess."

"Pleasant. You guess?"

A little giggle bubbled from her—the kind he'd wanted her to have. "Yeah. You need practice. Selah."

A mock growl rumbled in him. "I'm not pausing and thinking. I'm starting now." He rolled her over, poised above her with a dark scowl. "But before I teach you the meaning of *ecstasy*—again—you will tell me how you feel."

"Perfect."

"No weakness?"

"No. I'm healed." Her eyes widened. "I am. Koldo, I'm really healed! My heart didn't act up once."

She was…right. Not once had she displayed any symptoms of a defective heart. Her stamina had even surpassed his own. "The toxin is gone."

"Yes! But it's more than that, I think. I feel so clean. So…strong."

Yes, that did sound like more had happened. As if a spring from the Water of Life had formed inside of her, creating a well of health and vitality. But that would mean she was a Sent One.

He'd heard of that happening. But…was she?

"I'm so glad," he said.

"I—" Suddenly she frowned, rubbed at her chest. "Something's wrong. I need to check on Laila."

As many times as he'd sensed the danger Nicola was in, he knew not to discount her instinctual feelings. "Of course." He stood and dressed in the robe he'd torn. While the garment was once again in pristine condition, it was different than what he was used to. It opened in back and when he shoved his arms through the holes, the material had to fit itself around his wings and weave the seams together around them.

He tugged Nicola to her feet and pushed her own

robe over her head, covering her beautiful curves—a certain travesty. He kissed her temple, and said, "Whatever happens, we'll get through it together."

"I know." She was steady, her color high—welcome signs of her newfound well-being.

Koldo flashed her to Zacharel's cloud, the romance of his home giving way to the functionality of his leader's. "Zacharel," he called out.

"Back here. Hurry. I was just about to summon you."

Nicola burst into motion, dragging Koldo with her. In the living room, Zacharel and Annabelle crouched in front of the couch, where Laila still sprawled. Her skin had taken on a yellowish hue, and she was thrashing, moaning, her teeth coated with blood. She must have bitten her tongue.

Nicola rushed forward, pushed the couple out of the way and knelt beside her sister. "Oh, my love. No."

Zacharel met Koldo's gaze, stood and closed the distance. "Her heart stopped, but I was able to revive her," the warrior said quietly. "She won't last long."

"Don't you dare say that," Nicola threw at Zacharel, clearly fighting sobs.

Something in Koldo's chest constricted. He studied his wife's twin. To his surprise, the Most High once again allowed him to see past skin and bone and into her spirit.

There were now two demons inside her.

They'd managed to slip past her defenses, Koldo realized, his heart sinking. Or rather, her lack of defenses. How would Nicola react when her sister died? And Laila would die. She hadn't fought the toxin, but had welcomed more.

"The demons plaguing her…" Koldo began.

"They're gone," Nicola interjected. "I know that, but—"

"No," Koldo said, torn up inside. "They're inside her, love."

Nicola stiffened. "No. No!"

"I'm sorry."

Violently she shook her head, saying, "Feed her more of the Water."

"I cannot help her if she will not help herself."

"I'll talk to her. I'll make her understand." She shook her sister, trying to wake her up. "Listen to me, Laila, okay? You have to listen to me." Nicola shook her harder, her desperation evident.

Though an agonized moan was Laila's only response, Nicola began to talk, telling her sister everything she'd learned about spiritual warfare and overcoming demons. She talked and she talked and she talked, but Laila's condition never improved.

Eventually Nicola's voice cracked. Big, fat tears rolled down her cheeks. She twisted, looked to Koldo. "Tell me what to do," she croaked. "Please, just tell me what to do to help her, and I'll do it."

Spiritually, Laila was no stronger than she'd been the day he'd found her in the hospital. "Nicola—"

"No. Don't say it. Don't say there's nothing you can do." She swiped at her cheeks with the back of her hand. "There has to be something."

He hated seeing her like this, so broken, so sad. Losing hope. He couldn't bear it.

And he hadn't tried everything within his power to force Laila to listen, had he? He'd concentrated his efforts on Nicola. He had allowed life to distract him, every spare moment spent with his mother or chas-

ing after his father—even when he'd known the peril
Laila faced.

If he didn't try one last time, a wall could be built
between Nicola and him. Oh, she would forgive him for
any wrong she thought he'd done. If she even blamed
him at all. But every time she thought of this moment,
he would be cast in the role of failure.

He would have given up too soon.

He wouldn't have done all that he could.

And she would be right to think so.

Dread filled him, but still he looked to Zacharel. "I
must go. Guard the females."

"What are you—" The answer must have come to
his leader, because the male nodded. "Are you sure you
want to do this?"

"I am."

A nod of that dark head. "Will you come here afterward?"

"Only to give you the vial. If I stay, she'll try and
take care of me." And that would only negate what he
was about to do.

Again, Zacharel understood. "I see your essentia all
over her. You have claimed Nicola."

"I have."

He gave Koldo another sage nod. "I'll keep the females safe."

"Thank you. And…thank you for the gift," he said,
flaring his wings. He turned to Nicola. "I must go, but
I'll return with the Water of Life. It will buy her another
few weeks, and we can try again to teach her the truths
she needs to fight and win."

Hope sprang in her eyes and he gave her a quick kiss

before flashing to the realm of the Council. There was no time to waste.

An opulent palace made from silver stone appeared just in front of him, the tiered structure rising from a steep cliff, each layer topped by a dark red steeple. Snowcapped mountains were spread out behind it, mist falling from each of the peaks.

Last time he was here, he'd lost the hair on his head and the skin off his back.

Today, he would probably lose his wings.

Koldo pounded up the steps leading to the double doors in front, his boots thumping against the cobbles. Inside, the walls were painted with scenes of the victories the Most High had won. Battles against demons, human lives saved. Battles of good against evil, right against wrong, love against hate. For once, Koldo understood why the Most High had fought so valiantly to save the humans. There was nothing more precious than a devoted human heart.

Two guards were posted at the entrance to the tribunal chamber, their wings a rich cerulean. Angels aided Sent Ones and humans alike. Both males held a sword across the door, the lines of metal crossing in the center.

Koldo paused in front of them and offered his name, as was custom.

"Grata," they called, and clanged the swords together before flicking their wrists and twirling the metal behind them, creating an opening.

Koldo soared forward, pushing open the doors. An azure carpet stretched to the center of the spacious room. Above him arched a domed ceiling, angels and clouds visible through the crystal. The walls were draped with white velvet, and the floor polished ebony. The only furniture was a half-moon desk, and seven chairs. Seven council members peered at him expectantly, each wearing a decorative robe of a different color. Red, blue, green, yellow, cyan, magenta and violet. A rainbow of luxury. The Most High blessed His people with abundant wealth.

Four males, three females, and each appeared to be at the end of a human life—and Koldo wasn't sure why. No one was, though they were certain it had nothing to do with rot, as with the Nefas. As with Germanus, these beings had silver hair and heavily wrinkled skin.

Even still, they were powerful in ways Koldo could not fathom.

He inclined his head in greeting.

"So soon you return to us," Dominicus said.

"This surprises me," Isabella said.

"I have need of the Water of Life," Koldo announced.

Adeodatus tilted his head to the side, pondering him. "And you wish to give it to a human, rather than a comrade."

He wasn't startled by the fact that they knew his purpose. They always knew. "Yes."

"Why?" Christa asked.

Koldo gave them the entire story. How he'd met Nicola, what had happened with her, what had happened with her sister.

"One listened, and one did not," Benedictus said. "Interesting."

"Why should Laila Lane receive another chance?" Katherina asked.

"Because she deserves it? No," Koldo said. "Because she desires it for herself? No. But because I, a servant of the Most High, am asking."

A slow smile lit Dominicus's entire face. "You have gained confidence since last you were here. I approve."

Last time, he'd come for Zacharel and Annabelle. Last time, he'd come with anger and hate in his chest, determined to do whatever was necessary to capture his mother. He had kept his head bowed, his voice low, too afraid of being turned down.

Today, he knew he would not be turned down. He knew his rights. Knew he was in good stead with the Most High, his anger released, his past wiped away. There were no obstacles in his path. What he wanted, he wanted out of love. And it was always the Most High's will to heal. Never did He want a person to suffer, not even to learn a lesson.

"We have no need to convene and discuss. You are approved," Christa said with a nod.

As he'd known he would be. Now, to hammer out the details. "What must I sacrifice? I will give whatever you ask, but I wish to remind you that this is not the Most High's way. He doesn't require anything but the respect of His laws."

"But we require this, wanting our traditions to stand," Benedictus said sternly. "Do you still wish to proceed?"

No need to think about his answer. "I do."

A pause as the members looked to each other. In unison, they nodded.

"We could ask you to stay away from the human, Nicola," Katherina said.

His stomach twisted. No. Not that. Anything but that.

"But we will not," she added, and he breathed a sigh of relief. "We will take your wings. Leave them here. Then, you may go to Clerici's temple, where you will be whipped. Afterward, he will escort you to the river gate. Do you agree?"

Nicola's tearstained face flashed before Koldo's eyes. "I do," he said.

CHAPTER THIRTY-TWO

KAFZIEL STOOD BEHIND HIM, holding a dagger.

Koldo sat on a backless chair, leaned forward and gripped the edge of the table.

"You are a brave man, Koldo," the council member said. And then, as Koldo's mother had done all those centuries ago, he began the agonizing process of separating wing from muscle.

Metal pierced flesh. Warm blood trickled. Pain arced through Koldo's entire body. He gnashed his teeth and endured stoically. He'd gotten by without wings for a lifetime. He would get by again. But he mourned the fact that he would never again fly Nicola through the air. He would never again fly beside a fellow soldier. Once again he would be an oddity among his kind.

Better an oddity with love, than "normal" without it.

From the corner of his eye, he watched as one wing was placed on the floor, the beautiful feathers soaked in crimson, the muscles and tendons nothing more than raw meat.

"And now, the other," Kafziel said.

Koldo kept his mind on Nicola. Her beautiful, smiling face. Her storm eyes, twinkling. She hugged him, overjoyed. She kissed him, thankful.

Worth it.

It wasn't long before the second wing joined the first,

and Koldo was helped to his feet. His legs shook, and what was left of his back pulled and stretched and ached and stung—a back that would next be whipped.

"The human could spurn this gift," Isabella said sadly. "She could refuse the Water, fight its effects."

He knew that, but he couldn't regret his choice. He would give Laila a chance. That was all he could do. He would never have to look back and wonder what would have happened if only he'd tried.

"I won't stop now," he said.

"To Clerici you go, then," Adeodatus said with a nod.

"Many blessings upon you, Koldo," the members announced in unison.

With what little strength he possessed, Koldo flashed to the river gate at Clerici's temple. Already his eyesight was hazing. He knew the area by heart, however. There was no grass, only dirt. No trees, no flowers. Only more dirt and a fat stump that acted as the whipping post. In front of him stretched an iron gate he would soon bypass—if he could walk.

He expected a guard to be there, whip in hand, but it was Clerici who stepped forward to greet him.

"Hello, Koldo."

His knees buckled just in front of the whipping post, and he hit the ground hard. His breathing was choppy, but he could make out the scents of cinnamon and vanilla—a combination that sprang from his own skin. As much as he'd marked Nicola, she had marked him.

"I'm pleased with you, Koldo. You have placed another's well-being before your own." Clerici closed the distance. "You have no idea of the outcome, and yet still you do this."

Koldo closed his eyes and said not a word, asked not a single question.

"What you're doing is a true expression of love," Clerici said, "and I commend you."

Stop talking!

"This is your last chance to walk away."

A muscle ticked below his eye.

"Very well," Clerici said.

A pause…and then the first blow fell.

Leather against decimated flesh, and leather won, sending bits of skin, muscle and blood flying. Koldo locked his jaw. The second blow fell. The third. The fourth. His jaw hurt so badly from trying to contain his screams he was certain he'd popped the bones out of place.

This time, he imagined Laila rising from Zacharel's couch and shedding the sickness as if it were an unwanted winter coat. He imagined the two sisters hugging, laughing, then discussing spiritual laws, learning and growing and putting demons in their place— beneath their feet.

The fifth blow. The sixth.

He had no flesh left, he was sure. Every muscle in his body was tight, shaking, burning. Black spots winked through his vision.

The seventh. Eighth. Ninth.

Tenth. Eleventh. Twelfth.

Finally Koldo could hold back no longer. A cry of agony burst from him.

Thirteenth. Fourteenth. Fifteenth.

He breathed in through his nostrils, short, gasping pants, and breathed out through his mouth. The whip continued to fall. He couldn't pass out. He had to be able to get himself through that gate on his own. Had to get to the Water and back through the gate. Otherwise, all of this would have been for nothing.

After thirty blows, the whip at last stopped.

"Done. It's done."

Koldo's head lolled forward, his cheek resting on the stump.

"Never forget the Most High has girded you with strength," Clerici told him before stalking away.

The gate in front of him opened with a whine. Girded him with strength? Yes, that was true. The code was in his heart, burning as hotly as his back.

He could do this.

He crawled forward, black still winking through his line of sight. Once he passed the iron, dirt gave way to grass, cushioning his hands and knees. Yes, he could do this.

The sound of rushing water greeted his ears, and he forced himself to keep moving. Ruined skin pulled taut. Mutilated muscle tore further. One yard, two... he plodded along, flashing several feet when he could. Mist soon saturated the air.

There were two rivers. The River of Life and the River of Death. Everyone who entered the gates had a choice. Life or Death. Blessing or Cursing. One soothed with a cool breeze, the other smoldered with a stinging wind. One was clear and pure, the other dark and murky. There were those who had actually chosen death, deciding to sever their connection to the Most High. Willingly falling, wanting no part of the heavenly laws.

At the edge of the River of Life, Koldo withdrew a small vial from an air pocket and filled it to the brim, his hand shaking. *Can't drop it.* If he tried to take more than the allotted vial, even if he spilled the contents before leaving this area and sought only to replenish, the Council would know and he would lose everything he'd already sacrificed, plus the Water—and he would never again be allowed to this point.

He fit the cork in the center. The moment it was secure, he placed the vial in an air pocket and breathed a sigh of relief.

Now, to get the vial to Zacharel's cloud.

He couldn't manage great distances, would have to take this a little at a time. First, he crawled to the gate. Then, he flashed to the edge of the cloud. Then, he flashed to the next cloud over, then the next, hopping along, getting closer and closer to Zacharel's.

No, he realized a short while later. He wasn't. He was going in circles around Clerici's temple, ending up only where his gaze led him. Frustration joined a cornucopia of other emotions.

He pictured Zacharel's cloud. *I can do this.* Flashed—

And appeared in the middle of the sky, nothing to anchor him. He plummeted toward the earth, wind beating at him, and oh, did that hurt. If he landed at this speed, he would burst into too many pieces to put back together.

He pictured Nicola's home. It was closer, more manageable. If he could just get there, he could summon Zacharel. Not to help him, but to claim the Water and take it to Laila. Before it was too late.

Come on. One more time. He flashed—

Was still in the sky, only lower.

Flashed again—

This time, he appeared in Nicola's living room and

landed on his stomach with a heavy thump. He raised his gaze. There was the couch he'd left behind, the dark brown carpet with frayed and tattered edges. Oh, thank the Most High. Struggling to breathe, he reached up with a quaking hand and removed the vial from the air pocket.

Zacharel, he tried to project. As weak as he was, he couldn't quite manage it.

A shadow fell over him. "I wondered how long it would take you to fight off my poison and find us," a voice said—a voice he recognized. "I just didn't know you'd already be in the condition I wanted you."

Dread shot through him. Not her. Anyone but her. He tried to hide the vial, but he wasn't fast enough. Sirena stepped on his wrist, holding him immobile.

"I'm part Fae, and as you know, some Fae possess special abilities. I can block the power of others for short periods of time. That's why you couldn't flash—and why you couldn't find us." The container was ripped from his hand, and a stiletto was dug into the wounds in his back, making him hiss. "What do we have here?" A moment passed. She laughed heartily. "The Water of Life. How wonderful."

"Let me see that," another voice commanded.

No. No, no, no. Not anyone but Sirena, he corrected. Not his father.

Another shadow. Another laugh, this one deep, rumbling. "It certainly is. His woman must be sick. He must be trying to save her."

Pop. The cork fell to the floor and rolled just in front of him.

"Please," Koldo said, willing to beg.

Sirena's stiletto dug ever deeper.

"Oh, how I like that word on your lips," Nox said—
just before pouring the precious liquid on the floor.

No. No! After everything he'd suffered—everything
he would soon suffer at his father's hand—Laila's
chance was wasted. He squeezed his eyes closed. He
could do this again, and he would, but it might be too
late.

The Water splashed over Koldo's face, cool and
soothing, but he pressed his lips tightly together, not
allowing a single drop into his mouth. He wasn't to
partake of the Water until his back was totally healed.
To do so now was to suffer, unhealed, for all eternity.

Nox dropped to his knees, anchored his hand under
Koldo's chin and forced him to look up. "We're going
to have fun, you and I."

CHAPTER THIRTY-THREE

THANE LEFT THE HUMAN he'd just pleasured slumped on the floor of the bathroom stall and entered the night-club. The things he'd just done to her...the things she'd asked him to do... She was his third female that night. His eighth in the past three days. Usually he could control his desires. But here, this week, the more females he'd bedded, the more he'd wanted, even needed. Sex had become all he could think about.

He'd stopped hunting the demons entirely.

Something was wrong with him—and yet still he wanted another female. He wasn't sure his body could take it, however. His head was fogged, his limbs trembling.

A strobe light cast colorful rays over the dance floor. Loud, pounding rock music blasted from speakers, and bodies writhed all around, blurring together. Multiple perfumes and colognes scented the air, creating a sickening collage. He stalked from the building and the heat and into the cool of the night.

Pebbles along the sidewalk caused him to trip. The moon was a mere sliver, the sky dark, and only a few stars were visible. There were streetlamps, but the beams were weak, highlighting only small circles.

Currently, his wings were hidden in an air pocket. His robe conformed to his body in the shape of a T-shirt and pants, both black. A wave of dizziness hit him as he continued to surge forward, and he had to lean against the side of a building to remain upright.

Bjorn, Xerxes, he projected. He hadn't spoken to them since…his first few days in Auckland, he realized with a frown. That wasn't like him. That wasn't like them. Why hadn't they at least *tried* to converse with him?

They would come here and they would pull him out of this spiral. The three of them would track the demons together. Fight together. Win together.

Silence.

His frown deepened. They would never ignore him. They loved him.

Something had to be wrong with them, too.

"Hey, you," a female voice called.

He stopped at the entrance of a back alley and turned only because he recognized the voice. It was the woman he'd left in the bathroom. She looked different vertical. Her clothes were mussed, wrinkled, and her dark hair in the same condition. Brown eyes sparkled with excitement. Color was bright in her cheeks.

A sense of foreboding hit him as he struggled to concentrate on her.

"You left something behind," she said, almost within reach. She held out her arm, her fist closed.

A feather? "Show me."

Slowly her fingers uncurled. But…nothing rested on her palm.

"And that is?"

A smile curved the corners of her lips. "Your pride."

Anger slammed through him. He had been judged one too many times lately. "What of yours? I spoke only five words to you before you went to that bathroom stall with me."

Her amusement only increased. "Want to know a closely guarded secret of the Phoenix, Sent One? We can become anyone." As she spoke, her countenance morphed. Dark hair became gold and scarlet. Brown eyes became green. Rounded ears developed points at the end. Human teeth grew fangs.

The Phoenix.

His Phoenix. Kendra.

A second later, her image changed again. To the female he'd bedded earlier today. A second later, her image changed again. To the female he'd bedded before that. Another change. The female he'd bedded last night. On and on she morphed her appearance, until he saw all eight of the supposedly human females he'd taken.

He swallowed a mouthful of dark curses. "How did you know where I'd go?"

"I didn't. I followed you." She flicked her hair over her shoulder. "But you didn't know, did you, and didn't have any idea. That's not very soldierly of you, now, is it?"

Stealthily he reached behind him, into the air pocket he kept tied to his waist. His fingers closed around the hilt of a dagger.

"You took me back to my people, and they forced me to wed a warrior. But I ran away the morning after the ceremony and used the cash I'd stashed away to have my slave bands removed. There are people who specialize in that, you know."

"Your husband will come for you."

"Yes. He'll come for you, too." A tinkling laugh. "Want to know another well-guarded secret of the Phoenix? When we aren't slaves, we can enslave. Every time you slept with me these past few days, your need for me increased. Didn't it?"

The anger budded into sharp, jagged rage. She wanted him addicted to her body. He'd been a prisoner before, and he'd vowed never to endure such a hell again. Had vowed to destroy anyone who even tried.

He always kept his vows.

He didn't give himself time to think about his actions and how low he was about to sink—or the punishment he might face. He didn't waste time threatening the girl. Threats obviously wouldn't work with her.

"I'm no one's slave," he said.

And he struck.

In seconds, the tip of his dagger was embedded in her chest. Her eyes widened with…not confusion and pain, as he'd expected, but with glee.

"Thank you," she gasped out. "That was easier than I thought."

Her knees gave out, and she collapsed to the ground. She lay there, panting for breath, red blood spilling from her, her heartbeat no longer saving her, but killing her, pumping and pumping and pumping the life from her body.

"I'll catch fire, turn to ash and re-form… I'll be stronger…and you'll be forever mine."

"No," he growled. No. He wouldn't believe it.

A laugh sounded in the distance.

He swung around, fighting another wave of dizziness and watching as a shadow slunk from the roof of the building next to him and down the wall. Red eyes glowed from the center of the darkness. Another shadow followed, and then another. Then shadows began to slink from the roof of the other building.

Demons.

So many, more than he could count. Perhaps more than he could fight on his own, but he relished the challenge. To leave was to invite them to hurt the humans nearby.

"The pretty boy has been searching for me, I hear," an evil voice proclaimed. "He wants to punish me for helping to slay his precious king."

A chorus of chuckles echoed.

Thane stepped into the spirit realm and grabbed his sword of fire, the flames producing a crackling yellow-and-blue light far hotter than the ones found in hell, for it was pure. The creatures looked like motor oil that had been mixed with blood and congealed. They were blobs—and they were dangerous.

"I'll kill you," he vowed through clenched teeth. The dizziness had magnified rather than faded, and he was having trouble staying on his feet. Falling...falling... no, catching himself, once again leaning against the building.

"Let's find out," the evil voice cackled. "Last one standing wins."

Each shadow slithered from the buildings, soaring through the air, and aiming for Thane.

He twirled his sword to his left, his right, and arced through the center, slicing several creatures through the stomach. The shadows sizzled and hissed, but none fell from the air. They continued to come at him. He palmed a dagger with his other hand, but the metal did no damage, whisking through and causing the creatures to laugh more heartily.

A breeze blew behind him, and he knew something was trying to sneak up on him.

He flared his wings, knocking several shadows away from him, and hurtled into the air, flipping over the creatures that had thought to take him from behind. More shadows converged. He struck, taking what constituted heads. Rather than fall, however, they vanished.

Thane knew it would be better to remain in perpetual motion, never allowing anyone to get a lock on him. He darted to the side of a building, then to the other side, then to the ground, then to the roof, sword constantly swinging. They followed him. Three times he almost fell. Once he hit his knees, but he managed to bounce back up.

Suddenly Bjorn flew into view, followed by Xerxes. Both men landed at his sides, flanking him. He was so overcome with relief he willingly dropped to his knees.

"You don't call, you don't write," Bjorn said, leaping into motion, his sword of fire already drawn and swinging.

"Tried," he gritted. "Couldn't get through."

"After what we had to give up to get here, after what we had to do to find you, you owe us," Xerxes said, swiping at the shadows with short swords.

"I'll gladly pay the toll."

"The minions of strife," Bjorn said. "Always picking fights. Let's give them a spanking."

They split up, dividing the attention of the creatures, leaping, diving, flying this way and that, flipping, kicking, punching, but only the sword of fire caused any damage. One of the creatures finally managed to wrap itself around his head like a dark blanket, suffocating him.

Screams, screams, so many screams. They scraped at his ears, assaulted his mind. He thought he heard his friends shouting in the background, but…but…the screams, so loud, *so loud,* and they were his own, he realized, coming from him, from his past, from his present, blending together, bleeding so much, soaking him.

All too soon, scenes from his past sprang up and joined the party. The women he'd bedded and left. The humans he'd killed simply to get to demons. The warriors he'd betrayed after his return from the demon dungeon. The times he'd laughed when he'd wanted to cry.

Then suddenly, a blaze of light erupted and the darkness left.

Thane fell forward, landing on his face. He blinked rapidly, the haze around him slowly thinning, even as blood dripped into his eyes. He saw Xerxes and Bjorn, still fighting the shadow creatures, going low, straightening, taking out ankles and knees to hobble. The two warriors stayed close, shielding Thane as best they could.

Must have landed on the Phoenix, he thought. That had to be her still-warm skin cushioning him—no, not warm, but hot. Too hot. Somehow, in death, she was heating up, about to catch fire, all on her own.

Just as she'd promised.

One of the shadows slunk over, staying low, darting out of the way anytime Bjorn or Xerxes struck, and managed to latch on to Kendra's bare leg. The creature laughed manically—just before Xerxes beheaded it.

The shadow vanished, and Thane saw that a flame had finally sparked at the end of Kendra's toe. That flame intensified, spread. Soon, her entire foot was engulfed. Her ankle. Her calf.

The enemy thinned and the remaining few realized they couldn't win and backed up. They attached themselves to building walls and slithered up, up and over the roof.

Cowards!

Thane scrambled away from Kendra's body. Her thighs were the next to catch flame, then her torso, her arms, her chest. Her face. Her hair. Every inch of her was doused, crackling—and then she was gone, ash floating through the air.

She would re-form. She'd promised that, too. She would be stronger.

He would be her slave.

Every ounce of his being rejected the notion.

Xerxes stomped to Thane's side. "You all right, my man?"

His voice sounded far away. Thane tried to open his mouth to speak but he didn't have the strength.

Bjorn took a step toward him, stopped and frowned. He looked down at his wrist, where there was a black scratch, then back to Thane. Confusion gleamed in his rainbow eyes. His frown deepened. His knees collapsed.

Xerxes popped up to race to him, but—

Bjorn vanished.

Vanished as if he'd flashed—an ability he didn't possess. Or, as if someone or something had flashed him.

"What just happened?" Xerxes shouted. "Bjorn. Bjorn!"

Thane struggled to sit up. His friends. He had to help his friends. They were the world to him. Meant everything. He was nothing without them. But the dizziness returned, flooding his head, and weakness spilled into his limbs, and he could only lie there, panting—until he blacked out.

CHAPTER THIRTY-FOUR

NICOLA SAT BESIDE her sister's hospital bed. So much had changed since the last time they'd done this terrible dance, and yet, Laila still hurtled toward death.

If we're ever again in that situation, and I have a feeling we will be, I want you to let me go.

No, Nicola had said then.

Never, she said now.

Before, she had been without hope. Now, she was different. Stronger. Smarter. She knew there was a better way. But her sister didn't, and changing her mind was what mattered right now.

Her precious Laila, she thought, tears beading in her eyes. There were tubes in her sister's chest and arms. Her skin had already yellowed. She had slipped into a coma the doctors said she would never wake from. She was drugged but not without pain, her features pinched and her muscles tensed.

Every time Nicola repeated what she'd learned from Koldo, Laila's vitals strengthened—but the moment she stopped talking, those vitals plummeted. Sleep had become Nicola's enemy.

Zacharel had done what he could to keep Laila alive, but in the end, he'd needed help. So, he'd flown Laila to the hospital. He'd stationed two Sent Ones at Nicola's sides, and they were now standing in the hallway, giving her some time with her sister. To say goodbye.

Where are you, Koldo?

He'd been missing for two days. Zacharel was out looking for him.

Zacharel, who had told her that Koldo had gone to procure more Water, just because Nicola had asked, and that he should have returned by the end of the first day. That wasn't all he'd told her, of course. Even remembering the rest, Nicola shuddered.

Your man was whipped. Before that, he was commanded to give up something precious to him. His mind has to be a mess. I have asked our leader for the details, but they are not his to share.

So badly she had wanted to go back to those few minutes inside Zacharel's cloud and stop Koldo from leaving. But that's why he'd flashed without telling her where he was going. So that she couldn't. He was doing this for her. Suffering *for her.*

I have to find him. Yet, she couldn't leave her sister to…to… She just couldn't leave her sister alone.

And what if Koldo had been asked to give up Nicola?

Her stomach twisted into a thousand little knots, and she had to swallow back a moan of grief.

"This is it for me, Co Co."

Laila's voice pierced the silence of the room, and Nicola jolted with shock. Clear gray eyes watched her, no hint of pain evident.

Inside her, hope and confusion collided with the shock, creating a heady mixture that left her dizzy. "You're awake."

"Just for a moment." Chapped lips curved in a soft smile. "You have to let me go, my love. It's time."

No. Absolutely not! "I told you before. I can't. I won't." Nicola vehemently shook her head. "You can beat this."

A weak chuckle reverberated between them. "Always the strong one…as well as the sensitive one. I don't want you looking back on this and blaming yourself. You did everything you could. I refused to listen. And I don't want you afraid. I'm not. Not any longer."

"I'm not afraid, either." *I'm just devastated.* "You'll get better. Koldo went to get you special Water. It helped you before, and—"

"No, my love, I'm ready now. I've been hovering between the natural and the spiritual for a while, and I got some things worked out with the Most High. He really is wonderful, you know. I asked for a chance to say goodbye, and He granted it."

"Not goodbye. I want you to stay," she whispered brokenly.

"I know you do, but the fear… It was ugly and I let it ruin me. At least now I'm going to a better place, and one day we'll be together again. For now, you have a life to live. The things you're going to teach people… Look at what you've done for Koldo already."

"Laila—"

"I love you, Co Co." So softly spoken.

"Don't do this. Please."

"It's already done."

There would be no changing her sister's path, she realized. The tears escaped, flowing down Nicola's cheeks, one after the other, burning her skin. She reached out, took her sister's fragile hand and linked their fingers.

"I love you, too, La La."

Laila smiled again—and breathed her last.

NICOLA WALKED THE STREETS of her childhood neighbor-hood in a numbed daze. At her request, her guards had flown her here and now followed discreetly behind her. She couldn't stop picturing the way her sister's head had lolled to the side, the spark fading from her eyes, leaving them glassy, dull. Machines had beeped like crazy, and nurses had rushed inside. But that time, they hadn't tried to save the girl. They'd known they couldn't.

They'd turned off the machines, patted Nicola on the shoulder and left her alone.

Silence had surrounded her. Such heavy, oppressive silence. She had only been able to sit there, tears con-tinuing to slide down her cheeks.

How was she supposed to go on from here?

She was shaking by the time she reached the house they'd grown up in. The house where they'd laughed and talked and played. The house where they'd read storybooks to Robby.

Located in historic midtown, the house had yellow stucco and exposed red brick. There were bushes and flowers and bright green grass, plus a cement pathway leading to the steps of a wraparound porch.

The hospital faded from her mind, replaced by a vi-sion of Laila peering out from the window, watching for Nicola to return from the doctor. The moment she had emerged from the car, her sister had smiled at her through the glass, relieved to be together again.

Together again. Something they wouldn't have while Nicola was down here.

Nicola's knees collapsed. Grief was suddenly razor sharp inside her, cutting her up, ruining the numbness. For so long, Laila had been her only companion. Laila was the only one who had ever shared the many travesties of their lives. Laila had cried with her and mourned with her and hurt with her and helped rally her when she was at her lowest.

And now…now…

"Give me time alone," Nicola choked out to her guards. "Please."

A moment passed as they debated, but in the end they walked away and rounded the corner at the end of the street.

A fresh round of tears welled in her eyes and spilled onto her cheeks, one after the other, faster and faster, until she was sobbing, shaking uncontrollably, sorrow and despair rising up, consuming her. Sunlight beat down on her, but she couldn't feel the sting. She was cold inside. So cold.

Her sister was a part of her. There'd never been a Nicola without a Laila.

Her sobs increased until she was hunched over and heaving. Had she eaten, she would have thrown up all over the driveway. But she hadn't, and she could only gag and choke and remember and despair. The new owners and their neighbors must have been at work, because no one came out to check on her. She was glad.

Eventually, though, she calmed. She stayed there, crouched on the cement, her forehead pressing into her hands, her eyes swollen and nose stuffed. Death wasn't the end, she reminded herself. The grave couldn't win. She would see her sister again. She would.

But one thought arose, and refused to leave her. Things hadn't had to end this way. Demons had poisoned her sister, yes, but then, Laila hadn't fought back.

How many families had been affected by a similar situation, but just hadn't known it? How many had accepted what they thought was natural and inevitable, never knowing there was another way?

Too many.

She had to change that. She couldn't let another sister end up where she was, on all fours wetting the ground with a stream of fat tears. Or a mother. A father. A friend. Koldo had taught her how to fight, and she would teach others.

Out of her pain would come her purpose.

Yes. This was war.

The first stirring of hope hit her, and she straightened. The brightness of the light had her blinking. And then…then her heart began to pound in a wild, warped rhythm, as if the organ had just been strained beyond repair. Pain radiated down her left arm, as though she were having another heart attack.

Dying? she thought.

This is it. The end. Your sister is gone and you can't survive without her.

No. No, that couldn't be right.

But fear gobbled up every ounce of her hope, and the pain increased.

All alone. No one to help you.

No! Those thoughts couldn't be springing from her mind. They contradicted everything she'd just realized. So where could—

Demons, she realized. She couldn't see them, but demons must have sensed her despair and come running, hoping to poison her and feed. Well, she wasn't going to let them.

"I know you're lying to me. I know I'm well." As she spoke, her heart returned to its normal beat. "I'll never cave to your kind again."

Two scowling demons appeared in front of her and tucked their gnarled wings into their backs. She had seen them before—one had showed up at her office and then again with Koldo's father. One had a horn rising from his scalp and fur all over his body. The other had a horn in the center of his forehead and scales rather than skin. Their eyes were black, bottomless and pure evil, a match to their pungent scents.

She stood, saying, "You don't scare me."

"We should. We've been waiting for this day. For this moment."

"Where are your friends, huh?" the other asked. "They seem to have abandoned you."

"Then this moment isn't as it seems." She lifted her chin. "I always have help. And besides that, with or without them, you can't hurt me."

They grinned in unison, revealing sharpened fangs.

"We've been with you a very long time, Nicola. We know your weak spots."

"You need us." Uttered in a husky, seductive whisper. "If for no other reason than to keep other demons away."

One step, two, they approached her. She held her ground. At any other time she might have experienced horror. But not now. They'd been waiting for this moment, they'd said. Waiting for her sister to die, when Nicola's emotions would be wrecked. They'd planned this attack. Had probably strategized for days, weeks, laughing about what an easy target she would be. Well, they would get no satisfaction from her.

What do I do now? she wondered.

Now, I fight.

The thought rose from deep inside her, where instinct swirled. Yes. She'd decided to fight, and so she would.

They liked fear and despair—and so she would give them joy and hope.

She closed her eyes and thought about Koldo. Her husband. Her beautiful husband. He loved her, and she loved him. No matter what. She would hunt him down, and they would be together again. If he'd been asked to give her up, so what? She hadn't agreed to those terms. She hadn't promised to give *him* up.

They would fight this war together.

Her hand began to burn.

She glanced down—and watched as a sword of fire appeared in her grip. She yelped and almost dropped the weapon, so great was her surprise. But she somehow maintained her grip. The hilt was warm and light as she danced the crackling flames through the air.

Now the demons backed away from her, their big bodies trembling.

"Where did you get that?" one gasped.

"This can't be happening," the other cried.

They flared their wings, intending to fly away.

If I'm going to act, I have to act now.

"You picked the wrong target," she said. With a single swing of her arm, Nicola decapitated both of the creatures. Their heads rolled, and their bodies fell. Black blood pooled at her feet—and satisfaction pooled in her heart.

The battle had begun.

Magnus and Malcolm flew around the corner, both clutching their own swords of fire.

Hers was bigger.

They stopped when they spotted her.

"You…you…"

"How…"

"You're as shocked as I am, so let's discuss it later, all right? Do you know where Koldo is?" she demanded.

It was time to begin her hunt.

CHAPTER THIRTY-FIVE

KOLDO WAS CARTED to his father's underground nest—
which had been moved to Koldo's home in West India
Quay. The walls were comprised of dark, jagged rock,
the once-pure pool of water now dark in color. There
were around thirty Nefas soldiers dressed in loincloths,
standing around flesh-colored tents, waiting to praise
Nox for Koldo's capture.

"Strip him," Nox commanded coldly, never one to
delay the business of torture.

Eight females rushed to obey. Koldo was already
shirtless, so only the bottom half of his robe had to be
torn from him. Sharp nails sliced at his wounds, and
humiliation burned deep in his soul.

Once again, he was reduced to a puppet, under his
father's control, helpless.

"Tie him to the boulder and whip the rest of him."

Another command the females were happy to obey.

"But you better not like it," Sirena snapped, her possessive streak showing.

He couldn't go down like this. He couldn't. His life
couldn't end in defeat.

But Koldo was too weak to fight as he was dragged
to a large silver boulder and strapped down. A second
later, each of the females seemed to unfold a whip and
strike at him, over and over again. His arms, his legs,

and yes, even his decimated back. He gritted his teeth and bore it without a word, without a gasp, even when his skin was nothing more than tattered ribbons. He knew the rules of the Nefas.

A moment of frailty would be forever exploited.

He tried to flash, and failed. But even if he'd been at his strongest, he knew he wouldn't have been capable of the deed. During the journey, Sirena had dug her claws into many of his wounds and poisoned him, stealing his ability. "I'll have you yet," she'd whispered. He'd tried to project his voice into Zacharel's mind, but he wasn't sure he'd gotten through. There'd been no response.

At last the females finished with him. More of his strength waned, but he was determined to live. He had to live. He had to obtain more Water. Had to help save Laila. Had to see Nicola again. Had to be with her, hold her.

He'd often sensed when she was in danger, but just then, he thought he sensed…determination from her. And if that were the case, Laila had to be alive. Nicola had to be wondering where he was. Nothing else would elicit that much resolve from her.

"How do you feel, boy?" Nox asked with a laugh. "Well, I hope. But if not, no matter. Tonight, Sirena will claim you as her very own."

Cheers erupted.

"Take him to the cage."

Koldo was untied and carried to the very cage he'd locked his mother in. Only, now it was covered by a tarp. He was flashed inside and dropped. He remained on the floor and rolled to his stomach, every inch of him aching. He looked around, but his vision was too hazed to make out more than a dark blob in the corner. A human?

His father approached, saying, "Have you learned yet, boy? You cannot vanquish me."

Koldo pressed his lips together. He could rage, but what good would that do him? He could threaten—and amuse his father. He would rather wallow in the humiliation.

"I hear you let your mother go," Nox said. "Did I ever tell you the story of your conception? No, probably not. I liked that you thought she loved me and still wanted me. But you see, your mother was helping defend an impoverished tribe of humans I wanted as my slaves. I captured her, too. Oh, how she fought me."

Sickness suddenly churned in his stomach.

"I soon put her in her place, of course. Underneath me."

Rape, Koldo thought, his stomach now heaving.

His mother had been raped. Koldo had been the result. He should have guessed, even when she'd claimed to want the man, probably too ashamed to admit the truth. Instead, he'd been so blinded by his hatred and his need to make her suffer, he'd taunted her about obsessing over Nox. No wonder she had spat at him.

Guilt and shame joined Koldo's humiliation, the same toxic mix he'd dealt with most of his life. He wasn't excusing his mother's behavior. But she had hurt, and so she had lashed out. Koldo had hurt, and so he had lashed out. He should have broken the cycle.

"I enjoyed her over and over again, and decided to keep her," Nox continued. "The day she gave birth I made the mistake of freeing her bonds. She escaped, taking you with her. I looked for her, but she hid very well."

And that was probably one of the reasons she had never wanted her friends to see him, Koldo thought, not because she was ashamed of his ugliness. She hadn't wanted word to travel and reach Nox.

"Will…destroy…you." The words left him, unstoppable.

He would. Whatever he had to do.

He would strengthen. He would come out of this.

Nox snorted, and even that was smug. "You can't even protect yourself, and you think you'll take me down? No, Koldo, that isn't how this is going to work. You're going to heal, and you're going to marry Sirena. You will get her with child if I have to steal your seed myself. Once she has a son, I'll have no more use for you."

And he would be killed.

"Until then, meet your cell mate." Nox gestured to the shadow Koldo had seen in the corner of the cage. "I believe you know him. His name is Axel. He's a Sent One, just like you, and you're going to kill him if you want your Nicola to survive what I have planned for her."

Footsteps pounded…became fainter….

"Liar," Koldo tried to shout, but only managed to whisper. Nicola was safe. Axel was safe. He wouldn't believe otherwise.

"Not this time, he's not," he heard Axel say calmly.

What? Koldo tried to sit up. No…no! *Have to get Axel to safety. Can't allow him to suffer.* "You must escape. Now."

"No, none of that now." Warm hands stroked over his scalp. "I'm exactly where I want to be."

Koldo relaxed, but only slightly. "How were…you caught?"

"You know, the uze. I was strolling down an abandoned alley, pretending to be helpless, and boom, someone grabbed me."

So…he was here on purpose?

"The Nefas had been following me for days. I just let them catch me."

Koldo was astonished. "Why?"

"Like I really want to break in a new partner."

No. No, that wasn't it. Axel cared about him. Axel had placed Koldo's well-being above his own. And now, Koldo was supposed to harm him to save Nicola? "Shouldn't…be here. I want you gone."

"No way. I told you. I'm exactly where I want to be."

"Too bad. You're not allowed to help me. The Water…you'll suffer."

"Who said anything about helping you?"

Then what? What was the plan? What was the purpose of this?

"Just sit back and enjoy the show, bro," Axel said, and Koldo heard the amusement in his tone. "I have a feeling you're going to like this one. Your day is about to be saved, and by the most unlikely person."

"Who? How?"

"No way I'll ruin the surprise."

Koldo couldn't help himself. He pulled himself into a sitting position and draped his arm around Axel. "Thank you."

"Not afraid of a man hug, I see," the warrior said, clearly uncomfortable.

Koldo gripped him tighter.

"Really? This is happening?"

"I love you, male."

Axel cleared his throat and wrapped an arm around him, too. "I love you, too. But I'm going to pretend that's the pain talking—for both of us. And if you ever tell anyone you heard any kind of trembling in my voice, I'll kill you."

A few hours earlier

NICOLA STOOD in the center of the spacious room located in a palace high in the heavens. A lifetime seemed to have passed since she'd been brought here, but in reality, only a half hour had. Malcolm and Magnus had summoned Zacharel, told him what they'd witnessed, and the dark-haired warrior had gathered her close and flown her here.

He had yet to speak a word.

She was still raw over her sister's death, still wondering where Koldo was—and growing more determined to find him by the second. She needed to be out there, right now, searching for him.

He was hurt. She sensed it deep, deep inside, a knowledge her concern for Laila had shadowed. But it wasn't hidden anymore, and urgency was riding her hard. Whether he'd been hurt from the whipping or something more, she didn't know. But she would. Soon.

"I have to leave," she said.

Zacharel shook his head.

Frustrating man! "Just as soon as I figure out how to land on the earth without going splat, you won't be able to stop me."

She gazed around the room, looking for a window without a thirty-thousand-foot—or more—fall. She saw alabaster columns, with ivy twined from base to ceiling. The floor was ebony, the walls ivory, with gorgeous tapestries hanging throughout. But no windows. The only exit was the door, now guarded by two winged warriors with metal swords.

She breathed deeply. The air smelled clean and fresh, and pure. As if it had never been tainted by evil. She looked up. The ceiling was domed, with Sent Ones painted throughout—no, not painted, she realized. Not painted at all. The dome was made of crystal and peered into a higher realm of the heavens.

There she saw...no way...but there her precious Laila was, standing beside a handsome young man with red... hair...

Robby? Was that Robby, all grown-up? Nicola's eyes widened. The two were hugging and grinning and laughing, so happy it made Nicola's chest hurt.

They were together again.

Joy was deposited directly into her heart, filling her up, overflowing. One day, Nicola and Koldo would join them. She'd had knowledge of that before, but just then, it sank deep into her spirit, coming alive. Yes, one day.

But not today.

"Koldo needs me," she said. "I have to—"

An unassuming-looking man suddenly paced in front of her, claiming her attention. He had dark hair and kind, dark eyes. He wore a white robe, his hands anchored behind his back.

Oh, good. Someone else to pester about this. "Sir," she said. "My name is Nicola, I'm human, and I need—"

"My name is Clerici."

"Clerici. Hi. Nice to meet you. I have a problem and—"

"Sent Ones are not angels, you know," he said, interrupting her again. "We're often called angels, and sometimes we refer to ourselves that way, but if we break down the pieces, we aren't angels. Really, we are humans with special abilities. And yes, we have longer life spans and wings. We also fight evil."

O-kay. Trying again. "Sir. I know all that. It's been explained to me. But I really need to—"

"Our people serve the Most High, who is a Holy Trinity," he said. "The Merciful One, the Anointed One and the Mighty One. We—and you—were created in His image. We are spirits, we have a soul, and we live in a body. Your spirit is your power source, what lives forever, and your soul is your mind, will and emotions. I'm sure you're well acquainted with your body."

"I am. Now. I'd like to leave and—"

"The Most High gave each of us a sword of fire. A sword you wielded," he said, and stopped. Just stopped and stared over at her with an enigmatic expression.

"Hey, you can't be any more surprised than I was. But there's no time to ponder the reasons. Koldo is out there, and he needs me, and I'm going to find—"

"You didn't wield the sword because you married Koldo, although that plays a part, I think."

Argh! Would he never allow her to finish a sentence?

"You wielded it because you were adopted into the Most High's family. That adoption is the true origin of a Sent One. Perhaps one day you'll even grow wings. Now, however, you will fight for us."

Wait, wait, wait. She was now a supernatural being, meant to join this warrior's army? Head...spinning...

"I'm happy to help you. I am. But I'm going after Koldo first," she said in a rush before the male could stop her. She would do whatever was necessary to succeed. "We'll talk about all this other stuff when he's safe."

"I know where he is," Zacharel said. His first words since this had started.

Nicola spun to face him. "What! Why didn't you tell me? Where is he? What's happened?"

"There was nothing you could do to aid him. You would only have harmed him. And my attention was and is needed elsewhere, where I can do some good. Another of my warriors is missing, and his friends are near the breaking point."

"But—" Nicola began.

"The part about Koldo is true," Clerici said, cutting her off. Again. "Any Sent One who has been whipped for the Water of Life cannot be aided until their wounds have healed."

"That's insane!" she gasped.

"I agree. I have attempted to convince the Council to abolish the tradition, but they insist on continuing it the way Germanus did. I will continue to work on them, though. But until I succeed, to aid Koldo is to condemn one's self to the same pain he now suffers." He turned to Zacharel. "For all but her. *She* can aid Koldo. She's his other half, an extension of his being. Whatever she does to aid him will be as if he's doing it himself."

A muscle ticked in Zacharel's jaw. "To escort her to him is to die myself, for I cannot fight the Nefas. I'm not bound to the warrior, thus anything I do on his behalf before he is healed will be considered aid."

"I know. But you can aid and protect her."

Zacharel's shoulders straightened, and he jolted, as

if he'd just experienced a startling revelation. "That's true."

So…he and his men couldn't hurt the bad guys unless they threatened her? Otherwise they'd be helping Koldo. And they could help her, even though she was Koldo's other half, because she was also half…well, Nicola. Had anything ever been more confusing?

Clerici's head tilted to the side, returning to his study of her. "Are you ready for battle, Nicola?"

For the man she loved? "I am."

"Koldo will be upset if she's injured," Zacharel said.

"He can't be upset if he's dead," she said—and guess what? No one interrupted her.

Clerici brushed his knuckles across her cheek in the gentlest of caresses. "I like the way your mind works, female. Now, go get your husband."

CHAPTER THIRTY-SIX

Even the smallest light can grow until there's no darkness left.

NICOLA HAD NEVER been to war. Well, not in the natural realm, fighting with her physical body. But even if she had, she knew it wouldn't have prepared her for *this*.

Zacharel flew her toward the side of a building in— she wasn't sure where she was anymore. There were multiple structures, a bridge, water, black birds in every direction, and the air was supercold, even damp. There were about fifteen soldiers with him, flying beside him, and oh, they were a majestic sight.

The sky was dark, the moon high, stars twinkling from their perches. The Sent Ones had somehow colored their wings black with tiny diamond sparks throughout the feathers, and the long appendages blended perfectly into the night.

To the left, she could just make out Jamila's beautiful face. There was fear in her eyes, but also a little excitement. *My coworker is a Sent One, and I had no idea.* And what was that sound? The…rattle of snake tails? The rustle of unmowed grass? The hiss of an animal being threatened?

"Serp demons," Zacharel said. "As I'm sure you

know, they are almost as evil as the Nefas, and they are poisonous to all life. They feed upon destruction."

The Nefas were worse, and Koldo was related to one. But look at everything he'd done to overcome his heritage and his past. He might have been born to vileness, but he'd crawled out of it, was no longer a part of it.

Jade-green eyes locked on her. "These creatures wish to hurt Koldo. Can you kill them?"

"Yes." No hesitation. Evil wasn't to be tolerated.

"Good. Because they've sensed us, which means the starting bell has rung." To the others, he shouted, *Only kill those who approach the girl.*

Somehow, the words reverberated through *her mind* rather than her ears.

There was no time to question him, no time to marvel. He swooped down and dropped her on the street. She landed with a thud, dust pluming around her. Demons shot out of the shadows, headed straight for her—but Zacharel's men were there, their swords of fire lighting up the night and striking the demons before they could reach her. Grunts and groans sounded. Heads soon rolled.

So close…

Thankfully, there were no other humans around. It was too late, she supposed.

Before she had time to unfreeze from petrifaction—*thought I was prepared…thought wrong*—Zacharel scooped her up and resumed his breakneck pace toward the building, which was looming closer and closer. Closer still. He never slowed.

She squeezed her eyes closed, expecting to crash. But then he dived down. Farther and farther. Surely they would reach the ground any moment…now! Impact never came. The air chilled another degree, and she looked on. They were now *underground* and—going farther *dooown*. She swallowed a yelp of panic.

When they landed at the bottom of a cave, Zacharel set her on her feet and released her. Then, he and his men lined up behind her, making her a big fat target. Gasps of shock resounded through a now-active campsite, followed by growls of rage. Footsteps scrambled. Bald-headed warriors raced toward her. Just before they reached her, Zacharel broke formation and attacked, swinging his sword of fire. Shouts of pain and panic rang out. The gasps and growls were replaced by grunts and groans.

Baldies kept coming, and the rest of the warriors broke from behind her, as well, stepping beside her to save her from being run down...or decapitated. Their swords danced through the air, cutting, slicing. Flesh burned. Screams joined the chorus. The winged soldiers darted up, flipped in the air, plunged low, moving so quickly she had trouble tracking their progress. Some of the Nefas ran away. Some ran toward the action. But Zacharel and the others couldn't chase them.

"Nicola," Zacharel said from beside her. "Do something to draw attention to yourself. Get the rest of them to attack you."

Yes. Of course.

No, she thought a moment later. She was here to fight, not to watch the action from afar. Not to watch others be struck down defending her. She could do something. And she would.

She held out her arm and peered down at her hand. Her empty hand. What had she done to summon the sword before? She thought back. Laila had just died.

Oh, my darling Laila. The demons had just threatened Nicola. She had imagined her life with Koldo.

Joy had filled her.

Joy, then.

Nothing delighted her more than the thought of rescuing Koldo, of living her life with him, the way she'd been born to do. And she would.

Flames sparked to sudden life.

"You and your men gather as many of the enemy as you can," she said to Zacharel, "and I'll deliver the deathblows. Don't do this to help Koldo, but to save me from their wrath. You know they'll come after me if I survive." Hopefully, that would save everyone from any kind of penalty.

Zacharel gaped at her, but he asked no questions. He leaped into motion.

He quickly caught one of the Nefas and threw him in Nicola's direction. She acted immediately, swinging her sword. The tip slashed through the being's middle. He collapsed on the cave floor, writhing. She struck a second time, taking his head.

One down.

Zacharel sped back into motion. Determined, she marched forward. A male swooped in from the left, morphing from human to black smoke in seconds—before reappearing just in front of her, reaching for her. Again she swung the sword. He ducked and straightened. His hands fit around her neck. But at the moment of contact, he flew backward, as though she'd pushed him.

Was she...shielded again? By her tattoos? Even though she wasn't staring at them? Maybe. Maybe she had memorized the numbers, and they were now a part of her. Maybe there was another reason. Either way... this rocked.

He hit the ground, hard, losing his breath, allowing her to simply drag her sword up his middle as she walked past.

Two down.

Nope. *Three...four...five down.* Zacharel and the others constantly threw the Nefas at her and she easily ended their lives, never missing a step.

Six, seven, eight.

After that, she lost count.

She saw that tents had been erected at the far end of the cavern, a little river winding through the center. The man from the park, Koldo's father, rushed out of the biggest one, with another male and Sirena at his sides. Their eyes widened when they spotted Nicola and her sword.

Axel and Koldo stumbled from another tent. Both were covered in blood and bruises, their faces swollen, and they had to lean on each other to remain upright. Rage and concern nearly dropped her where she stood, but Nicola pushed the emotions back. Now wasn't the time to indulge.

The group of Nefas paused a few feet away from her, just out of striking distance.

"You're outnumbered, Nox," Zacharel called.

Sirena opened her mouth to speak. Nicola leaped forward and struck without issuing a warning.

The girl's head fell to the ground, and her body followed.

Twenty-six, maybe?

Unlike the girls in the late-night movies, Nicola wasn't interested in taking time to discuss what was about to happen, what problems they had with each other or anything like that. She was simply doing what needed doing to save her man.

Koldo's father peered down at the blonde's motionless body and shouted with fury. His gaze jerked up, landing on Nicola, and he pounded toward her—only to hit the same wall the other male had. He didn't fall, but stumbled back a few steps before catching himself.

As the remaining guard gaped, Nicola was able to strike at him.

Twenty-seven.

Koldo's father hurtled a mouthful of vile curses at her. "I'm going to remove my son's intestines through his mouth and force you to watch as he dies."

She laughed. "You'll do no such thing. You're surrounded. Your army is defeated."

He launched at her again, but again, he flew backward. When he straightened, he shook his head, as if to orient his thoughts. "How are you doing that?"

"Aw, is the evil man confused? Does he not understand he picked the wrong side?" One step, two, she approached him.

Paling, he backed up until he could go no farther, the jagged walls of the cave stopping him. "Stay away, or I'll find a way to rip out your throat."

Hardly. "I bet you wish you'd stayed in hiding," she said, continuing her forward march. "All your scheming and fighting, and you have to die knowing the good guys came out of this far stronger than when it started."

"I'm unarmed," he said, raising his palms. "You don't want to do this."

A lie. He was always armed with evil. And she *really* wanted to do this.

She struck, but he bent low, avoiding contact. The momentum spun her, leaving her back to him. He charged her, but hit that invisible wall for a third time and stumbled backward.

"That'll never get old," she said, and spun back around, facing him.

He tried to dart right, but Zacharel stopped him.

He tried to dart left, but another soldier stopped him.

"You did this to yourself," she said, and struck.

This time, he had nowhere to go. Her sword sliced through his stomach. Blood and intestines spilled out.

His knees collapsed, and he hit the ground. His mouth opened on a pained moan.

"Finish him," Zacharel commanded.

"With pleasure." Another slash of her arms, and his head was rolling toward her feet, minus his body.

Twenty-eight?

The Sent Ones erupted into cheers. Someone patted her on the shoulder, nearly drilling her into the ground. She let go of the sword, and it vanished.

"Koldo," she said, and raced toward him.

KOLDO BLINKED OPEN his eyes. His pain was gone, his strength having returned. He frowned. How was that possible? He was no longer in the cave. Instead, the white walls of his ranch surrounded him.

And what was that warm thing pressed up against him? He looked down, and saw the spread of Nicola's strawberry curls over his chest. Her beautiful face was tilted up, toward his, and her eyes were closed. Her breathing was even. The confusion magnified. He'd been trapped in that cage with Axel.

Axel! That's right. The warrior had been beaten, as

broken as Koldo, and yet, after hearing the sounds of battle, he and Koldo had somehow found the strength to tear the cage apart. Together, they had walked out of the slave tent. That's when he'd seen what he'd assumed was merely a hallucination: Nicola, holding a sword of fire, forcing his father to back down.

Then nothing. He must have passed out.

Then cheers had rung out, waking him, and he'd heard little bits of conversation.

"—never expected a former human to fight like that," someone had said. "And the fact that you have the tattoos, creating the force field, is even better. You better believe I'll be getting an outward sign of the Most High's promise, too."

"You can be my battle partner anytime."

"Koldo's a lucky man."

"Nicola," Koldo said now, his voice rougher than he'd intended.

Like him, she blinked open her eyes. Then, she jolted upright and faced him. "You're finally awake."

"Where's your sister?"

Sadness caused her features to fall. "She didn't make it."

No. He had failed her, then. Had failed the love of his life. And Laila, too. "I'm so sorry, Nicola. I tried—"

"I know you did." She offered him a soft smile. "I'll never be able to thank you enough for all you endured on her behalf."

"I should have… I wish…"

"No. Don't do that to yourself. We don't even know if she would have accepted the gift. And she's happy now. She's with Robby, and they're both so happy."

Koldo reached up with a hand shaky from disuse and caressed her cheek. Soft, warm. "I love you," he said.

"I love you, too. So much."

He breathed her in, savoring what he'd thought to never have again. "Tell me what happened."

"Well, for starters, the two demons you warned me about attacked me, trying to infect me with more toxin, and I killed them with a sword of fire. Then, the Most High adopted me. Or maybe He did before, and I just didn't know it. Then, I managed to kill your father and save the day. In a nutshell, I totally rocked it!"

"You...are a Sent One?" He'd had that one moment of suspicion, and yet, he was still shocked to his soul.

She nodded, pleased. "I am."

He could barely process the knowledge. It was just too amazing.

"Thank you," he said, to the Most High, to Nicola. Like the sword of fire, she was a gift from above, and he would be forever grateful for her. He kissed the line of her jaw. "We're in Panama, aren't we?"

"Yes." She angled her head, ensuring the next kiss was on her lips.

"How long was I out?"

"Two weeks, and a lot of things have happened."

"I can imagine. But wait. You helped me, and you shouldn't have helped me, love. It's against the—"

She placed a finger over his mouth, silencing him. "It's okay. I'm a part of you, and you're a part of me. It was like you were helping yourself. Clerici said so. And guess what? Your hair is growing back."

He frowned as he moved his hand to his scalp, and sure enough, there was stubble on his scalp, tickling his palm. "That's impossible."

"Nope. Clerici isn't fond of some of the rules the Council came up with. Rules that go against the Most High's desires. So, he's cut a few. He even ruled that all sacrifices for the Water be returned."

As Koldo moved, something dug into his back. He reached around, felt—

"Wing buds," he said, his shock deepening. His wings were growing back, too. He would no longer be bald like his father. He would once again be able to soar through the skies, taking his woman wherever she wished to go. "What could be better?"

A slow grin lifted the corners of her lips, but her amusement didn't last long. "I hate to be the bearer of bad news, but you have to be told. Bjorn is missing. Thane and Xerxes are going crazy as they search for him. Zacharel and the others are helping. And some guy named Kane was spotted in New York, but then he vanished again, and it's got everyone in a tizzy."

Kane. One of the Lords of the Underworld, and the keeper of the demon of disaster. He'd been lost in hell for weeks, though rumors of his torture had surfaced. The warrior's friends had come to the Army of Disgrace, asking for help locating him. A promise had been issued, but no one had had any luck, until now.

"I must help my people," Koldo said. "With Kane, and with Bjorn." And the six demons responsible for Germanus's death were still out there. Finding and dealing with them, before they could infect all of humanity, had to be a top priority.

"I had a feeling you'd say that. That's why I scheduled you a meeting with Zacharel in…two hours. He'll get you caught up on all the details I missed."

That was wonderful, but… "How did you know I would awaken?"

She grinned slowly. "A feeling. So, what are we going to do while we wait?"

Wonderful woman. Precious woman.

His woman.

He wound his arms around her, and rolled her to her back. "Words without action mean nothing. I'll show you."

And he did.

* * * * *

The Lords of the Underworld return
with Kane, the keeper of disaster,
and the woman he just can't resist….
Don't miss THE DARKEST CRAVING,
coming soon from Harlequin HQN!